WAR COMES TO BROAD RIVER

A NOVEL OF THE
WAR BETWEEN THE STATES
BASED ON THE DIARY OF ISAAC VAUGHN MOORE
OF GEORGIA

By Ron Jones

TATE PUBLISHING, LLC

ISBN: 1-9332905-9-5

THIS BOOK IS DEDICATED TO MY WIFE ANNETTE WITHOUT
WHOSE URGING, ENCOURAGEMENT AND SUPPORT IT WOULD
NEVER HAVE BEEN POSSIBLE

TO MY SON PHILIP WHO I HOPE ONE DAY WILL PASS ALONG TO
HIS FAMILY THE RICH HISTORY OF OUR ANCESTORS

AND
TO THE MEMORY OF MY FATHER HEBRON EDWARD JONES AND
MY GRANDMOTHER WILLIE THEOLA GINN JONES
THROUGH WHOM I CONNECT TO THE
PEOPLE OF BROAD RIVER

ACKNOWLEDGMENTS AND SOURCES

I would like to thank the following people for their help in providing source information and assistance with this book.

- Jeanne Arguelles, Coordinator of the Madison County Genealogical Website.
- Charlotte Collins Bond, Madison County Historical Society.
- All those who have contributed to the Madison County Genealogical Website.
- The many researchers with whom I have shared genealogical Data.
- William R. Scaife for use of his wonderful maps of the Atlanta Campaign.
- *"Georgia Confederate 7,000: The Barton Stovall Brigade"* Gary Ray Goodson Jr.
- My cousin Caroline Thompson Angelo, 3rd Great Granddaughter of Isaac V. Moore for photographs of Isaac Moore and the Moore family.

CONTENTS

FOREWORD

War Comes to Broad River is an unusual book about the civil war because it combines a primary source with creative fiction. The primary source is a diary kept by a soldier, Isaac V. Moore, Company E, 37th Georgia Infantry. In this diary Isaac covers his military experience from the early days of the war until the surrender of his regiment with the Army of Tennessee. The creative fiction is the contribution of the author who creates conversations and describes scenes which are alluded to, but not transcribed, in the diary. These additions are done with a high degree of skill and reflect a knowledge of the war gained by extensive study and reading.

While the diary of Isaac V. Moore could stand alone as a contribution to scholarship about the war, the "fleshing out" of the characters and situations by the author's imagination makes the book appealing to a wider audience than historians or history buffs.

Through the pages of War Comes to Broad River readers will make the acquaintance of a host of real people from our past whose ordinary lives were transformed by being caught up in the great drama of war. The reward of this knowledge is well worth the pleasurable effort of reading this unusual book.

Dr. Michael R. Bradley

Dr. Bradley is a professor of History at Motlow College in Lynchburg, Tennessee where he has taught for 34 years. He is the Author of several books on the War Between the States and a widely sought after speaker as well as the stated supply Pastor of First Presbyterian Church in Clifton, Tennessee.

INTRODUCTION

Six years ago I began my research into my Southern roots. Since an aunt had previously done a limited family tree on my Mother's Tennessee family, I turned to the Georgia family of my Father. Once again a family member, my Father's cousin, had done some research which was helpful in getting me started but offered little information past my Grandparents and their children. Very little was known of my Grandfather's parents other than their birth dates and approximate places of birth; therefore my Grandmother's parents seemed to be the place to begin my search.

Beginning with my Grandmother's birthplace, Elbert County, Georgia, and her parents William T. Ginn and Ophelia Moore, I began to make contact through the Internet with people researching these family names in Elbert, County. Very quickly, with the help of some very nice people who for the most part turned out to be distant cousins, and several visits to the outstanding Genealogical Library in Knoxville, Tennessee where I live, I began to discover a rich family history beginning in Southern Virginia as early as the 1640's.

Having had a strong interest in history and especially the period of the War Between the States since childhood, I spent hours searching for the service of my Georgia ancestors discovering more than I could have ever previously anticipated.

A short time after obtaining the service and pension records of my 2nd Great Grandfather William M. Moore and joining the Sons of Confederate Veterans to honor his service, I was surprised to receive as an e-mail attachment the diary or journal kept by his brother Isaac during his service in the Army of Tennessee which only served to intensify my interest to search other family lines for ancestors who served.

Some four years later after doing a little writing of my own on the war and being involved in several living history activities, I adapted Isaac Moore's journal to a first person presentation to give to various historical groups. The presentation was given in period clothes of the 1880's as if Isaac "Ike" Moore was telling the various groups of his experiences during his three years of service in the army.

After giving several of these presentations, it occurred to me that the diary/journal would be a marvelous framework for a historical novel. The following work is that novel. The story is true, the characters and events, with only a few exceptions are real, the campaigns and battles in which the men of Company B 9th Georgia Battalion later Company E of the 37th Regiment Georgia Infantry have been researched and represent historically accurate summaries of their battles and campaigns. I have taken liberties in the development of dialogue between the characters, letters between Ike and his wife Elizabeth and several of the events portrayed in the story.

The purpose of this work is not to attempt another history dealing with in-depth discussions of the battles and tactics of the armies involved, as I have neither the knowledge nor expertise to attempt such a work and the library and bookstore shelves are full of examples of these works much superior to anything I could possibly add, but merely to tell a story of a real person and his friends and family framed by his service to his country and participation as a soldier in the "GREATEST FIGHTING FORCE EVER ASSEMBLED."

Isaac V. Moore (1830 - 1913)

Isaac Vaughn Moore was born November 17, 1830 in Elbert County Georgia. He was the second son of John Nathaniel Moore and Martha Elizabeth Vaughn and one of six children, three sons and three daughters. The Moore and Vaughn families had both settled in the Broad River area of Northeast Georgia just prior to 1800, both coming from southern Virginia.

In October of 1852, Ike Moore married Elizabeth J. Simmons of Madison County, which lay just across the Broad River from his home in Elbert County. Ike and Elizabeth apparently settled near her parents who lived near the banks of Holly Creek which ran southeasterly through the county emptying into the Broad River, near the ancestral home of Ike's Grandparents.

Elizabeth J. Simmons Moore Isaac Vaughn Moore	Martha Elizabeth Tucker Moore Thomas A. Moore	Keziah H. David Moore William M. Moore	Martha Elizabeth Almond Moore John Nathaniel Moore

The above picture of John Nathaniel Moore and his sons and daughters-in-law was taken between 1880 and 1885. John Nathaniel died in 1887.

Ike's brother's William and Thomas both joined the service of the Confederacy in October 1861, enlisting in the Goshen Blues, a company of men being raised in the northwest corner of Elbert County where they lived. William, two years older and Thomas, four years younger both survived the war after serving in many of the battles and campaigns of Robert E. Lee's Army of Northern Virginia. William, the writer's 2nd Great Grandfather would be captured in January 1864, after transferring from the 38th Georgia to the 15th Georgia and would spend the remainder of the war in prison. Thomas would survive a wound at Fredericksburg and brief imprisonment after his capture and wounding on the first day at Gettysburg and eventually be one of twelve men in his company to surrender at Appomattox Court House in April 1865.

Excerpts from the journal are interwoven throughout the book and the journal is presented in its entirety at the end along with the roster of his company.

The final section is a genealogical study of six of the families most often mentioned in the journal and the story on which it is based, each of these families a direct family line of the author.

I hope the book will present enjoyable reading and give the reader a taste of the wonderful riches that often can be found during the process of genealogical research. To those readers who have not developed the interest or found the time to discover their roots I would suggest that it is one of the most rewarding hobbies or pastimes that one can ever take up.

PROLOGUE:

Seeing the Elephant

August 6th 1862

This was the day that the fight was at Tazewell. It commenced about eleven o'clock with heavy firing, continued until about one o'clock with small arms but the enemy shelled us until about six o'clock. Our sides loss is about 45 killed and wounded. The enemy's loss is about 160 killed and wounded. We also took about 75 prisoners. We gained the victory the enemy is all fled to Cumberland Gap. We fell back about one mile and to camp.

The 9th Georgia Battalion arrived near Tazewell, Tennessee on the 5th of August, 1862 forming a line of battle with the other units in the Department of East Tennessee along the cedar topped hills southeast of the town. The 9th had been brigaded with the 40th, 42nd and 52nd Georgia Regiments and others under General Seth Barton since leaving Camp Van Dorn in Knoxville, Tennessee in early June. It was Ike Moore's second time at Tazewell in the last two months and the second time Company B, his company, had been formed in battle lines on the hills which surrounded this sleepy little town in upper East Tennessee.

General Seth Barton

This visit would prove to be different than the previous one. The men of Company B were about to see their first action and the chance to prove themselves as soldiers under fire. "Seeing the Elephant" was the phrase many a soldier would use to describe the first time going into battle. Settling down among the cedars and pine thickets which covered the many hilltops around the small upper East Tennessee town and ordered not to build fires, they supped on the rations they had prepared the night before along the Clinch River and tried to get some sleep. Sleep came reluctantly to many, especially the younger boys as their minds filled with thoughts of possible injury or death in battle. Death's angel had visited Company B and the other companies of the 9th Battalion since their formation in Northeast Georgia that spring but not yet in the violent ways of battle and the prospect of battle was both fearsome and exhilarating.

Frank David and Tom Deadwyler, close neighbors of Ike and two of the younger men in the company were huddled with their friend Will Porterfield, another young soldier, talking quietly but excitedly about what the morning might bring. After a few minutes, Frank, who had been designated the group spokesman, moved close to Ike who was now 3rd Sergeant and asked:

"Sarge whatd'ya you think about tomorrow? Do you think the Yanks will run?"

Ike glanced quickly to his friend Sam Power and back to young David.

"Well Sarge, whata you think?"

Ike had heard reports from the battles in Virginia, which some troops from his part of Georgia had taken part in, but nothing first hand and he had no personal experience himself. In fact, Tom and Will had both joined the army a full two months before he had.

Ike thought carefully for a while then spoke with the calm one might expect of a family man with five children.

"No," he said. "I reckon most of them won't run. Will you?" He continued slowly, obviously choosing his word carefully and thoughtfully.

"No, some of them will run as some of us will but most of them will stand, I reckon."

Ike, who was a deeply religious man, had been wrestling internally for some time with his religious beliefs and his loyalty to his home state. He couldn't be sure how he himself would react when the air filled with the missiles of death.

He hoped he would simply do his duty. As an educated man, he could appreciate the brief history of the now eighty year old United States and the ideals on which it was founded and although he felt a sense of loyalty to the fledgling country, he could not understand Lincoln's haste to order up troops to suppress the secession of the Southern States. He was first and foremost a Georgian and he felt drawn to defend his native soil when the call for additional troops had come in early 1862. He would become a reluctant participant in "Mr. Lincoln's War."

The young men returned to their bedrolls after the brief conversation and Ike and his squad members settled down to try and catch a few hours sleep.

Shortly before daylight, word was passed along the line to form up and get ready to move when the order came down. Those men who had not yet been issued muskets were told to form up in the rear.

"Muskets would likely become available soon enough," according to Captain Gholston.

When dawn broke over the rolling hills around Tazewell it found the countryside blanketed in a dense fog. The misty covering settled in the cedar and pine thickets where troops on both sides had formed and was an eerie reminder to Ike of the late summer morning fogs along the Broad River near his home in Georgia. He was struck by his inability to recognize anyone more than a dozen or so feet away and wondered how a battle could be fought under these conditions. How would anyone know friend from foe?

An hour or so after sunrise the order came down to stand down from battle ready but to hold positions and remain alert to changing conditions which would surely bring new orders.

The men of Company B stretched out on the pine needle covered shale so prevalent in the area and waited for the word that would send them into the conflict that at one time seemed so glorious and thrilling. The reality of camp deaths and loss of friends in other theatres of the war had removed much of the luster from the idea of glory in battle.

About nine o'clock the big guns opened their exchanges. The initial exchanges were between batteries supporting troop positions a mile or so away from Ike and Company B and were little threat to most soldiers on either side. Casualties did include the Tazewell Court House, struck by an artillery round fired by one of the long range Confederate batteries. The old frame structure quickly caught fire and burned to the ground as the stunned town's folk watched in horror and disbelief from the places of safety they had gone to escape the battle. A short while after the big guns had opened up word began to pass along the Confederate lines that all units would step off at eleven o'clock. Men began to pray and talk in quiet hushed tones about their prospects for victory, as none would allow the possibility of defeat to enter their thoughts. Ike's personal thoughts went briefly to Elizabeth and the children at home, but were interrupted by his friend and neighbor Sam Power. Sam, Elizabeth's cousin, was married to Martha David whose sister Keziah was married to Ike's older Brother Bill. Sam and Ike had been close for some time and their children were daily playmates along with those of Bill Eberhart, who was in Virginia with Ike's brothers Bill and Tom.

"Are we ready Ike?" quizzed Sam.

"I don't know Sam, we'll just have to find out when the time comes. Stay close and maybe we can lookout for each other in some way."

"Yeah, I'll try to do that. You watch my back and I'll watch yours."

The quiet conversation between Ike and Sam was interrupted by the order to step off and the sound of isolated musket fire. Very quickly the isolated reports gave way to the sound of musket volleys, which was an indication that at least some of the Union troops had moved forward before the Confederates and had now run into the advancing gray lines. In short order, more Union troops were released to support their embattled brothers in blue. But by the time this second group of troops stepped off, a general advance had begun from the Confederate lines and a wall of gray was closing in on the Union lines which were not closed along the entire line, offering flanking opportunities to the advancing Rebels. The coordinated Rebel movement, quickly accelerating to the double quick, flanked and enveloped a number of Union Companies, capturing some units almost intact. Those who could quickly began a hasty retreat, which became a "skedaddle," a soldiers term describing a swift unordered departure from battle. The hard charging Rebels, many yelling defiantly and flushed with success, soon were slowed by a combination of exhaustion, caused by the now hot August day, stifling humidity, and the Federal artillery which had been quickly repositioned close to the town. The victorious Confederates unable to sustain their advance returned to the positions from which the Federals had been driven and took up positions along this line to await further orders. Union Artillery continued a covering fire until late afternoon as the Federal Army began pulling back to Cumberland Gap.

Ike and his Company B compatriots had been a part of the advance but encountered little opposition and had passed their first test in battle without casualties. As the push forward halted, Captain Gholston reformed the line and Company B fell in with the remainder of the 9th Battalion and withdrew to a position about a mile from the battlefield, camping in one of the many cedar covered hilltops surrounding Tazewell. Ike's thoughts, as he settled down to get some rest that evening, went back to his home on Broad River and to the roads that had brought him to the hills surrounding Tazewell for the second time in two months.

Map of Georgia 1855

CHAPTER I

GATHERING CLOUDS

In the spring of 1861 Ike's home in Madison County was a farming community in Northeast Georgia, bounded all along its eastern border by the Broad River, and its neighbor Elbert County on the opposite side of the river. In 1860 the total population of Madison County was approximately 5,900 people, of which 3,942 or 66% was white. Madison County was not an area of large plantations and cotton was less important than in many neighboring counties, thus 80% of the counties slave owners owned ten or less slaves and over half less than five. Most families did not own any as was typical in most of the South.

Many of the families along the Broad River had moved into the Northeast Georgia area in the late 1700's after the Cherokee Indians ceded to the Colonial Governor of Georgia. These families were in many cases from Virginia and many were veterans, receiving land grants for their service in the Revolutionary War. By 1860 these families had intermarried extensively and the communities were very tight knit and neighbors were often members of the extended family.

Although very patriotic, they were tied much more closely to the local area than to the Federal Government or the State. Very few knew anything of the Government in Washington beyond the mail service it provided and its issuance of currency, and were not interested in politics.

While great changes had occurred in the almost eighty years since the independence was finally won from King George, most of these changes had little effect on the people in rural areas of the South, so they paid them no mind despite the fact that many of these changes were shaping a new world. The issue of slavery had been a hotly discussed topic for years and through legislative actions had created a country divided by an imaginary line, the Mason-Dixon, running from east to west and establishing where slavery would be legal and where it would not. There was also a not so imaginary line separating the two sections and their peoples based on cultural differences, owing to the basis of the economy in each of the two regions; the north essentially mercantilist and industrial, the south almost exclusively agrarian. Tariff issues had also been divisive points and led to much bitterness between the political leaders of the two regions. As sectional division had fostered differences over slavery and the application of tariffs on imports and exports, this division had also caused the country to become separated with regard to politics and religion. The two paramount political ideologies had remained rooted in those of Thomas Jefferson and Alexander Hamilton and the political parties to which their philosophies gave birth. The Jeffersonians subscribed to his ideas of limited government and power resting in the hands of the governed, and eventually became the founders of the early Democratic Party of Andrew Jackson. Meanwhile many of the Hamiltonians, who believed in Hamilton's idea of a larger more powerful central government controlling much more of the daily lives of the independent states and their peoples, became members of the Whig party of Henry Clay and its successor the Republican Party of Abraham Lincoln.

Religion, a much deeper cause for division than most history books allude to, was divided again along philosophical differences. The Southern people, those primarily below the previously mentioned Mason-Dixon Line, were very Calvinistic in their approach to religion believing simply that God was sovereign, having dominion over all and playing an active role in everything. On the other hand, many of the New England sects and churches were developing a more Unitarian approach to religion putting much more emphasis on the role of the individual and relegating God to more of a caretaker role in man's daily affairs. Widening differences such as these caused the three major religions—the Presbyterians, the Methodist/Episcopal and the Baptist—to split in the years between 1835 and 1860.

These things affected the daily lives of the people of Madison County in ways many of them would simply have never realized. Just as we would today, they would all notice when prices roses on items imported from the north as well as from Europe, but few would realize that tariffs were the cause unless they were literate and read the newspapers of the day. It is reasonable to assume that these rural people would have had little interest in these political issues and would have wished simply to be left alone to live their lives.

These differences did not become issues with most common citizens until the election of 1860. The balance of power, which had been maintained through the two house system of the legislative branch of government despite the four or five to one population differential between the two sections, began to swing to the north as non-slave states began to outnumber the slave states and slavery became more of a political issue.

The anti-slavery and abolitionist movement was centered in New England and the stance taken there by many seems odd considering that the vast majority of slaves were imported into the Americas by New England merchants and ship owners. Many of these New Englanders had made their fortunes through the trade of slaves and rum and many continued to make fortunes on the exportation and distribution of southern agricultural products whose production was based heavily on the use of slaves.

The surprising election results of 1860 resulted in Abraham Lincoln being elected President with less than 40% of the popular vote. This was possible due to a rift in the Democratic Party which split the Democratic vote. Soon after the election, Congress passed the most harsh tariff legislation passed up to that point, the infamous Morrill Act. This new legislation increased the existing tariff rate by 150%, expanded the scope of items covered by the tariffs and nearly tripled the tax burden in the South. The effect would be a dramatic reduction in the profits of the southern planters and assurance that the small farmers and working class in the South would lose significant ground as necessities they must purchase would dramatically increase in cost. The issue of slavery, which is today put forth by many as the single reason for the War Between the States, was much less of an issue. In truth, the Republican platform stressed a policy of non-interference regarding slavery in the States where it already existed, and Lincoln in his Inaugural address said, *"I have no purpose, directly or indirectly, to interfere with the institution of slavery in the states where it exists. I believe I have no lawful right to do so."*

There was in fact a Constitutional amendment proposed and passed by both houses, but not ratified by the States prior to the outbreak of hostilities, which would have guaranteed the existence of slavery forever in the States where it currently existed. The article read as follows: "ARTICLE THIRTEEN, No amendment shall be made to the Constitution which will authorize or give to Congress the power to abolish or interfere, within any State, with the domestic institutions thereof, including that of persons held to labor or service by the laws of said State." This proposed amendment was signed by President Buchanan just prior to Lincoln's inauguration and was and is the only amendment ever signed by a President.

Seven States had seceded from the Union by the time this amendment was passed by Congress and thus the amendment was never ratified by the States. Ironically, it was later replaced by the current thirteenth amendment outlawing slavery. Georgia, although deeply divided, was one of the seven States having seceded.

The stage was now set and Madison County, like counties throughout the South, braced for war. The newly elected President's call for troops to invade the South and put an end to the newly formed Confederate States of America triggered four additional States to secede and join their Southern brothers and sisters. Georgia stood poised on the brink, and military units began to form in Counties throughout the State. Madison County and its neighbor to the east, Elbert County, were no exception. Three of the earliest regiments, the 7th, 8th and 9th Infantry Regiments, formed in late Spring of 1861 and very quickly joined other Southern troops in Virginia as part of the army being raised to block the Northern invasion. They all saw service at the Battle of First Manassas.

The first company raised exclusively in Madison County was the "Madison County Grays," later Company A of the 16th Georgia Volunteer Infantry, formed during July of 1861. Its formation was followed closely by the "Danielsville Guard," designated Company D of the same regiment and about two months later by the "Fireside Guards" and "Bowman Volunteers," formed just across the Broad River and including in their ranks several men from Madison County. These two companies would later be a part of the 15th Georgia Infantry and serve with the 1st Corp of the Army of Northern Virginia until surrendering at Appomattox, Virginia on April 9, 1865.

CHAPTER II

THE PEOPLE
OF BROAD RIVER

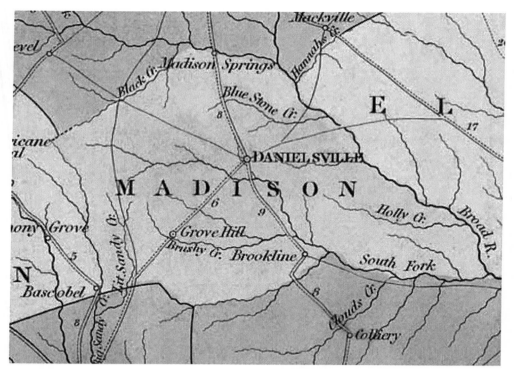

Map of Madison County Georgia 1839

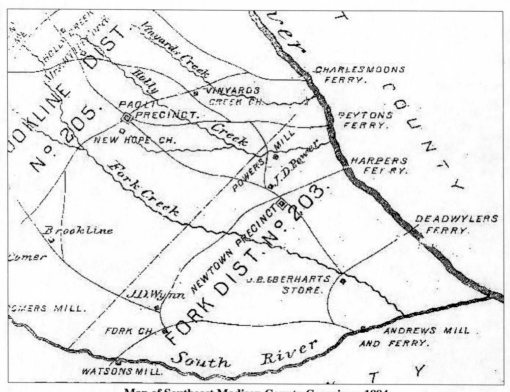

Map of Southeast Madison County Georgia ca 1884

Page. No. 45 179

SCHEDULE 1.—Free Inhabitants in _____ in the County of *Madison* State
of *Georgia* enumerated by me, on the *28* day of *June* 1860. *A.J. Patterson* Ass't Marshal.
Post Office *Danielsville*

		3	4	5	6	7	8	9	10	11	12	13	14
1		Jonathan Moon	6	M					Georgia				
2	328	328	Samuel B. Brown	59	M	Farmer	1	200	215	N.C.			1
3		Parthenia	53	F					Georgia			1
4		Mary J.	21	F					"			
5		Henry H	20	M	Farmer				"			
6	329	329	William A. Shelnett	63	M	Miller	1		210	"			
7		Parthenia	58	F					"			
8		Sally A	23	M	Farmer				"			
9		Sarah	18	F					"			
10		Jincy	11	F					"			
11	330	330	Frederick Thurman	47	M	Farmer		1200	395	Georgia			
12		Anna	46	F					"			
13		Lewis A	24	M	Farmer			40	"			
14		Martha J	12	F					"			
15		Mary J	10	F					"			1
16		John F	8	M					"			
17		Bertha Thurman	87	F					N.C.			
18	331	331	Logan Dudley	28	M	Laborer	1		295	Georgia			1
19		Sarah ?	24	F					"			1
20		Joel Ly	6	M					"			
21		John J	2	M					"			
22		Joseph Thomas J	5/12	F					"			
23	332	332	James McPherson	48	M	Bapt Clergyman	1	1000	1635	Georgia			
24		Eliza M	42	F					"			
25		Eliza J	15	F					"			
26		Sarah M	13	F					"			
27		Margaret J	11	F					"		1	
28		William L	9	M					"		1	
29		Ophelia	6	F					"			
30		Flora	4	F					"			
31		Lucy J Johnson	15	F					"			
32		John Page	24	M	Farmer	1		200	"			
33		Freeman Smith	35	M					"			
34	333	333	Luke H White	26	M	Farmer		400	217	Georgia			
35		Elizabeth A	37	F					"			
36		James M	2	M					S. "			
37	334	334	Elizabeth Thurman	41	F	Farmer			370	N.C.			
38		Isabel	45	F				400		Georgia			
39	335	335	Isley B Brown	35	M	Farmer		2075	580	Georgia			
40		Mary J	24	F					"			

No. white males, 74   No. colored males, ___   No. foreign born, ___   No. idiotic, ___   13,325   3,957   No. blind, ___   No. convicts, ___
No. white females, 58   No. colored females, ___ No. deaf and dumb, ___   No. insane, ___   No. paupers, ___

1860 Census page 179

SCHEDULE 1.—Free Inhabitants in _____ in the County of _____ 180 State of _____ enumerated by me, on the ___ day of _____ 1860. _____ Ass't Marshal

Post Office _____

		The name of every person whose usual place of abode on the first day of June, 1860, was in this family.	Description			Profession, Occupation, or Trade of each person, male and female, over 15 years of age.	Value of Estate Owned		Place of Birth, Naming the State, Territory, or Country				
1	2	3	4	5	6	7	8	9	10	11	12	13	14
		Esther A. Johnson	5	F					Georgia				1
		Eliza J.	2	F					"				2
		Mary E.	10/12	F					"				3
336	336	Elizabeth Moore	32	F		Farmer		120	Georgia			1	4
		John J.	6	M					"				5
		Benj. Martin Jones	6	F					"				6
		Barbary W.	4	F					"				7
		Geney L. Glaser	20	M		Farmer			"				8
		Sarah W.	3	F					"				9
337	337	John Simmons	35	M		Farmer	1500	1910	Georgia				10
		Milley W.	49	F					"				11
		Sydney C.	35	F					"			1	12
		Milley J.	11	F					"				13
		____ A.	10/12	F					"				14
338	338	John Fletcher	38	M		Mercer		150	Georgia				15
		Mary H.	30	F					"				16
		Mary J.	14	F					"			1	17
		Francis M.	10	M					"			1	18
		Benjamin	6	M					"			1	19
		Isaac	3	M					"				20
		Jane	1	F					"				21
339	339	James P. Owen	40	M		Merchant	400	10545	Georgia				22
340	340	Isaac W. Moore	29	M		Clerk		185	"				23
		Elizabeth J.	24	F					"				24
		John W.	6	M					"				25
		Frances A.	5	M					"				26
		Martha G.	2	F					"				27
		Ceci____ B.	10/12	M					"				28
341	341	James P. Earhart	26	M		Doctor	400	3660	Georgia				29
		Martha M.	23	F					"				30
342	342	William Chabert	35	M		Farmer	3500	17350	"				31
		Martha	28	F					"				32
		Frances C.	4	F					"				33
		____ ____	4	F					"				34
343	343	Samuel P. Owen	24	M		Farmer		2295	Georgia				35
		Martha A.	22	F					"				36
		Berry H.	5	M					"				37
		William H.	3	M					"				38
344	344	Elizabeth Davis	45	F		Farmer	1500	2650	Georgia				39
		Elizabeth J.	21	F					"				40

1860 Census page 180

Page No. 181

SCHEDULE 1.—Free Inhabitants in _____ in the County of *Madison* _____ State
of *Georgia* _____ enumerated by me, on the *29* day of *June* 1860. *W. J. Elder* _____ Ass't Marshal.
Post Office *Danielsville*

		The name of every person whose usual place of abode on the first day of June, 1860, was in this family.	Age	Sex	Color	Profession, Occupation, or Trade of each person, male and female, over 15 years of age.	Value of Real Estate	Value of Personal Estate	Place of Birth, Naming the State, Territory, or Country.	Married within the year	Attended School within year	Persons over 20 who cannot read & write	Whether deaf and dumb, blind, insane, idiotic, pauper, or convict.
345	345	Francis E Power	43	M		Farmer	400	465	Georgia				
		Elizabeth P.	59	F					"				
		John L.	17	M		Farmer			"		1		
		Mary J.	14	F					"		1		
		Martha A.	13	F					"		1		
		Elizabeth L.	10	F					"		1		
		William N.	8	M					"		1		
		James B.	6	M					"				
		Sarah C.	3	F					"				
		Martha Wood	62	F					"				
346	346	Jacob D Moon	37	M		Farmer		315	Georgia		1		
		Sarah	38	F					"				
		William M.	13	M					"		1		
		Stephen A	11	M					"		1		
		Delila A.	7	F					"		1		
		Jacob D	6	M					"				
		John L.	2	M					"				
		Aaron W.	1	F					"				
347	347	Lackey A Moon	63	F		Farmer	500		Georgia				
348	348	Peter Dowd	72	M		Farmer	4000	14700	Virginia			1	
		Elizabeth M Dowd	25	F					Georgia				
		Mary J.	40	F					"				
		Frances M David	72	M		Farmer			Alabama		1		
		Henry C	16	M		"			"		1		
		George A	14	M					"		1		
		John M Jr.	11	M					"		1		
349	349	John M David	42	M		Farmer	1700	5265	Georgia				
350	350	Lewis M David	31	M		Farmer	1700	1050	"				
351	351	Ida B David	58	M		Farmer	13741	11700	Georgia				
		Mary Ann J	40	F					"				
		Margaret	19	F					"				
		Thomas J	16	M		Farmer			"		1		
		John L	13	M					"		1		
		Martha	12	F					"		1		
		Ada P	7	M					"				
352	352	William Johnson	44	M		Farmer		170	Georgia				
		Frances H	78	F					"				
		Martha E	22	F					"				
		Mary J	20	F					"				
		Susan M	78	F					"			1	

No. white males 21 ... No. colored males ... No. freight born ... No. blind ... 17241 83723 ... No. white females 19 ... No. colored females ... No. deaf and dumb ... No. insane ... No. idiotic ... No. paupers ... No. convicts ...

1860 Census page 181

The Dogwoods and Red Bud blooms of spring 1861 were gone, replaced by the shimmering green leaves of summer. The cool breezy mornings of April and May had given way to the warm dewy mornings of June and now the warm mornings and sultry afternoon and evenings of July. Ike Moore had secured a position as clerk in the general merchandise store owned by James Duncan "Jim" Power in the late 1850's and as a result had become acquainted with almost everyone in the area. The use of his store as a satellite post office for the people in the Holly Creek area saved them the trip to the closest Post Office, several miles away at Brookline, and brought them all to his store.

Jim Power had been a bachelor in his late 30's when Ike came to work for him in the late 50's but was now beginning to court Ike's sister-in-law Mary Elizabeth David, who lived with her widowed mother near the store and next door to her sister Martha, who was married to Jim's cousin Sam Power. The women's older sister Keziah was married to Bill Moore, Ike's older brother, creating a very close bond between the Moore, Power and David families. As Ike swept the front porch of the store on a particularly warm morning in early July, Sam Power came hurrying up the road almost at a trot. It was obvious that he was coming to see Ike and that he had what he thought to be important news.

"Ike," Sam yelled as he neared the store. "What do you think Ike?"

"What do I think about what Sam?"

"About the Grays," Sam said excitedly, "about the Grays," referring to the company being raised around their home area.

"Did you hear Jas had joined?" Sam continued, referring to their neighbor James David. "He was made Sergeant. Danny Witcher, Bill Gholston, Tully Strickland and John King, too, they all joined."

All of these men were neighbors and often visited Jim Power's store.

"Is that right?" replied Ike. "Hadn't heard about Danny, that'll worry John and Mary."

Danny's older brother John was married to Ike's wife's sister and lived just up the road from the store.

"What're you gonna do Ike?" quizzed Sam.

"Reckon I'll wait a spell Sam. With the four we already have and Elizabeth expecting by year end I'm needed at home more than in some army."

"Guess you're right," replied Sam, "I'm sure Martha would whole lot rather have me here than off fighting Yanks. I believe she could manage the darkies and see everything was done, but I know she'd want me here with her and the kids. Hopefully these young bucks going in now will take care of things and us ole family men can stay home."

"Yeah, wouldn't that be nice," laughed Ike.

"Ike, Ike!" It was Elizabeth calling from inside the store.

"Be right in," Ike called out before turning back to Sam.

"Maybe we'll all get lucky and this thing will work itself out and we can all stay home."

"Yeah, that'd be nice," replied Sam, "But I reckon I wouldn't mind getting a crack at those meddlers if I got the chance."

"Be careful what you wish for," replied Ike as he stepped through the doorway on his way to find out what Elizabeth needed.

Ike and Elizabeth had married almost nine years earlier when Ike was almost twenty-two and Elizabeth just sixteen. Their family now numbered three boys and a girl and the boys, especially John and Frank the two oldest and typical boys, were into something all the time. Elizabeth, a strong self-reliant woman rarely asked for help from Ike with the children and the urgency in her voice had concerned Ike a little. He quickly discovered that the youngest, Ike's namesake thirty month old Isaac, had taken a tumble down the steps from the second story quarters in the back of the store, which was home for Ike's family. He had suffered a cut, which for a moment had frightened Elizabeth because of the blood; however, by the time Ike reached them she was well in control of things.

"Ike, I'm going to take Isaac next door and let Doc take a look," said Elizabeth.

"Alright," said Ike, "probably best to be safe but it doesn't look too serious."

Elizabeth was a dark-eyed, dark-haired, handsome woman nearly as tall as Ike, who, like his brothers Bill and Tom, was well under six feet tall. He felt he had made an excellent choice in Elizabeth. She was an excellent wife and mother as well as a big help to Ike and Jim in the store. She gathered young Isaac up and was off to the doctor's office which was just next to the store. Doctor James Eberhart was only twenty-seven years old by the summer of 1861, but he had begun his medical studies to become a doctor early in life and had graduated from a medical school in Philadelphia by 1857. Elizabeth caught he and his wife Milly finishing breakfast. They had married shortly after the new doctor had returned to Georgia from Pennsylvania. After taking a quick look at young Isaac, the doctor assured Elizabeth that the wound was superficial despite all the blood, and walked with her back to the store to buy some coffee.

Sam Power was gone by the time Elizabeth and the Doctor reached the store and they found Ike gathering up an order for John Witcher, Elizabeth's brother-in-law. John had married Elizabeth's older sister Mary and their farm was the next farm up the road from the store. Elizabeth could hear that the conversation between Ike and John was centered around the upcoming hostilities and the enlistment of close friends and relatives.

"I wish Danny had waited awhile, but he's full growed and it's his decision to make. I just hope he didn't let his hot-headed friends persuade him. I just got a bad feeling Ike," said John.

John felt much like Ike and Sam. Mary and the five children had to come first, plus he was just a year shy of forty years old. War was for younger men, John had decided, at least for the present.

Dr. Eberhart stopped and announced to Ike and John, "I've joined the Fireside Guards over in Elbert. We leave for camp in a couple of weeks."

"I didn't know," said Ike. "What made you decide to do that"?

"I wish I knew," said Jim. "It was just something I felt I was called to do. I take it you two are going to wait awhile?"

Ike and Sam indicated they were and the group broke up a few minutes later in order to get on with the day's work.

The summer wore on and the men who had joined the Grays and a new company called the Danielsville Guards had begun to leave home, marching away to camps of instruction and posts near the Georgia coastline. Their departures were always met with large crowds of friends and families, many waving the newly adopted Stars and Bars of the Confederate States. The younger children ran alongside the troops, trying to stay in sight of their father or older brothers as they disappeared down the dusty summer roads. By late July word had reached Northeast Georgia of the exciting victory won in Virginia at a railway junction named Manassas. The Northern invaders and been stopped and sent back toward Washington City in defeat. Sadly, along with the news of the victory had come the war's first battle casualty lists from the ranks of the 7th, 8th and 9th Georgia Volunteer Infantry. Although these lists did not contain the names of any soldiers from Madison County, they had included men from neighboring counties including adjoining Oglethorpe, which was just below the corner of Madison County where Ike and his neighbors lived.

As the men from Madison County continued to join the army and spread out over the southern states to various camps of instruction, the war began to extract casualties of a different kind. By the late fall of 1861, a dozen men from the Madison Grays had succumbed to the diseases that spread through the ranks. Diseases, including measles were widespread in the camps of instruction, as men who had been protected from many childhood diseases by their somewhat isolated lives on the farm, were thrown together in close and often unsanitary conditions.

On September 10, 1861 the following report was made in the Richmond, Virginia "Whig."

MORTALITY IN CAMP. - The deaths in the 16th Georgia Regiment, Col. Howell Cobb, (encamped at the Old Fair Grounds) during the week ending Sunday, the 8th ins., were as follows:

Privates, Jas. R. Lawless, Wm. Pinson, T. M. Falkner, Jas. Bradley, Co. A; Jeb Smith and L. D. Bowles, Co. B; James Byrd, Co. D; Gilham Wilbanks and Chas. Tankersly, Co. E; W. L. Tucker and T. L. Long, Co. F; M. J. Parks and J. W. Harwell, Co. G; Silas Kadle, Co. I; ___ Kidd.

One of the last named died at the General Hospital. Sickness prevails in this Regiment to such an extent, that it hardly musters half of its members on parade.

Illness in the camps was so prevalent that many companies, including those from Madison County, often had as many men confined to their beds or in hospitals as they had on the parade grounds drilling.

Most of Ike's friends and close neighbors were not included in the early enlistments of 1861; therefore, the sadness and horror that would visit almost every Southern household in the next four years was not seen in the immediate area around Jim Power's store during the summer and fall of 1861.

In October 1861, Ike's brothers Bill and Tom joined the Goshen Blues from across the river in Elbert County. They were joined by three of their mother's younger brothers and a number of Ike's cousins. This company became part of the 38th Georgia Infantry Regiment and after receiving their instruction was sent to Savannah as part of the coastal defense. As more and more of Ike's family and friends joined the southern forces and marched away to defend the besieged south, and reports of battles on the Carolina Coasts, in Northern Virginia, Kentucky and other locations along the borders of the new nation reached Georgia, Ike began to wonder how long he could remain uninvolved.

Winter passed with only a smattering of news of battles and conflict. As the first signs of spring began to arrive in North Georgia, along with them came the news of new battlefronts in Tennessee, Missouri and on the ocean. Reports of the fall of Forts Henry and Donelson in Northwest Tennessee and the loss of the first Confederate State Capital at Nashville brought a temporary sadness to the folks near Jim Power's store, but did little to dampen their patriotic spirit and resolve.

One warm Sunday afternoon in late April, a particularly patriotic and rousing sermon by Reverend James Mankin Power—Elizabeth's cousin and Sam's older brother–prompted a quite vigorous after church discussion among the men in attendance. Ike, and a number of his friends who had tried to remain level headed and place their families first, began to discuss the most recent news from the front and the new Conscription Act. This provision, for all men between 18 and 35 to serve unless they could provide a substitute or qualify for one of the exemptions, had left Ike and many of his friends with little choice but to consider enlistment. Word of the big battle at Pittsburg Landing on the Tennessee River had just reached the area, followed a day or so later by news of the fall of Fort Pulaski on the coast, and an invasion of Virginia in the James River area south of Richmond. It was now very obvious that this was going to be a lengthy struggle for the Southern States, and all her sons would eventually be needed.

The group included Ike, Sam Power, Sam's cousins Asa, Joe and Tom Power, who were Jim Power's half-brothers, Frank David and his younger brother Henry, who was not yet eighteen, Jimmy White and his little brother Stephen, both less than eighteen as well, the Wynn and Russell brothers and others. Several of the area men had already joined one of the two companies being formed in Madison and Elbert Counties, which would later be a part of the 9th Georgia Battalion. The four remaining companies in this battalion would come from the surrounding counties of Hart, Wilkes, Franklin and Muscogee. Neither company had been filled in the early March recruiting and were to be completed late the next month. Most of the local men seemed partial to the company of Captain Dabney Gholston of Madison County, and several already had brothers who had signed up. These men had been in Camp McDonald, north of Atlanta near Big Shanty, since mid March and were expecting to receive orders to move, possibly to East Tennessee, at any time.

"What are you gonna do Ike?" quizzed Sam his neighbor. "Reckon it's time for us to decide, now that we'll most likely get conscripted anyhow. Think I'd rather join up with my friends and kinfolks if I'm gonna go."

"I expect you're right," said Ike. "Look's like the time's come."

"Pete says they're moving out next week," said Frank David, referring to his older brother, who had joined in early March.

"Yeah, that's what Doc says too," echoed Sam, speaking of his cousin who was always called "Doctor" Frank to separate him from two older cousins of the same name.

Frank, or "Doc," was Junior Second Lieutenant of the Madison Company and had been by a week before recruiting to fill out the Company. Talk turned to Shiloh, as some called the fight at Pittsburg Landing a couple of weeks before, and the horrible loss of life on both sides.

"What kind of soldier do you think I'll make?" Sam asked Ike.

"You're a good man Sam, and I reckon you'll do your duty," replied Ike. "Don't suppose they can ask or expect any more than that."

"Well I reckon you're right, but I sure would rather not go. Not that I'm afraid," Sam lied, "but it just seems like a man with a family needs to be home providing for them."

"I know exactly how you feel Sam," said Ike. "I've got five now with little Mary and it just seems they need me more than the army. But I suppose we all know it's coming and we might as well set our minds to it." Ike felt a tug on his trouser leg and looked down to see John W., his oldest.

"Pa," he said, "Mama sent me to fetch you; she wants to go home."

Ike rubbed little John, who was named for his Grandfather John Nathaniel Moore, on the head and said, "Run along and tell your mother I'm coming." Ike watched for a few seconds as John ran back toward where his mother and the other ladies were gathered, and turned back toward the group and wondered out loud to no one in particular. "What do you suppose this war is gonna mean for them?"

Later, when the whole family—Elizabeth, John W., Frank, Martha (who was named after Ike's mother who had passed away two years before), little Ike and Mary, born only four months before—was in the buckboard heading home, Elizabeth spoke up, breaking several minutes of silence.

"What were you men talking about after preaching?"

"Oh, we were just talking about the progress of the war and how it seems to be spreading all over the South."

"When will you be going?"

"How did you know?" asked Ike.

"Ike you know you can't keep anything from me," she replied. "I've always known you'd go. Bill and Tom are gone; your friends from around here have all gone or will be going soon. I just knew your time would come."

Ike detected a sad tone in her voice and glancing at her caught her wiping away a tear.

"Elizabeth," Ike said, "I know it will be hard, but this conscription act doesn't leave me with much choice. I would rather volunteer and serve with men I know and trust. You know most of the local boys have joined Dabney Gholston's Company. I think that's probably the place for the rest of us. You and the children should probably go to live with your father and mother, they will be needing help. David has already joined (David Simmons was Elizabeth's cousin and had been working on her father's farm), and the two darkies are just kids and won't be that much help."

"I know Ike," said Elizabeth, struggling to not let her emotions show in front of the children. "But I just cannot bear the thought of something happening to you. What would I do?"

Ike tried to think of something reassuring to say but determined after a moment or two that any words he chose would be empty and no solace to Elizabeth.

"Elizabeth," Ike said. "You know me well enough to know that I'll be careful and take no chances, but I must do my duty as all Georgians must. Hopefully the latest terrible battles will bring the leaders of the Union to their senses and they will stop this terrible war and leave the South alone."

"Oh Ike," do you think that might actually happen?" asked Elizabeth wishfully.

"All we can do is just pray that it does," said Ike. "It's in God's hands."

The remainder of the trip home passed in silence. Less than a month later, Ike joined most of the men who were in that Sunday afternoon discussion group in joining Captain Gholston's Company.

CHAPTER III

SOLDIERS ALL

I enlisted May 9th, 1862 in Company B, 9th Georgia Battalion. There were six companies in the 9th Georgia Battalion. They were from Madison, Elbert, Hart, Wilkes, Franklin and Muscogee Counties of Georgia.

After traveling with the early May enlistees to Camp McDonald near Big Shanty, Georgia, Ike and his friends were quickly transported to Knoxville, Tennessee. They arrived in Knoxville in mid May and quickly moved to Camp Van Dorn, the large camp of instruction west of Knoxville. For many of the men it and been their first time on a train and the excitement level was high. At Camp Van Dorn they joined the rest of the men who had joined the Company two months before. The days at Camp Van Dorn, while they lasted only three weeks for Ike and Sam, were like nothing they had ever experienced. The May recruits received a quick lesson in drilling and movements to be used when on a battlefield and were quickly introduced to the crowded unsanitary conditions of the camps. Upon arriving at Knoxville, they had found Jesse Power sick with the measles and Peter David already dead from the same disease.

We were in camp first in and around Knoxville, Tennessee. Some time the last of May, 1862, Jesse Power relapsed with measles and died in Knoxville, Tennessee. (He went out one morning and got his feet wet and relapsed) S. P. Power and I bought his coffin and shroud and sent him home. I waited on him while he was sick.

When Ike heard that Jesse was sick and was told he was still in camp, he went looking for him. Ike found Jesse in his tent. Jesse coughed as he stirred from a fitful sleep when Ike entered the tent.

"Ike," he said weakly. "What are you doing here?"

"Sam and I joined up," said Ike. "So did Asa, Joe and Tom. We're all here. How are you doing Jesse?" continued Ike.

"I'm getting some better, Ike," said Jesse. "The hospital got so full they couldn't keep us all, so those of us who were the least sick were sent back to camp. Peter David died, Ike. Did you know that?"

"Yes they told me," answered Ike. "What did they do with his body?"

"I've heard they started a cemetery near town, I think they took him there."

"Did they tell Mary (Peter's wife) and his father? Surely they would have wanted him returned home?" Ike asked.

"I don't know," replied Jesse, his voice trailing off as he rapidly tired from the conversation.

"You're tired," said Ike. "Get some sleep and I'll look in on you tomorrow if I get a chance."

Ike, having had the measles as a child, took it upon himself to wait on Jesse until he was up and about. In the next few days Jesse improved and he began to move around camp once again. A few days later, following a couple of rainy days, Jesse got his feet wet walking around in camp and his fever returned. With the return of the fever he quickly relapsed and within a couple of days he was dead. Sam and Ike bought his coffin and shroud and sent him home to Georgia. Several other members of the battalion, not as well known to Ike as Peter David and Jesse, died during the days in Knoxville and were buried in cemeteries in and around the town. They included James R. Patterson from Ike's Company.

Back home, Elizabeth had continued to live above Jim Power's store after Ike's departure and eagerly sorted through the latest postings after each delivery for a letter from him. One morning in early June, she was elated to find a letter posted only a little more than a week before at Knoxville.

As the store was empty of patrons at this early hour, Elizabeth excitedly opened the letter, trying not to tear the precious contents. Wiping at her eyes to clear away the tears of joy, Elizabeth unfolded the paper and began to read.

June 4, 1862

My Dearest Elizabeth,

I have sat myself down at the end of a long day to write you a few lines that I hope find you and my beloved children well. I received your letter of May 22ⁿᵈ this morning and hope it will be the first of many. There is sad news from here as your cousin Jesse Power has died from measles on May 29ᵗʰ. I waited on him while he was sick and Sam and I bought his coffin and shroud and arranged to have his body sent home yesterday. His earthly remains may arrive there before this letter but knowing the man he was his soul is surely with his creator. If the letter arrives before the body please let his father know of his death. Peter David passed away before I arrived here and was buried in a cemetery here in town. If you see Mary his wife or his father please offer them my condolences.

Elizabeth, I miss the quiet times we shared together in the evenings after the children were asleep and holding you close before we went to sleep. I long for those times to return soon and it is my hope we are able to share a lifetime of these memories. How is little Mary? I regret that I probably will not be there when she takes her first step or speaks her first words. I cherished those memories from the other children so much. I pray my absence will not be a long one.

Elizabeth, if you see Father please tell him I am well and look forward to seeing him soon. Please kiss the *little ones for me and give them my love. I must close for now as we rise at four o'clock in the morning and it is after nine o'clock now. We are told that our orders are to leave this camp and join other troops before marching north. Please write when you can as our officers have assured us that mail will find us wherever we go.*

Your loving husband

Ike

In early June the 9th Battalion marched out of Knoxville, stopping briefly at Clinton on the Clinch River before turning north toward Kentucky. Their objective was Tazewell and Cumberland Gap, now in enemy hands. As the men marched the dusty roads leading up the valley toward Tazewell, many of them spoke with the bravado of untested soldiers about the quick work they would make of their enemies awaiting them. They would surely send the Yankees back where they came from and soon be on their wary back home. None dreamed that it would be almost three years before the war would end and that life for those who survived would never be the same.

On the evening of June 17, 1862, the men of the 9th Georgia Battalion, in addition to other units from Georgia, were placed in line of battle expecting their first action to come the next day with Union troops under General George Morgan, who had recently moved south of Cumberland Gap toward Tazewell. The anticipated battle did not materialize, and the next morning the Confederate forces began a withdrawal from the Tazewell area down the Kentucky Road, after camping briefly on the East side of the Clinch River.

June 18, 1862

We left on a march at eleven o'clock and crossed the Clinch River and camped, went in bathing.

Many of the men took this opportunity to wash themselves and their clothes in the river. This was the first bath for many of them since leaving home. Ike was very happy to get out of the smelly, dusty clothes he had worn since leaving Clinton almost two weeks before. Removing the bar of lye soap he had brought from home, he washed his clothes and laid them on one of the many large rocks that dotted the river bed. He slipped below a group of these rocks and relaxed in the quiet still waters of the pool created by the rocks diversion of the rapidly flowing river. After a few minutes, he stepped from the eddy into the faster moving water between the rocks to rinse the soapy lather from his body and longjohns. Soon he gathered up his clothes and waded toward the bank from where he had entered the river. Positioning of the units along the shoreline had placed Ike and the men in his Company at the lower flank of the Rebel Army as it spread out along the river. As he neared the riverbank, his attention was attracted to a group gathered down river a ways, along the river's edge. It was some of the younger men in the Company who generally hung together when the Company was in camp. The group included Frank David, Tom Deadwyler, the Power brothers, Will Porterfield and the Simmons brothers, David and Wiley. Something had attracted their attention and they were gathered around in a near circle, all looking down at the object which had caught their eye. It was awhile before any of them saw Ike coming toward them. Finally, David Simmons saw Ike as he approached the group.

"Sarge," David exclaimed in excitement. "Look at this. I think it's a dead Yankee."

As he moved closer to the group, he could see what had drawn their attention. Snagged among some tree limbs close to the riverbank was a body clothed in what had been a military uniform. At first glance the soldier's allegiance was hard to determine, but upon closer examination the uniform buttons confirmed that he had at least been wearing a Union sack coat.

"Yeah, it looks that way boys, but many a half naked southern boy has put on an enemy jacket," replied Ike. "Did you find anything else?"

"No," said David, the oldest in the group at twenty-four. "Looks like he washed downstream from up above and got caught up in these here tree limbs. He was gut shot Ike. Probably crawled to the river to drink and died along the edge. First good thunderstorm, the rising water just carried him along to here."

"You're probably right." said Ike, "poor soul."

The body was already decomposing, but the wound just above the top of the trousers was obvious. A Minnie ball left quite a hole.

"What's that under him?" Ike asked.

"Can't say," said young Simmons. "We ain't touched him."

Laying his freshly washed and dried clothes on a nearby rock, Ike broke a limb from the snagged tree and poked at a dark colored object under the body.

"Why it's his haversack," exclaimed Tom Power. "Can you get it Ike?"

Ike pulled the haversack from under the decomposing body and held it away from the decaying flesh.

"Cut the strap off the bag and let's see if it holds anything," said Ike.

As Ike held the mud covered bag away from the body, David cut the strap and pulled the bag from the water. Opening the canvas bag, which had been tarred indicating federal issue, the men found the contents little help. There had been some hardtack and pork, some badly deteriorated letters that had faded to the point that they were illegible, a pencil and a tintype, ruined by the exposure. The dead man was still a mystery. The men of Company B had seen death in the camps, but this was different. Here was a man with a large hole in his belly. The dead Yank had ripped at his shirt and wound until his internal organs protruded from the wound and had attracted various aquatic wildlife which had ripped at the exposed flesh. After a brief discussion, the men decided to leave the man where he was due to the advanced decomposition. Ike bowed his head and under his breath spoke a few words, and then, picking up his clothes, turned and left the dead man to the river.

The next day, the Southern troops crossed the Clinch Mountain and camped around the hotel at Bean Station on the Knoxville Road.

June 19, 1862

We marched and crossed the Clinch Mountain we were to be going over and camped at Bean Station on the Kentucky Road. There is a large hotel here, no town, it is large summer resort.

During the next few days, Ike and his fellow Georgians marched south on the road to Knoxville, camping near Rutledge until the 4th of July. On July 5, 1862 the 9th Battalion moved their camp to one of the many springs in the area where they remained for almost the remainder of the month.

July 27, 1862

Moved to Lea's Springs and camped. I was taken sick about the 17th of July with yellow jaundice. The Dr. gave me a pass to go out into the country to get a suitable diet for this disease. Ed Eberhart went with me. We stayed at the home of a good lady whose name (maiden name) was Lowe. She was very kind to us.

One morning, a few days after the anniversary of the Declaration of Independence from England, Ike woke with fever and stomach cramps. Ed Eberhart, who had been sharing a tent with Ike, hunted down the doctor who examined Ike and decided he had jaundice and needed a better diet than he could get in camp.

"Soldier," the doctor said to Ed, "take this man and see if you can find a local who will take the two of you in for a week or so. Maybe some home cooking will cure him. I'll talk to your Captain and write a pass for the two of you. He will need someone to go with him."

Ed and Ike left camp the next morning and walked the country roads near Rutledge. The Grainger County countryside near Rutledge was dotted with farms, large and small, all lush with vegetable crops of all kinds and many types of fruit. The second farm house they came upon sat on one of the rolling hills that were common in the valley. These hills stretched back to the mountains that ran southwestward on either side of the valley, like fingers extending back to the palm of a hand.

Ike found the shade of an Elm tree to rest in while Ed walked up the wagon path to the house. Approaching the house, Ed noticed a woman in her middle twenties hanging clothes on a line running behind the house. Startled when she caught sight of Ed, the young woman bolted toward an old shotgun propped against a nearby corn crib.

"Ma'am," Ed shouted, raising his hands above his head, "I don't mean you no harm, just want to talk a minute."

The young woman continued on until she felt the security of the old shotgun in her hands. Picking up the beat up old gun, she turned toward Ed with a look of terror in her eyes.

"I can shoot this thing, raised up doing it," she said. "What is it you want?"

"Ma'am," Ed continued, "I've got a real sick man down there by the road under the shade of that big Elm. We're camped up the ways at Sulphur Springs, as you likely know. The doctor sent us out to see if we could find someone who wouldn't mind feeding him something other than camp rations for a few days to see if it might help his condition. You wouldn't have to make no fuss about me, I'll eat my rations and I'll be glad to help you out with your crops and such."

"What kind of condition?" the young woman asked.

"Doctor thinks it's his liver, nothing contagious," replied Ed.

"Well, I don't want my young'uns exposed to nothin' they might catch, like the measles or such. My man caught the measles in camp. Might near killed him."

"No ma'am," Ed replied, "nothin' like that. We've seen our share of measles too."

"Well, I could sure use the help. I reckon I got more than I can say grace over."

Ed and Ike were fortunate that the young woman was the wife of a Confederate soldier serving in a cavalry unit in East Tennessee. She was trying to manage the one-hundred acres they had with the help of her brother, too young to be a soldier, and her two young children, both too young to be of any real help.

"You see the barn there? You'll have to sleep in there. I'll take a look at your friend and feed you if you will help out, it's a mite more than Josh and I can handle just now. Josh, that's my brother Joshua, he's fourteen. He tries hard, but he's got his heart set on being a soldier. Daddy just won't hear of it. Daddy, he's the preacher round here. Josh is in the upper field yonder. We're trying to get in some late crops for the fall. Tell your friend to come on up. What are you names by the way? Mine's Martha but folks call me 'Mattie.' My young'uns are Ben and Sarie. They're seven and four."

"Ed, my names Ed, Ed Eberhart and my friends name is Ike, Ike Moore. We're from Georgia. We sure do thank you Ma'am, it means a lot to be among friends. I'll go get Ike," replied Ed as he started back down the hill toward the Elm tree.

"Didn't think you sounded like you were from around here," Mattie said. But by this time Ed was too far down the path to hear her.

Ike had fallen asleep while Ed was gone and did not awake until Ed shook him by the shoulder.

"We can stay here. Lady here seems real nice. I'll tell you about it later," Ed said as he helped Ike to his feet and up the wagon path toward the barn.

"This here's Ike," Ed said to their benefactor as they approached where she was hanging the remainder of her wash.

"Good to know you Mr. Moore," said Mattie. "Bet you both are hungry. Got some biscuits left over from breakfast. I'll fry up a half-dozen eggs and a piece of ham and then ya'll can bed down in the barn."

"We'd be mighty grateful," replied Ed.

During the next two weeks, Ike's health slowly returned as Mattie's home cooking had been just what he needed. Ed had spent the two weeks helping with the crops already on the way to maturity and the various livestock on the farm. They had all developed a bond of friendship likely to be remembered a lifetime. After the first couple of days Mattie had become so trusting of Ike and Ed that they all ate around the table in the house together and talked of times before the war. Ike and Sam told Mattie about their wives and families and all about their home in Georgia. She shared with them the story of how her Great Grandfather, Isaiah, had come to Grainger County from Virginia in the late 1700's and settled on a tract of land he had received as a grant for his service in the war for Independence from Great Britain. She told them of her mother's people, who had arrived in the area about the same time from North Carolina receiving land for her mother's Grandfather's service in the war. She explained that her mother's people were pretty much Unionist, while her Father's people and those of her husband were strong secessionist. This had made for some unpleasantness between the families, but it was no different from many of the families of East Tennessee which was almost equally divided in its support for the two sides in the great conflict that was this War between the States.

Toward the end of July, the men received word that the camp was moving, and since Ike was feeling much better they said their goodbyes and returned to camp, grateful for the hospitality Mattie had shown them and pleased to have shared this time with someone so caring and generous.

A couple of days later the camp was moved to Lea Springs, a few miles down the road toward Knoxville, where they remained until the 3rd of August, 1862. On that day, the 9th Battalion moved back north toward Tazewell as part of a joint campaign into Kentucky by the armies of Braxton Bragg and Kirby Smith. The men of Company B crossed over the Clinch Mountain into Poor Valley, many camping near a small Baptist Church at Locust Grove. As was the case at many of the stops along the way, many of the men were to remain in the woods and fields around the church for eternity. By the evening of August 5, 1862, the 9th Georgia Battalion, along with troops of the 3rd Georgia Battalion and the 40th, 42nd, and 52nd Georgia Infantry Regiments as well as others from Alabama and Tennessee, were drawn in a line of battle in the cedar and pine thickets dotting the hills south and east of Tazewell. Company B was about to get its first test in battle.

CHAPTER IV

THE KENTUCKY CAMPAIGN

August 7, 1862

*This day I was out on a scout most of the day hunting
up the enemies that were cut off in the fight.*

The morning after the battle of Tazewell found Ike and a number of his friends scouting the area around the town, rounding up Yankees who had been separated from their units during the hasty Union retreat. Many were hiding in the dense thickets between the various rebel units and could not slip through to rejoin their units who had fallen back to Cumberland Gap. During that first day of scouting the battlefield, dozens of Union soldiers were captured by the net of Rebels advancing as skirmishers. Being a smaller unit of only six companies, the 9th Battalion would often be used in this role of skirmishers. It was in one of these thickets Ike Moore came face to face with his first "live" Yankee. The man was hunkered down among a group of small cedars not much taller that the average man. The branches at the bottom of the trees, owing to their lack of height, grew only a few inches from the ground and made for a perfect hiding place, or so the Yankee had thought. It had looked a good place to Ike and had been the very reason he had paid particular attention to it. Ike, Sam and Ed had been moving slowly only a few yards apart when the thick stand of cedars caught Ike's eye and drew his attention. Motioning Sam and Ed to move to the sides and rear of the thicket, Ike cautiously approached the trees, crouching to get a better view of the ground. In the darkness of the thicket, the white socks worn by the Union soldier offered the only indication of something out of the ordinary. The frightened Yankee was sitting on his heels with his arms clasped around his legs and his head buried between his knees. With bayonet fixed, Ike move closer to the cedars and thrust his bayonet into the trees.

"Hey Yank," he shouted, "come on out'a there." The Yankee slowly raised himself up and straightened out to his full height.

"Raise those hands up and step out of there," Ike continued. The blue clad soldier pushed his way through the cedar branches and stepped out into the less densely covered ground where Ike was waiting.

"Any more of you?" questioned Ike.

"No sir," the Yankee answered nervously. "I'm by myself."

While Ike continued to question their captive, Sam and Ed pushed their way into the cedars, thrusting their bayonets into the trees as they searched the thicket, and finding nothing more than the Union Soldier's haversack which he had discarded.

"Where's you musket?" Ike asked.

"I don't know," the man answered. "I threw it down when everybody started to run. My friend Jake was shot in the face right beside me. I had seen enough."

Continuing to question the wet and hungry Yankee, they learned he was a private in the 16th Ohio under DeCoursey and had been in the army for almost a year serving in Kentucky and the areas around Cumberland Gap. Two of the companies of the 16th, his and one other, had been flanked and cut off by the advancing Rebels, losing a number of men killed and wounded and over fifty captured. Most of those had been captured immediately by members of the 42nd Georgia, along with a significant number of weapons. Ike's prisoner was among the few that had slipped away and sought refuge in the dense stands of cedars.

Ike took his prisoner back a ways to an area Captain Gholston had established as a holding area for the enemy found and then returned to where he had left Sam and Ed and they continued their search. By the end of the day, Ike's Company had rounded up a half dozen prisoners and a considerable amount of supply left behind in the Yankees' hasty retreat. There would be no need for a soldier to be without a musket after that day. The scouting parties continued for the next two days and on August 9th the Southern troops moved closer and into Tazewell, the 9th Battalion camping around the grounds of the destroyed Court House. Corn, the principal crop in the area, was abundant and the men feasted on roasting ears during their stay in Tazewell.

August 9, 1862

We moved into Tazewell and camped around the Court House. Roasting ears were plentiful here.

During their stay in Tazewell, Ike chanced to meet a Mr. Hugh Graham, who was a prominent citizen of the town and whose home, "Castle

Rock," was a prominent feature on the landscape of Tazewell, sitting beside the main road from Cumberland Gap to Knoxville. Mr. Graham, it was said, watched the proceedings of the battle from a window on the third floor of his home while his family, neighbors and slaves took shelter in the cellar. The old man, "an ardent secessionist," was eager to converse with any rebel soldier whose duties did not interfere with their discussions. His daughter, Miss Ellen Graham, had quite a reputation in her own right as a Southern sympathizer, and the stories of her aiding the Rebel troops during their stays in the Tazewell area were numerous.

During the next month the Army of East Tennessee, growing almost daily by the influx of new units from the southern part of Tennessee, maneuvered into position to surround the smaller Union Army which was now confined to the natural fortress of Cumberland Gap.

On the 14th of August General Kirby Smith assigned General Carter Stephenson command of the troops besieging Cumberland Gap, including the Brigade of Seth Barton, and moved the remainder of his forces into Kentucky where they harassed and cut communication and supply lines to Union General Morgan at Cumberland Gap. Smith continued through mostly unfriendly country to Lexington and Frankfort, where they were more warmly received. This march was a very difficult one owing to the lack of supplies and a prolonged drought which had settled on the area.

August 16, 1862

Left Tazewell at eight o'clock and marched all night towards Cumberland Gap. Got to Powell River at seven o'clock on August 17th.

A day or so later, the 9th Battalion, along with the remainder of Barton's Brigade, moved to the Powell River some three miles southeast of the Cumberland Gap. After crossing the river and moving to within two miles of the Gap, a line of about three miles in length was formed and camps established. Due to the close proximity to the Union forces, clashes with Union foragers, scouts and skirmishers occurred on an almost daily basis. For Ike and his friends, the hot days of late summer were filled with picket duty, exchanges with their Union counterparts and the periodic cannonading from the Union batteries on the mountain above Cumberland Gap. These artillery rounds were noisy, but did little or no damage.

August 20, 1862

Some cannonading and firing with the picket all day and a good portion of the night.

August 21, 1862

I am on duty in sight of the enemy's tents and can view the Cumberland Mountains gap. Some firing with the pickets up to nine o'clock in the morning, firing continued over and after all day, but at long distance.

August 22nd 1862

Friday. Pickets commence early in the morning and by evening there was three or four Regiments engaged for two or three hours but not much damage done, some shelling from the enemy, at night all was quiet.

The cool mountain evenings were mostly quiet and Ike used these hours to write home to Elizabeth. He had not yet received anything from her but held out hope that once the business in Cumberland Gap was settled that mail might begin to catch up with them. Ike could find little to write of in his new life as a soldier so he filled his letters with reassurances that he was well and in minimal danger. He wrote of the kindness of the people he had met in Tazewell, and the dusty conditions due to the small amount of rainfall they had received. He described the view from his posts atop the ridges surrounding Cumberland Gap, which allowed him to see the tents of the enemy dotting the timberless mountain above the Gap. The Union soldiers at a distance of a mile or more reminded Ike of ants moving atop their hills of granulated dirt. Mostly, Ike wrote of the longing for home he felt and his love for Elizabeth and the children. He avoided dwelling on the loneliness of camp so not to add to the sadness he knew she felt during his absence. He mentioned familiar names of friends and neighbors to comfort her in knowing he was not alone. He did not write of the hunger they often felt or the lack of socks and shoes, as it seemed neither lasted very long due to the miles walked each day. The walking was almost a daily occurrence, whether the battalion was moving or merely on picket duty or patrol.

August 23, 1862

Today (Saturday) everything appears to be quiet. We move nearer to the Virginia line.

August 31st 1862

There was considerable shelling from the enemy today about ten o'clock but no damage was done.

As Ike was finishing a letter home on the evening of September 11th, huge explosions were heard coming from Cumberland Gap. Talk was that the Union Army had come to the end of its rope, knowing now that the Rebels had no intention of attacking such a stronghold and also knowing their choices were now limited to starvation, surrender or attempting an escape. Either choice meant that the large stores of war materials would fall into Southern hands and that was to be avoided. Thus, strong speculation was that the explosions were the result of the destruction of the magazine in Cumberland Gap.

September 17th 1862

Wednesday This is the day the enemy vacated Cumberland Gap.

A few days later, General Morgan and his troops slipped out of Cumberland Gap under the cover of darkness using the old Indian trail known as Warrior's Path. He continued his retreat with only slight harassment from Rebel forces until he reached Ohio.

September 18th

Today we marched into Cumberland Gap and took possession of that place. The enemy destroyed and left a large number of things there.

On the 18th of September, Rebel forces moved into Cumberland Gap finding that most of the military supplies had been burned when the Yankees had blown up the magazine a week before. The Rebels also found that the sick Yankee soldiers and those wounded in the fighting at Tazewell the month before and skirmishing since had been left in the hospital at the Gap.

September 19th 1862

Friday Today we marched over the mountain into Kentucky and camped right at the foot of the mountain right close to a creek.

September 20th 1862 Saturday

We commenced our march in Kentucky. We marched to Cumberland River Ford and walked through the water 3 or 4 feet deep and camped.

The evacuation and withdrawal by General Morgan allowed General Stevenson to move into Kentucky and move north toward Frankfort. This enabled the Army of Tennessee to move toward consolidation, as General Braxton Bragg had crossed into Kentucky during the early part of the month and was close to joining Kirby Smith near the State Capital in Frankfort.

September 23rd Tuesday

We continued the March past London Town, 50 odd miles from Cumberland Gap and struck camp at the forks of creek.

September 24th Wednesday

We continued our march fording the Rock Castle River. The men would ride in and examine the water before crossing.

September 29th 1862

Marched through Danville 130 miles from Cumberland Gap, also passed Harrisburg I saw the largest Rat here at this place that I ever saw. It was a wharf rat as large as a possum

Gen. Edmund Kirby Smith

Gen. Braxton Bragg

The 9th Battalion continued its march north through Kentucky passing London, Danville, Harrodsburg, Salvisa and Lawrenceburg.

October 2nd Thursday

We marched past Rough and Ready Town and camped near Frankfort at the stone bridge built by nature 20 or 30 feet long and wide enough for a wagon to cross.

On October 4th, Richard Hawes was inaugurated as Governor of Kentucky amid much pageantry and the attendance of both General Bragg and General Smith. In the distance could be heard the sound of enemy guns, marking that place as one of suspect safety for the new Governor. It had been hoped that the installation of the new Governor would bring thousands of new recruits into the Confederate Army, however Kentucky remained a confused and torn State despite its ratified secession.

October 4th 1862 Saturday.

We stayed in camp till very near night when orders came to March through Frankfort, the Capitol of the state. We marched very nearly all night to this place called Versailles, 13 miles from Frankfort, the Capitol. We burned bridges here to keep the Yankees from following us.

The Celebration in Frankfort was short-lived as much of the Confederate force marched through the Capitol that evening toward Versailles, burning bridges behind them to prevent their use by Federal forces. The Confederate forces were fresh from victories at Mumfordville and Richmond, where only small forces of a few thousand troops were engaged on both sides. These victories had give rise to hope that Kentucky would be won and thousands of Kentuckians would rally to the Southern cause.

By the early part of October however, General Don Carlos Buell had marched north from Middle Tennessee and with an army of about 55,000 stood in the way of the plan of Bragg and Smith to rid Kentucky of Union forces and establish a solid Confederate government in the state.

October 8th Wednesday.

We marched toward Lawrenceburg and formed in line of battle.

By the 8th of October, the Rebel army was spread out over the roads between Perryville and Lawrenceburg, a distance of about twenty miles. The 9th Battalion, along with most of the Regiments of Barton's Brigade, was formed in a line of battle near Lawrenceburg and escaped the bloody scene at Perryville.

Bragg's force of about 16,000 collided with approximately two-thirds of Buell's total force, and although outnumbered over two to one, the Confederates had the best of it in the vicious but short lived battle. Outnumbered and with the prospect of being outflanked by the superior Federal force, Bragg retired through Perryville toward Harrodsburg, hoping to consolidate the Confederate Army there and give battle. Casualties in this brief but bloody battle

numbered over 7,000 which, considering the length of the conflict, is stagger-
ing.

Most of the Confederate Army remained in line of battle and expected
an attack by Buell's forces, but that attack did not come. On the 12th of October,
to the surprise of both Union General Buell and his own Lieutenants including
his Co-Commander Kirby Smith, Bragg ordered a withdrawal from Kentucky
back through Cumberland Gap.

October 9th 1862

*We left at 2 o'clock and marched to Lawrenceburg, some
fighting going on today near this place, we marched
through Salvisa to Salt River and camped*

October 10th Friday

*Marched to Harrodsburg and formed line of battle. We
stayed all night west of Harrodsburg. A cold rain fell
all night.*

October 11th Saturday

*We marched back through Harrodsburg, eastward to
near Bryantsville and camped. Remained in camp till
dark on the 13th then marched through Bryantsville to
Lancaster.*

October 14th 1862 Tuesday

*We remained near Lancaster all day and past off the
time in line of battle. There was some fighting with the
cavalry today. We marched all night to Gum Springs,
leaving the enemy behind us.*

The march through Kentucky was a particularly hard one for Ike and
the 9th Battalion, as it was for the entire Southern Army. The weather was
unseasonably cold during parts of the march, and by some estimates a full third

of General Barton's Brigade was barefooted. They were hard pressed much of the march by the pursuing Union troops and were fired on, both while marching and on the occasions they stopped, by Bushwhackers in the night. All along the march south there were stories of the harsh treatment of civilians who sided with the Confederacy by these lawless bands, who raided the countryside committing murder and rape and stealing from supporters of both sides.

On one of the occasions when Ike and his Company had been able to stop and make camp, Lt. Power had ordered Ike to take a detail and bury a family that had been found near a small burned out cabin close to their camp by a group that had gone out foraging. The father had been shot as he milked the cow, judging from the pail found in front of him in their small barn. The mother had been dragged into the yard where her partially clothed body was found. An older child about five was found shot in the ruins of the house, while a baby had simply been smothered in its crib, most likely to silence its crying.

As they silently dug the graves in the backyard of the small farm in the rough Kentucky hills, Sam Power broke the silence.

"Who or what manner of man would do such a thing? What has this war turned into? What has it made of men?"

Ed Eberhart, who unlike most of the older men was a bachelor, simply muttered without pausing in his digging, "I hope our Cavalry finds them. Lieutenant Power said they were on the lookout for them."

Ike, who was standing guard a few feet away, replied to Sam, "This isn't the war's work Sam. The evil in the men who did this didn't come from the war; it was in them all along. We've all heard of these types back home, we just never had to come face to face with it before."

"Reckon your right," said Sam, "but it don't make it set any easier."

Without further words being spoken, the men went back to their gruesome task until the three graves were filled. (The baby had been buried with its mother.) After rocks were placed to mark each grave, Ike read a few words from his new testament and the men returned to camp. Two days later as they continued their march south through the Kentucky hills, they came across two bodies stripped to their long-johns and hanging from an old oak tree near their route of march. It was said the Cavalry had caught the two men who had boasted of the killing, and hung them for all to see.

October 23rd 1862

Continued our March and crossed over Cumberland Gap. We were in Kentucky from the 20th of Sept. to the 23rd of Oct. We marched to the Cumberland River and camped.

October 24th 1862 Friday

We past Tazewell, marched to Clinch River and camped after crossing the river.

By the 24th of October, the 9th Battalion found itself once again in the now familiar area southeast of Tazewell along the Kentucky Road. As the march was continued, an early snow began to fall.

October 25th 1862 Saturday

We marched across the Elk River and camped near Rutledge, Tenn.

October 26th and 27th 1862

At Rutledge today. Stayed here today, considerable snow fell yesterday.

On the 26th of October, the army once again camped in the area of Rutledge where they had been just three months before. The deepening snow had accumulated to four inches and intensified the suffering of the once proud sons of Georgia, now demoralized by the retreat from a battle they thought had been a victory and their ragged condition. The sudden turn in the weather caught many of the men without shoes and with only the summer clothes they had left Knoxville with five months before. After two days of rest near Rutledge, the march continued down the Knoxville Road and on through Knoxville to their destination of Lenoir Station, Tennessee, twenty miles south of Knoxville where it was hoped the army could be resupplied.

November 1st 1862 Saturday

Reached our camp here near Lenoir Station 22 miles from Knoxville.

November 2nd

*Stayed at this camp from Sunday through Thursday,
the 13th All at ease, no trouble at all.*

The first two weeks of November 1862 passed with relatively little activity. This was a time for the Army of Tennessee to rest and lick its wounds. Men who had made the trip from Kentucky with nagging wounds or illness were sent to hospitals in Knoxville, Atlanta and other locations depending on their needs. Soldiers who lacked the necessities of shoes, uniforms and equipment lost or worn out in the past five months of campaigning, were supplied with these items when they could be obtained.

The autumn days were spent healing, cleaning muskets, washing threadbare clothes, which in many cases had not been changed in weeks for lack of anything to change into, and writing letters. Many of the men who could not write would ask those that could to write letters for them and to read for them the letters they had received.

While at Lenoir Station, mail began to catch up with the army. New deliveries found the 9th Battalion on an almost daily basis as letters written weeks before now found a stationary army and could finally be delivered. It was one of these late fall days in this small river town when Ike received his first mail from home. The bundle, tied tightly together by a piece of string, included a dozen letters written between mid May and early August. The first was dated in May, only a few days after Ike's departure. The remaining letters were dated at first in three or four day intervals and then finally a week apart. They were generally written and dated on a Sunday afternoon after church services, and almost always including a reference to the sermon of the day and a congregational prayer for the men in service of their country. The first few letters always began with the same sentiments if not the same words.

My Dearest Husband,

*I hope this letter finds you well. We are all very well
here. I miss you and pray daily for your safe return
to me at the earliest possible moment. Each day without
you here seems to pass as slowly as an eternity . . .*

The remainder of the letters were filled with news of the area. There were few men remaining in Madison County and most of those remaining had joined home guards or reserve units raised to protect the citizens and to aid in maintaining law and order, so there was not much news of Ike's friends serving in other units in other theatres of the war. Elizabeth had decided to remain at the store to help Jim and his new bride Mary Elizabeth, who was tied to the families of both Ike and Elizabeth. The bond between the two Elizabeths, for everyone called Mary Elizabeth by her middle name, seemed to ease the loneliness they all felt. Ike's Elizabeth had reported in one of her letters the death of James W. V. David, brother to Mary Elizabeth, Sam Power's wife Martha and Ike's sister-in-law Keziah. This had been a particularly hard blow for the sisters as they had lost their only other brother Henry and their father Berry in the years just before the war.

Another letter informed Ike of the deaths of his sister's husband Stephen White, who had died in Savannah, and his Uncles Jacob and John Vaughn, his mother's younger brothers who had died in Savannah and Virginia. They and another of his mother's brothers, Alex, had joined the Goshen Blues, along with his brothers Bill and Tom and several of his Booth and Vaughn cousins. The Blues, now part of the 38th Georgia Infantry, were in Virginia and Elizabeth's letters spoke of the battles they had participated in as well as the death of his cousins W. H. Vaughn and Gabe Booth at a place called Cold Harbor during the Federal campaign against Richmond in late June and early July. There was also sad news from the Madison Grays, now part of the 16th Infantry and Cobb's Legion, serving in Virginia with the 38th and 24th and 15th Regiments, which all numbered men from Madison County. Turner Simmons, Elizabeth's uncle, had died of disease as had five of the Thompson boys and Ben Witcher, brother of Ike's friend John, who was married to Elizabeth's sister Mary. Madison County was giving up her sons at an alarming rate.

Ike read and re-read the letters until the paper was torn and soiled by his hands, which he never seemed to be able to keep clean, feeling a closeness with home and family each time he read them. Ike received a second package of letters just days before leaving Lenoir Station. Written less frequently, they had covered the months of August and September. Ike had heard talk of the great battle at Manassas, Virginia for the second time and the bloodiest battle yet a small town in Maryland called Sharpsburg, but few or no details. The last of Elizabeth's letters, dated the last day of September, reported the death of Ike's friends James David, know by everyone as "Jas," and Tolly Strickland. Both had been killed near Sharpsburg at a place called Crampton's Gap. Ike's brothers and his uncle Alex had been involved in both battles, but somehow escaped injury. The letter had said the one day battle at Sharpsburg, fought along a creek, had cost the lives of over 5,000 men on both sides. It seemed to Ike that the two countries were now determined to battle it out until all the young men on both sides were either dead or maimed.

CHAPTER V

CAMPAIGN FOR MIDDLE TENNESSEE

On the 9th day of November 1862, General Carter L. Stephenson was promoted to Major General and ordered to move his forces from Lenoir Station to Manchester, Tennessee between Nashville and Chattanooga.

November 14th 1862 and 15th

Left camp and left Kingston and crossed the Clinch and Emery Rivers just below the Fork.

On the 14th and 15th the Army of Tennessee broke camp at Lenoir Station and began their march into Middle Tennessee. The march carried them through Kingston where they crossed the Clinch and Emory Rivers just below the fork and through an old community called Post Oak.

November 17th 1862 Monday

This is my Birthday. I am 32, years old. We marched past Post Oak a noted place.

Passing Walden's Valley and over the ridge or mountain of the same name, they marched down into the Sequatchie Valley and turned south. As the troops marched south down the valley Ike thought to himself what a beautiful area this must be in the spring and summer in contrast to the wintry veil spreading over the countryside now.

November 21, 22, & 23, 1862 Friday & Saturday

We marched past Jasper and camped. Sunday we stayed in camp which is 11 miles from Lone Oak Station.

Pausing only one day near Jasper, at the southern end of the valley, the army turned west, crossing over the Cumberland Mountains and passing near the University of the South before moving on to Manchester.

November 26th to December 5th

We marched to Manchester and camped and stayed here for some time.

Near the end of November, the weather turned bitter cold and snow began to fall. Because of the unexpected harshness of the weather, it was determined to remain in Manchester for a period of time before moving any further toward the ultimate destination of Nashville.

December 5th 1862

I received clothes from home today, the first that I have got since leaving home.

While camped at Manchester, mail again began to catch up with the army and Ike received another bundle of letters. This group contained several from Elizabeth and one from his youngest sister Martha who was just now fourteen.

She had heard from Bill and Tom who were now in Northern Virginia south of Washington City. Accompanying the coveted letters was a package containing clothes. Elizabeth had found time in the evenings to knit three pair of wool socks, which she enclosed with two cotton shirts and a pair of trousers dyed with shell from the hickory and walnut trees in the area. These brown butter-nut colored clothes were rapidly replacing the gray worn by the troops due to the shortage of gray dye created by the Yankee blockades. Elizabeth had written that many items were becoming scarce, expensive or unavailable at any price. Flour was nearing $40 a barrel, salt was becoming scarce and coffee sometimes could not be found at any price. Chicory often replaced coffee in the pots in Madison County.

The rising costs had made Jim Power unpopular with some of his customers, but most knew he could only pass along his price increases or go out of business. It did require that Elizabeth keep a watchful eye on those that might try to take small things without paying. These instances were very rare but Jim had cautioned both she and his wife to be watchful just the same. After passing along news such as this, Elizabeth's letters were full of the news of the children and the rapid growth of little Mary, now approaching her first birthday. It was now clear that Ike would not see her first steps or hear her first words. She also always mentioned the money that Ike would periodically send home to help Elizabeth provide for the children.

December 6th 1862

I sent $100 home.

December 7 & 8

We marched to camp at Readyville.

December 9th through 17th 1862

Was stationed at Readyville.

A few days later the army was on the move again, marching to Readyville over ground frozen and covered with snow. Many of the men were still without shoes and prospects for them less likely while on the move. Ike heard rumors of desertions in other companies but his company had not experienced any since returning from Kentucky. Readyville was still some 40 miles from Nashville which was reportedly their objective but the weather was holding up their progress.

The army arrived in Readyville on the 8th of December and remained in place with only slight movements until the end of December. While at Readyville, General Stevenson's Division was ordered to Vicksburg to reinforce General John C. Pemberton's army there. The 9th Georgia Battalion was at that time transferred to the Brigade of General James E. Rains of North Carolina which included the 3rd Georgia Battalion, commanded by Lt. Col. Marcellus Stovall, the 9th commanded by Major Joseph T. Smith, the 29th North Carolina, Colonel R. B. Vance commanding, the 11th Tennessee under Colonel G. W. Gordon and the Eufaula Alabama Lt. Artillery commanded by Lt. W. A.

McDuffie. The new Brigade was a part of the Division commanded by John P. McCown.

General James E. Rains

December 18th 1862

The Georgia Battalion was transferred from Barton's Brigade to Raines Brigade and one mile.

This reorganization separated the 9th Battalion from the Georgia Brigade of General Seth Barton with which they had campaigned for over six months.

The weather leading up to Christmas turned unseasonably warm for the time of year and was in stark contrast to the harsh conditions the army had endured for the previous two weeks.

December 25th Christmas Day 1862.

Christmas day passed quickly and lonely for the men of Company B. Thoughts of home did little to cheer them up and only increased their feelings of homesickness and sadness. Two more of these Christmases away from loved ones would be endured before this war would be over and the next two would be far more harsh and desperate than the first.

December 26th and 27th 1862

We marched 12 miles to Murfreesboro, Tennessee

December 27th, 1862, Saturday

We formed a line of battle along a fence here today.

On the day after Christmas 1862, the 9th Battalion and the rest of the newly formed Brigade marched the 12 miles to Murfreesboro and camped. The Brigade was formed in line of battle on Saturday December 27th but passed the remainder of that day and the Sabbath day in relative quiet.

December 29th Monday

We moved across Stones River and formed a line of battle in a large field. There was some firing with pickets

On Monday December 29, 1862 the Rain's Brigade along with the rest of the army, with the exception of the troops on the far right commanded by Breckenridge, crossed the Stones River and established a battle line along the edge of a large field. The report of musket and artillery exchanges could be heard by Ike and his friends in Company B for most of the next day, but no movement was made by the lines of Confederate Infantry to their right except those movements required to fuse the line and properly position them for the battle which was to come.

December 30th 1862 Tuesday

There was considerable battle today near us.

As the men of Company B lay in line of battle and anticipated, based on the size of the armies assembled, the momentous struggle that was ahead, the talk again turned to prospects for victory and soul searching with regard to expectations of their individual performances. Although the company had been in existence for ten months and the large majority of the men now in the Company had served either that period or seven and one-half months for the men who had joined in May at the urging of the Conscription Act, their combat involvement had been minimal. Save the battle at Tazewell almost five months previous, circumstances had left the 9th Battalion with little actual experience under fire. This was about to change.

Relaxing against a stone wall traversing the field where they were positioned, the conversation of Ike and his friends speculated on the next day's outcome. They had all been touched in some way or another by the reports of casualties from the battles in Virginia, where most of them had families or friends, and the fear of similar results the next day could hardly be removed from their minds. The overriding concern of all was to be maimed in some horrible way so as to be invalided and a burden to their families for life. "How do you think it must feel for a ball to tear into you?" asked Elizabeth's cousin Wiley Simmons of anyone who was listening. "I hope I never find out," answered his brother David. David Simmons's wishes would be realized as he would serve the next two and one-half years without injury, surrendering in late April of 1865 with the remainder of the Army of Tennessee. Unfortunately, Wiley would experience his questioned fears almost two years later at nearby Franklin, Tennessee, where he would suffer a wound that would result in the loss of a foot and render him a cripple.

"If their gonna get me, I hope they kill me outright," replied Bird Moon, who eerily would suffer that fate three weeks shy of two years later at the second engagement fought at Murfreesboro on nearly the same ground. Premonitions of death or injury seemed not to be uncommon but given the risks of battle were well within the bounds of expectation.

Ike, deep in thought of home and family, only half heard the morbid conversation and paid it little mind. The angel of death had passed over Company B in battle up to now and would do so again tomorrow.

December 31st

Today was the day of the great battle of Murfreesboro. We killed wounded and imprisoned about 16,000 men, so it is said. Our loss was 5000. General Raines was killed, one was killed out of Bates Battalion, ten wounded.

As the night wore on, a blustery winter wind whistled through the trees and across the fields chilling many of the still ill-clothed southern troops huddled together for protection. Only a few hundred yards away, the Union commanders mostly ignored the sounds of troop movements on the Confederate left. In a stroke of coincidence that would deliver an early set back to the

Federal forces, both commanding generals had made plans for an attack on the other army's right flank, beginning the next morning. Bragg's decision to attack at dawn turned out to be a well played trump card, as the attack of McCown's Division, with Rain's Brigade on the extreme left caught the unsuspecting Yankees totally unprepared and due to their westerly facing positions sent them cascading back one smashed unit upon another. Unfortunately for the Rebels, however, this overwhelming success had resulted in McCown's troops drifting away from Cleburne's Division on his right and had ultimately contributed to the change in the course of the battle. As a result of the Confederate success, the Union right had bent back at an angle in front of the Nashville Pike. Un-coordinated thrusts against this line, including one by Rain's Brigade in which the gallant North Carolina General was killed, threw confusion into the Rebel ranks and blunted the continuation of the advance.

These factors, along with the stiffening resolve in the Union center in the area called the "Round Forest" by some and "Hell's Half Acre" by others, stabilized the Union line which had now been aided by reinforcements from the left. Originally intended for the planned attack on the Confederate right, these troops were now available since the Rebel attack on the other flank had forced the cancellation of their attack. By evening the Union forces, driven back as far as two miles, had developed a firm defensive position which had repulsed the later Rebel attacks. Both armies remained on the field the evening of the 31ˢᵗ, uncertain of their next move.

January 2nd 1863

There was some shelling and some fighting yesterday and today.

The first day of the New Year passed with little activity save that of General Joe Wheeler's Confederate Cavalry, which harassed the Federal lines of communication back to Nashville. On the 2ⁿᵈ of January, 1863, General Bragg ordered an attack by the division of General John C. Breckenridge on the Union left approximately one hour before dark. Breckenridge outlined what he determined to be the futility of the action and protested the attack due to the presence of Federal troops to the north of his point of attack and situated on higher ground than his objective. Bragg insisted and about 4:00 P.M.

Breckenridge's troops charged into a situation exactly as he had described in his protest. While initially gaining their objective, well placed Federal artillery decimated the Rebels and forced them back to their point of departure. The ill-advised attack, delivered in miserable weather conditions, cost almost forty per-cent of Breckenridge's 4,500 man force and the life of Brigadier Roger Hanson, who died leading his "orphans."

January 3rd 1863

We retired from the battlefield at midnight yesterday. Heavy cannonading today.

Once again, the men of Ike's company had been spared the worst of the action. The 9th being a battalion and about half the size of the regiments in the brigade, they had been detailed as skirmishers before McCown's assault and in reserve of the North Carolina and Tennessee regiments during the morning attack. Although seeing battle for the second time, they had not as yet suffered a battle casualty.

Casualties for the remainder of the Army of Tennessee and that of the Union Army were horrific. Rosecrans, fighting essentially on the defensive, had suffered a casualty rate of twenty-nine per-cent, while Bragg in very case the aggressor had lost twenty-six per-cent. While a tactical victory, in that it blocked the Union Army's advance, it was a strategic defeat putting an end to Bragg's hope of driving the Union Army from Middle Tennessee and the Capital of Nashville. The Southern soldier, knowing little of the plans, strategies and objectives of their leaders, only knew they had once again met the enemy and had driven them from their positions. They were not prepared for and did not understand Bragg's next move.

General William S. Rosecrans

"Why're we leavin?" Sam asked Ike. "We whipped 'em didn't we?"

"Damned if I know," replied Ike, using an expletive which for Ike was very unusual, indicating his frustration with the curious response the army's commanders seemed to have to winning a battle.

"I don't know why once we have them whipped we don't finish them off," he continued. "It's kinda like wounding a deer and then not going after it. What's the point in fighting if we're not gonna complete the job. I just hope they know what they are doing. It's just like Kentucky. Marched all that way, whipped 'em and then turned tail. Damnest thing I ever saw. We ain't ever gonna get this thing done like this."

By this time, several of the other boys had gathered round listening to Ike and echoing his sentiments. Nevertheless, the Army of Tennessee was withdrawing south but there seemed to be uncertainty as to exactly where. The men in gray and butternut withdrew in a torrential downpour adding to the misery already felt by the confused Rebel soldiers.

Major General William Joseph Hardee

Eventually it was determined that General Polk's Corp would occupy Shelbyville and General Hardee's Corp would make camp at Tullahoma.

January 4th 1863, Sunday

Marched to Shelbyville 25 miles and camped

January 5th through the 10th

Stayed in camp at Shelbyville.

During the next four months the Army of Tennessee remained near Shelbyville, periodically moving their camp to a different location within the area.

January 11th 1863

Moved one mile to better place.

Snow fell on several occasions but spells of warm weather were also enjoyed before winter released its grip for good in April. It was also a time for sending and receiving mail and packages to and from home and receiving the occasional visitors whose presence broke the monotony of drilling and the routine duties of camp.

January 12th

I received a bottle of peach brandy from Father today. It was made by old man Charles Moon and daughter Cush.

January 29th

Preacher J. P. Rowe visited our camp today. He came from home.

Those who were literate read the bibles that many carried in their haversacks. Others played card games, some for fun and some to relieve those who were unskilled from their pay.

January 31st 1863 through February 8th

Still in camp here, sent $50.00 home Feb 3d

Family men, whose families were dependant on their monthly pay sent their pay home, as their needs for money were few if they were not gamblers and were unable to get to a town or a traveling sutler, from whom they might get clothes. Some arrived at unusual means of increasing the monies sent home.

March 8th 1863

Drew two months pay today. Also had inspection of arms.

March 9th and 10th 1863

In camp at Shelbyville, but we moved from this place at midnight and marched 8 miles north of Shelbyville and camped at a creek.

March 14th and 15th

It was reported that the Yankees were advancing but it was a mistake, on the 15th we resumed to our camp at Shelbyville.

March 17th 1863 Sent $75.00 home today.

March 18th through March 28th

We were in camp here for some time. Sam Power and myself made and baked apple pies (rights and lefts) and sold them to the Soldiers at $1.00 a piece, some of the Soldiers were simply too lazy to cook for themselves, if they had any money to buy anything with.

During one period in late March, Ike and Sam received a pass to go into Shelbyville to look for a shirt for Sam and something Ike might send home to the children. While shopping for what they needed, they overheard a conversation between the store proprietor and a lady who was looking to swap her canned good for item needed from the store. The store owner was willing to trade only a small number of her jars of fruits and vegetables she had put up the year before and it left her needing items she had no money for.

"Sam," said Ike, "I've got an idea how to make some money. We could buy some of her jars of apples and get some things here at the store and make some pies and sell them to the boys in camp."

"I don't know Ike, do you really think that will work?"

"Why not," said Ike, "They're always hungry and money seems to burn a hole in their pockets."

"Well, you just may be right," agreed Sam. "Let's try it."

After settling on a price for two dozen quart jars of apples, Ike and Sam bought the other ingredients they needed and set off for the camp. The men baked pie halves and sold them to the men in the company for a dollar each. The men eagerly bought the pies as it was simply easier to part with their pay than it was to put out the effort to cook something like a pie for themselves. Many of them would have parted with their money in the games of chance that always sprung up around the camps anyway. Often, after drawing their pay they would not even make it back to their tents before losing it to someone smarter and more skilled in the ways of the outside world, unknown before the war to many of these farm boys. The prospect of a hot homemade pie seemed a better alternative.

Letters received from Elizabeth during this time reported the big victory at Fredericksburg, the wounding of Ike's brother Tom and the death of his cousin Miles Vaughn. From another letter Ike learned that Bill, his older brother, had transferred form the 38th Regiment to the 15th and the Bowman Volunteers. She also wrote that Ike's Stepmother Sarah, who his father had married after his mother's death, was ill and her survival was feared for.

As was always the case, her letters brought Ike up to date on his children and were filled with the longing in her heart for Ike's safety and her prayers for his return home. Ike's return letters were always full of reassurance of his continued well being and assurance to her that he would be vigilant with regard to his safety. He spoke of his love for her and the children and how much her letters lifted his spirits and kept him going during the harsh winter evenings.

April 11th through 20th

Fair weather, big drill, still at Shelbyville.

Near the last of April, the company moved its camp to Flat Creek. It was always a welcome change to move to ground with fresh vegetation and away from an area which had been worn down and reduced to mud. A new camp would always improve the sanitary conditions for at least awhile and this was always welcome.

May 6th 1863

The 9th and 3rd Battalion consolidated into Regiment

Toward the end of the first week of May, the 9th Battalion and the 3rd Battalion were combined into a new regiment designated the 37th Infantry Regiment and Ike's company became Company E. This was part of a reorganization of the Brigade following the battle at Murfreesboro and the death of General Rains. The 11th Tennessee and the 29th North Carolina Regiments were transferred to other units and replaced by the 20th Tennessee, the 15th and 37th Tennessee, which had been combined, the 4th Georgia Sharpshooters and the 58th Alabama. This new Brigade was placed under the command of General William B. Bate who had helped raise the 2nd Tennessee and served as Colonel until he was wounded at Shiloh in April 1862. He had been promoted to Brigadier while recuperating from his wounds. This was his first Brigade assignment and he was to prove an able commander.

General William B. Bate

May 29th 1863

Moved 14 miles north east of Shelbyville to Fairfield

May 30th

Moved 2 miles towards Hoovers Gap and camped near Fairfield

Toward the 1st of June 1863, the Brigade broke camp and marched fourteen miles to Fairfield. Fairfield lay to the northeast of Shelbyville and was situated near the eastern most of four gaps through the Cumberland Mountains called Hoover's Gap.

June 3rd and 4th

Made long march through Hoovers Gap and returned to camp.

June 14th 1863

Had a visit from Charles Witcher, (the Charles Witcher that killed Cal Edwards between Carlton and Broad River near Bridge)

June 23rd 1863

Drew two months wages $34.00.

For the next three weeks all was quiet, until the 24th of June when Rosecran's, under the urging of his superiors in Washington, broke the six month stalemate and sent a force of 2,000 Mounted Infantry under Colonel John T. Wilder to attack and open up Hoover's Gap while most of the army demonstrated on the right to divert Bragg's attention.

June 24th through 28th

The fight commenced at Fairfield on the 24th. Several were killed and wounded on our side. Some skirmishing on the 25th and 26th and 27th, we fell back to Tullahoma and camped.

The plan had the dual purpose of ensuring Bragg did not move to reinforce the besieged army of General John Pemberton at Vicksburg, and at the same time to begin a move on Chattanooga. Wilder's men, armed with seven shot Spencer repeating rifles, easily pushed through the Gap which was defended by the 3rd Kentucky Confederate Cavalry. General George Thomas' Union forces moved through the opened up Gap, but were met by the Infantry Brigades of Generals Bate and General Bushrod Johnson of Major General Alexander P. Stewart's Division of Hardee's Corp. The Union forces were checked until near noon on the 26th when Bate and Johnson were notified by General Stewart of his intention to fall back on Tullahoma.

July 1st 1863

We vacated Tullahoma, left there at one o'clock in the morning and marched to Elk River.

On July 1st General Bragg began to withdraw his Army of Tennessee for a third time in nine months. Once again the Southern Army had held their ground but was forced to withdraw by their commanding General.

The furious fighting at Hoover's Gap had cost old Company B, now E in the new Regiment, its first battle death as Private Henry Dudley fell victim to the hail of lead laid down by Wilder's repeating rifles.

July 2nd

We marched to the top of Cumberland Mountain and camped.

The Army of Tennessee continued its march to the southeast on a route similar to the one that had carried them into Middle Tennessee. From Jasper, near the southern end of the Sequatchie Valley, the weary Southern Army marched to the Tennessee River west of Chattanooga where they camped until a pontoon bridge could be completed to allow them to cross.

July 6th

Crossed the river on a Pontoon bridge and camped 6 miles below Chattanooga, Tenn. at Lookout Station.

After gaining the southeast side of the river, the army camped at Lookout Station at the foot of the mountain of the same name until railroad cars were assembled and a train put together which carried them north of Chattanooga. Their destination was Tyner's Station on the Knoxville road where the next month and a half was passed in relative quiet.

July 11th 1863

We took the RR Cars (railroad cars) today and passed Chattanooga and camped 10 miles above on the Knoxville Road at Tyner's Station.

July 12th through August 22nd

While at Tyner's Station everything was quiet. I sent $40.00 home by George Eberhardt. (Lamar's father)

CHAPTER VI

THE HOME FRONT

During this time letters once again began to catch up with Ike and his Company E companions. Letters from Elizabeth and Sam's wife Martha were full of the news of the battle at Chancellorsville, Virginia where the courageous "Stonewall" Jackson had fallen, reportedly shot accidentally by his own men during a great victory. Later letters carried disturbing news of the loss of Vicksburg and the capture of General Pemberton's entire command, as well as the vicious three days of fighting at a small town in Pennsylvania called Gettysburg, where Lee's Army of Northern Virginia had suffered a major blow and had been forced to retreat back to Virginia. It was reported that the two armies had suffered 50,000 casualties. *Fifty-thousand,* Ike had thought. How could that be? Great cities like Charleston, Mobile and Richmond had populations less than that. In fact, that number was two and one-half times the population of Savannah, Georgia's largest city, and five times that of Atlanta.

Elizabeth had included the names of men lost by the two companies from Madison, County serving with the 16th Georgia as casualties mounted in an ever increasing fashion.

Those lost at Chancellorsville included:
From Company A

George Key—killed
John King—killed
Joshua Mason–killed
Milt Strickland–killed
Perry Williams - wounded
Stephen O'Kelly–wounded
Robert Sorrells–wounded
John Burroughs–wounded
Sterling Chandler–wounded
William Clements–wounded
William Glenn–wounded
Henry Herring - wounded

From Company D

James D. Williams–wounded
Thomas Thompson–wounded
Lum Martin—wounded

Those lost at Gettysburg included:
From Company A

Thomas Aaron–captured
Albert Allen–wounded & captured
James Baugh–captured
Ellis Harper–captured

From Company D

D. M. Bray–captured
A. H. Coker–captured
J.B. Ginn–captured
Walter Ginn–captured
M.D. Long–wounded
J. C. Nunn–captured
J. S. Smith–captured
S. M. Swindle–captured

Luke Smith had also been captured at Gettysburg. He was a close neighbor and had been serving with Ike's brother Bill in the 15th Georgia. A letter from Elizabeth also carried the news of the capture of Ike's brother Tom, their uncle Alexander Vaughn and cousin A. W. Vaughn who had all been wounded and left behind at Gettysburg. He wondered how his Grandfather, Alexander Vaughn Sr., now nearing his eighties had reacted to the news. He had already lost two sons and several grandsons to the war.

Elizabeth tired desperately to remain cheerful or at least avoid melancholy in the tone and substance of her letters but the news she reported spoke for itself. The People of Broad River were suffering terrible hardships created by the loss of their sons and husbands but also economically due to the strangling blockade, now all but shutting down any trade with Europe by the Confederacy. The blockade was creating a shortage of most purchased items and a complete lack of others.

On July 21, 1863, under an order of Governor Joe Brown, the families of soldiers serving, or who had served in the Confederate Army were supplied with a ration of salt. At the time of this order, there were 76 widows of Confederate Soldiers in Madison County, along with 184 wives of soldiers and 32 widows with sons serving in the armies (see Part III Exhibit I). Many other mothers, whose husbands were too old to serve or were in units of the Home Guard or State Troops, had lost sons or had sons currently serving. These families, many now with fatherless children, were living in desperate situations, many with no income and no prospects for things to improve. Prices on the very staples such as flour, sugar and salt were more than the common people could afford so they simply did without. The money Ike sent home helped Elizabeth considerably and Jim's store provided employment and a roof over her family's head, but some things were just too expensive or simply not available. Shoes had become very expensive, so the children generally went barefooted and Elizabeth made do with what she had rather than spend the money Ike sent home on shoes for herself. She had not had a new dress in sometime but Jim and just received some bolts of cloth and she was thinking of making herself something new so she would have something nice to wear if Ike ever got to come home. He had now served over a year without a furlough or leave, but she knew he was not the only one and so she made no complaint.

Keziah and Betsy, her sisters-in-law, had not seen Bill and Tom in over a year either and now Tom had been captured. Just in case however, she had her eye on a particular bolt of cloth the color of a robin's egg. She knew she could dress it up with a little bit of lace and make something real pretty. Nothing too fancy, for she did not want Ike to think her too extravagant in these hard times. The children had accepted Ike's absence slowly. They only knew he was away fighting to keep their home safe. She had assured them of his love for them despite his inability to be with them and that he would soon come marching down the road leading past Jim Power's store and gather them up in his arms. They kept a watchful eye when not doing chores, playing with their friends or attending the school in the area. Each time a unit of men marched by they searched the unshaven dirty faces for their father. Little Martha, now nearly five, would pull on men's coats and ask them if they had seen her daddy. John and Frank, now nine and seven, would ask question after question: Did the men know him? Had they seen any Yankees? When was the war going to be over? And always they would tell the soldiers: If you see our father tell him we miss him and to hurry home. It broke her heart to see them disappointed each time, but how could she stop them from going. They would not understand how she would know he would not be with these old men and boys of the Reserves and Home Guard.

Time wore on as the pages of summer turned slowly one by one. The families of Broad River shouldered their loads and made the best of things as well as they could. Crops were planted, tended and gathered in the continuing cycle of the farmer. The fields were not all tended as in years past, and those that were did not receive the attention they would have received from the hands that normally guided the plow. The harvests that resulted fell short of those of less turbulent times; however, it was more from lack of experience than effort that the fields seem neglected.

CHAPTER VII

THE BATTLE
FOR CHICKAMAUGA

August 23rd

Moved camp from Tyner's to Chickamauga River at the Bridge.

August 25th

We moved up the Tennessee River 4 miles of Harrison at Big Spring. It ran a mill below.

Near the end of August, part of the Army of Tennessee was again on the move. This movement took them north this time, back toward their old camp at Lenoir Station. There was a threat on Knoxville and their move was part of a shifting of troops to block the Union advance on the strategic rail center in Knoxville.

August 28th through August 30th

Moved and took RR cars to Loudon, Tenn.

The Confederate Army went only as far north as Loudon, some eight to ten miles below Lenoir Station and on the south side of a big bend in the Tennessee River separating the two small towns. Upon reaching Loudon, there was a sudden reversal in plans and the troops returned to Charleston along the river on the same railroad cars that had brought them north. They remained camped along the railroad at Charleston for three days before beginning a march back the way they had come through Big Springs toward their previous camp at Tyner's Station.

September 1, 2, & 3rd

We camped here on the Railroad at Charleston.

September 4th

Left Charleston and marched 6 miles to Big Springs.

September 6th 1863 Sunday

We marched to Ooltewah Station 6 miles above Tyner.

Their march continued past their former camps at Tyner and on into North Georgia. The next few days were spent in the area of Lafayette, Georgia, south of Chattanooga.

September 8 1863

We marched past Tyner and past Chickamauga to Graysville Station, Georgia.

September 9th

We marched through Catoosa County, Georgia into Walker and camped at a Church.

By this date, Rosecran's Army of the Cumberland had reached the Chattanooga area and was spread out west of the Rebel Army. Scattered clashes occurred between September 10th and September 17th, but they were of little or no consequence, simply the normal clashes between scouting parties and skirmishers who chance to run into each other during their sorties. During this time Ike was able to write a letter home.

September 10, 1863

My Dearest Elizabeth,

I set down to write you a few lines to let you know that were are now on home soil in Georgia. We arrived here last night and have camped around a church near Lafayette in Walker County. Rumors have it that the Yankee Army having pursued us in our march from Middle Tennessee has now arrived to our west and is in Chattanooga and the area just to the south of that place.

Although we have been told nothing, we expect that a clash of the armies will happen soon, possibly within the week. I am thankful that Almighty God has laid his hands on me and kept me safe through the battles in which I have participated til now. My prayers continue to be to him that if is his will, I will continue to be safe and one day when this terrible conflict is ended can return to you and my dear little ones.

I received your letters and with them the reports of the losses on men from Madison County in the battles in Virginia and Pennsylvania. I am sure there is much sadness in the homes along Broad River. I know that our company cannot expect the continuance of the good fortune we have had to date on the battlefield. To have lost only one man in battle in the time we have served is truly remarkable indeed and I do not think that we can continue to expect that outcome as we continue to struggle against the invading forces.

I was especially saddened to hear of the capture of Thomas, Uncle Alexander and A.W., our close neighbor Luke White and the death of John King. Please express my condolences to their wives and families for

me. If you see father tell him I'm very sorry for his loss
of Sarah. She was a good woman and a good companion to him.

If we do see a battle in a few days, I may not be able to
write you for a spell. Please continue to write, as your
letters seem to find me even though many are weeks old
when they arrive. Give my love to all our precious children. Tell them that their father is well and that I love
each and every one of them.

I will close for now and try to get some rest as we do not
know what tomorrow might bring.

Your loving husband,

Ike Moore.

September 17, 1863

Dear wife, I am adding these lines to my letter because
I have not had a chance to post it as yet. I wanted you
to know we have just been told to prepare three days
rations as we are moving tomorrow up the Chattanooga
Road and it is expected that we will meet the enemy
within those three days. I will write again when I am
able.

Ike

September 12th

Marched to Lafayette and camped.

September 17th 1863

*We left Lafayette and marched up Chattanooga Road
8 miles and camped at a Church*

On the morning of September 17, 1863, Bate's Brigade broke camp at Lafayette and marched eight miles up the road toward Chattanooga, camping near a church where they drew cartridges. As they sat around the fires in their camp that evening and ate what would be their last hot meal for the next three days, the men of Company E shared their expectations of the battle which was to come, possibly as early as the next day. Men wrote letters to their wives, their sweethearts or their fathers and mothers. Those who could not write asked others to write a few lines for them. Many of the letters had a very familiar theme.

They professed their love for the one to whom the letter was addressed. They spoke of their faith, the joy of home life, their admiration for those at home and for their comrades.

Ike and the other non-commissioned officers of Company E had been summoned to Captain Gholston's tent to receive their squad's assignments for the next morning so as to ensure a timely movement when the order to move came down. When the briefing broke up, Ike and Lieutenant Frank Power walked back toward the area where Sam and his cousins Asa and Tom Power were huddled around a fire to avert the chill in the early fall evening. They had been discussing the prospects for the next day and wondering how it might compare to the carnage at Murfreesboro nine months before. Ike and Lieutenant Power found a couple of open spots in the group of men and sat down.

Sam spoke up immediately.

"Well, what's it look like? Is there gonna be a fight?"

"I reckon there will be," answered Lt. Power. "I suspect it will be a good one. Seems both armies are concentrated so close I don't see how it can be avoided."

"We will move out behind the Sharpshooters (The 4th Battalion Georgia Sharpshooters) and the Artillery. Things may be rough for the next few days. I suggest those of you who are religious might want to have a few words with your maker, I intend to. I don't look to make it through the next few days."

"Ah, you're just a little nervous about this right now," replied Sam, his cousin and outside of Ike the oldest in the group.

"Heck Frank, we're all a little skeered. Don't think we'd be right in the head if we weren't. I'm sure you will be fine."

"Oh, I'm not afraid to die," continued the Lieutenant. I am prepared and ready to die, when God calls. I do not dread the next fight, but I know that I will be killed."

"Well, we'll see," said Sam as he stood up and dusted himself off. "Right now I'm gonna get some sleep." The group broke up one by one, moving off to their bedrolls to get what sleep might come.

The morning of the 18th of September was very much like any other fall morning in the North Georgia woods except for the stillness of everything but the bustling of an army readying itself for a march. The sounds of wildlife, which would be expected in a dense forest such as the one surrounding Chickamauga Creek, were not to be heard. The arrival of the troops the night before had driven off all of the animals before it to areas offering more serenity and protection. The only remaining inhabitants were a few birds who serenaded the troops as they sipped on the chicory blends which had all but supplanted the coffee enjoyed so much by the soldiers.

September 18th

We marched to Chickamauga Creek. Heavy firing commence, the enemy shelled us heavy.

After finishing a very early breakfast, Company E and the rest of the 37th Regiment assumed their position in line and the Brigade began its march toward Alexander's Bridge with their objective to take and hold Thedford's Ford about a mile to the south of the bridge. After marching to a point near the creek, the command double quicked to a wooded area overlooking the ford, where General Bate placed the artillery. While the remainder of the brigade remained in reserve but not out of harm's way, the Sharpshooters were sent forward against the enemy holding the ford. After a brief skirmish, the Sharpshooters drove the enemy across the stream and secured the ford. Meanwhile, the remainder of the brigade was positioned north of the ford and exposed to the Union Artillery above Alexander's Bridge on the northwest side of the Chickamauga. The Union batteries were eventually driven off by the well placed rounds of the Eufaula Artillery, but not before one was killed and five or six wounded in the brigade. This action, though minor, was the opening action in what was to become a very bloody affair, adding additional credence to the Chickamauga's Indian name, "River of Death." The evening of the 18th of September, Bate's Brigade bivouacked on the ground just contested and won from the enemy, and in a position to command the Thedford Ford and another which General Bate referred to as the "Bend Ford" in his official report.

Lee and Gordon's Mills. Chickamauga Battlefield, Ga., 1863

Early the next morning, the brigade crossed the creek at the fords they had secured the afternoon before, forming battle lines in rear of the brigades of Brigadier Generals John C. Brown and Henry D. Clayton. The division moved in that order some two miles north of the fords where they halted and remained until early afternoon. During this period of inactivity, Ike's squad huddled together in soft hushed tones. During this time Lieutenant Power, seeking out his cousin Sam, came upon Ike and Sam who as usual were together and talking quietly.

"Sam," Lt. Power interrupted. "I need to talk to you."

"Sure," replied Sam.

Ike and a few others began to rise when Lt. Power quickly motioned them to remain where they were. Frank Power sat down in front of where Ike and Sam were sitting side by side and knowing the group he was with asked that they pray together. Ike, who would later serve as a deacon in the Carlton Baptist Church for 45 years, began the prayers with each man offering his own unique message to God. Lt. Power, the last to pray, prayed for his country, his comrades and for the whole Army. He prayed for the Church and the world, his wife and children and lastly for himself, commending himself to his Lord both soul and body. As he rose from his knees, he extended his knife, watch and pocket book toward Sam, saying: "Sam, I am confident this fight will be my last. Keep these things and send them home to my wife after my death. Tell her that I died happy, trusting in the Lord and that I want her to meet me in heaven and that it is my wish that she raise our children right, that we may meet an unbroken family in heaven."

[The words of Lt. Francis E. Power were taken from "Historical sketches" pgs. 154–156 by Groves Harrison Cartledge (1820–1899)]

Sam at first tried to refuse the items extended to him but was assured by Lt. Power, who at home was known as "Doctor Frank," that he was quite certain of his wishes. Reluctantly, Sam placed the keepsakes in his haversack along with those of his own. The men were reminded eerily of the Lieutenant's words of two days before.

"I do not dread the next fight but I know that I will be killed."

As Lieutenant Power moved slowly away from the group to find Captain Gholston, he left them with the following words:

"Be strong men, trust in the Lord and do your duty."

Within a few minutes, they would hear his voice again.

"Up men, fall in and form battle lines."

Lieutenant Power and Company E were on the threshold of their greatest engagement of the war up to that point. For many, it would be the last.

September 19th 1863

This is the day of the great battle. Our Brigade got into the battle about 3 o'clock, killed and wounded in our Regiment about 140, three in Company E. They were Lieut. Power, Corporal Morris and R. T. Power, 93 wounded. Myself wounded in the right side. Ball struck cap box, did not go through. W. A. J. Brown (Jesse Brown's Grandfather) carried me off the battleground. (He had a sick certificate) and he followed us and carried me behind a log to protect us from bullets.

As in their previous alignment, the brigade was formed in line behind the brigades of Brown and Clayton and held in reserve. As these brigades were sent forward, Brown's troops were subsequently repelled by the enemy and thrown back through Bate's command. Again the men of Company E heard the voice of their friend and Lieutenant, as he drew his sword and, turning to the men of his squads, who were a part of the eighty or so left in the Company out of the one-hundred and fifty plus who had joined a year and one-half ago, shouted:

"At the double quick forward."

The words would be his last as within moments, among the angry buzzing of the Minnie balls fired from the entrenched Federal line, one would find its way to the chest and heart of another of Dixie's finest. The prophetic words of Lieutenant Francis E. "Doctor Frank" Power, spoken only a short time before had come true. Close behind Lt. Power, Ike Moore urged his squad on.

"Let's go men, come on," he shouted, turning to see if someone had come to the Lieutenant's aid. As Ike turned back toward the distant blue line, obscured to some extent by the dense growth of trees in which it was anchored, a second volley burst forth from the darkness of the woods. There was a muffled thud as Ike's body was spun to the right. His legs gave way and before he knew it Ike was on his knees. Looking down, Ike could only see the hole in his cap box where the lead projectile had hit him. Instinctively, he prostrated himself on the ground to avoid the whistling missiles of death. Examining his side with his fingers, Ike felt the warmth of his blood seeping from under the remnants of the cap box. As he tried to find something with which to press into the wound in his side, he found himself in a struggle to maintain consciousness. As he searched his pockets for a handkerchief, a dark form settled over him and he heard the familiar voice of Bill Brown. Bill was a neighbor and was married to Polly Simmons, Elizabeth's first cousin.

"Ike," he heard Bill shout over the roar of the cannons and muskets.

"Are you all right? Where is it, where are you hit?"

Without answering, Ike pointed to his side and the shattered cap box. Bill removed Ike's belt and tried to determine the extent of the wound. The blood and sweat had formed a moist, sticky mixture, soaking Ike's shirt and jacket, making it difficult to get a good look at the wound.

"Let's get you out of here," said Bill, lifting Ike over his right shoulder. Bill struggled with his load back toward the area where the brigade had formed less than an hour before. Finding a large fallen tree, Bill laid Ike behind it and after getting the bleeding stopped, went to look for a stretcher bearer. There were men down everywhere and there would be a need for lots of stretcher bearers.

The battle raged until the rapidly approaching darkness brought the first full day's action to a close. Bate's Brigade and the 37th Georgia slept on the field among the enemy dead.

The following description of the involvement of his Brigade on September 19th is from the Official Report of General Bate written after the battle:

"The whole command moved forward with spirit and zeal, engaging the enemy hotly before it had proceeded 200 yards, his lines extending in front and to the right and left of us. A battery in front of my extreme right played constantly and with terrible effect upon that wing until my right pressed within less than 50 paces of it, when it was rapidly removed to prevent capture. Another revealed its hydrahead immediately in rear of this, supported by a second line, hurling its death-dealing missiles more destructively, if possible, upon our still advancing but already thinned ranks. Having driven the first line back upon its support, a fresh battery and infantry were brought to play upon my right, which, by its advanced position had become subject to an enfilade fire, and gave way, but not until Major Caswell, Colonel Smith, and Colonel Rudler, the three officers commanding, respectively, the three right battalions, were wounded, and at least 25 per cent of their numbers killed and wounded."

The following report of Colonel Rudler commanding the 37th Georgia is copied from the Official Records of the War Between the States.

Report of Colonel A. F. Rudler
Thirty-seventh Georgia Infantry
MISSIONARY RIDGE, NEAR CHATTANOOGA, TENN.,
September 28, 1863.

MAJOR: I have the honor to submit the following as my report of the part which my regiment took in the battle of Chickamauga on the 18th, 19th and 20th instant:

On the afternoon of the 18th, my command was hastily formed in a skirt of the woods fronting the brigade across the creek near Mr._____ house, where the enemy's battery was stationed throwing shell and shot, during which time I lost 2 men wounded.

On the morning of the 19th, my regiment, with the brigade, was held in reserve in line of battle in rear of Clayton's and Brown's brigades.

About 2 o'clock the regiment, with the brigade, was ordered to advance to the front. General Brown's brigade at the time was engaging the enemy. While in close supporting distance General Brown's brigade was driven back through my command. At this critical juncture the command was given to forward, which was done with spirit, engaging the enemy within 150 yards. After engaging the enemy with considerable success, the order was given to charge a battery immediately in my front. My regiment, the Twentieth Tennessee, and Caswell's sharpshooters drove them from their guns. As soon as the enemy sheltered himself behind a second battery in the rear of the one from which we drove him, he opened with grape and canister, which was so destructive that the regiment became divided, a large portion moving forward to the left and the others to the right.

At this time I received a slight wound in my right foot which disabled me from participating further in the battle. For the subsequent action of the regiment in the battle, I respectfully refer to Lieutenant-Colonel Smith's report, on whom the command devolved, which I herewith forward.

I carried into the engagement 400 men and came out with 206, sustaining a loss of 194 men. Killed, 19; wounded, 168; missing, 7; a report of which has been forwarded.

The officers and men behaved with such gallantry I am unable to make any distinction among either officers or men, all being entitled to credit for having nobly done their duty as becomes good and true soldiers.

Very respectfully, your obedient servant,
A. F. RUDLER,
Colonel, Comdg. Thirty-Seventh Georgia Regiment.

Colonel Rudler received a wound which incapacitated him during the remainder of the battle and passed command of the regiment to Lieutenant Colonel Joseph T. Smith, whose report follows.

Report of Lieutenant Colonel Joseph T. Smith
Thirty-seventh Georgia Infantry.
Missionary Ridge, near Chattanooga, Tenn.
September 28, 1863.

SIR: The command of the Thirty-seventh Georgia Regiment having devolved upon the undersigned during the battle of the evening of September 19, I have the honor herewith to transmit a report of what occurred while I thus remained in command:

The regiment on charging the enemy about 4 P.M. Saturday, September 19, became mixed up with a regiment of Law's brigade, and in the confusion incident to such a state of things about 50 men, several line officers, and myself became separated from the other portion of the regiment (we being on the right flank) and pursued the fleeing enemy in a right oblique direction some 400 or 500 yards, when, perceiving what appeared to me to be a brigade of Federals making a charge to the rear of our right flank, with the evident intention of cutting us off, I gave the order to the few men with me to fall back rapidly. This was done with a loss of 4 or 5 men captured by the enemy, our whole party barely escaping from our exposed and critical position. In a few moments we rejoined our regiment, which we found moving back from the left with Clayton's brigade. A short time afterward, the battle not being renewed, we encamped upon the battle-field for the night.

(end of first day's report)

During the evening of the September 19, 1863, the two divisions of General James Longstreet of the Army of Northern Virginia (ANV) completed their arrival at Chickamauga and formed battle lines along side their Southern brothers of the Army of Tennessee.

Ike was taken to a field hospital near General Bragg's headquarters and just west of Chickamauga Creek. Only slightly more than a mile from the battle lines, Ike could hear the sounds of battle resume the next morning about 8:00 A.M. To him it sounded like the unholiest of Sabbath mornings.

General James Longstreet

September 20th 1863 Still fighting.

The report of Colonel Smith commanding the 37th after the wounding of Colonel Rudler, and the casualty statistics for the Regiment are a testament to the fighting done by this gallant band during these two autumn days.

(Lt.Col. Smith's report continued)

At an early hour on Sunday morning (September 20), the regiment, under my command, moved from their camp by the right flank to the position assigned them. Here, under, we erected slight breastworks out of the fallen timber, stones, &c. Our line of battle at this point was not exceeding 400 yards from the batteries and formidable breastworks of the enemy erected the night previous and concealed from our view by the undergrowth. We had been at this position but a short while before the enemy opened upon us with shell, canister, and grape. We remained steadily under this fire until between 1 and 2 P.M., losing a number of men wounded.

At about the above-stated time we received an order from General Bate to charge the enemy's batteries, which had been annoying us so much. The regiment moved forward at once in gallant style with a cheer and at a double quick. The enemy at once perceiving our movement opened upon us from all his guns, firing very rapidly canister and grape, and in a few seconds afterward his whole line of infantry from their breastworks poured upon us the most terrific volleys. The regiment moved steadily forward and pushed up to within 50 yards of the enemy's artillery and breastworks. Here the smoke from the enemy's guns was so dense that I could only see my command at intervals. I was not able to perceive that I was supported upon my left flank by any troops whatever. I now think it probable that the regiment on our left moved so far to the left that I was unable to see them, or it is possible that we moved farther to the right than it was intended we should. One thing is sure, neither the officers of my regiment nor myself saw any support to our left while we were so near the enemy's lines.

On our right, the little Spartan band of the Twentieth Tennessee Regiment went forward with us and gallantly stood by us. Being subjected to a very heavy fire upon our right flank from an angle of the enemy's breastworks and to a raking fire from front, and also from a left-oblique direction, the regiment was in a manner compelled to retire, being easily rallied at the breastworks by General Bate in person. Coming up a moment afterward, I reformed the regiment, which was by no means in a demoralized condition.

Our loss in this charge was very heavy, 5 or 6 of our gallant fellows being afterward found dead within less than 40 paces of the enemy's guns.

At about 5.30 P.M., same evening, we were again called upon to charge the enemy. The order was responded to with the utmost enthusiasm, and moving forward rapidly the enemy were driven from their position in disorder and confusion, we capturing many prisoners, arms, &c. Night intervening closed the contest.

The officers and men of the regiment acted throughout the engagement with conspicuous coolness and gallantry.

**I was particularly indebted to Major M. Kendrick,
who was in charge of the left wing of the regiment, for the
skill displayed by him in discharging his duties, &c.
I am, very respectfully, your obedient servant,
JOSEPH T. SMITH,**

Additional excerpts from General Bate's report covering the action on the second day follow along with a summary of the losses of his Brigade:

"My right, as upon the evening previous, became hotly
engaged almost the instant it assumed the offensive. It was
subject to a most galling fire of grape and musketry from
my right oblique and front, cutting down with great fatal-
ity the Twentieth Tennessee and Thirty-seventh Georgia at
every step, until they drove the enemy behind his defenses,
from which, without support either of artillery or infantry, they were unable to dislodge him. General Deshler's
brigade not having advanced, I called on Major-General
Cleburne, who was near my right and rear, for assistance;
but he having none at his disposal which could be spared,
I was compelled to retire that wing of my brigade or sacrifice it in uselessly fighting thrice its numbers, with the
advantage of the hill and breastworks against it. I did so in
good order and without indecent haste, and aligned it first
in front and then placed it in rear of our flimsy defenses."
My command entered the fight Friday evening with
1,055 guns and 30 provost guard and a fair complement of
officers, out of which number it lost 7 officers and 59 men
killed and 541 wounded, 61 of whom were officers; making a total of 607. It is seen that every field officer in the
brigade excepting three were wounded.

The additional excerpts from General Bate's report which follow below describe how ill-equipped the Southern Army seems to have been going into this tremendous battle. It seems inconceivable, considering today's military might, that an army could send a full two-third of its men into battle lacking the most fundamental armament of the infantryman.

"My brigade went into the fight with muskets in the
hands of one-third of the men, but after the first charge
Saturday evening every man was supplied with effect on

their original owners the next day. The dead and wounded
of the enemy over which we passed in driving them back on
Saturday and Sunday give an earnest of the telling effect
produced upon them in both days' fight. Besides arming
itself with Enfield rifles, a detail from my command, under
supervision of my ordnance officer, James E. Rice, gathered upon the field and conveyed to the ordnance train
about 2,000 efficient guns. The pieces captured by Colonel
Tyler and those in which Colonel Jones participated in the
capture were taken to the rear and turned over to proper
officers."

The desperate struggle continued on all fronts on the 20th, with the
fortunes of battle ebbing and flowing until a mix up in orders in the Union
command created an opportunity quickly seized by the Division of General
John Bell Hood of Longstreet's 1st Corps of the Army of Northern Virginia.
The attack by Hood split the Union forces and sent the right flank of that army
reeling back toward Chattanooga with Rosecrans accompanying the rout. At
this point, the commander of the Army of the Cumberland thought his whole
army to be in retreat and was concerned only with falling back to Chattanooga
and attempting to form a defensive position to prevent the total destruction of
his command. He was later to find out that General Henry Thomas was holding on precariously on the Union left wing and in effect covering the complete
collapse on his right.

Longstreet, whose troops had won the day, seeing a golden opportunity ordered General Joseph Wheeler to drive between the Federals and
Chattanooga and cut them to pieces in their disorganized rout. No sooner than
Wheeler had begun his movement, he was ordered by General Bragg to stop
and pick up arms and stragglers. Longstreet protested and asked for permission to advance. He was refused.

General Nathan Bedford Forrest, who had observed the rout and seen
the same opportunity as Longstreet, directed an aide to: *"Tell General Bragg
to advance the whole army. The enemy is ours."* But Bragg, apparently the
only man who had not realized that a great victory had been won and a golden
opportunity presented, halted his army. Even in the days following he made no
move to take advantage of his victory.

The reluctance of Bragg to pursue and the stubborn defense of Thomas
near Snodgrass Hill almost certainly saved the Union Army from complete
annihilation and led to the loss of Chattanooga by Bragg a month later.

General Nathan Bedford Forrest

Thus was born the rift between Bragg, arguably the most ineffective commander of his rank in either army, and nearly all of his commanders in the Army of Tennessee.

September 21st

I came to the railroad at Dalton on my way to Hospital

Ike's wound was not serious and he remained at the field hospital until the morning of September 21st, when he was moved with the other wounded to the railroad at Dalton to be transported to the hospital in Atlanta. His wound had cost him an opportunity to see his older brother Bill, who was now with the 15th Georgia in General Henry "Rock" Benning's Brigade. The two brigades had slept on the field for two nights and had been less than a half mile apart. This quite possibly would have allowed them to visit after the Union retreat to Chattanooga.

September 22nd and 23rd

Got to Atlanta on 22nd, and left for home night of 23rd and got on the 24th 1863. Stayed at home till October 27th, 1863.

On the 22nd of September, Ike was transferred by railway car to the hospital in Atlanta and after treatment was allowed a leave to go home.

Back at Chickamauga, both armies were licking their wounds and the command structure of the Confederate Army was in chaos. Longstreet and General Leonidas Polk met secretly and determined to beseech Richmond to act. In a letter written to Secretary of War Seddon, Longstreet said:

> *"Our chief has done but one thing that he ought to have done since I joined his army—- that was to order the attack upon the 20th. All other things that he has done he ought not to have done. I am convinced that nothing but the hand of God can save or help us as long as we have our present commander."*

He suggested that Davis should replace Bragg.

On October 4th, a document signed by the majority of the Corp and Division Commanders was sent to President Davis. It expressed the complete lack of faith in their Commanding General and asked for his removal.

A now famous confrontation between Bragg and Forrest had occurred a few days earlier, when Bragg ordered Forrest to turn over command of his troops to Wheeler. After sending a letter indicating his displeasure with Bragg, Forrest rode to Bragg's headquarters. As reported by Forrest's Medical Officer, Dr. Cowan, they entered Bragg's tent where, after finding Bragg alone and refusing Bragg's offered hand, Forrest began:

> *"I am not here to pass civilities of compliments with you, but on other business. You commenced your cowardly and contemptible persecution of me soon after the battle of Shiloh, and you have kept it up ever since. You did it because I reported to Richmond facts, while you reported damned lies. You robbed me of my command in Kentucky, and gave it to one of your personal favorites—men that I armed and equipped from the enemies of our country. In a spirit of revenge and spite, because I would not fawn upon you as*

others did, you drove me into West Tennessee in the winter of 1862, with a second brigade I had organized, with improper arms and without sufficient ammunition, although I had made repeated applications for the same. You did it to ruin me and my career.

When in spite of all this I returned with my command, well equipped by captures, you began your work of spite and persecution, and have kept it up. And now this second brigade, organized and equipped without thanks to you or the government, a brigade which has won a reputation for successful fighting second to none in the army, taking advantage of your position as the commanding general in order to further humiliate me, you have taken these brave men from me.

I have stood your meanness as long as I intend to. You have played the part of a damned scoundrel, and are a coward, and if you were any part of a man I would slap your jaws and force you to resent it. You may as well not issue any more orders to me, for I will not obey them. And I will hold you personally responsible for any further indignities you try to inflict upon me. You have threatened to arrest me for not obeying you orders promptly. I dare you to do it, and I say that if you ever again try to interfere with me or cross my path, it will be at the peril of your life."

After exiting Bragg's tent, Dr. Cowan told him, *"Well, you are in for it now."* Forrest turned and replied, *"He'll never open his mouth. Unless you or I mention it, this will never be known."* Many regard it as the greatest act of insubordination ever by any American officer.

Davis could not ignore the situation and on October 9th arrived at Bragg's Headquarters. Despite the pleadings of Longstreet, Buckner, Hill and Cheatham in the presence of Bragg, Davis amazingly ignored their advice and instead circulated a letter chastising the commanders for their lack of confidence. Davis then allowed Bragg to dismiss all the dissenters save Longstreet, who was considered "untouchable," and Forrest who was later reassigned and promoted. Others including General Thomas Hindman were either removed or reassigned to less responsible positions. Upon Davis' departure, the Army of Tennessee was left in total confusion with no plan for the future of the fall campaign.

Late in October, Davis decided it might be a good plan to dispatch Longstreet to Knoxville to dislodge Burnsides and open up the route from

Virginia to the South. This would also separate Longstreet and Bragg who Davis had finally decided would never work in concert. Cooperation between Longstreet and Bragg had essentially ended and this lack of cooperation and breakdown in morale of the Rebel forces were certainly factors in the upcoming failures at both Chattanooga and Knoxville.

Confederate President Jefferson Davis

CHAPTER VIII

AT HOME

Ike left Atlanta on the night of September 23rd, after being briefly examined by a doctor in the hospital there, he caught a train heading East through Athens and on to Elberton. Ike got off near Comer and walked the remaining distance to his home along Holly Creek. As Ike drew nearer to his home, he began to meet with familiar faces. The older men still at home left their work in the fields, which by now was cleaning up after the harvests, and met Ike at the fence rows along the roadside. Ike hurried along, eager to see Elizabeth and his children. Topping the slight rise in the road that descended on the other side down toward Jim Power's store, Ike could see a small group gathered on the front porch of the store. The group had been alerted by a neighbor boy sent ahead by his mother who had recognized Ike as he passed their farm. Soon Ike's family broke away from the group and began running up the slight incline. The two oldest boys, John and Frank, led the way as might be expected, followed by Martha, little Ike and Elizabeth who was carrying Mary and was slowed by that added burden. Ike dropped to one knee to receive John, the first to reach him and who in his exuberance would have most likely have jumped into Ike's arms, straddling Ike's waist and the wound in his side with his legs. As tears of joy flowed from all eyes, Ike greeted each child and then stood to receive Elizabeth and Mary into his arms. Ike's heart was bursting with joy as he embraced Elizabeth and Mary and kissed each of them lovingly. The other children surrounded their parents attempting to wrap their short arms around them. After awhile, the family, with each member trying to maintain contact with Ike, moved down the road toward home. Almost a year and a half after leaving, Ike Moore was once again at home.

The days at home passed all too rapidly for Ike. Refusing to sit and rest, Ike drew visitors to the store who just wanted to talk. Everyone wanted to hear Ike's stories from the war and reluctantly, he obliged many of them, usually answering their questions but offering little if not asked. Many had loved ones still on the front and were looking for reassurance as to their well being. Many of Ike's friends had returned home within a few days of Ike's return, several wounded only slightly like himself, and others more seriously. Ike had traveled to Atlanta with those killed and wounded on the 19th, where the more severely wounded were hospitalized and the dead prepared for their journey home. Those wounded in the fighting on September 20th followed a couple of days later.

A few days after Ike arrived home, the following list of casualties of Chickamauga was published in the Athens Banner Herald.

Athens Banner Herald, Athens, Ga. 1863
Battle of Chickamauga
List of casualties in Co. "E" 37th Ga. Reg.
On the 19th and 20th Sept. 1863
Editor Banner

Sir
You will please publish the following list of killed and Wounded in our company, and oblige many Of their friends.

Killed

2nd Lieut. Frances Power,
2nd Corp. William A. Morris,
Private, Robert T Power

Wounded

1st Lt. J B Eberhart, in ankle slight;
1st Serg't G A Gloer, on head, slightly;
2nd Serg't Y A Daniel, right arm slight;
3rd Serg't I V Moore, in side slight;
5th Serg't D Wayne, on toe slight;
4th Corp. M H Pittman, left leg slight;
Private J H Burroughs, left leg severely;
T G Deadwyler, thigh severely;
W J Dudley right leg severely;
Isaac D? Eberhart, bowels severely;
J. Drake, left hand slight;
J C Kirk, right arm slight;
B A Moon, jaw and shoulder slight;
T B Power, right leg severely;
A G Power, right leg slight;
G P Gentry, finger slight;
R T Russell, arm severely;

Wm. R? Smith, left leg severely
Caleb M Stephens, breast slight;
Wm. A Tolbert, ankle slight;
J B Thompson, left arm slight;
J W White, right leg, severely

By that time, the bodies of Sam's brother Robert and Sam and Elizabeth's cousin "Doctor Frank" Power had arrived in Madison County. Their funerals were officiated by Reverend James M. Power who was Sam and Robert's brother.

Ike spent the days at home as close as possible to his family. He took the older boys fishing along the Broad River, something he had done when time permitted before the war. Now it seemed very important to be with them as much as he could. On one of the fishing trips, while keeping a watchful eye on their bobbers in the still eddy created by the large rocks that reached from bank to bank in broken groups all along the river, Ike's thoughts went back to another river a year before and the dead Yankee soldier. His quiet thoughts were interrupted by his oldest son John.

"Pa, have you killed any Yankees?" he asked.

"I don't rightly know son. I've shot at them a number of times, but It's hard to know for sure in all the smoke and confusion. Why do you ask, John?"

"I don't know, I just wondered."

Ike thought back. He really could not be sure he had ever shot anyone. He had fired his first shots at Murfreesboro and really taken aim at an individual for the first time at Hoover's Gap. It was quite possible he had never shot anyone. Nothing more was said and except for the big catfish Frank caught, the afternoon passed uneventfully.

The little ones, Ike held on his lap as much as he could and told them stories he remembered from his own childhood, and read to them children's stories from the few books available.

The evenings he spent with Elizabeth, walking in the autumn moonlight, talking softly as they rocked on the porch of the second story of the store where they lived, or often just watching her as she mended the children's clothes, combed her long dark hair or took care of things that had to be done in the quiet time when the children were asleep. They talked of times before the war, of the days of their courtship when she was just a young girl of sixteen. He remembered how beautiful she was when he had first seen her and she remembered how handsome he looked in the new suit he wore when he came to call on she and her family the first time. They still felt the magic they had felt ten years before. At night they lay close, holding each other without the passing of many words. Ike felt at these times as if he had never been away. He slept soundly and deeply beside her as he had not slept since leaving home the year before.

Ike was very much aware that in a few days it would be exactly ten years since they were married, October 18, 1852. Ike knew Elizabeth had closely managed the money he had sent home and had spent little on herself during his absence. He had seen the pretty blue dress and had not remembered it from before. She had not worn it since he had been home and Ike suspected she was keeping it for their anniversary. He wanted very much to find something to go with the dress that she would not have bought for herself.

One day while Elizabeth was bathing the little ones, Ike had sought out Jim's wife, Mary Elizabeth, to get some advice. Ike approached Mary Elizabeth, who was also his sister in law, as she checked the store's inventories.

"Mary Elizabeth, I need to find something for Elizabeth for our anniversary. Can you suggest something?"

She looked up from her inventory list and toward Ike.

"Why Ike, I'll be happy to help you. Did you have something in mind?"

"Well, yes and no. I saw the blue dress she is working on and I thought maybe something to go with that. I just don't know."

Mary Elizabeth thought for a minute and said, "What about a nice lace collar or a fan?"

"No, I was thinking of something a little more special than that."

Scratching her head, Mary Elizabeth tried to think of something else, something she was sure Elizabeth would like.

"I know," she exclaimed excitedly. "I know exactly what she would like. It came in last week. It's a little expensive and Jim was not pleased that I had ordered it, but I thought it might fit someone's special needs when I saw it in the catalog. She's seen it too Ike and even tried it on. She thought it was beautiful but a little extravagant."

"Well what is it?" said Ike chuckling. "Are you going to show it to me or just go on and on about it?"

Mary Elizabeth laughed and replied, "Why sure. I was just caught up by the coincidence and how perfect it would be."

They walked to the side of the store where the counter was and she withdrew a small velvet covered box. Inside the box was a heart shaped gold locket and matching chain, which opened up to allow for placement of small photographs.

"That's perfect! Could you wrap it in some pretty paper for me?"

Mary Elizabeth assured Ike she would tie a pretty ribbon around it and that she felt the box it was in was pretty enough not to need wrapping paper. Ike agreed and was very pleased with the locket and with himself. She had assured Ike that although moderately expensive, he could have it for the price they had paid from the catalog and that Jim would be glad that it was sold and that he had not been stuck with it.

Before Ike knew it, the eighteenth was on him. He rose early that morning and took the children the short distance to the home of Elizabeth's parents, Frank and Elizabeth Simmons. The eighteenth fell on a Sunday and he felt some guilt in not going to preaching, but he wanted this day for just himself and Elizabeth. He knew his God would understand. If he were to be less fortunate the next time he went into battle he wanted a special memory to carry with him. Elizabeth's mother had prepared a picnic basket for them so Elizabeth would not have that to worry about. He planned to take her to some of the quiet wooded places along the river where they had walked on Sunday afternoons during their courtship. He had only told her to be ready when he got back from her parents.' When he returned she was sitting on the porch waiting, wearing the beautiful new blue dress. Around her neck was the gold locket and chain. He had left the velvet box, its contents and a note in a conspicuous place before leaving with the children. Her beautiful brown eyes showed signs of having recently shed tears, but the smile on her face was radiant. Her long hair fell gently on her shoulders as she descended the steps and into his waiting arms.

"Oh Ike, what a wonderful surprise."

Despite feeling the gift extravagant under the current conditions, Elizabeth said nothing. Ike was a wonderful man, father and provider and she could not and would not question his decision or judgment.

"I love you so very much," said Ike kissing her softly and lifting her into the buckboard he had borrowed from Jim. The day had dawned cool and crisp, and the remainder of the day would equal or surpass the morning. God had blessed Ike and Elizabeth once again. Their special day would be all Ike had hoped for and more.

The remaining days of Ike's leave passed so quickly they seemed a blur to him. His wound had healed and his strength, which had been reduced considerably by his seventeen months of meager and unhealthy rations, was restored. He had gained back a portion of the weight he had lost and felt a new man. A few days before he was to leave, his father John Nathaniel paid him a visit. They talked of his mother, his brothers Bill at Chattanooga and Tom, who they had learned had been paroled in September along with Ike's cousin A. W. Vaughn, and returned to duty. The wounded A. W. had returned home.

Unhappily, the news had not been good for Ike's Uncle Alexander, who had died of his wounds a few days after Gettysburg and had been buried there. He learned his Uncle Joel, his father's brother, and Joel's young son William had joined the 1st Georgia Infantry under Olmstead and had left the first of the month for the coast. They spoke of the war, politics, their faith, but mostly they just enjoyed each others company. His father indicated his intention of finding another wife after a respectful length of time. Ike thought this to be wise as he felt his father would live a longer, happier life if he had companionship.

Before Ike knew it, the day had come for him to pack up what he would need for the winter and return to his company. He said goodbye to the children the night before he was to leave and the next morning he kissed Elizabeth lovingly and held her tightly in his arms for several minutes. Quickly pulling away, wiping the tears from his eyes and kissing each of her cheeks wet with tears, he picked up his gear and left by the rear entrance and down the steps at the back of the store. Jim met him at the front of the store where he had his buckboard waiting. Jim had promised Ike he would take him to the railroad junction near Comer. Jim was contracted to carry the mail to and from the post office at Brookline near Comer to his store for the convenience of the people who lived along Holly Creek near his store, and he needed to make the trip anyway.

October 27th

Left home and got to Atlanta.

October 28 and 29th

Got to Chickamauga on the 28th, and rejoined my company near the point of Lookout Mountain.

CHAPTER IX

CHATTANOOGA

By evening, Ike was in Atlanta and two days later he had rejoined his company at the foot of and near the point of Lookout Mountain. For the next month Ike's company, now part of Breckenridge's Division, was positioned in the valley to the east of Chattanooga near the foot of the mountain. This new alignment was part of the total reorganization of the Army of Tennessee that had come from the command meetings between Bragg and President Davis. (General Patrick Cleburne's Division had been the only division untouched by the reorganization.

Chattanooga looking toward Lookout Mountain
Photographed by George N. Barnard

On the 24th of November, Confederate forces abandoned Lookout Mountain after a brief engagement with the forces of General Joseph Hooker, of Chancellorsville infamy. Giving up the mountain made the valley a very difficult area to defend and increased the potential for a flanking attack from the south. For these reasons, the troops in the valley were moved further eastward and into the fortified line extending along Missionary Ridge.

November 24th 1863

Considerable fighting on Lookout Mountain. It was taken by enemy. We left the Valley.

Action at Orchard Knob on November 23rd convinced Bragg that Grant, who was now in overall command, intended a breakout of Chattanooga. Bragg had added to his problems by dispatching the Divisions of Generals Bushrod, Johnson and Patrick Cleburne to join Longstreet, now in the vicinity of Knoxville. He attempted to recall these divisions, but found Johnston was already too far up the valley. Cleburne, who was still in the area, was recalled and placed on a position on the northern most part of Missionary Ridge.

Also on the 24th of November, General W. T. Sherman, whom Grant had chosen as his right hand by now, attacked Cleburne's hastily thrown up defenses on the Confederate right. Failing to achieve any success against Cleburne's determined defenders, Sherman's attack was stopped and resumed the next morning with the same results. True to his form throughout the war, when confronted by a fighting force anywhere close to similar strength, Sherman had failed again. In this case, his four divisions had failed to even gain a foothold on the ridge against the solitary division of Cleburne.

General Patrick R. Cleburne

North end of Missionary Ridge looking south
Photographed by George N. Barnard

As the thrust by Sherman was intended to be the major attack and the flanking maneuver which would drive Bragg's Army off Missionary Ridge, the attacks on the center and left of the Rebel lines were intended primarily as diversions.

November 25th 1863

We came to the top of Missionary Ridge and had a big fight. We vacated the Ridge and fought one mile from it. M. David was killed. We lost several pieces of cannon, the enemy shot our own cannon. We marched towards Cleveland, past Chickamauga, and camped 3 miles of Graysville.

Inexplicably, the attack on the center by Thomas' Army of the Cumberland, beaten so badly the month before at Chickamauga, succeeded. Designed initially as a diversion and to drive the Rebels from the rifle pits at the foot of the ridge, the attack gained momentum and breached the Confederate line in the area defended by troops from the Divisions of Anderson and Bate, both newly organized and led by new commanders.

November 26th 1863

*We lay in line of battle most all day at Cross Roads. We
then marched past Ringgold to Catoosa Spring and
camped*

Badly outnumbered, the Confederates had no reserves to throw into the
breach and consequently many of the Rebels broke and retreated rather than
be flanked and captured, as many of their compatriots were to be. The Battle
of Missionary Ridge is a contradiction to the rule of battle which provides that
a defending force will in most case hold their ground against a force twice its
size. Many factors led to the overturning of this rule of battle at Missionary
Ridge, but the low morale of the Southern troops unquestionably played a
major role.

Post battle casualty reports more often than not give a clear indication
of the victors and vanquished of a battle. Those from the Battle of Missionary
Ridge and Ringgold Gap would suggest an entirely different outcome for the
battle until the huge numbers of Rebel troops who simply gave up are factored
in. Excluding the category of Missing/Prisoner, the casualty rates were 9.7%
for the Union and only 5.5% for the Confederates. These results are very similar to the statistics at Fredericksburg with a totally different outcome. The fact
that almost 9% of the Confederates simply surrendered seems to be entirely
the reason for the results of the two battles differing so greatly.

The beaten Confederate Army withdrew to the east, past Chickamauga toward Graysville, and formed a line of battle expecting pursuit from the
Federals. A holding action by General Cleburne's Division at Ringgold Gap
thwarted the expected pursuit and on the 27th of November, the Confederate
Army marched the twenty odd miles to Dalton, Georgia and dug in.

November 27th 1863

*We marched to Dalton, Georgia and camped at the new
Hospital where they put our wounded and sick Soldiers.*

Once again, Braxton Bragg had proven his inability to manage a battlefield and in fact had almost surely doomed his army before the fighting even
began. This time it would be his last opportunity. Under tremendous public
pressure Bragg asked to be relieved of command in December. His replace-

ment would be General Joseph E. Johnston, who had commanded the Confederate Army in Virginia before his wounding in the 1862 Peninsula Campaign and his subsequent replacement by General Robert E. Lee. Ironically, it had been Johnston that Longstreet had pushed for command less than a month earlier in a meeting with Davis.

General Joseph E. Johnston

CHAPTER X

WINTER 1864

November 28th 1864.

We built little Shantys and took up winter quarters here, the weather is very cold here.

Georgia Governor Joseph E. Brown

When it became obvious that the Union Army was going to remain in and around Chattanooga and not attempt a winter campaign, Ike and the rest of the army settled in around Dalton and began to construct shelters against the cold of a winter come early. During the next few months, the new Commander was able to develop a congenial relationship with Governor Joe Brown of Georgia, which was beneficial in seeing that the troops, especially those from Georgia, were re-supplied and re-outfitted. Additionally, the ranks of Johnston's army would be increased by the availability of the various units of

Georgia State Troops raised by Governor Brown for service only in Georgia. He also received the support of the Governor of Tennessee Isham G. Harris in the following letter written to the Secretary of War James A. Seddon:

Tennessee Governor Isham G. Harris

HEADQUARTERS ARMY OF TENNESSEE,
Dalton Ga., January 9, 1864.

Honorable JAMES A. SEDDON:

SIR: From an intimate acquaintance, and much intercourse with the Army of Tennessee and especially the Tennessee troops of that army, I am satisfied that the reorganization of the army, breaking up State divisions, &c., at Missionary Ridge, proved an element of weakness in the battle fought at that place. I need not resort to argument to satisfy you that men will fight better when supported upon the right and left by men with whom they have passed through many hard-fought battles than they will when supported by entire strangers. It is equally true that they will fight better when led by officers whom they have known long and well and followed through hard-fought and victorious fields than when led by strangers. I know that the reorganization has produced much dissatisfaction, and so far as I can see has produced no one good result. I understand that the reorganization was required by an order of the President, which prevents General Johnston from interfering with it hence I address you alone for the purpose of asking that General Johnston may be permit-

ted to organize the Army of Tennessee in such manner as he may think will best promote the efficiency of the army he commands. From a verbal interview which I had with you when at Richmond, in December, I was satisfied that the Department would not be disposed to control General Johnston in a matter of organization. Being fully impressed with the fact that the Tennessee troops will be much better satisfied, and therefore more efficient, in their old organizations and under their old generals, I venture to urge most earnestly the policy of immediate reorganization so far as practicable. It is proper that I state that this letter is written without the knowledge or consent of General Johnston.

Very respectfully,

ISHAM G. HARRIS.

Clearly, Harris' letter indicates that the dissention in and subsequent reorganization of the Confederate Army, between the victory at Chickamauga and the defeat at Chattanooga, played a significant role in the divergent outcome of these two battles, fought only twenty-nine days apart. The fact that the Confederate Army had never shown a proclivity to collapse under pressure before and that the one division, that of Cleburne, which had remained intact without reorganization, stood its ground on North Missionary Ridge despite being faced with the largest disadvantage in terms of opposing troop strength seems to add substance to the opinions of Governor Harris who had taken an active role in the war in Tennessee and in fact was with General Albert Sidney Johnston when he died at Shiloh.

During late December and early January, the weather turned unseasonably warm, improving the roads and due to the proximity of Dalton to Madison County, allowing several of the members of Ike's Company to take well earned leaves and go home. It also gave Ike a means of sending money home and in a two week period he sent $200 home. It also allowed the people back home to visit their friends and relatives in camp.

During this same period a significant revival of spirit and faith took place in the ranks of the Southern Armies both at Dalton and near Fredericksburg, Virginia. Visiting Ministers and Army Chaplains spoke to large groups of men at each service and thousands of men were either converted or experienced a rebirth of their Christian beliefs. Ike and Sam, who had both been raised Christians and regular attendees of services before the war, and others from the Thirty-Seventh were often included among the worshipers. Many of the visiting ministers traveled from the counties of North Georgia, having congregational members numbered in the soldiers on the Army of Tennessee. Similar religious movements occurred in the camps of the Union armies, as soldiers found faith in God and belief in a better life to come to be all the more important during these troubled and perilous times.

December 17th 1863

I sent $30.00 home to Wife by Sargt. J. A. Glore.

December 23rd 1863

Drew $169.00 Sent $100 home by J. B. Eberhardt

December 25th Christmas Day.

I sent $70.00 home by Capt. D.L. (Dabney) Gholston.

January 2nd and January 5th

Warm and pleasant. Visit by J. G. Power.

During a particularly nice period of weather in early January, Jim Power came up to Dalton and spent a few days with Ike, Sam and his other friends in the company. During the visit, Jim suggested that he might bring Elizabeth with him on a later trip if Ike thought it was alright. Eager to see Elizabeth again he told Jim that if Elizabeth felt comfortable in leaving the children for a few days that he had no objection.

February 6, 1864

Wife started with J. G. Power to visit me came as far as Union Point, but had news that the enemy was advancing and went back home.

In early February, Elizabeth started from home with Jim Power but, hearing of an advance by the Union forces from Chattanooga, turned back at Union Point. Jim continued on and spent another few days with Ike and Sam in camp.

February 10th 1864

J. G. Power went home. On Feb. 13th was beautiful weather.

Toward the latter part of February, the weather turned cold and several inches of snow fell. Rumors begin to circulate of Union troop movements and near the end of February the Rebel troops made ready to move to block this advance.

February 23rd 1864

We left our camp and moved 2 miles toward Tunnel Hill and camped

February 23rd & 25th

We had considerable fighting on our right and heavy fighting in this Gap at the Railroad

A few days later, reports of Union movement toward Dalton and the tunnel at Rocky Face Ridge, or Buzzard's Roost, were received and Bate's Division and others were moved toward the tunnel where they camped. Over the next few days, February 23rd through the 26th, there was a considerable amount of skirmishing with little change in the overall situation in North Georgia. Casualties on both sides amounted to under 300 and General George Thomas commanding the Union forces realized the strength of the Confederate positions and withdrew his army back toward Chattanooga and his camps near Ringgold.

Union Troops drilling near Ringgold, Ga.
Photographed by George N. Barnard

February 26th 1864

Fighting is not so heavy today. The enemy retreated toward Chattanooga during the night.

February 27th 1864

Returned to our old camp. Rainy weather.

On the 27th of February most of the troops, who had moved to the tunnel, returned to their camp in Dalton. Over the next two months, all was quiet for the men of Bate's old Brigade, now under the command of General Thomas Benton Smith. Supplies continued to roll into Dalton and the army became re-supplied with both men and materials.

General Thomas Benton Smith

A letter received from Elizabeth during this time informed Ike that his brother Bill and been captured in East Tennessee after the battles around Knoxville, and had been sent to a Northern prison camp in Illinois. Her letters also informed Ike of the death of Isaac Simmons, her cousin and a brother to David, and Wiley Simmons of his company. Isaac Simmons was one of several Madison County men serving in the 16th Georgia lost in the Battle of Knoxville.

Time passed with the men involved in the normal pursuits of an army at rest. It was a time to heal the wounded, catch up on letters home for those not lucky enough to receive a leave, and to refresh the understanding of the basic military drills, formations and battlefield maneuvers. The drilling was necessary in order that the new recruits coming into the ranks would have an understanding of what to do in all situations under fire. Most of the men in the Southern Army when the war began had been familiar with firearms, if not military drills, and needed little instruction in the handling and care of a musket. Now, however, many of the new recruits entering the army as a result of changes in the laws regarding substitutes and the new Conscription Act of that February (which had lowered the minimum age to seventeen and increased the upper age to fifty) were less familiar with firearms, and Ike found himself spending more time conducting drills and in weapons instruction. The lack of a standard musket made the job a little more difficult but by 1863 the muskets, although different in manufacture, were similar in design and often the same or very close to the same caliber, allowing for interchangeable cartridges. This was true of the British made Enfield, used extensively by the Southern Infantryman, and the U.S. made Springfield, the most common Union rifle as well as its Southern counterpart the Richmond Rifle. In addition to the Enfield Ike carried, he had also been fortunate to find a 36 caliber Colt revolver, for which he procured a holster and began to carry as a sidearm. His pistol not of Southern manufacture (some copies of this model Colt were made in southern Georgia at Griswoldville) was a U.S. issue and was carried by many Union and Confederate Infantry Officers, making the cartridges readily available. The additional weapon would serve him well during the upcoming months.

April 6th through April 26th 1864

Pleasant weather, all quiet on front, but expecting a move soon.

The soldiers were blessed with warm, pleasant weather during April, and this spring would have been difficult to tell from a typical North Georgia spring had it not been for the barren landscape, which was stripped clear of trees in the Dalton area as well as the area near Rocky Face Ridge. Small flowering trees budded and opened their blooms of many colors to the warm spring showers and the sunshine that followed.

April 29th 1864

Orders to be ready to move at any time.

April 31st

Went to the Gap today, some skirmishing.

CHAPTER XI

ATLANTA CAMPAIGN

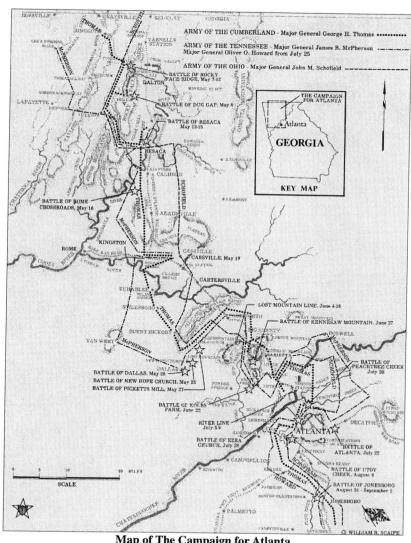

Map of The Campaign for Atlanta
used with the permission of William R. Scaife

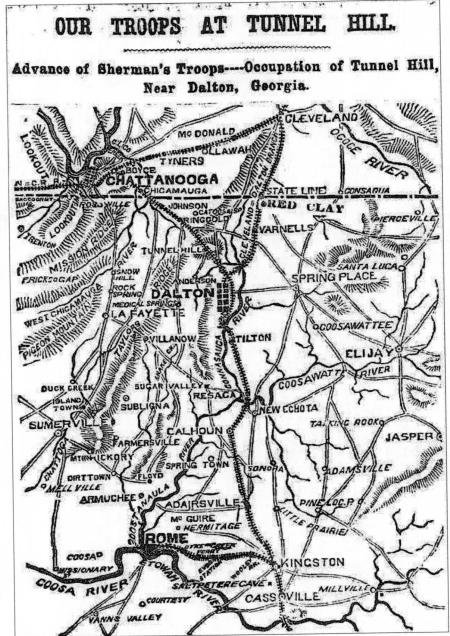

Map of Tunnel Hill area from New York Herald ca. 1864

By the end of April, most units were expecting to receive the call to move. For Smith's Brigade, these orders came on April 31st. The Division of General Bate returned to the area near the Gap and awaited a move by their enemy in blue. The anticipated move came on May 7th as General William T. Sherman, now commander of the Military Division of the Mississippi, began his advance on Johnston's Army of Tennessee, which was entrenched along Rocky Face Ridge extending eastward across Crow Valley.

May 7th 1864

Moved to the front. Cavalry with infantry at Mill Creek Gap on Rocky Face Ridge.

Pass in the Raccoon Range
Photographed by George N. Barnard

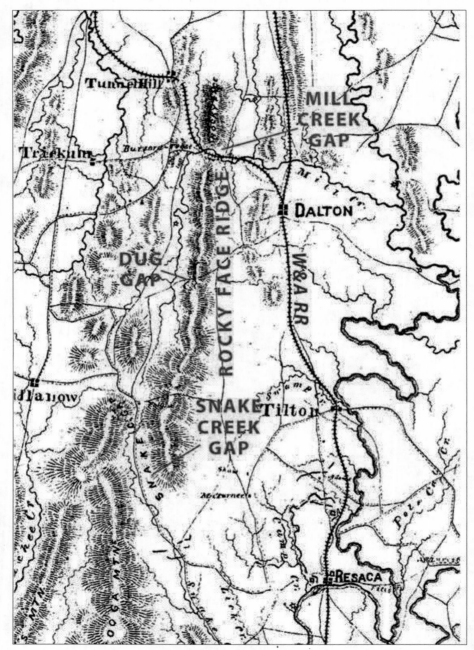

Union Map of area around Dalton

Sherman's three column attack was split, with two columns engaging Johnston head on at breaks in the ridge at Mill Creek Gap and Dug Gap, while a third under General James McPherson was sent around the confederate left flank through the Gap at Snake Creek, in an effort to capture Resaca. Finding Resaca well defended and fearful of bringing on an engagement unsupported, McPherson withdrew to the Snake Creek Gap.

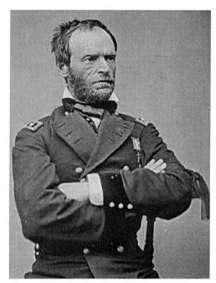

Maj. Gen. William Tecumseh Sherman

May 8th and 9th 1864

There was considerable skirmishing and cannonading for the two days with little effect.

May 10th 1864

Heavy skirmishing and cannonading most all day. There were heavy cannonading in the evening with a storm of rain and wind.

May 11th

There was heavy skirmishing and cannonading in the evening on the north side of the Gap. We had a big rain and very hard wind last night.

Sherman, seeing the hopelessness of trying to dislodge the Confederates from Rocky Face Ridge and the two Gaps which were well defended, withdrew his forces from in front of the ridge and began a flanking maneuver toward Resaca.

May 12th 1864

There has been skirmishing going on today. We are very closely confined in the ditches The general opinion is that the Yankees are moving to our left. Their line is in full view. At eight o'clock in the night we left the Gap going toward Resaca moving very near all night.

May 13th 1864

We reached Resaca, Forming line of battle west of that place and built breastworks.

Left with little choice, Joe Johnston pulled his troops from their entrenchments on the ridge and retired toward Resaca. Sherman's demonstrations against Johnston's fortified position had been a costly one in terms of casualties but had succeeded in forcing the Rebels off Rock Face Ridge.

On May 13, 1864, the two armies began three days of fighting which in the end were inconclusive in results, but left nearly 5,600 casualties divided almost equally among the combatants. The first day's fighting was light as the Union Army probed the Confederate lines looking for a weakness. Sending his troops against the entrenched Rebels the next day, Sherman found little success, while again suffering significant losses.

May 14th 1864

A very heavy fight commence at one o'clock it kept up

till dark Our loss was light, the enemy was heavy. Our Brigade was held in reserve but was under heavy fire all the time and several of our men were wounded. J. W. Patton was wounded in the leg and it killed him

Ike and his dwindling band in Company and the rest of Smith's Brigade were held in reserve, but the heavy artillery bombardment preceding the Union advance took a heavy toll just the same. Ike moved along the entrenchments behind which his men had taken up position urging everyone to remain as still as possible. Despite his warnings, a number of men were wounded by the shrapnel from the exploding shells.

As he moved along, Ike found John Patton screaming in pain and his friends trying desperately to stop the bleeding from a wound caused by a goose egg sized piece of shell which had torn through his leg, all but severing it from his body. The men tried everything they could to stop the flow of blood without success. As the precious life blood flowed from the pulsating artery into the red Georgia clay, he lost consciousness and little by little his body became more lifeless until he was gone. After this, Ike had little trouble in convincing the remainder of the company to cover as best they could and remain still.

Resaca battlefield
Photographed by George N. Barnard

May 15th

Fighting commence again early today, heavy fighting all day with small arms and artillery. Our loss in killed is very light. As the enemy is flanking us on the left, we took up a line of march at 10 o'clock in the night, marching southward along the railroad to Calhoun.

Again Sherman began to move his army to the left of the southern entrenchments and once more, unmoved from their breastworks, the Rebel Army was forced to retire, fighting as they withdrew southward along the railroad toward Calhoun.

May 16th 1864

Considerable fighting with the enemy today. We left the place at one o'clock in the night and marched the balance of the night.

General Joseph Wheeler

Continuing to move south looking for a suitable place to make a defensive stand, the troops met once again at Adairsville where heavy fighting occurred between Major General Oliver O. Howard's IV Corps and the entrenched infantry of Lieutenant General Joseph Hardee. Finding the ground at Adairsville unsuitable for attempting a stand, Johnston pulled his infantry back to Cassville, while the Confederate Cavalry of Major General Joseph Wheeler skillfully covered his withdrawal.

May 17th 1864

We reached Adairsville, rested the most of the day, late in the day we had some heavy fighting, made breast-works. Then marched all night and reached Kingston at day.

May 19th 1864

We were marching and forming line of battle all day. Had some very heavy fighting near Cassville. We stayed at Cass Station this night.

May 21st 1864

We are stationed at Etowah, these days between Dalton and Atlanta. Sherman's Army fought and flanked us so that they could surround

Johnston's Army. Johnson tried to save his men, and some blamed him for not going on ahead but he did the best he could.

May 25th 1864

We marched 2 miles east of Dallas and formed line of battle.

As the Confederate Army fell back toward Dallas, which appeared to be the destination of the Union Army as it continued to move around the Confederate left, Federal assaults were made at both New Hope Church on May 25th, and Pickett's Mill on May 27th. In each case, Sherman miscalculated the strength of the Rebel defenses and the Union offensives were repulsed with heavy Union casualties.

May 26 & 27th

Built fortification, and fighting started. There was heavy skirmishing all day and night on our right. Company out on picket.

By May 28th and 30th, both armies had reached the Dallas area and this time Sherman decided to entrench his troops as well. In a reversal of the defensive tactics he had employed during the almost constant fighting beginning at Rocky Face Ridge, Johnston chose to seize the initiative and ordered Lieutenant General William Hardee to test the Union entrenchments. Much like the outcomes at New Hope Church and Pickett's Mill, the aggressor was repulsed, only this time the shoe was on the other foot and it was the Rebel Army that suffered high casualties.

May 28th 1864

Very heavy skirmishing today. Bates' Division made a charge in the evening killing and wounding and taking several prisoners. Sargt. Griffeth was killed. Ned, A. Spurlock was killed, William Wood, and J. Dudley were wounded and died from their wounds.

Company E. stepped off as part of Bate's Division, which anchored the left flank of Hardee's assault. There was initial success, as a number of the Federal skirmishers were caught by the rapid Rebel advance and a good number were killed, wounded and captured by the initial Rebel thrust. As Ike and the rest of the company closed on the Union entrenchments, a hailstorm of lead erupted from a solid line of blue clad troops, who rose above their breastworks and poured a destructive volley into the double-quicking Rebels. Out of the corner of his eye, Ike saw Walton Griffith, who had recently been promoted to Sergeant, spun around by a Minnie ball which struck him in the chest and dropped him to his knees. A second ball quickly finished the deadly work. Men began to drop at a more rapid rate as the firing from the Union line now became more constant if less furious, as the men in blue loaded and fired at will. A second projectile now claimed the life of Augustus "Ned" Spurlock, who had only been in the army since the past October and had accompanied Ike from Atlanta back to Chattanooga at the end of Ike's leave. As Ike paused to check on the wounded Will Wood, he heard Captain's Gholston's voice ring out over the din of the row of muskets to their front.

"Fall back, fall back," he shouted. "Ike, move your men back, we cannot go on."

Turning to the men in his squad and those of Sgt. Griffith, Ike screamed in a voice louder that he had ever employed before.

"Fall back, fall back, check the wounded as you go."

As Ike urged his men back he came across Lem Dudley on his knees, holding his head in his hands. A ball had struck him in the forehead above the left eye and his face was covered with blood. Blinded by the force of the impact and the blood streaming into his eyes, he was repeating over and over in a strange, calm voice, "I can't see, where is everyone?" Sam had stopped to help the stunned, frightened man and between the two of them they got him to his feet and moving back toward the safety of the Confederate trenches. As Sam urged the badly wounded man along, Ike tried in all the confusion to make sure everyone had heard the orders and was falling back. It seemed all had turned and were moving as rapidly as possible, while staying as low as possible to avoid the occasional ball still coming form the Union lines, now fading in the distance. Ike moved to help J. G. Seagraves who was trying to pick up the mortally wounded Will Wood, a pre-war neighbor, and get him back to safety. Ike helped young Seagraves get Wood across his shoulder and stayed with them as they struggled back to their own lines. The company returned to their lines and counted the wounded, dead and missing. The company had lost Sgt. Griffith and Ned Spurlock killed, and the badly wounded Will Wood and Lem Dudley would not survive their wounds. A number of others had received minor wounds and several were unaccounted for. Some would find their way back to the company during the night, while others would have to be numbered among those whose fate was never known.

May 30th 1864

Skirmishing all night. David Seagraves was wounded, several wounded today, and 2 were killed in the Regiment. Lieut. Sheppard was killed

Fighting continued around Dallas until June 5th when Sherman, who continued to attempt to get on Johnston's flank, abandoned his entrenchments at Dallas and moved his infantry to the railroad at Allatoona Pass, which his Cavalry had occupied a few days before. During that period, the fighting claimed additional casualties from the ranks of the 37th Georgia including David Seagraves, who was wounded and later died in the hospital in Atlanta.

May 31st

Skirmishing is not so heavy as usual today. The enemy is falling back beyond Dallas. I was taken severely sick today, reported to Dr. Galloway.

June 2nd 1864

I was sent to Marietta and from there to Atlanta

On May 31, 1864, Ike became very ill and reported to the Doctor who, being unable to treat him there, ordered that he be sent to the Hospital in Macon. His illness seemed to be a reoccurrence of the liver ailment he had suffered nearly two years before, only much more severe. He was suffering greatly from fever, headaches, nausea and violent intestinal cramping and there was nothing that could be done for him in a field hospital. Two days later Ike was sent to Marietta and on to Atlanta, where he was transferred by rail to Macon.

June 3rd

From Atlanta I was sent to Macon. W. H. (Billy) Smith is with me. We are in the City Hall Hospital.

While in the City Hall hospital in Macon, Ike was reunited with Billy Smith who had received a severe leg wound at Chickamauga and was still receiving treatment. (Author's note: Muster documents indicate William Smith was still in the hospital at the close of the war). Their hospital beds were side by side at Ike's request and they spent much of the time, when Billy's pain allowed it, talking quietly about home, families and their experiences over the last two years. Ike took advantage of the time to write letters home to Elizabeth and to his father. He assured them he was getting better and that his life was not threatened by whatever his infirmity was, for even the doctors were uncertain.

June 13th 1864

I was transferred to Eufaula, Ala. Been raining for 10 days

Ike remained at Macon for about ten days and then was sent to a hospital in Eufaula, Alabama where rain fell nearly every day during his stay. Confined much of the time inside by the wet weather, the days passed slowly and Ike was subjected to sights that would haunt him the remainder of his days. Men were recovering from wounds that many would carry the rest of their lives. There were men maimed in unimaginable ways by the horrors of war. Men who had lost limbs were too numerous to count. Others had been transformed from handsome youthful figures to disfigured and pathetic creatures that would be the object of pity and curiosity the remainder of their lives. Many of these men would never again be able to live a productive life and many would have to be hospitalized for the remainder of their lives. There were men who had been struck in the face and who were transfigured into objects of horror. Others, while saved from death by medical practices emerging out of necessity, were living with injuries which would make them dependent on someone to help them for the rest of their lives.

Shortly after his arrival at Eufaula, Ike was adopted by a young soldier from Alabama named Wesley Goins, whose lower jaw had been all but blown off by a ball at Missionary Ridge the past November and whose recovery had been extremely painful and slow. His mouth and jaw had been rebuilt to the best of the surgeon's ability, but he was still horribly disfigured. He was able to chew only very soft foods, so his diet was almost exclusively soups and other soft things which would not be painful to his healing jaws. He was relearning to talk to where he could be understood and he was almost constantly with Ike, chattering away in some unintelligible gibberish that Ike was only able to pick a few understandable words from. After a few days, Ike had listened to so much of the man's incessant ramblings that he was able to understand him better than anyone and began to relay to the doctors and nurses what Wesley was trying to tell them when they talked to him about his wound. Without effort and only through Ike's Christian kindness he had become Wesley's best friend, and Wesley had followed him nearly everywhere he went on the days that the rainy weather broke enough for them to walk the grounds around the hospital. Ike had learned that Wesley was from near Tuscaloosa and that he had joined the army when he was sixteen, two years before. He was the youngest in a large family and was living with his widowed mother when the war broke out. He had not written her or any of the folks at home of his injury for he could not find the proper words. The folks at home included a girl that Wesley was sweet on and he was concerned how she would react to his wounds when he recovered enough to go home. Wesley talked to Ike like a boy would talk to his father. He shared with him his concern for what life would be like for him after the war was over and his hopes that he might be returned to duty. This concerned, Ike for he felt Wesley's fear for the life he might have after the war would provoke him into a disregard for his safety that might lead to his death.

Ike recovered quickly at Eufaula and after a week and a half, the doctors pronounced him fit for duty and told him he would return to Macon the next morning. As Ike packed up the few belongings he had brought with him to the hospital, Wesley approached, curious as to what Ike was doing. When Ike explained that he had been released to return to duty the sadness in Wesley's horribly disfigured face and his eyes, moist with the tears he was attempting to hold back, broke Ike's heart and he shook Wesley's hand and embraced him in the manner men embraced one another. The next morning Ike was on his way back to Macon and then on to Marietta and the war.

While Ike had been away, the fighting had continued at Marietta until Sherman, extending his lines beyond those of the Rebels and threatening their supply line, forced Johnston to move to a position he had previously selected at Kennesaw Mountain. A futile attack by General John Bell Hood, who after recovering from the loss of his leg at Chickamauga had been reassigned to the Army of Tennessee, led Sherman to believe that the under manned and thinly stretched out Rebels would be susceptible to a frontal attack and on June 27th, he attacked Kennesaw Mountain.

Sherman's attack met with some initial success, driving Rebel pickets and skirmishers back to the main entrenchments, but the attack stalled against the strongly defended Confederate line and their withering fire. After horrific losses, reaching at one stretch about sixty casualties a minute, Sherman called off the attack. Once again, Sherman had miscalculated and was left with little to show but casualties for his effort.

Major General John Bell Hood

**Union entrenchments near Kennesaw Mountain, Ga., 1864
Photographed by George N. Barnard**

July 1 & 2nd

Heavy skirmishing, we fell back 8 miles, giving up Marietta.

By the 1st of July, Ike had rejoined his company in the defensive line north of Atlanta, near Kennesaw Mountain and Marietta. Once again Sherman was moving on the Confederate flank, forcing Joe Johnston to retire from a well conceived and well constructed defensive position so that he was not flanked on the left. Johnston retired several miles, constructing temporary breastworks while a more solid line of defense was built behind him along the Chattahoochee River, and protecting its various crossing points.

Defensive positions along the Chattahoochee River
Photographed by George N. Barnard

This line was one of the strongest defensive positions constructed during the Atlanta Campaign, but it eventually fell victim to the same fate of many others, that of abandonment.

Sherman finally had learned his lesson and this time he avoided being drawn into another attack on a well fortified position. His movement both east and west along the river and beyond the six mile length of the Confederate line again flanked Johnston's position and forced yet another withdrawal, this time to within five miles of Atlanta along the south side of Peachtree Creek, which extended from east to west on the north side of the city.

Battlefield of Peachtree Creek
Photographed by George N. Barnard

July 9th

Moved in facing Atlanta, gave up the Chattahoochee River.

July 12th and 13th

We are in 4 miles of Atlanta, on the Railroad.

From this position, Johnston planned to make an offensive move against Sherman in hopes of winning a victory decisive enough to force the Union Army back toward Chattanooga, thus relieving the besieged city of Atlanta and keeping the Georgia Railroad, running east through Decatur, open and connected with the lines north to Virginia. Before Johnston was able to initiate his plan, Davis, who was tired of Johnston's defensive tactics, removed him from command and replaced with John Bell Hood. Hood, who had been no higher than Division Commander in the Army of Northern Virginia, had been given one wing of Johnston's reorganized Army of Tennessee, after his recovery from the loss of a leg at Chickamauga and subsequent transfer to the western theatre. Many believed that Hood, who was very ambitious, had formed an alliance with Braxton Bragg, now the military advisor to President Davis, in order to get Johnston removed.

July 14th 1864

We moved 4 miles north of Atlanta to Peachtree Creek, Johnson was relieved and Hood was put in command

Davis had now replaced a cautious leader, admired and respected by his troops for his interest in their well being, with a man known for his hard fighting but also for his recklessness and disinterest in the high number of casualties in which his reckless tactics often resulted. Rumors had begun to surface about the 14th or 15th of July of the change but the official telegram did not reach General Johnston until the 17th. Johnston remained one day to discuss with Hood the current positioning of the army and to acquaint him with the plans he would now not be able to put into action.

With the departure of Johnston the Army of Tennessee, reeling from successive strategic set backs, suffered another serious blow to its morale. Many of the senior officers, friends of Johnston and distrustful of Hood, were convinced that Hood had purposely undermined Johnston's efforts and was complicit in his removal. The men in the ranks, lacking confidence in Hood's leadership began to desert in increasing numbers.

July 20th

We fell back to our breastworks and made a charge.

Eager to please his new Commander in Chief and prove his decision to be correct, Hood began to look for an opportunity to show his aggressiveness. Lacking time to formulate a new plan of his own, Hood adopted the plan which Johnston had hoped to use. On July 20th he launched an attack against the left wing of Sherman's Army, commanded by General Thomas, as it crossed Peachtree Creek. Sherman's Army, split into three wings under Thomas, Schofield and McPherson, was separated between the three wings and this separation allowed Hood to achieve early success in his attack against Thomas on the Union left. Thomas' artillery, placed very strategically, proved ultimately to be the deciding factor and the determined Confederate attack was eventually repulsed, with the Rebel Army suffering two and one-half times as many casualties as their foe.

July 21st

We moved to the right at night to the east of Atlanta

July 22nd

We made a charge and lost several men. J. W. Griffith was killed, and four others were wounded This was called the Blackberry Charge.

Two days later, on July 22nd, Hood, hoping to catch another of Sherman's wings unsupported, sent a force against the Union left wing commanded by McPherson, who was attempting to flank Atlanta on the East and destroy the railway link through Decatur. Much like at Peachtree Creek, Hood's troops were initially successful but once again they were stopped by overwhelming Union firepower. General McPherson, killed in the fighting, was one of the 3,600 Union casualties, but once again Hood's losses exceeded twice those of Sherman's Army.

Although his losses were high, Hood had succeeded in preventing Atlanta's capture from the East and Sherman was forced once again to change tactics. This time Sherman, who had promoted General O. O. Howard to replace McPherson, pulled this wing of his army still on the Union left flank, and sent them on a march around to the right to test the Confederate left and cut the last remaining railroad supply line between Atlanta and East Point. Hood anticipated a Union shift to his left and sent troops to block the movement at Ezra Church. These troops, under Lt. Gen. Stephen D. Lee and Lt. Gen. A.P. Stewart, met an entrenched Union force and were bloodily repulsed, suffering six times the casualties of the Union forces. In the eleven days since his elevation to command, Hood had reduced the strength of his army by almost one-third.

July 23rd through 26th.

Moved back to the west of Atlanta, worked on breastworks all day the 24th.

August 2nd and 3rd

Moved to the right one mile and back to the Sandtown Road. Heavy fighting today.

In early August, still determined to cut the rail line between Atlanta and East Point, Sherman moved Schofield from his position on the Federal left to the right of Howard's troops, where he encountered Hardee's Corp at Utoy Creek.

August 6th

Our division was in a considerable fight today, killing, wounding and taking prisoners a good many, our Losses was light. W. M Perry was killed and D. R. Mosely better known as Dick was wounded

In three days of fighting, Schofield's troops not only failed to cut the railroad, but suffered heavy casualties in an attack on the Division of General Bate, including the 37th Georgia and Ike's company. Although the losses in Company E were relatively light at Utoy Creek, their numbers continued to shrink as W.M. Perry and Dick Moseley were added to the list of casualties. Although he survived his wounds, Private Moseley was permanently disabled and did not return.

August 10th

General Bate was wounded today in the leg by riding in too far.

Another casualty of the fighting around Utoy was the Confederate Commander himself. Wounded in the leg while on a ride forward to observe the Federal positions, General Bate would be lost to the Rebel army for a little over two months. After their lack of success at Utoy Creek, the Union forces moved toward the main Confederate line in front of Atlanta and remained entrenched until the end of August.

CHAPTER XII

STONEMAN'S RAID

While the fighting raged around Atlanta, the war was also coming frighteningly close to Broad River. In late July, Major General George Stoneman convinced Union Commander in Chief Sherman to allow him to take his Cavalry command, numbering 2,800 men, south toward Macon to free Union soldiers held in prison nearby and disrupt the Confederate supply line from there. On July 30th, Stoneman attacked a collection of 2,500 boys, older men and recovering wounded from the hospital in Macon, assembled by Governor Joe Brown, General Howell Cobb and General Joe Johnston who was now living in Macon. Stoneman's attack was repulsed and the next day his command was surprised by 1,300 cavalry, commanded by General Alfred Iverson. Iverson was somehow able to convince Stoneman he was outnumbered and after ensuring the escape of two of his Brigades, under Adams and Capron, Stoneman surrendered along with 600 of his troops. Ironically they would be imprisoned in the very prisons they sought to liberate. Adams and Capron moved north toward Athens, intending to re-supply and attack Confederate government facilities there. On August 2nd, Confederate Home Guard, aware of the approach of the Union cavalry and armed with artillery, removed enough planks to render the bridge south of Athens unusable and turned Adams' approaching brigade west toward Atlanta where he rejoined Sherman's Army on August 4th. Capron, whose brigade was trailing Adams' Brigade, attempted to close up on Adams and follow but became separated and surprised by William's Kentucky Brigade, who captured over 400 of Capron's men. A handful of the Yankee troopers escaped, including Capron, finding their way back to the Union lines near Marietta. The captured troops were sent to Athens, creating much excitement in the area.

General George Stoneman

Along Broad River, people had been following the news of the progress of the battles around Atlanta and concern grew as the war reached closer and closer to their homes. Some families had gathered up all they had and moved to areas where they had family and were a safer distance from the war's devastation. Since mid May when the war began to creep south through Georgia, Company E had lost seven men killed and many others wounded and unaccounted for. The casualties would only mount as the battles continued.

Now word had come that Yankees had reached as close as Athens only 30 miles away, and that some who had escaped might well be in the countryside near by. There was no panic, but greater precautions were taken by everyone.

As people gathered after church service the Sunday following the Athens affair, the conversation was dominated by talk of the possibility of Yankee fugitives loose in the area. The Captain of the Madison Home Guard, R. W. Milner, had visited that day and Reverend Power had invited him to speak to the congregation after the service. He had simply warned people to secure their homes as much as possible until the threat had passed. The children had been sent out to play while Captain Milner had addressed the congregation but some of the older boys including John Moore, now ten, had listened at the windows.

Later, when the adults had begun to split up from their after church visiting, John came to Elizabeth curious about what he had heard.

"Are the Yankees here Mama?" asked John with a look of genuine concern in his eye.

"No son. They captured several over at Athens but they're not close to us," assured Elizabeth.

"Well, what was the Captain talking about?"

"He just wants us to be vigilant and cautious."

"What does that mean?"

"Well, he says we need to make sure our doors are secure at night and that we should be suspicious of any stranger, regardless of what uniform he might be wearing."

"Oh! I just wondered. He's never come to church before."

"Yes, I know. But it's nothing to worry about. The guard is going to increase patrols in the area for awhile."

Not fully understanding what he had heard, but satisfied with the calm tone in his mother's voice that he did not need to worry, John rushed off to tell his news to his young friends.

One could not say that things returned to normal for they did not. The threat of the Union Army, now only 75 miles from the homes along Holly and Fork Creeks in the southeast corner of Madison County, was all too real. The war had truly come to Georgia.

In other ways, the war had already imposed increasing hardships on the people of Madison County and for that matter most of the South. The paper money issued by the Confederate States was now worth a mere fraction of its face value, and goods to purchase with it were practically non-existent. Someone once said in another time of inflation that "one went to market with their money in a shopping basket and came home with their purchases in their pocket book." Times were such in Georgia.

Clearly the Confederate States were a shattered remnant of the proud and determined group that had broken away from what they felt was a tyranny equal to that of Great Britain almost ninety years before.

CHAPTER XIII

THE FALL OF ATLANTA

Toward the end of August, 1864 Sherman decided that in order to force Hood to evacuate Atlanta, he would have to sever all his supply lines. He had cut them in the past using cavalry and small infantry detachments on raids, but they were always restored in a matter of two or three days.

August 26th and 27th 1864

The enemy moved from the right still farther.

Beginning about August 25th, Sherman began to move against the supply lines still operating, the Macon & Western and the Atlanta & West Point, with six of his seven Infantry Corps. To counter this, Hood dispatched Hardee with two Confederate Corps. (Note: due to a somewhat different organization, Union Corps tended to number around ten-thousand total including artillery while a Confederate Corp could sometimes number twice that many).

Badly outnumbered, Hardee's advance was easily thwarted and, fearing an attack on Atlanta itself, Hood recalled one of Hardee's Corps.

August 30th 1864

We stayed there all day and at night we marched to Jonesboro.

August 31st 1864

Today there was considerable fighting. A great many were killed and wounded Capt. Gholston was killed; Lieut. J. B. Eberhardt was wounded, other wounded were Lieut. Young Daniel, Dan Flynn, A. Flynn, D. Patton, E. Dudley, W. A. J. Brown J. C Nichols was killed He did not hear the report of a gun for he was killed by a stray

Bate's Division was involved heavily in the fighting on August 31st and September 1st, and Company E suffered severely. Lost to the Company were Captain Gholston and Private J. C. Nichols, who were killed, as well as Lieutenant Jacob Eberhart and Privates E. J. Dudley and David Wynn, who were severely wounded and never returned. Wounded less severely were Lieutenant Young Daniel and Privates Hezekiah Patten, Hezekiah Wynn and Bill Brown, who had carried Ike from the field at Chickamauga.

That evening as the men of Company E lay in the trenches awaiting the renewal of fighting that was sure to come at daylight, Ike and his friends talked quietly of what had happened over the last month. Most of the talk centered on the leadership of the army and the losses sustained by the company. Some one-hundred forty men had joined the company in the spring of 1862. They were joined that summer, while the Battalion was camped near Rutledge, Tennessee, by a dozen replacements for those who had been rejected or had died in camp, and another eighteen had been added since just before Chickamauga. Altogether, some one-hundred seventy-five men had at one time been a part of the company. The number was now less than forty. Ed Eberhart, Ike's friend who had looked after him during his first illness two years before at Rutledge and had joined as a private, was now First Lieutenant and with the death that day of Captain Gholston, he would most certainly now be Captain as he was well liked and had proven to be a good officer.

"Ike, what do you make of Hood?" asked Sam. "Can't see how he's such an all fired improvement over old Joe."

"No, it sure doesn't look much like it does it," replied Ike. "Seems like nothing much has changed but the casualty rate."

John Brown, a neighbor of Ike and Sam before the war who had been with them since the beginning and was sitting close by, chuckled and said sarcastically:

"Well with Hood in command we'll have less and less to share rations with."

"That's a fact," replied Sam. "If things keep going like they are there won't be any of us left."

Their discussions continued and everyone agreed; about all they could do was try to do their duty and keep their heads down when it counted. The next day under a heavy attack, Hardee's remaining Corp was forced to retreat and that evening, September 1, 1864, General Hood evacuated Atlanta.

September 1st 1864

There was considerable fighting today. The Yankees made a charge on our line and the loss on both sides was heavy. We gave up a part of our line at Jonesboro and made a new line at Lovejoy Station. Hood vacated Atlanta.

September 3rd and 4th

Moved to Bear Creek Station and stayed 2 days, the Yankees fell back from Lovejoy.

After withdrawing from Atlanta, Hood concentrated his army near Lovejoy Station to the south. There was no significant action for the next few days and about the 4th of September, Sherman withdrew his army from in front of Lovejoy. He had achieved the first part of his mission, that of capturing Atlanta. After securing Atlanta he would begin the next part. The second part included cutting the Confederacy in half by marching to the sea and capturing Savannah. This part of his plan also included breaking the will of the people of the South by destroying everything in his army's path between Atlanta and Savannah. There was little to stand in his way.

September 8th

Returned to Jonesboro, stayed till the 19th Drew three months wages $34.00.

On the 8th of September, Confederate emissaries went out under a flag of truce to begin attempts to exchange prisoners captured by both armies during the campaigns around Atlanta. The following day word was received that Sherman would agree to the exchange of all prisoners still on hand. The Official Records indicate he wished the exchange to be regulated by the stipulations of the old cartel in place before the exchange process was halted. Sherman further indicated in a letter to General Hood that he "deemed it to be the interest of the United States that all citizens now residing in Atlanta should remove, giving them the choice of going north or south, as they may prefer." Those preferring to go south would be sent to Rough and Ready where they would be met by Confederate authorities and sent out by rail. In a letter to Sherman, Hood made known his displeasure with this order: "This unprecedented measure transcends in studied and ingenious cruelty all acts ever before brought to my attention in the dark history of war." Hood was left with little choice but to protest in this manner, and later that day a flag of truce went out to arrange for the completion of this inglorious act.

Two days later, on September 11th, negotiations were suspended in the exchange process as Sherman refused to receive those Union prisoners whose term of service had expired. This disregard for their own troops was to be evidenced over and over again by the government in Washington in the last months of the war. The most notable examples were the refusal by Secretary of War Edwin Stanton to send doctors, medicine and supplies to prisoners at Andersonville Prison when that was proposed by the Confederate Government to alleviate the suffering there, and later to send ships to Savannah to pick up sick prisoners who had been moved there in a humanitarian gesture until after the elections of November 1864. There was much bitterness by Union soldiers after the war because of these betrayals, which were well known and documented, by the leaders of their government.

On the 12th, the removal of the people of Atlanta began and all available wagons were sent to Rough and Ready to help move the exiles to Lovejoy Station. A truce existed for period of about ten days while these events were being undertaken extending until near the end of September.

September 19th

We marched from Jonesboro west 20 miles to the West Point Railroad

September 20th 1864 through September 28th

We built breastworks near Palmetto Station. Stationed here till the 29th. Received letter from home. Cloudy and rainy, wrote letter home on 23rd.

At this point, Sherman's interest in what remained of the Army of Tennessee was secondary to securing Atlanta and removing the threat of a hostile populace. The next few days were a period of quiet for Hood's Army as it remained in the vicinity of Lovejoy Station and Jonesboro until September 19th. On this date, Hood began to move his army west toward Palmetto Station where breastworks were erected in case the Union Army chose to pursue them.

Sherman, satisfied at least for the moment with his capture of Atlanta and what looked to be an open path to Savannah, made no move to follow the Army of Tennessee. During their stay at Palmetto Station, Ike received a letter from home. The news Elizabeth reported was both good and bad.

September 10 1864

My Dearest Husband,

I am exceedingly hopeful that this letter finds you well and fully recovered from your recent illness. We have learned of the horrible fighting around Atlanta and received the casualty reports of the men from Madison County. Such horrible news of poor Dabney. I am sure he is missed both as an officer and a friend. I have spoken with his wife Lucinda and she is uncertain what she will do now. The farm may be more that she can manage. I am pleased to tell you that your father has married Martha Almond of Elbert County. They were married August 23. The news from Virginia is not good. The fighting has been almost constant there since May. Tom has been promoted to Corporal and has taken part in all this action. I believe Keziah has received a letter or two from Bill who is in prison at a place called Rock Island. She says he has drawn duty as a cook in his barrack but is given little with which to accomplish his duties. The fighting in Virginia has cost the life of a number of boys from the area. Included among them are Danny Witcher and John Ginn. Many others were wounded and several captured. Those known to be taken prisoner are Bill Gholston, Willis Gholston, Bill

Hunt and Jim Bond. I believe they were all imprisoned somewhere in New York.

We received quite a scare last month as some Yankee Cavalry attempted to attack Athens. They were driven off and I hear that several hundred were taken prisoner in Athens. A few reportedly escaped and there was a time when it was feared that they might find their way to our area. Captain Milner and the Guard were more obvious with their presence for a few days and in a short time the threat was forgotten.

Ike, I do not mean to add to your worries but I feel I must tell you that little Ike has been feeling poorly and I am worried that he shows little improvement. With Dr. Eberhart serving in the Army, I have sought help from Milly. She thinks I should get him to a Doctor in either Danielsville or Athens. I will see if Jim will take me.

Ike, I try to remain in good spirits and hopeful about our cause but the news now seems always to be bad and it is hard to remain optimistic of our chances. My thoughts now are only with you my dearest and if it is God's will that we are not to win this war I pray for its quick conclusion and your safe return home to me and our beloved children. If God wills it otherwise I will look forward to reuniting with you in the glorious land above.

I remain your loving wife,

Elizabeth

(Author's note: Danny Witcher was a brother of John Witcher who was married to Elizabeth's sister)

That evening Ike found some time, after cooking his supper and cleaning his musket and pistol, to write some words of his own to Elizabeth.

September 23, 1864

My Dearest Elizabeth,

I received your letter and its news of home this morning. I am very troubled to hear of Isaac's illness. Take him wherever you must to see a doctor. I know it has been awhile since I have been able to send money home but it has been several months since we received pay. We finally received three months pay a few days ago and I will try to get it to you at the earliest opportunity. I hope you have been able to put some money away so that you may see he has the best possible care. Please write and tell me of his progress.

Everything is quiet here. Once we were forced to give up Atlanta the Yankees seemed not to be concerned with us. We have had no contact save for some between the cavalries. Please give Father my congratulations. I know the Almond family and they are good people. I am sure he will be happy.

It is hard to believe it has been almost a year since last I held you in my arms. Those days of last October are often in my thoughts during the day and in my dreams at night. I too pray for a speedy conclusion to this war that has torn us from each other and disrupted our peaceful happy life. Please continue to hold me in your thoughts and prayers as I will you.

The army's next move is uncertain but our recent movements would suggest a move back to the north of Georgia toward Chattanooga. If that is the case it would seem we would be moving away from the enemy's main army, to what purpose I do not know.

I will write again as soon as I am able. In the meanwhile I can tell you that I am well and am suffering no lingering effects from my recent hospitalization. My thoughts are ever with you and our beloved children and I long for the time we are united.

Your loving husband,

Ike

On the 25th of September, President Davis paid a visit to General Hood and the next morning, accompanied by their respective staffs, they rode out to the front lines to visit the troops. The reception received by them from the soldiers is described in the Official Records as "enthusiastic" and, following a "short and spirited speech," the "assemblage manifested by their loud and continued cheering that they would support him in the remarks he made."

Some reports indicate the reception was quite cold with at least some of the troops shouting "give us back ole Joe."

An overzealous attempt by General Hardee to have Davis remove Hood and reinstate Johnston cost Hardee his command in the Army of Tennessee and resulted in his transfer to command the department of South Carolina, Georgia and Florida, with the task of collecting at Savannah forces to operate against Sherman's advance. The army had lost another fine field commander to politics.

Ike and the members of Company E were on hand for the speech of President Davis and remarks by Generals Hood and Howell Cobb, as well as Governor Brown. Letters and diaries suggest that the response from the troops might not have been so enthusiastic. A letter from Jeremiah Hall of the company to his wife contained his impressions of the visit:

> "the President came around this morning and he did not gain much applause. Last year he came around and all the hollowing I ever heard of it was then but there was little cheering done. The troups seem to be all out of heart."

The letter continued as Jeremiah Hall expressed his feelings on the state of things:

> "I am out of heart I don't deny it. They have ten men to our one that is a clear case. If they have a notion to drive us farther they can do it easily now. If we attempt to fight them here they will over power us by November as they can flank us back in the level country. It is a rich mans war and a poor mans fight but if they want the Negroes all free we will only have to keep fighting twelve months longer and they will force their way all over our country and free them without any law. There is but one way to prevent the freeing of every Negro in the south. A great many people are expecting a rupture in the Lincoln government in about the time of the election but that is all stuff. Lincoln is sure to be the next President and now is the best time to make peace that will ever be again. With Lincoln as President we may expect the war to continue four more years or come to his terms. I have no sympathy for a Yankee and will fight then as long as any other person but I am not in favor of putting myself up for a target when I see I can

do no good by it. I will close for the present. I am full.
I could sit and talk a week. I am pestered.

Farewell my dear. "

Jeremiah Hall's words no doubt reflected the feelings of many a southern soldier. Those in the Army of Tennessee had seen few positive results from their two and one-half years of sacrifice save the victory at Chickamauga, which was rendered meaningless by the events which followed.

CHAPER IV

HOOD MARCHES NORTH

September 29th 1864

*We marched from Palmetto to the Chattahoochee River,
crossed and camped.*

Near the end of September, the Army of Tennessee began a movement to the northwest and around Atlanta. By moving around to the north, Hood's intention was to disrupt Sherman's supply line running south from Chattanooga. For the next two weeks the marching was almost continuous as Hood moved his army north to accomplish this goal.

October 8th, 1864

*Marched to Cedartown and camped. The enemy met at
Cedartown*

The weary Confederate soldiers marched past Kennesaw Mountain and Dallas to Cedartown, where a small engagement occurred on the 8th of October as part of Sherman's forces continued to follow the Army of Tennessee as it continued north.

On the 10th of October, now recovered from his wounds, General Bate returned to his command and the Division took part in the capture of Dalton and Mill Creek Gap and the destruction of the railroad at the tunnel.

October 12th and 13th

*Marched 18 miles to Sugar Valley, then on to Dalton.
Took Dalton, also Mill Creek Gap and captured 700
prisoners, tearing up the Railroad at the Tunnel.*

Ike and his companions, as part of Bate's Division, advanced on Mill Creek Gap and, after capturing the block house at the Gap, set about destroying as much of the railroad as possible. Advancing against Tunnel Hill, Bate found the tunnel's defenders had been evacuated, leaving behind a storehouse of supplies, both quartermaster and commissary, so large that all could not be transported leaving much to be destroyed.

With the capture of Dalton, the Rebels now had a new problem as three fourths of the nearly eight-hundred prisoners taken at Dalton were troops of the 44th U. S. Colored Infantry Regiment, which had been organized at Chattanooga the previous spring. The colored prisoners were put to work destroying the railroad and later moved with the Army while their officers and other white soldiers were paroled and returned to Chattanooga.

Ike and members of the 37th were among those troops assigned to the destruction of the railroad at the tunnel and guarding these colored prisoners.

"What'dya you think they'll do with those fellas, Ike?" asked Bill Brown.

"I couldn't say. I suspect they will try to return them to their masters but that's gonna be a big job. Those that they can't return to their masters are likely to be put to work on some detail for the army or put in prison if they seem to be too troublesome to keep an eye on," replied Ike.

"You don't think they'd shoot them do you?"

"No, I doubt it, that'd bring on more trouble than we already got. I sure wouldn't participate in any firing squad and I don't think many of the other boys would. Looking back I wish we had just freed all the slaves and sent them up north and let the folks up there take care of them. They might have just left us alone to form our own country, but I doubt it. Seems like they were more interested in making sure they could still get their tax money than freeing anybody when this damned war started."

"Did your Father own any slaves?" Bill asked.

"He has a house servant that's not much more than a girl, but she's more like family than a slave. Since mother died she has taken care of the house and seen that he eats right and such. My Grandfather Vaughn owns some and of course Elizabeth's father owns two."

The talk of the colored prisoners gave way to talk of what was to be next for them. Now that Sherman had Atlanta, where would Hood take the army? Some thought they might try to retake Chattanooga and others thought they might head toward Knoxville first.

As for the colored prisoners, some were returned to those who claimed to have owned them before they were freed, while others were sent to work on fortification projects in Alabama and Mississippi. Many ended the war as prisoners in Columbus and Griffin, Georgia, where they were released during May 1865.

After finishing their work at the tunnel and along the railroad, Bate's troops fell in at the rear of the army now moved toward Lafayette where it caught up with the rest of Hardee's Corp, now under Major General Benjamin Cheatham.

Maj. Gen. Benjamin F. Cheatham

October 16th.

Marched past Lafayette on the Rome road 4 miles, camped.

For the next two weeks the Army of Tennessee was almost constantly on the move. The movement carried them southwest from Lafayette and into Alabama, where they stopped briefly at Gadsden. After two days in Gadsden, they resumed their march northwest toward Decatur, surrounding the Union garrison there on October 27th.

October 27th 1864 and 28th

Surrounded Decatur, Alabama and stayed here the next day.

In action around Decatur on October 28th, a number of men from the 37th Georgia were captured including several from Company E and others from Company G. Those captured from Ike's company were C. V. Collins, C. B. Duncan and Jesse Pierce, the latter a neighbor who lived only a short distance from Ike and Sam. The men from both companies were shipped north, where they were imprisoned at Camp Douglas and where several died, including Privates Collins and Duncan.

On the 29th of October, the Army of Tennessee began the twenty-five mile march to Tuscumbia where they arrived on October 31st.

October 30th and 31st

Passed Courtland 20 miles to Tuscumbia and camped.

Rain was an almost constant companion in those last days of October and the first few days of November, making any further movement very difficult at best, so for the next two weeks the Army of Tennessee camped at Tuscumbia on the south side of the Tennessee River. During this time the Army rested and re-supplied itself as best it could. The people of the area were very supportive of the soldiers, feeding them and offering all they could spare including clothes and second-hand shoes. At this point in the war, the Confederacy could do very little to supply its troops in the field with either commissary or quartermaster supplies, and very much depended on the land and its people for its subsistence. Despite the oncoming winter, the Army of Tennessee was very much a barefooted and underfed army.

During the two weeks of relative inactivity around Florence and Tuscumbia, mail began to catch up with the army once more and soldiers again had the time to write to their loved ones at home. There was, however, very little joy expressed in the letters written or those received. In each case, the writers tried hard to avoid transmitting through their words the sadness and melancholy that was pervasive throughout the Confederate States in both the armies and the general populace. For this reason, letters that had once covered several pages full of news of victories and hope were now replaced by letters of only a few lines, assuring the recipient of the letter that the writer was well and hopeful that a reunion with their loved ones would soon be possible. On the 2nd of November, Ike sat down to pen such a letter to his beloved Elizabeth.

November 2, 1864

My Dearest Wife,

We have arrived near Tuscumbia, Alabama along the Tennessee River. It has been very rainy and has such restricted our movements which seem now to be directed north, possibly toward Nashville, that being a major Union supply depot. The Army was able, under the protection of artillery, to cross the swollen river and drive the Union troops away from Florence on the north side of the river. The people here have greeted us with the warmest of welcomes and have generously supported us in everyway possible. They have done this while suffering from the lack of many things taken for granted three years ago.

Thanks to the blessing of Almighty God I continue to be reasonably healthy and have suffered little from the elements and my past infirmities. I hope everything is such with you and my beloved children.

We once again have a new Corp Commander, as Gen. Hardee was removed and replaced by Gen. Cheatham. We were saddened by the departure of Gen. Hardee for we know but little of Gen. Cheatham.

My love and admiration for you is endless and my thoughts of you are constant. These thoughts of you sustain me and help me through each successive day. Please

*kiss each of my beloved children for me and assure them
I will see them soon.*

*Please write me soon and let me know how little Isaac
is faring.*

Your Husband,

Ike

A few days later, while in Tuscumbia, Ike received a letter from home. The contents of the letter bore the worst of news.

November 7th 1864

Got word of the Death of my Son I. D. Moore.

October 1864

Dearest Ike,

*I am heartbroken to bring you the news of the death of
our son Isaac. He passed away in his sleep last night.
The Doctor was unable to determine the cause of the
fevers that he repeatedly suffered over the past weeks. He
would show improvement and the fevers would subside
for a time only to give us false hope for his recovery and
then when our hopes were high the fever would again
return.*

*Jim and Mary Elizabeth have been wonderful support
and Jim is helping father make arrangements for his
burial. They have taken him to Father and Mother's so
that the other children are spared the anguish of having
him lie here until we can complete the burial arrange-*

ments. I have asked that we only have a service at the grave site which will be in the Simmons' family cemetery.

I am torn between the desire to have you here with me at this saddest of all times in a parents life and the contentment in knowing that with all that you are facing there that you will be spared the sight of him dead and will always have pictures of him in your mind in happier times.

I am troubled as to how to end this sorrowful message to you but hopeful that you will understand there is so much to do here and that I have our other four precious children to consider and care for.

My heartfelt thoughts are with you and I continue to be hopeful that these tragic times will soon be at an end.

Your loving wife,

Elizabeth

After reading the first few lines, Ike's head dropped into his hands and he exclaimed "Oh No!" almost under his breath but loud enough that Sam, who was sitting nearby cleaning his musket, took notice.

"What is it Ike? You are pale as a ghost."

"He's dead Sam. Little Ike's dead."

"Dead? How can that be? I thought he was getting better?"

"It was the fever. Elizabeth says they could not control it and it finally killed him."

"I am so sorry Ike. I can't imagine how it must feel. Is there anything I can do?"

"No Sam, I thank you for your thoughts, but I reckon there ain't anything can be done."

Sam returned quietly to his gun cleaning, not knowing if he should move away to give Ike some time alone or stay put doing what he was doing. Sam had only to wait a couple of minutes for the answer to his dilemma, as Ike moved away toward the tent they shared. He reappeared after a short time with the book he had carried with him since leaving home two and one-half years before. Ike quickly leafed thorough the worn and water spotted book until he found what he was looking for and quietly began to read to himself the first few verses from the 14th Chapter of the Gospel of John.

Let not you heart be troubled: ye believe in God, believe also in me. In my father's house are many mansions: if it were not so, I would have told you. I go to prepare a place for you. And if I go and prepare a place for you, I will come again, and receive you unto myself; that where I am, there ye may be also. And whither I go ye know, and the way ye know. Thomas saith unto him, Lord, we know not whither thou goest; and how can we know the way?

Jesus saith unto him, I am the way, the truth and the life: no man cometh unto the Father, but by me.

He then turned back to the Book of Psalms and read to himself from Psalms 23.

The Lord is my shepherd; I shall not want.

He maketh me to lie down in green pastures:

He leadeth me beside the still waters.

He restoreth my soul:

He leadeth me in the paths of righteousness for His name' sake.

Yea, though I walk through the valley of the shadow of death,

I will fear no evil: For thou art with me;

Thy rod and thy staff, they comfort me.

Thou preparest a table before me in the presence of mine enemies;

Thou annointest my head with oil; My cup runneth over.

Surely goodness and mercy shall follow me all the days of my life, and I will dwell in the House of the Lord forever.

While at Tuscumbia and Florence, Ike would find comfort in reading scriptures from the worn New Testament he had placed in his haversack almost three years before. His testament like many of the day included the Psalms, which were the very passages Ike turned to in his hour of need. During the next week Ike held his suffering within, sharing the news with only Sam and a few close friends. The news eventually circulated through the company and soldier after soldier stopped by to offer their condolences.

November 13th

We Crossed the Tennessee River to Florence, 5 miles Tuscumbia.

An attempt was made to cross the Tennessee River into Florence about the 10th of November but the river, swollen by the rain, had risen so high the pontoons bridge was in danger of destruction and the orders had to be revoked and the crossing delayed. As the weather cleared, the Army made ready to cross the Tennessee which it did on November 13th.

November 14th through the 20th Stayed at Florence.

The week following the river crossing was spent camped at Florence preparing for a movement north into Tennessee, which began in a snowstorm on the 21st of November.

CHAPTER XV

THE CAMPAIGN FOR TENNESSEE

November 21ˢᵗ

Marched north 10 miles. Cold, snow.

November 22nd

We marched 16 miles to Tennessee line. Very cold and snow.

As they marched north, crossing into Tennessee on November 22nd, snow fell and temperatures plummeted, adding to the misery of the ill clothed, underfed and barefooted army. They arrived at Waynesboro in southern Tennessee on November 22nd, finding the town deserted. They had marched past many deserted homes since leaving Atlanta, but this was the first abandoned town they had encountered.

The march north into Tennessee was made especially harsh by the weather and the lack of proper clothing and footwear. Footprints left in the accumulating snow often were outlined in red from the blood of many a shoeless soldier. The devotion to duty and country of this ragged group of men and its counterpart with Robert E. Lee in Virginia is unsurpassed and possibly unequaled by any army in the history of man, save possibly the American Army around Bastogne in December eighty years later, and the Colonial Army with Washington at Valley Forge nearly ninety years before. Those armies would number among their members many ancestors and descendants of men now serving in this band of Southern Brothers.

Receiving word of Hood's advance, Union General Schofield abandoned his position at Pulaski, Tennessee and fell back toward Columbia, constructing defensive positions south of the town. Hood advanced on the Union positions there but rather than attack, he sent two Corps to move around Columbia to position themselves across Schofield's line of communication to Nashville, and to block his path should he withdraw toward that place. Arriving at Spring Hill on November 29th, Hood's troops found elements of Schofield's army holding the crossroad there. Uncoordinated attacks failed to dislodge the Union forces from the crossroads and evening brought a close to the action as the Confederate troops camped in the fields along the road to Franklin and Nashville. The remainder of Hood's army, including Ike and the 37th Georgia, remained in Columbia, hoping to bottle up the majority of Schofield's army still entrenched there.

November 28th

The Yankees slipped out and left Columbia.

On November 28th Schofield withdrew his forces across the Duck River and on the 29th began to move up the Nashville road toward Franklin.

November 29th

We marched across Duck River to Spring Hill.

Arriving at Spring Hill the evening of the 29th, the Union army marched past the sleeping Confederates and on to Franklin where they prepared to receive the Rebel army. The breakdown in Confederate orders allowing the Federals to slip past at Spring Hill has been blamed by many historians on Hood, who many believe simply retired for the evening without issuing orders as to which command was responsible for securing the road north. Regardless of who the responsibility for this lapse rests on, it was a major blunder by the Confederate forces allowing Schofield to consolidate his forces and set up a defensive line at Franklin, against which Hood threw his army in a series of assaults which achieved very little save adding to the Confederate casualty list.

November 30th

We marched to Franklin in Williamson, County, where a great battle was fought. It commenced at 5 in the evening and lasted all night. The Yankees gave up

and left after the turn of the night. It was a bad time,
our loss 423 killed. The Yankees loss was 313 killed on
the field.

Hood's pursuit struck the perimeter of the Union defenses at about 4:00 P.M. forcing the Union troops back to the main lines where, after brutal fighting lasting most of the night, the Union line ultimately held.

When dawn broke on the morning of December 1st, the Rebel army found its adversaries gone. Schofield had retreated to the safety of Nashville to consolidate with General Thomas there. This engagement had opened the road to Nashville but cost the Army of Tennessee six Generals killed or mortally wounded including General Patrick Cleburne, arguably the finest Division Commander in the Army of Tennessee.

December 1st 1864

We buried the dead today. We buried the Yankees in
their own ditches.

The next day was spent burying the dead from both sides. The Yankee soldiers were simply buried in the fortification trenches they had dug the day before. They had literally dug their own graves. Ike's company had participated in the charge on the interior Union line and like most other units included several casualties among their numbers. Jeremiah Hall, who had written to his wife only two months before expressing his concerns about the turn the war had taken, fell in the attack as did Thomas Wilson. Young Wiley Simmons, who had expressed his concern of being wounded almost two years before at Murfreesboro, was wounded severely in the foot and would lose a leg and live the remainder of his life a cripple. In a bizarre twist of fate, Captain Tod Carter, serving on the Staff of General Thomas B. Smith, received a mortal wound near the Union fortifications and very near the home of his father on the Nashville turnpike. His bravery was paid special mention in the following excerpt from the report of General Bate: "His gallantry I witnessed with much pride, as I had done on other fields, and here take pleasure in mentioning it especially."

December 2nd

I went with the Guard and Lieut. to Columbia with prisoners, and it took most all night to get there.

On December 2nd Ike was ordered to accompany Lieutenant Daniel and a squad of men in taking a group of Union prisoners to Columbia. The detail took almost two days and upon returning, Ike found his company readying to march to Murfreesboro with Bate's Division, now numbering about 1,600 men. The objective of their mission was to seize and destroy the bridges along the railroad running north to Nashville and the block houses defending them, and to destroy as much of the railroad between Murfreesboro and Nashville as possible.

Bate's Division moved to the north and east across country to intersect the Nashville Turnpike and the railroad which ran parallel, and thus avoid being cutoff by the much larger Union force within the fortress northwest of town.

December 5th

Battle at creek near Murfreesboro.

On December 7th Bate's troops were joined by units of Cavalry and Infantry commanded by General N. B. Forrest and proceeded to seize and destroy several bridges and the blockhouses protecting them and to destroy a portion of the railroad. The Rebel troops moved toward the fortress near Murfreesboro and the old battlefield near Stones River. Bate's Division and the two Brigades brought by Forrest then attacked the fortified Union works but were driven back by the superior Union numbers.

December 7th

Moved to the right. A considerable battle on the old battlefield. Sargt. Griffeth and B. A. Moon were killed and left in the hands of the enemy. We marched back to the Nashville Pike road

The dwindling ranks of Company E were further reduced in this action by the deaths of Sgt. Griffith and Bird Moon. That evening, as they sat huddled around a small fire on the snow covered ground, Sam reminded Ike of Moon's words, spoken in a similar setting on the same ground almost two years before: "If their gonna get me, I hope they kill me outright." Those word would probably have sent cold chills down Ike's spine had he not already been shivering from the cold.

December 8th 1864

Destroyed the Railroad.

The next day the Rebels moved back toward the railroad where they continued to work on destroying the railroad with minimal success. This activity is described in General Bate's report:

> **"Next day we engaged again in the destruction of the railroad; but little progress was made, in consequence of the extreme bad weather; the snow fell rapidly and the ground was freezing. In consequence of the recent marches many of the men were barefooted; all were shod, however, when we left Florence."**

December 10 and 11th

Marched above Lebanon near Nashville.

December 14th

Heavy fighting today on the left. We moved to the left.

On the evening of December 15th Bate's Division moved into the line of battle near Shy's Hill where the Rebels had reformed after being forced to retreat earlier in the day by Union attacks on both flanks. When the fighting resumed the next morning, the over matched Confederate forces were flanked on their left and driven from Shy's Hill in disarray. Bate's Division, being positioned on the western slope, was caught by the flanking move on the left and took fire from three directions. As a result of this casualties in some companies of the 37th were very high. Company E, not on the left of the regiment, was not as hard hit as others but lost W.F. Strickland killed and James P. Hall and John Seagraves captured.

December 16th

Heavy fighting today, and we retreated to Franklin, from Nashville. W. F. Strickland was killed here. This is the roughest time we have had.

The collapse on the left eventually caused a similar collapse on the right flank at Overton's Hill and a disorganized retreat south along the road toward Franklin. As the defeated Confederate Army retreated south on the Franklin Road, Thomas' Cavalry pursued and continued to harass the rear guard commanded by Forrest.

Over the next few days, the army retreated to Columbia with all troops crossing the Duck River by the morning of December 20th. Here the Army of Tennessee turned down the Pulaski road, reaching the Tennessee River on Christmas Day.

December 26, 27, and 28th

Crossed the Tennessee River, marched to near Tuscumbia, Ala., remained here through the 28th.

The next two days were occupied in crossing the pontoon bridge at Bainbridge and on the 28th the pontoons were removed. At this point the Union troops gave up their pursuit and the Army of Tennessee crawled off to lick its wounds. After crossing the river, the army moved south to Burnsville where each of the three army corps received orders. Ike and members of the 37th Georgia, now under a new Brigade Commander, moved with the rest of Cheatham's Corp to Corinth, Mississippi. A new organization of the command structure was made necessary by the losses of ranking officers at Franklin and Nashville. One of the losses was General Thomas B. Smith, whose brigade Ike had served in since just after Chattanooga. In one of the most bizarre stories of the war, indicative of the cruelty often displayed, Smith, the youngest Brigadier General in the Confederate Army when promoted in July 1864, was confronted by Colonel William Linn McMillen of the 95th Ohio Infantry while being escorted from the field at Nashville as a prisoner of war. According to several sources, McMillen began to berate the young General and curse him. To this General Smith made no reply except to explain his position as a prisoner of war. At this point, McMillen drew his saber and struck Smith repeatedly on the head, cutting into the skull. After McMillen's vicious and cowardly attack,

Smith was taken to a Union field hospital where he was told he would not live as his skull had been split, exposing his brain. As death did not take him, Smith was sent north to Fort Warren in Massachusetts where he survived until war's end. Released at the end of the war, he returned to his home State of Tennessee where, unable to resume his prior duties with the railroad, he became a patient of the Tennessee State Hospital for the Insane in Nashville. General Smith, who was in his mid-twenties, lived another fifty-eight years before dying in 1823 at the age of 85. Colonel McMillen received no discipline.

January 1st 1865

Marched to Corinth, Mississippi, camped.

January 2nd 1865 through the 9th

Stationed here at Corinth, Miss.

Cheatham's Corp remained at Corinth while the Corps of Stephen D. Lee and Alexander P. Stewart moved on toward Tupelo, Mississippi on the 3rd of January. On the 10th of January, Cheatham's Corp followed the others to Tupelo, arriving on January 12, 1865. The fighting was now over for Ike Moore and Company E, but not the marching.

CHAPTER XVI

THE ROAD TO SURRENDER

January 12th through January 23rd

In camp at Tupelo, Mississippi

On the 13th of January, 1865, General John Bell Hood, after consolidating his command in Tupelo, asked that he be relieved from his command of the Army of Tennessee. The reply from Richmond granting his request was received four days later and he was ordered to report to Richmond. He was replaced on January 23rd by General Richard Taylor; son of President Zachary Taylor and soon after the once proud Army of Tennessee was broken apart and sent to other theatres of the conflict. Most of what remained of the army, including Cheatham's Corp, would begin a trek across the South ending in North Carolina, while other troops would be sent to Mobile.

Ike's company began their long journey on January 26th. Marching south, they reached Meridian, Mississippi on January 31st.

January 31st

Marched to Meridian, Miss.

February 1st 1865

Marched to Demopolis (Alabama)

The next day, they crossed into Alabama and marched to Selma where they were transported by steamboat to Montgomery on the Alabama River.

February 3rd and 4th

Went to Montgomery on steam boat on Alabama River.

The ride to Montgomery by Steamboat was a welcome change to the rigors of marching and a welcome respite for the war weary men taking their minds off their hopeless situation and the despair they all felt. Sitting with their backs against the main cabin of the boat, Ike and Sam watched the shoreline pass by and their thoughts drifted into the future to better days, when they would be able to return home to their families and all thoughts of this terrible war could hopefully be put aside.

"How much longer do you think we'll have to go on Ike?"

"Wish I knew Sam, I just hope they (the government in Richmond) see the futility of continuing and put this madness to an end before many more of us lose our lives. We can't win. There is no way we can win. There are Yankee armies everywhere and there are so few of us left. We are now no more than one good size Corp. They must be twenty to our one if you figure all the different armies they have all over the South. If we go on much longer there won't be any men to rebuild all the damage done down here. The railroads are tore up the bridges are all burned and many towns are simply gone. The South may never be the same. But we have to go on Sam. We can't quit, couldn't live with myself if I quit. Just goes against my nature."

"I know what you mean. I don't see how they do it, the deserters I mean."

"I reckon some just feel differently, Sam. It's scary enough to think about getting caught and shot as a deserter, but I couldn't live with the shame. Look at what Bill and Tom have gone through. Bill, he's been in that prison for over a year and Tom, well he's been wounded twice and captured. I could never face them or the rest of my family. How do you tell your boys? How do you bring them up to be honorable men if you turn your back on your friends and your country?"

Quickly changing the subject, Ike pointed to the shoreline where seemingly endless fields stretched into the distance. The fields were bare except for the remnants of the cotton plants that had been harvested the previous year, and hundreds of white fluffy balls clinging to the plants like small children cling to their mother.

"Looks like lots of cotton just gets left in the field these days. Guess the folks could still get it picked but I don't suppose they have anywhere they could sell it. Sometimes this just all seems like a nightmare. Like we're gonna wake up one day and everything will be just like it was three years ago, but we know that ain't gonna be. Don't reckon things will ever be like they were three years ago."

Sam pointed off in the distance to a huge house with dozens of smaller buildings surrounding it, sitting on what passed for a hill in the flat river county through which they were passing.

"How do you suppose those folks are passing the war?" Sam asked. "Doesn't seem like the war has reached this part of the country does it? Do you think they are seeing hard times too? Makes me wonder about Holly Creek, I hope the Yankees haven't torn up our part of the world."

"We'll know pretty soon how Georgia has fared," replied Ike. "Seems were headed in that direction."

"I've heard talk of furloughs," said Sam. "Maybe we'll get to go home when we get close enough."

"Yeah, maybe, but I wouldn't get my heart set on it. They seem to be trying to get us to North Carolina in a pretty big hurry, if that's where we're headin.'"

Their steamboat ride was all too brief and soon they were on foot once again marching toward Columbus, Georgia. As they resumed their marching and movement by railcar, they began to encounter hundreds of refugees on the roads, moving west to escape Sherman's Army which had left Atlanta the fall before on its path of devastation toward Savannah.

By the 5th of February, Ike and his fellow Georgians had reached Columbus and were once again on their native soil.

February 5th 1865

We marched to Columbus (Georgia) and at night went to Macon, Ga.

As they continued across Georgia, through Macon and Milledgeville toward Augusta, they began to see the devastation that had fallen on Georgia as the Union army devoured and destroyed everything before it as it rumbled to the sea. The men in the ragged southern army could not believe what they were seeing. War was supposed to be between armies. They could accept the hardships they had been forced to endure over the last three years, but this was something totally different. This was a war against civilians. Forcing the citizens of Atlanta to leave their city had been bad enough and now the Yankee army was on a vengeful, destructive rampage.

A refugee family leaving a war area with belongings loaded on a cart.
Photographed by George N. Barnard

Homes everywhere lay in ruin, many burned to the ground leaving only the chimneys standing. Conversations with the people who had been in the path of the Yankee army left little doubt that it had now become Sherman's intent to prosecute the war beyond that of a conflict between armies, and to now carry the war to the civilians as well. The burned and barren landscape was a testament to Sherman's aim. People who had stayed and attempted to protect their homes were in many cases assaulted or killed and their possessions, regardless of the value, stolen. Foraging for food had often become secondary to the indiscriminate confiscation of anything they could haul off and later sell, if having enough value, or just keep as souvenirs.

"What kind of war has this become?" Sam said to no one in particular. "When did it become part of an army's job to treat civilians like they were part of the war?"

"This is not about war Sam," replied Ike. "This is punishment. The war went badly for the Yankees for so long that they have apparently developed a stronger hatred for us than we ever had for them. This is retaliation for three years of our standing up for ourselves and our rights and not just accepting whatever the northern states wanted."

"Do you think anything like this has gone on at home Ike?" said Bill Brown, who was walking nearby.

"The last letters I got from Elizabeth didn't say anything about any Yankees being in the area. We've seen how big a place the South is. I reckon they may not have enough troops to be everywhere. Let's hope that most of their men are Christian men and that they won't all do what you see here. Maybe we'll get one of those furloughs Sam has heard about and we'll be able to see for ourselves."

The next few days of marching were very demoralizing for the men, as each mile traveled exposed new horrors and more and more people who had lost everything.

Periodically negroes, still true to their masters, would be encountered along the road begging for food for their white families, too proud to speak for themselves. Others, obviously freed by the Union Army and trying to avoid capture by the Southern soldiers, could be seen ducking behind cover or running into the fields or woods.

February 6th

Went to Milledgeville, Ga.

February 7th and 8th

Went to Mayfield, Ga.

February 9th to 17th

Came home, left home, and went back to camp.

Beginning during the latter part of January and continuing into February and March, many of the men of the Army of Tennessee had begun to receive furloughs, after initial objections from Richmond that such a move would compromise the Army's safety if Thomas pursued across the Tennessee. When it became obvious that Thomas would not pursue, the furloughs were granted and Ike and many others were able to return to their homes for short periods while the rest of the Army moved on to Augusta.

Ike's furlough began on the 9th of February and he was accompanied on his trip home by his friend Sam Power who like Ike had seen little time away from camp in what was now approaching three years. The ten day furlough, although brief, was a welcome change from the hardships of camp and the constant marching and discomfort of riding in dirty, overcrowded railroad cars.

This time, unlike Ike's trip home almost a year and one-half before, there was no one to alert Elizabeth and Martha that their husbands were on the way home and the men walked into town virtually unnoticed, as the cold of the wet and dreary February day had kept most folks inside. Separating in the road near Jim Power's store, Ike and Sam quickly went toward their homes. Expecting to find Elizabeth at work in the store, Ike climbed the steps from the road, shook off the water from his slouch hat and poncho and opened the door to the store. Two lamps hanging from the ceiling of the building along the middle of the store, and a smaller table lamp on the counter behind which Jim transacted business offered little illumination to the cold dark interior of the store, made even darker by the cloudy, rainy winter day. The store seemed almost barren as Ike glanced around looking for Elizabeth. The shelves, which had once held almost anything one could expect to find in a general merchandise store of the time, were now almost empty. A man's voice finally came from behind the dimly illuminated counter and Ike now recognized Jim Power as he moved closer to the dim light of the small oil lamp.

"Can I help you?" Jim said, not recognizing the gaunt bearded figure clothed in the dark rain covering and wide brimmed hat pulled down for protection.

"Jim, it's me Ike."

"Ike, my God what are you doing here? Is the war over?"

"I sure wish that it was, but I'm just home on furlough. Is Elizabeth around?"

"She sure is. She just went next door to check on things. My Elizabeth has been trying to continue the older children's learning. She wants to make sure they don't miss out on learning to read and write just 'cause there's a war on. Elizabeth has seen to it that John and Frank have been attending. Are you OK? You're skin and bones."

"Yeah, I'm alright, just tuckered out. It'll be nice to be home for a few days and get some home cooking. I hope there's something here to eat, looks like the store is pretty bare."

"Yeah, it's hard to get things these days. Coffee, salt, tea and sugar are scarce as hen's teeth. I don't know if people could buy anything even if I had what they needed. Prices are unbelievable. Flour is over a hundred dollars a barrel and salt, if you can find it, is close to a hundred twenty-five dollars a bag. There is no coffee to be had and I couldn't sell it if I could find it. People just drink chicory or some blend they concoct themselves, but we'll find something for you to eat. Did you come by yourself?"

"No, Sam's was with me, he went on down to his house. Think I'll go find Elizabeth now and the kids. Are the little ones with her?"

"Yeah, I think so. They're usually pretty close."

As Ike walked back toward the door Jim called behind him: "Ike, be watchful, I hear there's a bunch riding around further north that have pro-union sentiments or just like killing or the bounty money they can get from catching and turning in men they suspect of being deserters."

"I'll watch out Jim, thanks for letting me know. See you a little later."

It was true that men on furlough had to be careful as there were many deserters and men who had been exchanged, who simply did not want to rejoin the fight, slipping back into their home areas and Ike knew the importance of not being far from where he was supposed to be while on leave. The last thing he wanted was to be shot while at home by some over zealous home guard who might shoot before asking any questions. Fortunately for those on leave in Madison County, Captain Milner and the Madison Home Guard operated much more like regular army troops than some of the roving bands in the North Georgia and Southeast Tennessee mountains, who were concerned only with the bounty they might collect on a deserter and less with how he was returned or if he was returned to duty. Ike and Sam had returned home to be with family and had no plans to venture very far in any event.

Putting the poncho he had removed while in the store back on and pulling his hat down over his ears, Ike stepped back out into the dismal weather. He found, at least for the moment, that the rain had stopped but that the wind had now begun to blow and the temperature seemed to be dropping very quickly. Hurriedly walking to the home of Jim and Martha just a short distance from the store, Ike climbed the steps and knocked on the heavy wooden door. As he waited, he again removed his wet poncho and draped it over a rocker sitting nearby on the porch. His hat he held in his hand. He soon heard the sound of someone moving toward the door and in a moment the door was opened and there was Elizabeth, with Mary holding on to her mother's dress.

"Ike, Oh Ike," Elizabeth exclaimed as she threw her arms around his neck.

"Watch out, I'm soaking wet."

Paying no attention to Ike's warnings, Elizabeth only hugged him closer until her clothes were nearly as wet as his.

Dropping his hat, Ike wrapped his arms around her and they both began to cry. Mary, not recognizing the father she had seen only once in three years, began to cry as well.

"Mary it's your father. Your father has come home."

With her mother's reassurance Mary's tears began to dry up and she too threw her arms around her father, wrapping them tightly around his leg.

"Tell me you're home for good. I don't want to let you go again."

"I wish it was true my love, but I only have a few days and then I have to go back."

"Well, we'll just have to make the most of those few days. Are you hungry? I'll bet you're starving. Let's get the other kids and go home."

Elizabeth shouted to Jim's Elizabeth, "It's Ike, he's home!" The other Elizabeth came running into the room, followed by a bunch of children including Ike's sons John and Frank and young Martha, who had been pretending as a student although still only seven years old.

"Ike it's so good to see you home and safe," exclaimed Jim's Elizabeth. We have all been so worried about you and Sam. We heard how bad it was in Tennessee and we have all been praying for your safety and the safety of the other boys from around here. Are you home for good?"

"No just for a week, I have to be back next Friday."

"Well it's good to have you here for that time anyway. We'll all have to get together on Sunday afternoon for a big family dinner. Now you take your family on home and get you something to eat, I'll bet you're starved."

Ike hadn't thought about it but she was right, he was very hungry as he had not stopped to eat since the day before except for a cold biscuit he ate along the way.

The Ike Moore family gathered together and walked the short distance back to their home above the store. The rain had stopped and the cold February breezes had blown away the cloud cover, leaving blue sky and the puffy white clouds which often followed. Elizabeth heated water and after he had eaten Ike took a warm bath and the family gathered together once again before the children went to bed. Ike and Elizabeth talked for awhile, catching each other up on the events since their last letters to each other and about eleven o'clock they went to bed. Ike took Elizabeth in his arms and held her tightly as if he would never get another chance. He kissed her tenderly and stroked her long dark hair as they made love. Later Ike held her in his arms as they dropped off to sleep. He slept soundly until late the next morning, as Elizabeth ensured the children would not disturb him. When he woke he found Elizabeth in the kitchen preparing his favorite dishes, pork chops and collards. After eating, they resumed their conversation of the prior evening, talking of happier times before the war and their hopes that the days ahead would be as happy.

The arrival at home, although joyously received by their immediate families, was almost completely ignored by others in the area, now so war weary and disheartened that they found little reason to celebrate the return of a few when so many would never return. On Sunday as Mary Elizabeth Power had promised, the families of Sam Power, Jim Power and Ike Moore along with Elizabeth's parents Francis and Mary and Mary Elizabeth and Martha's mother Elizabeth David, gathered at Jim and Mary Elizabeth's for a Sunday afternoon dinner. It would be one of several family gatherings while Ike was home.

Later in the week, Ike's father John Nathaniel and his new bride Martha Almond Moore paid a visit. They were accompanied on the trip by Bill's wife Keziah, the older sister of Martha and Mary Elizabeth, and her two children as well as Ike's youngest sister, also named Martha like her mother.

Their visit lasted two days, which allowed Ike and his father to do a lot of whittling and talking and Ike's children to visit with their Grandfather and their cousins Berry, who was John's age and Ophelia, who was nearly the same age as Ike's Martha. It also allowed Keziah to spend time with her sisters and her mother, who she had seen infrequently since the beginning of the war. The commotion created by so many people being about and so many youngsters running in and out almost took the war from Ike's thoughts, but of course it was the war that his father wanted to hear about.

They had talked late into the night the evening before John Nathaniel was to return home and it was obvious his father was deeply concerned for Ike's brother Bill, who was still in a Union prison and Tom, who when last heard from was in the trenches near Petersburg, Virginia. A letter from Tom had described the horrible conditions of the troops around the besieged Confederate Capital and the horrific fighting and slaughter of men on both sides that had taken place there the previous summer and fall. The harsh winter and the severe shortage of supplies had taken a horrible toll on the Army of Northern Virginia and what remained of Tom's Company of Elbert County men. The next morning, after the departure of his family, Ike began to make preparations for his own return to camp and two days later Ike and Sam were back in camp in Augusta. They remained in Augusta until the 23rd of February, allowing those that had been on furlough to reassemble before the Brigade crossed the Savannah River into South Carolina. While much of what remained of the Army of Tennessee moved into North Carolina, joining with the troops there under General Joseph Johnston, who had been called on once again, Ike's company and the rest of the 37th Georgia remained in South Carolina.

February 24th

Stationed in S.C till March 18th

Johnston had recently been elevated to command of all the armies south of Virginia by Robert E. Lee, who was now Commander of All Confederate armies in the field. Johnston was to consolidate forces from Carolina, Georgia and Tennessee in order to mount an attack on Sherman, who was marching west toward Raleigh.

While a small force had remained in South Carolina, the rest of the troops from the Army of Tennessee had moved into North Carolina where they fought along side the men from the Department of North Carolina at the Battle of Bentonville. Initially successful in the first day's action against the left wing of Sherman's Army, the Confederate forces were eventually overwhelmed by Sherman's superior numbers when his right wing arrived on the field. Johnston had no choice but to withdraw his army west toward Raleigh, where he expected additional troops to join him.

Ike's command, which had been part of the force which had remained in South Carolina near the Savannah River, began their move across South Carolina on March 18th. By March 30th, they had reached Chester and the railroad there.

March 30th

Marched to Chester, and took train at Chester and passed through Charlotte to Salisbury, N.C

After arriving in Chester, the men of the Thirty-Seventh Georgia along with units detached from other Army of Tennessee Divisions were loaded on railcars and transported through Charlotte to Salisbury and on to Lexington, North Carolina.

April 2nd

Went from Lexington to Greensboro. Were at Greensboro through 4th.

By April 2, 1865 they had arrived in Greensboro where they remained until the 4th. On that date General Beauregard wired the following message to President Davis at Danville, Virginia, where Davis and members of his cabinet had set up headquarters: *"I consider railroad from Chester to Danville safe at present. Will send today 600 more men to latter point. Twenty-five hundred more could be sent, if absolutely needed, but they are returned men of various commands in Army of Tennessee, temporarily stopped and organized here."*

April 5th through 13th In Danville, Virginia.

The 37th Georgia, now numbering about one-hundred fifty men was part of the command sent to Danville under the command of General Charles Shelley to help protect the President until General Robert E. Lee, who was withdrawing his army southwestward from Petersburg, could arrive there. On April 9th, while Davis and the Confederate Government awaited his arrival in Danville, General Lee surrendered his ragged starving army, ending any hope of consolidating the Army of Northern Virginia and the Army of Tennessee for a push against Sherman. Beaten but undefeated, the proud Army of Northern Virginia had fought its final battle.

Upon receiving word of Lee's surrender, Davis and members of his cabinet made arrangements for a movement to Greensboro and left for that location on April 12th. On the 14th, the Confederate forces in Danville began withdrawing toward Greensboro. By April 16th, these troops had completed their march to Greensboro, rejoining the Army of Tennessee there.

April 14th

Left Danville, Marched 5 miles

April 15th and 16th　.

Marched 25 miles on the 15th and on to Greensboro.

April 21st and 22nd

Moved south to the Brigade.

On April 22nd, Ike and the men of the 37th Georgia, now consolidated along with the Sharpshooters with whom they had served so long into the 54th Georgia Infantry, rejoined their Brigade and their Division. The consolidation into the 54th had been part of a total reorganization of Johnston's Army on April 8th. Although now officially designated the Army of Tennessee, Johnston army included troops from several different departments and hardly resembled the proud Army of Tennessee which had fought together for three years.

By the April 18th, hostilities had been suspended and the commanding Generals were in the process of arranging a surrender agreement.

April 26th 1865

Moved to within 6 miles of High Point, N.C

April 27th 1865

Surrendered and stacked arms in the Public in High Point, N.C. Johnson was back in Command before the Surrender.

On the April 26, 1865, Johnston agreed to the terms offered by Sherman and the Army of Tennessee began to lay down arms and surrender. The following day, Ike, Sam and twenty-three others from Company E marched into the town square of High Point, North Carolina, where they stacked their arms and surrendered. They were all that remained of the approximately one-hundred seventy-five men who at one time had been members of Company B 9th Georgia Battalion and later Company E of the 37th Georgia Infantry.

Over the next week the men were fed and provided for under the terms of the surrender and paperwork was processed indicating their surrender.

May 3rd 1865

We were ordered to Lexington, N.C

May 6th to May 13th

Marched from Salisbury to Chester on to Newberry then past Oak Station, S.C

On May 3, 1865, the surviving members of the small band from Madison County began the long journey home. Tracing closely their route to North Carolina, they marched steadily for the next eleven days until reaching and crossing the Savannah River into Georgia on May 14th.

May 14th 1865

We crossed the Savannah River and camped near Ruckersville in Georgia.

The tired men spent the night camped near Ruckersville and the next day disbursed to their respective homes. Ike, Sam, and a few of their close neighbors including William A.J. Brown, John S. Brown, John Russell and Thomas Mitchell completed their journey mid-afternoon the next day.

May 15th 1865

Monday. We reached home at 3 o'clock.

For Ike and Sam it had been almost three years exactly since they had joined in May, 1862. Their world had changed dramatically in those three years and would never be the same as it had been in the years before the war. The next few years of Reconstruction would be hard years, but Sam and Ike were of hearty stock and would be respected members of the community for over forty years after the close of the war. In 1870 Ike, who had not been a land owner before the war, bought his first farm from his friend John Witcher in the area along Holly Creek where he had lived for years.

In the seventeen years following the war, Ike and Elizabeth became the parents of an additional seven children and the family became one of the prominent families in the Fork Creek area of Madison County. During the remaining fifty-three years of his life, Ike served as a Justice of the Peace in Madison County and was a deacon in his church at Carlton, Georgia for forty-five years. Elizabeth died on February 17, 1897 and four years later Ike married Sarah Frances Almond Bentley, the widow of Joseph Bentley of Elbert County. Ike Moore died November 29, 1918 in Madison County at the age of eighty-eight and was buried near his home in the Fork Creek Cemetery. His descendants were quite obviously numerous and many of them still live near his home in the Fork Creek Community very near where Ike's Great Grandparents settled over two hundred years ago.

Isaac Vaughn Moore and Sarah Frances Almond Bentley Moore

**Tombstone of Isaac V. Moore and Elizabeth Simmons Moore
Fork Creek Cemetery near Carlton Georgia**

**Family of John W. Moore and Mary Isabelle Stamps
Oldest son of Isaac and Elizabeth Moore**

PART II

**THE DIARY OF
SERGEANT I. V. MOORE OF CARLTON, GA.
MEMBER OF COMPANY E, 37TH REGIMENT,
GEORGIA VOLUNTEER INFANTRY, C S. A.**

I enlisted May 9th, 1862 in Company E, 37th Georgia Regiment. There were 6 Companies in the 37th Georgia Regiment. They were from Madison, Elbert, Hart, Wilkes, Franklin and Muscogee Counties of Georgia.

We were in camp first in and around Knoxville, Tenn... Some time the last of May, 1862, Jesse Power relapsed with Measles, and Died in Knoxville, Tenn. He went out one Morning and got his feet wet, and relapsed) S. P Power and I bought his Coffin and shroud, sent him home, I waited on him while he was sick.

June 1862 We marched to Clinton and then reached Tazewell, stayed in camp at Tazewell.

June 17th 1862 At dark we were drawn in line of battle.

June 18th 1862 We left on a March at 11 O'Clock and crossed the Clinch River and camped, went in bathing.

June 19th 1862 We marched and crossed Clinch Mt. We were 2 be going over, Camped at Bean Station on the Kentucky Road. There is a large hotel here, no town, it is a large summer resort.

June 20th 1862 We marched down the valley past Rutledge and camped on the creek.

June 21st 1862 marched in 19 miles of Knoxville and camped

June 22nd 1862 marched back over Ky. road to within 2 miles of Rutledge, stayed here till the 4th of July.

July 5th 1862 Moved and camped at Sulphur Springs till 27th of July.

July 27th 1862 Moved to Lee's Springs, and camped. I was taken sick about the 1th of July with yellow jaundice; the Dr. gave me a pass to go out into the country to get a suitable diet for this disease. Ed Eberhardt went with me. We stayed at the home of good lady whose name (Maiden name) was Lowe. She was very kind to us

August 3rd 1862 We left Lee's Springs. Sent 30.00 home.

August 4th 1862 marched to Clinch River.

August 6th 1862 This was the day that the fight was at Tazewell: it commenced about eleven o'clock with heavy firing, continued until about one o'clock with small arms but the enemy shelled us until about six o'clock Our side loss is about 45 killed and wounded. The enemy's loss is about 160 killed and wounded We also took about 75 prisoners, we gained the victory the enemy is all fled to Cumberland Gap. We fell back about one mile and to camp.

August 7th 1862 This day I was out on a scout the most of the day hunting up the enemies that were cut off in the fight.

August 9th 1862 We moved in to Tazewell and camped around the Courthouse. Roasting ears were plentiful here.

August 10th Remained at this camp, I was on picket.

August 11th On duty today.

August 12th, 13th, 14th, 15th On duty.

August 16th Left Tazewell at eight o'clock in the night and marched all night towards Cumberland Gap, got to Powell River at 7 o'clock on Aug 17th

August 17th Firing commenced from the enemy at half past seven o'clock and continued all day with cannon not gaining.

August 18th 1862 Firing going on all day with pickets.

August 19th Firing still going on with pickets and some cannonading all day

August 20th 1862 Some cannonading and Firing with the pickets all day and a good portion of the night.

August 21st I am on duty in sight of the enemy's tents and can view the Cumberland Mountains gap. Some firing with the pickets up to nine o'clock in the morning, firing continued over and after all day, but at long distance.

August 22nd 1862 Friday Pickets commence early in the morning and by evening there was three or four Regiments engaged for two or three hours but not much damage done, some shelling from the enemy, at night all was quiet.

August 23, 1862 Today (Saturday) everything appears to be quiet. We move nearer to the Virginia line.

August 24th 1862 Sunday, some firing with the pickets up to 2 o'clock. I am on guard today. Everything quiet all through the night.

August 25th Monday There was some firing with the pickets today, but not very much.

August 26th 1862 There was firing with the pickets today, and also cannonading from the enemy. Tonight all is quiet.

August 27th Wednesday. There has been some firing with the pickets today.

August 28, 29, 30. All quiet.

August 31st 1862 There was considerable shelling from the enemy today about ten o 'clock but no damage was done.

September 1, 2, 3, & 4th All quiet.

September 5th Friday. This was the day the dispatch came. Everything quiet.

September 6th Through Tuesday the 16th All quiet.

September 17th 1862 Wednesday. This is the day the enemy vacated Cumberland Gap.

September 18th Today we marched into Cumberland Gap and took possession of that place. The enemy destroyed and left a large number of things there.

September 19th 1862 Friday. Today we marched over the mountain into Kentucky and camped right at the foot of the mountain right close to a creek.

September 20th 1862 Saturday. We commenced our march in Kentucky. We marched to Cumberland River Ford and walked through the water 3 or 4 feet deep and camped.

September 21st Sunday. We continued our march today for about 23 miles to Goose Creek.

September 22nd Monday We marched 12 miles and struck camp at 1 o'clock night.

September 23rd Tuesday We continued the March past London Town, 50 odd miles from Cumberland Gap and struck camp at the forks of creek.

September 24th Wednesday We continued our march fording the Rock Castle River. The men would ride in and examine the Water before crossing.

September 25, 26, & 27th March each day, passed London Town.

September 28th 1862 marched and struck camp near Danville

September 29th 1862 marched through Danville 130 miles from Cumberland Gap, also passed Harrodsburg I saw the largest Rat here at this place that I ever saw. It was a wharf rat as large as a possum

September 30th, October 1st 1862 Wednesday We marched past Salvisa also Lawrenceburg.

October 2nd Thursday We marched past Rough and Ready Town and camped near Frankfort at the stone bridge built by nature 20 or 30 feet long and wide enough for a wagon to cross.

October 3rd Friday We stayed today in camp.

October 4th 1862 Saturday We stayed in camp till very near night when orders came to March through Frankfort, the capital of the state. We marched very nearly all night to this place called Versailles, 13 miles from Frankfort, the Capitol. We burned bridges here to keep the Yankees from following us.

October 5th Sunday. Stayed at Versailles today, it is a beautiful level country.

October 6th Monday. I am on picket duty today.

October 7th Tuesday. Remained at camp today.

October 8th Wednesday. We marched toward Lawrenceburg and formed in line of battle.

October 9th 1862 We left at 2 o'clock and marched to Lawrenceburg, some fighting going on today near this place, we marched through Salvisa to Salt River and camped

October 10th Friday, marched to Harrodsburg and formed line of battle. We stayed all night west of Harrodsburg. A cold rain fell all night.

October 11th Saturday. We marched back through Harrodsburg, eastward to near Bryantsville and camped.

October 12th 1862 Remained in camp. Also on Oct. 13, till dark then marched through Bryantsville to Lancaster.

October 14th 1862 Tuesday. We remained near Lancaster all day and past off the time in line of battle. There was some fighting with the cavalry today. We marched all night to Gum Springs, leaving the enemy behind us.

October 15th 1862 Wednesday. We marched on about five miles from Gum Springs and camped in a nice grove near a school house.

October 16th 1862 Thursday. We marched today to the foot of a big hill and camped.

October 17th 1862 Friday We marched from big hill to Rock Castle River and camped.

October 18th Saturday We marched about 25 miles to the left of the State road.

October 19th Sunday Continued to March.

October 20th Monday 1862 We marched on and came to the same road that we went up. We camped at Flatlick.

October 21st 1862 Tuesday We marched about 2 miles to the Cumberland River and camped.

October 22nd Wednesday We crossed the Cumberland River and camped.

October 23rd 1862 Continued our March and crossed over Cumberland Gap. We were in Kentucky from the 20th of Sept. to the 23rd of Oct. We marched to the Cumberland River and camped.

October 24th 1862 Friday We past Tazewell, marched to Clinch River and camped after crossing the river.

October 25th 1862 Saturday We marched across the Elk River and camped near Rutledge, Tenn.

October 26th 1862 Sunday At Rutledge today.

October 27th Monday Stayed here today, considerable snow fell yesterday.

October 29 & 30th 1862 Continued our March through Knoxville, Tenn.

November 1st 1862 Saturday. Reached our camp here near Lenoir Station 22 miles from Knoxville.

November 2nd Stayed at this camp from Sunday through Thursday, the 13th All at ease, no trouble at all

November 14th 1862 and 15th Left camp and left Kingston and crossed the Clinch and Emory Rivers just below the Fork.

November 16th Stayed in camp today.

November 17th 1862 Monday This is my Birthday. I am 32, years old. We marched past Post Oak a noted place.

November 18th 1862 Tuesday Company marched today. I rode on 2 wagons.

November 19th Wednesday We left Walden's Valley and crossed Walden's Ridge

November 20th 1862 Continued our march and came to Sequatchie Valley.

November 21, 22, & 23, 1862 Friday & Saturday We marched past Jasper and camped. Sunday we stayed in camp which is 11 miles from Lone Oak Station.

November 24th Monday 1862 We marched to Cumberland Mountain and camped there.

November 25th We marched over Cumberland Mountain to Elk River and camped

November 26th to December 5th We marched to Manchester and camped and stayed here for some time.

December 5th 1862 I received cloths from home today, the first that l have got since leaving home.

December 6th 1862 I sent $100 home.

December 7 & 8 We marched to camp at Readyville.

December 9th through 17th 1862 Was stationed at Readyville.

December 18th 1862 The Georgia Battalion was transferred from Barton's Brigade to Rain's Brigade and one mile.

December 25th Christmas Day 1862.

December 26th and 27th 1862 We marched 12 miles to Murfreesboro, Tenn..

December 28th, 1862, Saturday We formed a line of battle along a fence here today.

December 29th Monday We moved across Stones River and formed a line of battle in a large field. There was some firing with pickets

December 30th 1862 Tuesday There was considerable battle today near us.

December 31st Today was the day of the great battle of Murfreesboro. We killed wounded and imprisoned about 16,000 men, so it is said. Our loss was 5000. General Raines was killed, one was killed out of Bates Battalion, ten wounded.

January 1st 1863 and 2nd There was some shelling and some fighting yesterday and today.

January 3rd 1863 We retired from the battlefield at midnight yesterday. Heavy cannonading today.

January 4th 1863 Sunday. marched to Shelbyville 25 miles and camped

January 5th through the 10th Stayed in camp at Shelbyville.

January 11th 1863 Moved one mile to better place.

January 12th I received a bottle of peach brandy from Father today. It was made by old man Charles Moon and daughter Cush

January 13th thru 27th 1863. Continued to camp near Shelbyville. Considerable snow fell on the 14th

January 29th Preacher J. P. Rowe visited our camp today. He came from home.

January 31st 1863 through February 8th Still in camp here, sent $50.00 home Feb 3d

February 9 through 12th 1863 Fair and warm rain on the 12th

February 13th 1863 through March 7th Remain in camp at Shelbyville, warm rain.

March 8th 1863 Drew two months pay today. Also had inspection of Arms.

March 9th and 10th 1863 In camp at Shelbyville, but we moved from this place at midnight and marched 8 miles north of Shelbyville and camped at a creek.

March 12 and 13 Fair weather, still in camp.

March 14th and 15th It was reported that the Yankees were advancing but it was a mistake, on the 15th we resumed to our camp at Shelbyville.

March 17th 1863 Sent $75.00 home today.

March 18th through March 28th We were in camp here for some time. Sam Power and myself made and baked apple pies (rights and lefts) and sold them to the Soldiers at $1.00 a piece, some of the Soldiers were simply too lazy to cook for themselves, if they had any money to buy anything with

March 29th 1863 Snow today.

April 1st to 4th Very cold. April 5th big frost.

April 11th through 20th Fair weather, big drill, still at Shelbyville.

April 21st 1863 Moved to a new camp at Flat Creek

May 6th 1863 The 9th and 3rd Battalions consolidated into Regiment

May 9th 1863 Sent $30.00 home to Wife.

May 23rd Moved down creek about 2 miles

May 28th Near Shelbyville.

May 29th 1863 Moved 14 miles north east of Shelbyville to Fairfield

May 30th Moved 2 miles towards Hoover's Gap and camped near Fairfield

June 3rd and 4th   Made long march through Hoovers Gap and returned to camp.

June 6th Moved 1 mile toward Fairfield

June 14th 1863   Had a visit from Charles Witcher, (the Charles Witcher that killed Cal Edwards between Carlton and Broad River near Bridge)

June 16th   Moved to new camp 1/2 mile up the creek.

June 23rd 1863 Drew two months wages $34.00.

June 24th through 28th   The fight commenced at Fairfield on the 24th. Several were killed and wounded on our side. Some skirmishing on the 25th and 26th and 27th, we fell back to Tullahoma and camped.

June 29th   Went out in line of battle and remained there the next day

July 1st 1863 We vacated Tullahoma, left there at one o'clock in the morning and marched to Elk River.

July 2nd   We marched to the top of Cumberland Mountain and camped.

July 3rd marched down the mountain to Marion Valley.

July 4th marched to Jasper and camped

July 5th marched to the Tennessee River and camped.

July 6th Crossed the river on a Pontoon bridge and camped 6 miles below Chattanooga, Tenn..

July 7th At Lookout Station.

July 1th 1863 We took the R R Cars (railroad cars) today and passed Chattanooga and camped 10 miles above on the Knoxville Road at Tyner's Station.

July 12th through August 22nd While at Tyner's Station everything was quiet. I sent $40.00 home by George Eberhardt. (Lamar's father)

August 23rd Moved camp from Tyner's to Chickamauga River at the Bridge.

August 25th We moved up the Tennessee River 4 miles of Harrison at Big Spring. It ran a mill below.

August 28th through August 30th Moved and took R R cars to Loudon, Tenn..

August 31st We took cars back to Charleston.

September 1, 2, & 3rd We camped here on the Railroad at Charleston.

September 4th Left Charleston and marched 6 miles to Big Springs.

September 6th 1363 Sunday We marched to Ottewah Station 6 miles above Tyner.

September 8 1863 We marched past Tyner and past Chickamauga to Graysville Station, Georgia.

September 9th We marched through Catoosa County, Georgia into Walker and camped at a Church.

September 10th marched west 6 miles and camped on creek

September 11th We had a little fight today in the valley.

September 12th marched to Lafayette and camped.

September 13th marched 5 miles up the Valley and back. We were dodging the enemy.

September 14, 15, and 16th. Rested in camp at Lafayette

September 17th 1363 We left Lafayette and marched up Chattanooga road 8 miles and camped at a Church

September 18th We marched to Chiccamauga Creek. Heavy firing commence, the enemy shelled us heavy.

September 19th 1863 This is the day of the great battle. Our Brigade got into the battle about 3 o'clock, killed and wounded in our Regiment about 140, three in Company E. They were Lieut. Power, Corporal Morris and R. T. Power, 93 wounded. Myself wounded in the right side. Ball struck cap box, did not go through. W. A. J. Brown (Jesse Brown's grandfather) carried me off the battleground. (He had a sick certificate) and he followed us and carried me behind a log to protect us from bullets.

September 20th 1863 Still fighting.

September 21st I came to the railroad at Dalton on my way to Hospital

September 22nd and 23rd Got to Atlanta on 22nd, 26th and left for home night of 23rd and got on the 24th 1863. Stayed at home till October 27th, 1863.

October 27th Left home and got to Atlanta.

October 28 and 29th Got to Chickamauga on the 28th, and rejoined my company near the point of Lookout, Mountain.

October 31st and November 1 through 10th Was on picket duty.

November 11th Sent $30.00 home by Corporal Allen.

November 16th We moved to the right.

November 17th 1863 This is my Birthday, 33 years old today.

November 18th 1863   The enemy shelled us a good bit today.

November 23rd 1863 Considerable fighting with pickets.

November 24th 1863 Considerable fighting on Lookout Mountain. It was taken by enemy. We left the Valley.

November 25th 1863 We came to the top of Missionary Ridge and had a big fight. We vacated the Ridge and fought one mile from it. M. David was killed. We lost several pieces of cannon, the enemy shot our own cannon. We marched towards Cleveland, past Chickamauga, and camped 3 miles of Craysville.

November 26th 1863 We lay in line of battle most all day at Cross Roads.   We then marched past Ringgold to Catoosa Spring and camped

November 27th 1863 We marched to Dalton, Georgia and camped at the new Hospital where they put our wounded and sick Soldiers.

November 28th   We remained in camp in Dalton til February 23, 1864. We built little Shantys and took up winter quarters here, the weather is very cold here.

December 17th 1863 I sent $30.00 home to Wife by Sargt. J. A. Gloor.

December 23rd 1863 Drew $169.00 Sent $100. home by J. B. Eberhardt

December 25th Christmas Day and December. I sent $70.00 home by Capt. D.L. (Dabney) Gholston.

January 2nd and January 5th Warm and pleasant. Visit by J. G. Power.

February 6, 1864 Wife started with J. D. Power to visit me came as far as Union Point, but had news that the enemy was advancing and went back home.

February 10th 1864 J. D. Power went home. On Feb. 13th was beautiful weather.

February 18th 1864 Very cold weather with heavy snow.

February 23rd 1864 We left our camp and moved 2 miles toward Tunnel Hill and camped

February 23rd & 25th We had considerable fighting on our right and heavy fighting in this Gap at the Railroad

February 26th 1864 Fighting is not so heavy today. The enemy retreated toward Chattanooga during the night.

February 27th 1864 Returned to our old camp. Rainy weather.

March 5th Sent $5.00 home to Wife by S. P. Power.

March 16th through April 3rd Cold with some snow

April 6th through April 26th 1864 Pleasant weather, all quiet on front, but expecting a move soon.

April 29th 1864 Orders to be ready to move at any time.

April 31st Went to the Gap today, some skirmishing.

May 7th 1864 Moved to the front. Cavalry with infantry at Mill Creek Gap on Rockyface Ridge.

May 8th and 9th 1864 There was considerable skirmishing and cannonading for the two days with little effect.

May 10th 1864 Heavy skirmishing and cannonading most all day. There were heavy cannonading in the evening With a storm of rain and wind.

May 11th There was heavy skirmishing and cannonading in the evening on the north side of the Gap. We had a big rain and very hard wind last night.

May 12th 1864 There has been skirmishing going on today. We are very closely confined in the ditches The general opinion is that the Yankees are moving to our left. Their line is in full view. At eight o'clock in the night we left the Gap going toward Resaca moving very near all night.

May 13th 1864 We reached Resaca, Forming line of battle west of that place and built breastworks.

May 14th 1864 A very heavy fight commence at one o'clock it kept up till dark Our loss was light, the enemy was heavy. Our Brigade was held in reserve but was under heavy fire all the time and several of our men were wounded. J. W. Patton was wounded in the leg and it killed him

May 15th Fighting commence again early today, heavy fighting all day with small arms and artillery. Our loss in killed is very light. As the enemy is flanking us on the left, we took up a line of March at 10 o'clock in the night, marching southward along the Railroad to Calhoun.

May 16th 1864 Considerable fighting with the enemy today. We left the place at one o'clock in the night and marched the balance of the night.

May 17th 1864 We reached Adairsville, rested the most of the day, late in the day we had some heavy fighting, made breastworks. Then marched all night and reached Kingston at day.

May 18th We stopped at Kingston three hours for rest and then marched three miles toward Cassville and stopped for rest, staying all night.

May 19th 1864 We were marching and forming line of battle all day. Had some very heavy fighting near Cassville We stayed at Cass Station this night.

May 20th We were up soon and marched through Cartersville to Etowah River, crossed over going about 2 mires and stopped for rest.

May 21st 1864 We are stationed at Etowah, these days between Dalton and Atlanta. Sherman's Army fought and flanked us so that they could surround Johnson's Army. Johnson tried to save his men, and some blamed him for not going on ahead but he did the best.

May 23rd 1864 We marched toward Dallas and stopped. May 24th Had a little skirmish fight at this place.

May 25th 1864 We marched 2 miles east of Dallas and formed line of battle.

May 26 & 27th Built fortification, and fighting started. There was heavy skirmishing all day and night on our right. Company out on picket.

May 28th 1864 Very heavy skirmishing today. Bates' Division made a charge in the evening   killing and wounding and taking several prisoners. Sargt. Griffeth was killed. Ned, A. Spurlock was killed, William Wood, and I. Dudley were wounded and died from their wounds.

May 29th Heavy skirmishing all day and heavy all night. We moved ½ mile to the left.

May 30th 1864 Skirmishing all night. David Seagraves was wounded, several wounded today,   and 2 were killed in the Regiment. Lieut. Sheppard was killed

May 31st Skirmishing is not so heavy as usual today. The enemy is falling back beyond Dallas. I was taken severely sick today, reported to Dr. Galloway.

June 1st 1864 Very little fighting today, the enemy is falling back I

June 2nd 1864 I was sent to Marietta and from there to Atlanta

June 3rd From Atlanta l was sent to Macon. W. H. (Billy) Smith is with me. We are in the City Hall Hospital.

June 4th through 12th Was in City Hall Hospital at Macon

June 13th 1864 I was transferred to Eufaula, Ala. Been raining for 10 days

June 28th Went back to Macon.

June 29th Went to Atlanta and on to Marietta, Ga.

June 30th 1864 We were in battle near Marietta.

July 1 & 2nd Heavy skirmishing, we fell back 8 miles, giving up Marietta.

July 3rd and 4th Built breastworks anti heavy skirmishing, fell back 3 miles

July 5th through 8th Was on picket duty. Heavy skirmishing.

July 9th Moved in facing Atlanta, gave up the Chattahoochee River.

July 10th 1864 Resting today.

July 12th and 13th We are in 4 miles of Atlanta, on the Railroad.

July 14th 1864 We moved 4 miles north of Atlanta to Peachtree Creek, Johnson was relieved and Hood was put in command.

July 15th through 18th Still at this place, with little picket fighting

July 20th We fell back to our breastworks and made a charge.

July 21st We moved to the right at night to the east of Atlanta

July 22nd We made a charge and lost several men. J. W. Griffith was killed, and four others were wounded This was called the Blackberry Charge.

July 23rd through 26th. Moved back to the west of Atlanta, worked on breastworks all day the 24th.

July 27th I was put on provost duty.

July 29th A fight on our left.

August 1st 1864 We moved to the left on the Sandtown Road.

August 2nd and 3rd Moved to the right one mile and back to the Sandtown Road. Heavy fighting today.

August 6th Our division was in a considerable fight today, killing, wounding and taking prisoners a good many, our Losses was light. W. M Perry was killed and D. R. Mosely better known as Dick was wounded

August 7th 1864 Very heavy picket fighting today.

August 10th General Bates was wounded today in the leg by riding in too far.

August 11th through 13th Heavy skirmish fighting, very quiet on 16th

August 23rd Little skirmish fighting today.

August 26th and 27th 1864 The enemy moved from the right still farther.

August 28th 1864 Our Division moved to the left and past East Point, going to Rough and Ready.

August 29th Stayed at this place tonight, then marched to Mount Gilead Church

August 30th 1864 We stayed there all day and at night we marched to Jonesboro.

August 31st 1864 Today there was considerable fighting. A great many were killed and wounded Capt. Gholston was killed; Lieut. J. B. Eberhardt was wounded, other wounded were Lieut. Young Daniel, Dan Flynn, A. Flynn, D. Patton, E. Dudley, W. A. J. Brown J. C Nichols was killed He did not hear the report of a gun for he was killed by a stray

September 1st 1864 There was considerable fighting today. The Yankees made a charge on our line and the loss on both sides was heavy. We gave up a part of our line at Jonesboro and made a new line at Lovejoy Station. Hood vacated Atlanta.

September 2nd 1864 Stayed at Lovejoy.

September 3rd and 4th Moved to Bear Creek Station and stayed 2 days, the Yankees fell back from Lovejoy.

September 5th Moved one and half miles up the Railroad

September 6th Stayed here over night and returned to Lovejoy and Bear Creek

September 8th Returned to Jonesboro, stayed till the 19th Drew three months wages $34.00.

September 19th We marched from Jonesboro west 20 miles to the West Point Railroad

September 20th 1864 through September 28th We built breastworks near Palmetto Station. Stationed here till the 29th Received letter from home. Cloudy and rainy, wrote letter home on 23rd.

September 29th 1864 We marched from Palmetto to the Chattahoochee River, crossed and camped

September 30th Marched up the River to the Villa Rica road and camped.

October 1st 1864 Marched up the Villa Rica Road in sight of Kennesaw Mountain and camped there.

October 2nd We marched 4 miles past Dark Oak Post Office and camped.

October 3rd Marched 8 miles today, camped.

October 4th 1864 Built breastworks 4 miles east of Dallas

October 6th Marched about 8 miles today, camped

October 7th Marched 17 miles today, camped.

October 8th, 1864 Marched to Cedartown and camped. The enemy met at Cedartown

October 9th Marched to Cave Springs, camped. Frost this morning

October 10th Marched across Coosa River.

October 11th 1864 marched over Omucha (Armuchee) Creek, north of Rome.

October 12th and 13th Marched 18 miles to Sugar Valley, then on to Dalton. Took Dalton, also Mill Creek Gap and captured 700 prisoners, tearing up the Railroad at the Tunnel.

October 14th 1864 marched on the Lafayette Road 8 miles

October 15th 1864 Marched 10 miles, crossed Taylor's Ridge and camped.

October 16th Marched past Lafayette on the Rome road 4 miles, camped.

October 17th Marched down Broomtown Valley to Alpine 17 miles and camped

October 18th Marched in Alabama 15 miles on the Jackson road.'

October 19th 1864 Marched west 15 miles to cross roads and camped.

October 20th Marched 18 miles to Gadsden, camped.

October 21st Rested at Gadsden today.

October 23rd Marched on top of Sand Mountain.

October 23rd 1864 Marched past Lickskillet to Brookville.

October 24th . Marched 14 miles northeast.

October 25th 1864 Went to the top of mountain near Summerville.

October 26th marched near Decatur. Rainy today.

October 27th 1864 and 28th Surrounded Decatur, Alabama and stayed here the next day.

October 29th Marched 8 miles toward Courtland

October 30th and 31st Passed Courtland 20 miles to Tuscumbia and camped.

November 1st to the 3th Stayed at this place; rainy.

November 7th 1864 Got word of the Death of my Son I. D. Moore.

November 8th Very rainy and cold.

November 9th Clearing and cold. Moved

November 10th 1864 Moved near the River.

November 13th We Crossed the Tennessee River to Florence, 5 miles Tuscumbia.

November 14th through the 20th Stayed at Florence.

November 17th Birthday today, 34 years

November 21st Marched north 10 miles. Cold, snow.

November 22nd We marched 16 miles to Tennessee line. Very cold and snow.

November 23rd Marched to Warrenton in Waynes County.

November 24th Marched into Lawrence County and camped.

November 25th 1864 Marched past Henryville.

November 26th We marched past Mount Pleasant in Murry County to Columbia.

November 27th 1864 We surrounded Columbia.

November 28th The Yankees slipped out and left Columbia.

November 29th We marched across Duck River to Spring Hill.

November 30th We marched to Franklin in William. County, where a great battle was fought. It commenced at 5 in the evening and lasted all night. The Yankees gave up and left after the turn of the night. It was a bad time, our loss 423 killed. The Yankees lost was 313 killed on the field

December 1st 1864 We buried the dead today. We buried the Yankees in their own ditches.

December 2nd I went with the Guard and Lieut. to Columbia with prisoners, and it took most all night to get there.

December 3rd 1864 Returned to Spring Hill

December 4th marched near Nashville.

December 5th Battle at creek near Murfreesboro.

December 6th We built breastworks on the old battlefield.

December 7th Moved to the right. A considerable battle on the old battlefield. Sargt. Griffeth and B. A. Moon were killed and left in the hands of the enemy. We marched back to the Nashville Pike road

December 8th 1864 Destroyed the Railroad.

December 9th Marched to the spring.

December 10 and 11th Marched above Lebanon near Nashville.

December 12th 1864 Marched to the line of battle.

December 13th Some skirmishing today.

December 14th Heavy fighting today on the left. We moved to the left.

December 16th Heavy fighting today, and we retreated to Franklin, from Nashville. W. F. Strickland was killed here. This is the roughest time we have had.

December 17th, 18th, 19th Moved to Spring Hill, then to the creek and to Columbia.

December 20th Marched to Linville, then on to Pulaski, then reached Tennessee River on 25th.

December 26, 27, and 28th Crossed the Tennessee River, marched to near Tuscumbia, Ala., remained here through the 28th.

December 29th 1864 We marched to Cherokee Station.

December 30th We marched to Iuka.

December 31st marched 12 miles.

January 1st 1865 marched to Corinth, Mississippi, camped.

January 2nd 1865 through the 9th Station here at Corinth, Miss.

January 10th Marched to Brooksville.

January 11th marched to Cow Town.

January 12th through January 23rd In camp at Tupelo, Miss.

January 24th Moved in near town.

January 26th Marched to Artesian Well, stayed here till January 31st.

January 31st Marched to Meridian, Miss.

February 1st 1865 marched to Demopolis (Alabama)

February 2nd Went to Selma.

February 3rd and 4th Went to Montgomery on steam boat on Alabama River.

February 5th 1865 We marched to Columbus (Georgia) and at night went to Macon, Ga.

February 6th Went to Milledgeville, Ga.

February 7th and 8th Went to Mayfield, Ga.

February 9th to 17th Came home, left home, and went back to camp.

February 18th to 22nd 1865 In Augusta.

February 23rd Moved to South Carolina.

February 24th Stationed in S.C till March 18th.

March 24th 1865 Marched to Laurens S.C.

March 26th Marched to Glenn, S. C (This could possibly be Glenn Springs but if so would be out of the way if continuing on to Chester)

March 27th to 29th Marching.

March 30th Marched to Chester, and took train at Chester and passed through Charlotte to Salisbury, N.C

April 1st 1865 Saturday. Arrived Salisbury, and took train to Lexington, N.C

April 2nd Went from Lexington to Greensboro. Were at Greensboro through 4th.

April 5th through 13th In Danville, Virginia.

April 14th Left Danville, Marched 5 miles

April 15th and 16th Marched 25 miles on the 15th and on to Greensboro.

April 21st and 22nd Moved south to the Brigade..

April 26th 1865 Moved to within 6 miles of High Point, N.C

April 27th 1865 Surrendered and stacked arms in the Public Square in High Point, N.C. Johnson was back in Command before the Surrender.

May 3rd 1865   We were ordered to Lexington, N.C

May 4th and 5th 1865   Marched 20 miles on to Salisbury, N.C

May 6th to May 13th   Marched from Salisbury to Chester on to Newberry then past Oak Station, S.C

May 14th 1865   We crossed the Savannah River and camped near Ruckersville in Georgia.

May 15th 1865 Monday We reached home at 3 o'clock.

Moore J. V.

Co. E, 37 Georgia Infantry.

(Confederate.)

Sergeant Sergeant

CARD NUMBER.

Number of medical cards herein 2

Number of personal papers herein 0

Book Mark:

See also 9 Battn. Ga. Inf.

(CONFEDERATE)

M   37   Ga.

J. V. Moore

Sgt., Co. E., 37 Reg't., Ga. Inf.

Appears on a

LIST

of casualties, of the 37th Ga.
Reg't., in the battles of
Chickamauga, Ga., Sept. 18, 19
and 20, 1863.

List dated near Chattanooga, Tenn.
Sept. 21 , 1863.

Remarks:
     wounded slight

Series 1, Vol. 30, part 2, page 367.

N. Herring
Copyist.
1371

Muster Roll of Company B, 9th Battalion
Georgia Volunteer Infantry
Army of Tennessee C.S.A.
Clarke and Madison Counties

OFFICERS

GHOLSTON, Dabney L. - Captain Mar. 4, 1862. Transferred to Co. E, 37th Regt. Ga. Inf. as Captain May 6, 1863. **Killed at Jonesboro, Ga. Aug. 31, 1864.**

OSBORNE, Nelson C. (or Osburn) - 1st Lieutenant Mar. 4, 1862. Resigned on account chronic bronchitis Dec. 1862. Resignation accepted Jan. 6, 1863.

MEADOWS, Isaac J. - 2nd Lieutenant Mar. 4, 1862. Roll dated Jan. 14, 1863, last on file, shows him present. No later record.

POWER, Francis - Jr. 2d Lieutenant Mar. 4, 1862. Elected 2d Lieutenant in 1862. Transferred to Co. E, 37th Regt. Ga. Inf. as 1st Lieutenant May 6, 1863. **Killed at Chickamauga, Ga. Sept. 19, 1863.**

CRAWFORD, Charles Gresham - 1st Sergeant Mar. 4, 1862. Sent to Atlanta, Ga. hospital Nov. 12, 1862, where he died in 1863.

GLOER, Joseph A. - 2nd Sergeant Mar. 4, 1862. Transferred to Co. E, 37th Regt. Ga. Inf. and appointed 1st Sergeant May 8, 1863. Wounded Chickamauga. Elected Jr. 2nd Lieutenant Sept. 26, 1864. Surrendered at Greensboro, N.C. Apr. 26, 1865.

DANIEL, Young A. - 3rd Sergeant Mar. 4, 1862. Transferred to Co. E, 37th Regt. Ga. Inf. as Jr. 2nd Lieutenant May 6, 1863. Wounded Chickamauga. Elected 2nd Lieutenant Jan. 21, 1864. Wounded Jonesboro Ga. August 31, 1864. Surrendered at Greensboro, N.C. Apr. 26, 1865. (Born in Ga. Mar. 1843.)

DEADWYLER, Martin V. - 4th Sergeant Mar. 4, 1862. Appears last on roll for Apr. 17, 1862.

EBERHADT, Jacob B. (or Eberhart) - 5th Sergeant Mar. 4, 1862. Transferred to Co. E, 37th Regt. Ga. Inf. May 6, 1863. Elected 2nd Lieutenant June 2, 1863; 1st Lieutenant Sept. 19, 1863; Wounded Chickamauga September 20, 1863. Captain Aug. 31, 1864. Pension records show he was wounded near Atlanta, Ga. July 1864. Enlisted in Co. K, 3rd Regt. Ga. Militia while home on wounded furlough. Surrendered at Macon, Ga. May 1865. (Died in Madison County, Ga. Jan. 23, 1910.)

EBERHART, Edward P. - Private Mar. 4, 1862. Transferred to Co. E, 37th Regt. Ga. Inf. May 6, 1863. Elected 2nd Lieutenant Sept. 19, 1863; 1st

Lieutenant Aug. 31, 1864; Captain. Surrendered at Greensboro, N.C. Apr. 26, 1865.

MOORE, I. V. - Private May 10, 1862. Appointed 2nd Sergeant in 1862. Transferred to Co. E, 37th Regt. Ga. Inf. May 6, 1863. Surrendered at Greensboro, N.C. Apr. 26, 1865. (Born in Ga. in 1830.)

MORRIS, Stephen P. - 1st Corporal Mar. 4, 1862. Appointed 3rd Sergeant 1862. Transferred to Co. E, 37th Regt. Ga. Inf. May 6, 1863. Roll for Apr. 1, 1864, last on file, shows him present. No later record.

CRAWFORD, James Benjamin - 2nd Corporal Mar. 4, 1864. Appears on pay roll dated Apr. 12, 1862. Died in Madison County, Ga. Nov. 4, 1907.

GRIFFETH, Walton H. - 3rd Corporal Mar. 4, 1862. Transferred to Co. E, 37th Regt. Ga. Inf. May 6, 1863. Appointed 5th Sergeant. Roll for Apr. 1, 1864, last on file, shows him present. No later record. (Killed Dallas, Ga. June/July 1864)

ALLEN, Thomas - 4th Corporal Mar. 4, 1862. Appointed 1st Corporal in 1862. Transferred to Co. E, 37th Regt. Ga. Inf. May 6, 1863. Roll for Apr. 1, 1864, last on file, shows him present. Pension records show he "Was discharged at surrender." (Born in Madison County, Ga. in 1827.)

INFANTRY

ALLEN, Henry J. - Private May 10, 1862. Deserted July 14, 1862.

ALLEN, Joel S. - Private Mar. 4, 1862. Transferred to Co. E, 37th Regt. Ga. Inf. May 6, 1863. Roll for Apr. 1, 1864, last on file, shows him present. Captured and paroled at Athens, Ga. May 8, 1865.

ALLEN, William M. - Private Mar. 4, 1862. Transferred to Co. E, 37th Regt. Ga. Inf. May 6, 1863. Roll for Apr. 1, 1864, last on file, shows him present. No later record.

ALLEN, W. Thomas - Private July 20, 1862. Transferred to Co. E, 37th Regt. Ga. Inf. May 6, 1863. Roll for Apr. 1, 1864, last on file, shows he was discharge, date not given.

ANTHONY, Thomas B. - Private Mar. 4, 1862. Sent to Chattanooga, Tenn. hospital Dec. 26, 1862. Transferred to Co. E, 37th Regt. Ga. Inf. May 6, 1863. Sent to hospital Mar. 27, 1864. Appointed Sergeant. On detail with Co. B, 2nd Battn. Troops & Defenses at Macon, Ga. Dec. 31, 1864. Captured thre Apr. 20-21, 1865.

BARNETT, James F. - Private Mar. 4, 1862. Transferred to Co. E, 37th Regt. Ga. Inf. May 6, 1863. Roll for Apr. 1, 1864, last on file, shows him present. No later record.

BARNETT, Leonard C. - Private May 10, 1862. Died on march through Kentucky in 1862.

BARNETT, William B. - Private Mar. 4, 1862. Sent to Atlanta, Ga. hospital Nov. 12, 1862. No later record.

BATTLE, W. J. - Private May 10, 1862. Died at Chattanooge, Tenn. Nov. 15, 1862.

BAXTER, W. Henry - Private Mar. 4, 1862. Discharged on account of chronic rheumatism, at Chattanooga, Tenn., Nov. 26, 1862.

BENNETT, C. W. - Private May 10, 1862. Transferred to Co. E, 37th Regt. Ga. Inf. May 6, 1863. Captured at Chickamauga, Ga. Sept. 19, 1863. Died of diarrhoea at Camp Douglas, Ill. Oct. 11, 1863.

BRAY, George W. - Private Mar. 4, 1862. Transferred to Co. E, 37th Regt. Ga. Inf. May 6, 1863. Appointed Corporal. Surrendered at Greensboro, N.C. Spr. 26, 1865.

BROWN, John S. - Private Mar. 4, 1862. Transferred to Co. D, this Battn; to Co. E, 37th Regt. Ga. Inf. May 6, 1863. Surrendered at Greensboro, N.C. Spr. 26, 1865. (Born in Elbert County, Ga. in 1832.)

BRUCE, John M. - Private Mar. 4, 1862. Roll dated Jan. 14, 1863, last on file, shows him present. No later record.

BURROUGHS, James H. - Private Mar. 4, 1862. Transferred to Co. E, 37th Regt. Ga. Inf. May 6, 1863. Wounded at Chickamauga, Ga. Sept. 19, 1863. Died from wounds, at Atlanta, Ga., Oct. 29, 1863. Buried there in Oakland Cemetery.

CARITHERS, Berry T. - Private Mar. 4, 1862. Transferred to Co. E, 37th Regt. Ga. Inf. May 6, 1863. Surrendered at Greensboro, N.C. Spr. 26, 1865.

CHEEK, O. P. - Private Mar. 4, 1862. Roll for Dec. 1862 shows he deserted; "left in Kentucky and has not returned."

CLEGHORN, O. C. - Private May 10, 1862. Transferred to Co. E, 37th Regt. Ga. Inf. May 6, 1863. Roll for Apr. 1, 1864, last on file, shows him present. Captured and paroled at Athens, Ga. May 8, 1865.

COLBERT, James F. - Private Mar. 4, 1862. Appears last on roll for Dec. 1862.

COLLINS, Charles V. - Private Mar. 4, 1862. Transferred to Co. E, 37th Regt. Ga. Inf. May 6, 1863. Captured at Decatur, Ala. Oct. 28, 1864. Died of Smallpox at Camp Douglas, Ill. Dec 15, 1864.

COLLINS, James Willis - Private May 10, 1862. Transferred to Co. E, 37th Regt. Ga. Inf. May 6, 1863. Wounded. Admitted to Ocmulgee Hospital at Macon, Ga., wounded in left thigh, July 24, 1864. Furloughed Aug. 5, 1864. No later record.

COLLINS, John E. - Private May 10, 1862. Died prior to Feb. 11, 1863.

COLLINS, L. W. - Private May 10, 1862. Transferred to Co. E, 37th Regt. Ga. Inf. May 6, 1863. Roll for Apr. 1, 1864, last on file, shows him present. No later record.

COLLINS, L. W. - Private May 10, 1862. Transferred to Co. E, 37th Regt. Ga. Inf. May 6, 1863. Roll for Apr. 1, 1864, last on file, shows him present. No later record

COOPER, Thomas C. - Private Mar. 4, 1862. Died prior to Dec. 1862.

CRAWFORD, E. S. - Private July 20, 1862. Transferred to Co. E, 37th Regt. Ga. Inf. May 6, 1863. Discharged, diability, at Dalton, Ga. July 11, 1863.

CULBERTSON, George W. - Private Mar. 4, 1862. Deserted July 14, 1862. DAVID, Francis M. - Private May 10, 1862. Sent to Atlanta, Ga. hospital Nov. 12, 1862. Died Jan. 9, 1863.

DAVID, Francis M. - Private May 10, 1862. Sent to Atlanta, Ga. hospital Nov. 12, 1862. Died Jan. 9,1863.

DAVID, Morrassett - Private Mar. 4, 1862. Transferred to Co. E, 37th Regt. Ga. Inf. May 6, 1863. Died at Missionary Ridge, Tenn., November 25, 1863.

DAVID, Peter - Private Mar. 4, 1862. Received $50 bounty Apr. 17, 1862. Died in Knoxville, Tennessee in May of 1862 buried there in Confederate Cemetery.

DAVID, William G. - Private Mar. 4, 1862 Appointed 4th Corporal in 1862. Transferred to Co. E, 37th Regt. Ga. Inf. as 4th Corporal May 6, 1863. Surrendered at Greensboro, N.C. Apr. 26, 1865. (Born in Madison County, Ga. Aug. 24, 1839.)

DEADWYLER, Thomas J. - Private Mar. 4, 1862. Transferred to Co. E, 37th Regt. Ga. Inf. May 6, 1863. Wounded Chickamauga September 19,1863 Died Oct. 15, 1863.

DOWNES, Anderson H. (or Downs) - Private Mar. 4, 1862. Rejected on account of disability Mar. 1862. Enlisted as a private in Co. E, 37th Ga. Inf. Oct. 25, 1863. Roll for Apr. 1, 1864, last on file, shows him present. No later record.

DRAKE, Josiah - Private July 20, 1862. ransferred to Co. E, 37th Regt. Ga. Inf. May 6, 1863. Wounded at Chickamouga, Ga. Sept. 19, 1863. Roll for Apr. 1, 1864, last on file, shows him present. No further record.

DUDLEY, Henry - Private Mar. 4, 1862. Transferred to Co. E, 37th Regt. Ga. Inf. May 6, 1863. Killed at Hoover's Gap, Tenn. June 24, 1863.

DUDLEY, Lawson - Private Mar. 1862. Wounded. Transferred to Co. E, 37th Regt. Ga. Inf. May 6, 1863. Surrendered at Greensboro, N.C. Apr. 26, 1865.

DUDLEY, Lemuel - Private 1862. Received $50 bounty June 1, 1862. No later record. Transferred to Co. E, 37th Regt. Ga. Inf. May 6, 1863. Wounded over left eye, causing concussion of brain, at Dallas, Ga. July 1864. Died from wounds.

DUDLEY, Willis J., Jr. - Private Mar. 4, 1862. Received $50 bounty June 1, 1862. No later record.

DUDLEY, Willis J. - Private Nov. 3, 1862. Transferred to Co. E, 37th Regt. Ga. Inf. May 6, 1863. Wounded in right leg and permanently disabled at Chickamauga, Ga. Sept. 19, 1863. Sent to hospital Sept. 20, 1863. Pension records show he was at home, wounded, close of war. (Born in Ga. Jan. 14, 1831.)

DUNCAN, Charles B. - Private Mar. 4, 1862. Transferred to Co. E, 37th Regt. Ga. Inf. May 6, 1863. Captured at Decatur, Ala. Oct. 28, 1864. Died of consumption at Camp Douglas, Ill. Apr. 6, 1865. Buried there in Confederate Cemetery.

EBERHART, Isaac H. - Private Mar. 4, 1862. Roll dated Jan. 14, 1863, last on file, shows he deserted, "left in Kentucky and has not returned." Authors note: (Records were in error. Isaac Eberhart was among those wounded at Chickmauga in September 1863.)

FAULKNER, George W. - Private Mar. 4, 1862. Roll dated Jan. 14, 1863, last on file, shows he "Deserted; absent since July 1862."

FAULKNER, James V. - Private May 10, 1862. Transferred to Co. E, 37th Regt. Ga. Inf. May 6, 1863. Captured at Decatur, Ala. Oct. 28, 1864. Released at Camp Douglas, Ill. June 17, 1865.

FLOYD, J. P. - Private Mar. 4, 1862. Died at Tazewell, Tenn. Nov. 5, 1862.

FLOYD, William A. - Private Mar. 4, 1862. Roll for Apr. 17, 1862 shows he was rejected, under-age.

FLOYD, William P. - Private Mar. 4, 1862. Received $50 bounty Apr. 17, 1862. No later record.

FREEMAN, James L. - Private Mar. 4, 1862. Died of typhoid fever at Murfreesboro, Tenn. Dec. 15, 1862.

GENTRY, Grandison P. - Private Mar. 4, 1862. Transferred to Co. E, 37th Regt. Ga. Inf. May 6, 1863. Wounded Chickamauga September 19/20 1863. Sent to hospital Feb. 1, 1864. Died in Atlanta, Ga. Mar. 31, 1864. Buried there in Oakland Cemetery.

GLENN, John W. - Private Mar. 4, 1862. Received $50 bounty Apr. 17, 1862. No later record.

GRAHAM, Charles C. - Private May 10, 1862. Sent to hospital as nurse Jan. 4, 1863. Died of chronic diarrhoea, at home in Madison County, Ga. May 25, 1863.

GRIFFETH, James - Private Mar. 4, 1862. Transferred to Co. E, 37th Regt. Ga. Inf. May 6, 1863. Roll for Apr. 1, 1864, last on file, shows him present. Killed near Atlanta, Ga. July 22, 1864.

GRIFFETH, Jesse W. - Private Mar. 4, 1862. Transferred to Co. E, 37th Regt. Ga. Inf. May 6, 1863. Surrendered at Greensboro, N.C. Apr. 26, 1865.

GRIFFETH, Oliver P. - Private Mar. 4, 1862. Appointed 3rd. Corporal in 1862. Transferred to Co. E, 37th Regt. Ga. Inf. as 3rd Corporal May 6, 1863. Appointed 1st Sergeant. Surrendered at Greensboro, N.C. Apr. 26, 1865.

GUNNELS, Junius Z. - Private Mar. 4, 1862. Transferred to Co. E, 37th Regt. Ga. Inf. May 6, 1863. Roll for Apr. 1, 1864, last on file, shows him present. No later record.

HALL, James P. - Private Mar. 4, 1862. Transferred to Co. G, 37th Regt. Ga. Inf. May 6, 1863. Captured at Nashville, Tenn. Dec. 16, 1864. Released at Camp Chase, O. June 12, 1865.

HALL, Jeremiah - Private Mar. 4, 1862. Transferred to Co. G, 37th Regt. Ga. Inf. May 6, 1863 Killed at Franklin, Tenn. in 1864.

HALL, Jeremiah W. - Private Mar. 4, 1862. Appears last on pay roll dated Apr. 17, 1862.

HALL, J. S. - Enlisted as a private, Co. __, ___ Regt. June 20, 1862. Transferred to Co. B, 9th Bttn. Ga. Inf. Dec 15, 1862. No later record.

HAMPTON, H. H. - Private July 20, 1862. Transferred to Co. E, 37th Regt. Ga. Inf. May 6, 1863. Roll for Apr. 1, 1864, last on file, shows him present. No later record.

HEMPHILL, Oliver W. - Private Mar. 4, 1862. Roll dated Jan. 14, 1863, last on file, shows him present. No later record.

HICKS, Nathaniel - Private July 20, 1862. Transferred to Co. E, 37th Regt. Ga. Inf. May 6, 1863. Sent to hospital Feb. 1, 1864. Pension records show he was disabled by measles. (Born in Ga. Apr. 9, 1840.)

HIGGINBOTHAM, Woodson - Private Mar. 4, 1862. Appears last on roll dated Apr. 17, 1862.

KELLUM, John W. - Private Mar. 4, 1862. Appears last on roll dated Apr. 17, 1862. KIRK, John C. - Private Dec. 15, 1862. Transferred to Co. E, 37th Regt. Ga. Inf. May 6, 1863. Roll for Apr. 1, 1864, last on file, shows him present. Captured and paroled at Athens, Ga. May 8, 1865.

KIRK, John C. - Private Dec. 15, 1862. Transferred to Co. E, 37th Regt. Ga. Inf. May 6, 1863. Wounded Chickamauga September 1863. Roll for Apr. 1, 1864, last on file, shows him present. Captured and paroled at Athens, Ga. May 8, 1865.

LANDERS, John M. - Private May 10, 1862. Transferred to Co. E, 37th Regt. Ga. Inf. May 6, 1863. Killed near Atlanta, Ga. July 6, 1864.

LANDERS, Russell R. - Private Mar. 4, 1862. Died Apr. 29, 1862.

LAWRENCE, Thomas A. - Private May 10, 1862. Transferred to Co. E, 37th Regt. Ga. Inf. May 6, 1863. Roll for Apr. 1, 1864, last on file, shows him present. No later record.

LIVELY, S. J. - Private May 10, 1862. Died at Knoxville, Tenn. Sept. 20, 1862.

MARTIN, A. M. - Private May 10, 1862. Died at Atlanta, Ga. Sept. July 13, 1862.

MATHEWS, F. J. - Private May 10, 1862. Roll dated Jan. 14, 1863, last on file, shows him sent to Knoxville, Tenn. as Hospital Steward. No later record.

McELROY, Francis C. - Private Mar. 4, 1862. Died Sept. 17, 1862. (Born in Madison County, Ga. in 1834.)

MESSER, Jacob (or Mercer) - Private May 10, 1862. Died at Atlanta, Ga. Aug. 1, 1862. Buried there in Oakland Cemetery.

MITCHELL, Thomas C. - Private July 20, 1862. Transferred to Co. E, 37th Regt. Ga. Inf. May 6, 1863. Surrendered at Greensboro, N.C. Apr. 26, 1865. (Born Jan. 13, 1833.)

MOON, Bird A. - Private May 10, 1862. Transferred to Co. E, 37th Regt. Ga. Inf. May 6, 1863. Wounded Chickamauga September, 1863. Killed at Murfreesboro, Tenn. Dec. 24, 1864.

MORRIS, George A. - Private May 10, 1862. Died of chronic diarrhoea, at home in Madison County, Ga., Feb. 16, 1863.

MORRIS, William A. - Privare Mar. 4, 1862. Roll dated Jan. 14, 1863, last on file, shows him present. Pension records show right arm disabled. (Athens Banner Herald reported him killed at Chickamauga. This is confirmed by I.V. Moore's Diary.)

MOSELEY, D. R. - Private May 10, 1862. Pension records show he was wounded, right arm permanently disabled, at Utoy Creek, Ga. Aug. 6, 1864. (Born in Ga. Jan. 10, 1835.)

MUSE, Marcus D. L. - Private Dec. 15, 1862. Transferred to Co. E, 37th Regt. Ga. Inf. May 6, 1863. Roll for Apr. 1, 1864, last on file, shows him present. No later records.

PATTERSON, James R. (or Paterson) - Private May 8, 1862. Died at Knoxville, Tenn. May 26, 1862.

PATTERSON, John R. - Private May 8, 1862. Died June 8, 1862.

PATTON, Hezekiah D. (or Patten) - Private Mar. 4, 1862. Transferred to Co. E, 37th Regt. Ga. Inf. May 6, 1863. Wounded Jonesboro, August 6, 1864. Surrendered at Greensboro, N.C. Apr. 26, 1865.

PATTON, J. W. (or Patten) - Private July 20, 1862. Transferred to Co. E, 37th Regt. Ga. Inf. May 6, 1863. Roll for Apr. 1, 1864, last on file, shows him present. Wounded Resaca May 14th 1864 and died from wounds.

PIERCE, James A. (or Pearce) - Private Mar. 4, 1862. Transferred to Co. E, 37th Regt. Ga. Inf. May 6, 1863. Roll for Apr. 1, 1864, last on file, shows him absent, detailed shoemaker by order of Gen. Bragg Apr. 7, 1863. No later record.

PIERCE, Jesse M. (or Pearce) - Private Mar. 4, 1862. Transferred to Co. E, 37th Regt. Ga. Inf. May 6, 1863. Captured at Decatur, Ala. Oct. 28, 1864. Released at Camp Douglas, Ill. June 17, 1865. (Born in Franklin County in 1839.)

PIERCE, John M. (or Pearce) - Private Mar. 4, 1862. Roll dated Apr. 17, 1862, shows he was rejected, disability. No later record.

PITTMAN, Martin H. - Private Mar. 4, 1862. Appointed 2nd Corporal in 1862. Transferred to Co. E, 37th Regt. Ga. Inf. as 2nd Corporal May 6, 1863. Wounded Chickamauga, Septmeber 1863. Roll for Apr. 1, 1864, last on file, shows him present. *Martin Hughes Pittman died in the battle of Franklin, Tennessee in December 1864 at a Confederate hospital, of infection from a gunshot wound. His wife was Hulda J. Nunn; they were married on 20 Oct 1859 in Madison County.*

PORTER, William H. H. - Private Mar. 4, 1862. Appears last on roll for Apr. 17, 1862.

PORTERFIELD, Ephraim - Private May 10, 1862. Transferred to Co. E, 37th Regt. Ga. Inf. May 6, 1863; to Co. C, 4th Battn. Ga. Sharpshooters in 1864. Sent to Marietta, Ga. hospital June 20, 1864. Captured and paroled at Hartwell, Ga. May 18, 1865. (Born in Ga.)

PORTERFIELD, James W. - Private May 10, 1862. Transferred to Co. E, 37th Regt. Ga. Inf. May 6, 1863. Wounded, date and place not given. Admitted to St. Mary's Hospital at West Point, Miss., account of wounds, Jan. 10, 1865. No later record.

PORTERFIELD, King W. - Private Mar. 4, 1862. Transferred to Co. E, 37th Regt. Ga. Inf. May 6, 1863. Surrendered at Greensboro, N.C. Apr. 26, 1865.

PORTERFIELD, Robert L. T. - Private Mar. 4, 1862. Transferred to Co. E, 37th Regt. Ga. Inf. May 6, 1863. Surrendered at Greensboro, N.C. Apr. 26, 1865. (Born in Madison County, Ga. Sept. 17, 1830. Died in 1930.) In pension application filed in Wilkes County, Ga. in 1897, he stated "right arm was broken during war. Left knee broken during war."

PORTERFIELD, William J. - Private Mar. 4, 1862. Roll dated Jan. 14, 1863, last on file, shows him present. No later record.

POWER, Asa G. - Private July 20, 1862. Transferred to Co. E, 37th Regt. Ga. Inf. May 6, 1863. Wounded at Chickamauga, Ga. Sept. 20, 1863. Sent to hospital. Received pay at Atlanta, Ga. Apr. 30, 1864. No later record.

POWER, Jesse G. - Private Mar. 4, 1862. Died May 29, 1862.

POWER, Joseph B. - Private May 9, 1862. Died of chronic diarrhoea, at home in Madison County, Ga., Nov. 23, 1862.

POWER, Josiah W., Sr. - Private Mar. 4, 1862. Transferred to Co. E, 37th Regt. Ga. Inf. May 6, 1863. Sent to hospital Aug. 10, 1863. Received pay May 3, 1864. No later record. (Born in Ga. in 1840.)

POWER, S. P. - Private May 10, 1862. Transferred to Co. E, 37th Regt. Ga. Inf. May 6, 1863. Surrendered at Greensboro, N.C. Apr. 26, 1865.

POWER, Thomas B. - Private July 1862. Transferred to Co. E, 37th Regt. Ga. Inf. May 6, 1863. Wounded Chickamauga September 1863. Surrendered at Greensboro, N.C. Apr. 26, 1865.

RHODES, James W. - Private May 10, 1862. Transferred to Co. E, 37th Regt. Ga. Inf. May 6, 1863. Roll for Apr. 1, 1864, last on file, shows he was detailed shoemaker by order of Gen. Johnston Mar. 10, 1863.

RUSSELL, John - Private Mar. 4, 1862. Transferred to Co. E, 37th Regt. Ga. Inf. May 6, 1863. Surrendered at Greensboro, N.C. Apr. 26, 1865.

RUSSELL, J. E. M. - Private July 1862. Transferred to Co. E, 37th Regt. Ga. Inf. May 6, 1863. Roll for Apr. 1, 1864, last on file, shows him present. No later record.

RUSSELL, J. J. - Private Mar. 4, 1862. Died June 6, 1862. Buried in Hollywood Cemetery at Richmond, Va.

RUSSELL, Joseph. T. - Private July 20, 1862. Sent to Atlanta, Ga. hospital Dec. 28, 1862. No later record.

RUSSELL, Robert T. - Private May 10, 1862. Transferred to Co. E, 37th Regt. Ga. Inf. May 6, 1863. Wounded at Wounded at Chickamauga, Ga. Sept. 20, 1863. Sent to hospital. No later record.

RUSSELL, W. J. - Private May 10, 1862. Transferred to Co. E, 37th Regt. Ga. Inf. May 6, 1863. Surrendered at Greensboro, N.C. Apr. 26, 1865.

SAILORS, Crawford C. - Private May 10, 1862. Transferred to Co. E, 37th Regt. Ga. Inf. May 6, 1863. Roll for Apr. 1, 1864, last on file, shows He was sent to Atlanta, Ga. hospital July 7, 1863. Captured and paroled at Athens, Ga. May 8, 1865.

SAILORS, W. C. - Private May 10, 1862. Died Aug. 9, 1862.

SCROGINS, George W. - Private Apr. 17, 1862. Rejected, diability.

SEAGRAVES, John G. (or Segraves) - Private Mar. 4, 1862. Transferred to Co. E, 37th Regt. Ga. Inf. May 6, 1863. Captured near Nashville, Tenn. Dec. 16, 1864. Released at Camp Douglas, Ill. June 20, 1865.

SEAGRAVES, R. B. (or Segraves) - Private July 20, 1862. Transferred to Co. E, 37th Regt. Ga. Inf. May 6, 1863. Wounded in 1864. Died of wounds, in Ocmulgee Hospital at Macon, Ga., Sept. 13, 1864.

SEAGRAVES, William D. (or Segraves) - Private Mar. 4, 1862. Transferred to Co. E, 37th Regt. Ga. Inf. May 6, 1863. Died of Disease in Gilmer Hospital at Atlanta, Ga. June 5, 1864. Buried there in Oakland Cemetery.

SEGAR, J. A. - Private May 10, 1862. Detailed railroad guard, Knoxville, Tenn., Nov. 1, 1862. Transferred to Co. E, 37th Regt. Ga. Inf. May 6, 1863. Roll for Apr. 1, 1864, last on file, show he was on detail as railroad guard. No later record.

SEGAR, S. D. - Private May 10, 1862. Detailed guard at Chattanooga, Tenn. in 1862. Transferred to Co. E, 37th Regt. Ga. Inf. May 6, 1863. Captured at Chattanooga, Tenn. Oct. 25, 1863. No later record.

SHINN, G. W. - Private July 20, 1862. Roll dated Jan. 14, 1863, last on file, shows him present. No later record.

SIMMONS, David T. - Private Mar. 4, 1862. Transferred to Co. E, 37th Regt. Ga. Inf. May 6, 1863. Surrendered at Greensboro, N.C. Apr. 26, 1865.

SIMMONS, Wiley J. - Private Mar. 4, 1862. Transferred to Co. E, 37th Regt. Ga. Inf. May 6, 1863. Wounded in foot at Franklin, Tenn. Nov. 30, 1864, and captured there Dec. 17, 1864. Released at Point Lookout, Md. June 5, 1865. Admitted to U.S.A. Post Hospital at Savannah, Ga., on account of debility from amputation of right foot, June 22, 1865. Discharged July 8, 1865. (Born in Madison County, Ga. Jan. 25, 1842. Died at Confederate Soldier's Home at Atlanta, Ga. Jan. 8, 1910.)

SMITH, Stephen - Private Mar. 4, 1862. Transferred to Co. E, 37th Regt. Ga. Inf. May 6, 1863. Surrendered at Greensboro, N.C. Apr. 26, 1865.

SMITH, William - Private Mar. 4, 1862. Transferred to Co. E, 37th Regt. Ga. Inf. May 6, 1863. Wounded in leg at Chickamauga, Ga. Sept. 19, 1863. In hospital, wounded, close of war. (Born in Ga. Dec. 2, 1843.)

STEPHENS, Caleb M. - Private Mar. 4, 1862. Transferred to Co. E, 37th Regt. Ga. Inf. May 6, 1863. Surrendered at Greensboro, N.C. Apr. 26, 1865.

STRICKLAND, Kinchen M. - Private Mar. 4, 1862. Roll dated Jan. 14, 1863, last on file, shows him present. No later record.

STRICKLAND, Milton J. - Private Mar. 4, 1862. Received $50 bounty Apr. 17, 1862. No later record.

STRICKLAND, Samuel G. - Private Mar. 4, 1862. Roll dated Jan. 14, 1863, last on file, shows he was sent to Chattanooga, Tenn. hospital Oct. 15, 1862. No later record.

STRICKLAND, Wilson B. - Private July 20, 1862. Transferred to Co. E, 37th Regt. Ga. Inf. May 6, 1863. Died July 4, 1863.

STRICKLAND, W. F. - Private May 10, 1862. Transferred to Co. E, 37th Regt. Ga. Inf. May 6, 1863. Roll for Apr. 1, 1864, last on file, shows he was on furlough. Killed Franklin,Tn. November 1864.

THOMPSON, Joel B. - Private May 10, 1862. Transferred to Co. E, 37th Regt. Ga. Inf. May 6, 1863. Wounded Chickamauga September 1863 Surrendered at Greensboro, N.C. Apr. 26, 1865.

THWEATT, Thomas C. (or Threatt) - Private Mar. 4, 1862. Received $50 Bounty Apr. 17, 1862. No later record.

TOLBERT, William A. - Private Mar. 4, 1862. Transferred to Co. E, 37th Regt. Ga. Inf. May 6, 1863. Wounded at Chickamauga, Ga. Sept. 20, 1863. Surrendered at Greensboro, N.C. Apr. 26, 1865.

TUCKER, James R. P. - Private Mar. 4, 1862. Transferred to Co. E, 37th Regt. Ga. Inf. May 6, 1863. Captured at Missionary Ridge, Tenn. Nov. 25, 1863. Died of fever at Rock Island, Ill. Mar. 25, 1864.

WHITE, James W. - Private May 10, 1862. Transferred to Co. E, 37th Regt. Ga. Inf. May 6, 1863. Wounded in right thigh at Chickamauga, Ga. Sept. 20, 1863. Roll for Apr. 1, 1864, last on file, shows him absent, wounded. No later record. (Born in Ga.)

WHITE, Stephen R. T. - Private Mar. 4, 1862. Discharged, disability. Enlisted as a private in Co. E, 37th Regt. Ga. Inf. Feb. 18, 1864. Wounded, date and place not given. Admitted to Way Hospital at Meridian, Miss., Jan. 12, 1865; remark, "Furloughed, wounded."

WHITWORTH, Turley S. - Private Mar. 4, 1862. Received $50 bounty Apr. 17, 1862. No later record.

WHITWORTH, Winston - Private Mar. 4, 1862. Wounded in 1862. Transferred to Co. E, 37th Regt. Ga. Inf. May 6, 1863. Discharged Jan. 30, 1864.

WILHITE, Thomas M. - Private Mar. 4, 1862. Received $50 bounty Apr. 17, 1862. No later record.

WILLIAMS, J. J. - Private July 1862. Received $50 bounty June 1, 1862. No later record.

WILSON, James W. - Private Mar. 4, 1862. Died at Manchester, Tenn. Nov. 29, 1862.

WILSON, Samuel B. - Private Mar. 4, 1862. Received $50 bounty Apr. 17, 1862. No later record.

WILSON, Thomas - Private Mar. 4, 1862. Transferred to Co. E, 37th Regt. Ga. Inf. May 6, 1863. Killed at Franklin, Tenn. Nov. 30, 1864.

WOOD, John P. - Private Mar. 4, 1862. Sent to Tazewell, Tenn. hospital Sept. 15, 1862. Transferred to Co. E, 37th Regt. Ga. Inf. May 6, 1863. Roll for Apr. 1, 1864, last on file, shows he was sent to hospital Sept. 15, 1862.

WOOD, William J. - Private Mar. 4, 1862. Transferred to Co. E, 37th Regt. Ga. Inf. May 6, 1863. Roll for Apr. 1, 1864, last on file, shows him present. Killed at Dallas, Ga. May 28, 1864.

WYNN, David Z. - Private May 10, 1862. Appointed 2nd Corporal in 1862; 5th Sergeant in 1862. Transferred to Co. E, 37th Regt. Ga. Inf. May 6, 1863. Appointed 4th Sergeant. Wounded in left index finger in 1864. Admitted to Floyd House & Ocmulgee Hospitals at Macon, Ga. on account of wound, Aug. 29, 1864. No later record.

WYNN, Hezekiah S. - Private May 10, 1862. Transferred to Co. E, 37th Regt. Ga. Inf. May 6, 1863. Appointed Corporal. Surrendered at Greensboro, N.C. Apr. 26, 1865. (Born in Ga.)

THE FOLLOWING MEN JOINED COMPANY E OF THE 37TH GEORGIA INFANTRY BEGINNING IN LATE 1863.

ALLEN, Matthew S. - Private Jan. 6, 1864. Roll for Apr. 1, 1864, last on file, shows him present. Pension records show he was at home on sick furlough Feb. 1865, to close of war. (Born in Madison County, Ga. in 1844.)

BROWN, W. A. J. - Private Aug. 6, 1863. Wounded Jonesboro Ga. August 8, 1864. Surrendered at Greensboro, N.C. Apr. 26, 1865. (Born in Oglethorpe County, Ga. in 1825.)

BULLOCK, W. S. - Private Aug. 6, 1863. Sent to hospital Feb. 21, 1864. Captured and paroled at Atlanta (or Athens), Ga. May 8, 1865.

DUDLEY, E. J. - Private Mar. 4, 1864. Roll for Apr. 1, 1864, last on file, shows him present. Wounded Jonesboro Ga. August 8, 1864. No later record.

LAWRENCE, James M. - Private May 20, 1863. Captured at Decatur, Ala. Oct. 28, 1864. Died of pneumonia at Camp Douglas, Ill. Feb. 4, 1865. Buried there in Confederate Cemetery.

MASSEY, James E. - Private Oct. 23, 1863. Pension records show he was at home disabled close of war.

MEAD, M. M. (or Meade) - Private Oct. 23, 1863. Died in Atlanta, Ga. hospital Jan 12, 1864. Buried there in Oakland Cemetery.

NICHOLS, J. C. - Private Mar. 21, 1864. Roll for Apr. 1, 1864, last on file, shows him present. Killed Jonesboro Ga. August 8, 1864.

OWENS, E. P. - Private Oct. 28, 1863. Roll for Apr. 1, 1864, last on file, shows he was sent to hospital Jan. 10, 1864. No later record.

PERRY, M. P. - Private Feb. 4, 1864. Roll for Apr. 1, 1864, last on file, shows him present. Killed Jonesboro, Ga. August 6, 1864.(Diary of I.V. Moore)

PIERCE, Franklin M. - Private feb. 15, 1864. Wounded in hand, necessitating amputation, at Kennesaw Mountain, Ga. June 11, 1864. Captured at Macon, Ga. Apr. 30, 1865, and paroled there May 1865. (Born in Ga. in 1845. Died at Talking Rock, Ga. May 9, 1935.)

PULLEN, James M. (or Pullin) - Private Mar. 3, 1864. Surrendered at Greensboro, N.C. Apr. 26, 1865.

PULLEN, Major M. (or Pullin) - Private Mar. 5, 1864. Died July 10, 1864.

SAILORS, A. J. - Private Jan. 6, 1864. Surrendered at Greensboro, N.C. Apr. 26, 1865.

SCARBOROUGH, S. M. (or Scarbrough) - Private Oct. 30, 1863.Surrendered at Greensboro, N.C. Apr. 26, 1865.

SEAGRAVES, James C. (or Segraves) - Private Nov. 30, 1863. Roll for Apr. 1, 1864, last on file, shows him present. No later record.

SIMMONS, I. D. - Private Feb. 22, 1864. Roll for Apr. 1, 1864, last on file, shows him present. No later record.

SMITH, Jasper J. - Private Aug. 10, 1863. Surrendered at Greensboro, N.C. Apr. 26, 1865. (Born in Madison County, Ga. Aug. 3, 1845. Died at Confederate Soldiers' Home in Atlanta, Ga. Nov. 15, 1915.)

SPURLOCK, Augustus - Private Oct. 23, 1863. Roll for Apr. 1, 1864, last on file, shows him present. Killed Dallas, Ga. May 28, 1864.

STANDIFER, Luke R. - Private Aug. 3, 1863. Died of chronic diarrhea at Athens, Ga. Dec. 1, 1863.

PART III

EXHIBIT 1

MADISON COUNTY, GEORGIA
Names of Soldiers Families Supplied with Salt
dated July 21 1863 Under the Order of Govenor

Names of widows of deceased Soldiers

Mrs. Samuel Davids
" George S. Key
" J C bonds
" Catherine Stephens
" C G Crawford
" Louise Williams
" Safronia Chandler
" Mary Chandler
" Nancy Patton
" Susan Parton
" Elizabeth David
" Letty Pendleton
" Letty Wilhite
" Caroline Shields
" Melissa Swindle
" Louisa Chandler
" Caroline Martin
" S. F. Echols
" Mary Barnes
" William L Glenn
" Martha Glenn
" Martha williams
" Mary Pittards
" Adaline Williams
" Aletha chandler

" Selina Bone
" Sarah Clements
" Sarah Chandler
" Mary Freeman
" Harriet Seagraves
" Moses Sailors
" Fanny Bradley
" Nancy Smith
" Mary Payton ?
" Mary David
" Hariet King
" Lela Collins
" Fanny Mead
" Elizabeth Cooper
" Mary A. L. Rattliff
" Lucinda Thompson
" Mary McCurdy
" Emily Evans
" Dicey E. Simmons
" ? Thompson
" Louisa Cooper
" Lucy Pierce ?
" Mary Thompson
" Elizabeth Evans
" Amanda Collins
" Mary Thompson
" S. Farmer ?
" J. R. Patterson
" N. J. Allen
" Martha Sartain
" Emily Sartain
" Artemissia Stricklands
" Nancy Bragg
" Mary Strickland
" Sarah Pierson
" Martha Thompson
" C. C. David
" Caroline David
" C. C. David
" W. P. Floyd
" S. Threatt ?

" E. Wilson
" S. Thompson
" A. King
" A. Williams
" Mary Freeman
" Nancy Bone
" P. Porterfield (Patience C. Hall m. Horatio Porterfield, 28 Dec 1854)
" G. A. Morris (George A. Morris m. Cynthia E. Thompson, 5 Dec 1855)
" Rosannah Hall (Rosannah King m. 16 Dec 1858 Isaac S. Hall, d. CSA)
" Rebecca McGee (Rebecca Dudley m. 1 Dec 1853 Chiles McGee)
Total 76

Names of wives of Soldiers now in the Service

Mrs. B. Sanders
" I. Anthony (Ian P.
Anthony)
" D. B. Meadows
" P. C. Smith
" Thomas Wilson
" W. G. David
" H. H. Daniels
" J. J. Carithers
" James Griffeth Junr
" Jesse Griffith
" Walton J. Carrithers
" Joseph J. Key
" John A. McCurdy
" John M. Landers
" William rice
" Asa Coker
" James W. King
" D. R. Mosely
" K. M. Strickland
" E. J. Hering
" W. H. Griffeth Junr
" Maria Herring
" Samuel H Hardeman
" Marshal David
" W. H. Anthony
" W. H. Bowles
" James Wills
" S. F. Ware ?
" T. Mead
" E. S. Crawford
" L. Stephens
" M. E. Strickland
" Mary Streeman
" J F. Fitzpatricks
" W. E. Cain
" John T. Burroughs
" B. F. Mercier
" Frances Allen Dobbs

" A W McCurdy
" Joab Collins
" A. E. Barnett ?
" James Thompson
" W. C. Hitchcock
" G. L. Boltin
" James H. Bullock
" Wiley G. Eberhart
" John R Winkley
" Samuel Kilburn
" Jacob L. Bryant
" B. A. Cunningham
" John R. Patterson
" Thomas B. Thompson
" Geo. Morris
" Joel B. Thompson
" James A. Thompson
" John J. Cheatham
" W. S. Busbin
" James W. Kirk
" James K. Patterson
" James Gallaher
" G. W. Winfrey
" R. H. Bulloch Junr
" William C. Bridges
" M. Kellum
" John T. Adams
" George W. Culbertson
" O. W. White
" H. L. Hering
" Robert Power
" B. J. Carrithers
" Crawford Woods
" M. J. Woods
" Josiah Drake
" James Brooks
" ? C. Mitchell
" A. M. Power
" Samuel Wood
" Frances Alexander
" J. Parks ?

" G. Davis
" William Gunnells
" John Decker
" Henry Rowland
" Crawford Sailor
" James B. Crawford
" Charles S. Madden
" E. F. Baxter ?
" M. W. Talbot
" J. C. Nelms
" ? A. Meadows
" Lucy Linsey
" F. O. Williams
" James Baugh
" Nathaniel Hix
" J. S. Gholston
" H. Bray
" J. L. Patton
" J. M. Bird
" J. L. Bird
" E. Bray
" W. P. Alexander
" H. C. Nash
" J. A. Montgomery
" John Wood
" O. Cleghorn
" E. W. Martin
" J. S. Smith
" J. Hill
" G. J. Rice
" J. C. Campbell
" ? Williams
" A. Fitzpatrick
" J. H. Anderson
" ? Cramer ?
" A. H. Nix
" Frances Perry
" Cynthia Bray
" L. Dudley
" J. A. Moore
" M. A. Moon

" J. T. Witcher
" Y. D. Wynn
" W. W. Sims
" Samuel Power
" M. Wiley
" J. G. Eberhart
" S Smith
" Martin Tilman
" R. W. Tillman
" ? Williams
" W. H. Bullock
" R. J. Carrithers
" J. R. Faulkner
" W. A. Collins (Wesley
" A. H. Hampton
" Samuel W. Patten ?
" A. J. Thompson
" Eph Thompson
" H. Haywood ?
" J. A. Seagers
" Elizabeth McDuff
" Celia Ginn
" E. A. White
" Sarah Pierson
" Prudence Cheek
" Frances Dean
" Sarah Higgenbotham
" James F. Porterfield
" J. W. Patton
" R. Porterfield
" S. S. Chandler
" W. S. Sailor
" F. Culbertson
" H. Segar
" Martha Scarborough
" H. H. Brown (m. Sarah W. Whitworth 25 Jul 1861)
" P. L. B. Wilder (Peter L. B. Wilder m. July Ann O'Kelley 25 Oct 1848)
" Moses Sailors (m. Susan Sailors 12 Nov 1857
" Willis J. Dudley (m. Elizabeth Porterfield 28 Dec 1848)
" L. A. Dudley (Lawson A. Dudley m. Sarah E. Simmons 20 Jan 1853)
" J. A. Gloer (Joseph A. Gloer m. Sarah E. Thompson 13 Dec 1858)

" J. W. Roads (m. Margaret P. Power 25 Feb 1858)
" John L. Cartledge (m. Suntha Ann McCurdy 24 Dec 1850)
" James W. Gunnells (m. Sarah F. Tolbert 3 Nov 1853)
" H. H. Brown (m. Sarah W. Whitworth 25 Jul 1861)
" P. L. B. Wilder (Peter L. B. Wilder m. July Ann O'Kelley 25 Oct 1848)
" Moses Sailors (m. Susan Sailors 12 Nov 1857
" Amanda Sartain (Alfred Sartain married
" Helica Scarborough (Helica Sartain m. Lewis Scarborough 24 Jan 1856)
" L. M. Sartain (Lewis Sartain m. Martha Auntney Beard
" Mary J. Scarborough (Mary Jane Scarborough m. W. B. Scarborough 22 Oct 1849)
" Cynthia Scarborough (Cynthia Bragg m.W. B. Scarborough 22 Oct 1849)

Names of widows having a son or sons now in the Service July 24, 1863

Mrs. Eliza Carrithers
" Delilah Coker
" Emily ?ane
" Polly Bauman ?
" Mesiah Stgephens
" Letty Black
" Eliza Williams
" Judah Bone
" Mary A Shinn
" Malinda Moon ?
" Martha Anderson
" Kesiah Vaughn
" Mary Hix
" Nancy Segraves
" Dicey Tucker
" Martha Sims
" Harriett Stephens
" Elizabeth Mercer
" Mary Collins
" Caroline Bullock
" Permelia ?
" Nancy Sims
" Rebecca Gallaher ?
" H. Haywood
" Millie ?
" M. A. Boltin
" Permelia Burroughs
" Sarah Higginbotham
" Sarah Jordan
" Mary Hix

" Harlow S. Strickland (Harlow Gholston m. Willis Strickland 18 Jan 1826)
Total 32

FAMILY HISTORIES

The following family histories represent six of the families most prominently discussed in the this work and are all direct family lines of the author. Each of these families had ties to the Holly Creek area of Madison County and many of the members of these families served in the 9th Battalion and the 37th Georgia Regiment. The family histories are incomplete in some cases as information is not available for all descendants.

DESCENDANTS OF THOMAS MOORE

Generation No. 1

1. THOMAS MOORE was born May 07, 1782 in Virginia, and died January 10, 1845 in Elbert Co Ga. He married JUDITH ANN BOOTH about 1801, daughter of NATHANIEL BOOTH and ELIZABETH JOHNS. She was born June 05, 1781 in Amherst County, Virginia, and died March 05, 1864 in Elbert County.

    Children of THOMAS MOORE and JUDITH BOOTH are:

2.	i.	WILLIAM J MOORE, b. April 18, 1803, Elbert Co Ga; d. December 05, 1865, Elbert Co, GA.
3.	ii.	JOHN NATHANIEL MOORE, b. March 31, 1807, Elbert Co Ga; d. January 27, 1887, Elbert Co
4.	iii.	FRANCES A MOORE, b. Abt. 1812, Elbert Co Ga.
	iv.	ELIZABETH MOORE, b. Abt. 1814. never married
	v.	NANCY M MOORE, b. Abt. 1816, Elbert Co Ga; d. Aft. 1865, Elbert Co. Ga; m. HENRY HARDEN, October 08, 1865, Elbert Co Ga.
	vi.	MARY MOORE, b. September 17, 1818, Elbert Co Ga; m. JOHN JAMES JOHNSON, December 19, 1939, Elbert Co Ga.
5.	vii.	JOEL WASHINGTON MOORE, b. Oct. 10, 1821, Elbert Co Ga; d. June 16, 1913, Elbert Co

Generation No. 2

2. WILLIAM J. MOORE *(THOMAS)* was born April 18, 1803 in Elbert Co Ga, and died December 05, 1865 in Elbert Co, GA. He married ELIZABETH BOOTH September 20, 1832, daughter of JOHN BOOTH and ANNA FAULKNER. She was born January 21, 1814, and died February 26, 1891.

    Children of WILLIAM MOORE and ELIZABETH BOOTH are:

6.	i.	THOMAS JEFFERSON MOORE, b. October 08, 1833; d. October 04, 1912.
	ii.	JOSEPH MOORE, b. Abt. 1835; m. MARY SANDERS; b. Abt. 1836.
7.	iii.	JOHN N. MOORE, b. December 22, 1836; d. October 27, 1859, Madison Co Ga.
8.	iv.	WILLIAM MOORE, b. Abt. 1838.

       v.   MAHULDA "HULDY" MOORE, b. Abt. 1840; m. WILLIAM J SANDERS, October 13, 1859, Elbert Co, GA; b. Abt. 1840.

9.   vi.   MARY E MOORE, b. June 10, 1843, Elbert Co, GA; d. July 03, 1897, Madison Co, GA.

10.   vii.   WOODSON V MOORE, b. 1845, Elbert Co, GA.

     viii.   MARTHA H "MATTIE" MOORE, b. Abt. 1847; m. WILLIAM NUNN, August 17, 1865, Elbert Co, GA; b. Aft. 1835.

11.   ix.   NANCY CATHERINE MOORE, b. November 14, 1848; d. Abt. 1925.

      x.   ROBERT JUDSON MOORE, b. October 25, 1854, Elbert Co, GA; d. January 28, 1904, Madison Co, GA; m. SARAH A "SALLIE" HAMPTON, June 15, 1876, Madison Co, GA; b. February 16, 1856, Madison Co, GA; d. November 24, 1908, Madison Co, GA.

3. JOHN NATHANIEL MOORE *(THOMAS)* was born March 31, 1807 in Elbert Co Ga, and died January 27, 1887 in Elbert Co Ga. He married (1) MARTHA ELIZABETH VAUGHN March 06, 1828, daughter of ALEXANDER VAUGHN and ELIZABETH DAVID. She was born March 04, 1812 in Elbert Co Ga, and died July 17, 1860 in Elbert Co Ga. He married (2) SARAH R JOHNSON February 20, 1862 in Elbert Co Ga. She died April 02, 1863. He married (3) MARTHA E. ALMOND August 23, 1864, daughter of W.M. ALMOND and S. THORNTON. She was born April 27, 1834 in Elbert Co Ga, and died December 27, 1908 in Elbert Co Ga.

     Children of JOHN MOORE and MARTHA VAUGHN are:

12.   i.   WILLIAM M. MOORE, b. May 03, 1829, Elbert Co Ga; d. May 09, 1907, Franklin Co. Ga.

13.   ii.   THOMAS A MOORE, b. January 13, 1834.

14.   iii.   ELIZABETH MOORE, b. August 05, 1836.

15.   iv.   JUDAH ANN MOORE, b. November 11, 1840, Elbert Co Ga; d. February 27, 1858, Elbert Co

      v.   MARTHA J. MOORE, b. Dec 24, 1852; m. CHARLES JESSE VAUGHN, October 15, 1868.

16.   vi.   ISAAC "IKE" VAUGHN MOORE, b. November 17, 1830, Elbert Co, GA; d. November 29, 1918, Madison Co, GA.

     Child of JOHN MOORE and MARTHA ALMOND is:

17.   vii.   PRISCILLA TULULLAH[3] MOORE, b. December 27, 1865, Elbert Co Ga; d. September 28, 1948, Elbert Co Ga.

4. FRANCES A MOORE *(THOMAS)* was born Abt. 1812 in Elbert Co Ga. She married WILLIAM J JOHNSON September 02, 1837 in Elbert Co Ga. He was born Abt. 1810.

Children of FRANCES MOORE and WILLIAM JOHNSON are:
i.JOHN TURK JOHNSON, b. Aft. 1837; m. SIS EBERHART; b. Abt. 1840.
ii.WILL JOHNSON, b. Aft. 1837; m. HATTIE BOOTH; b. Abt. 1840.

5. JOEL WASHINGTON MOORE *(THOMAS)* was born October 10, 1821 in Elbert Co Ga, and died June 16, 1913 in Elbert Co Ga. He married SARAH ANN HEWELL December 16, 1847 in Elbert Co Ga, daughter of WILLIAM HEWELL and CATHERINE. She was born January 14, 1823, and died September 03, 1891. **Military service: Private Co H 1st Ga St Troops**

Children of JOEL MOORE and SARAH HEWELL are:

18.   i.   WILLIAM THOMAS MOORE, b. October 03, 1848; d. January 04, 1928.

19.   ii.   MARY CATHERINE MOORE, b. October 10, 1850; d. December 24, 1922.

       iii. JOHN HENRY MOORE, b. August 05, 1852; d. August 25, 1930; m. MARY CAMPBELL, December 03, 1879; b. March 24, 1862; d. November 13, 1951.

       iv.   ISSAC JEFFERSON MOORE, b. December 24, 1854; d. August 01, 1946; m. MARY E. MIZE; b. July 24, 1863; d. May 30, 1930.

       v.   JAMES WASHINGTON MOORE, b. September 16, 1857; d. April 02, 1949; m. VICTORIA C. BURDEN, November 12, 1884; b. September 19, 1857; d. October 30, 1928.

       vi.   GEORGE BENJAMIN MOORE, b. September 03, 1860; d. October 28, 1942; m. SALONIA GILMER, December 15, 1889; b. May 28, 1866; d. May 13, 1961.

       vii. ALEXANDER JOEL MOORE, b. September 02, 1863; d. April 29, 1951; m. MARTHA C. MIZE, December 19, 1890; b. October 23, 1863; d. February 21, 1945.

Generation No. 3

6. THOMAS JEFFERSON MOORE *(WILLIAM J, THOMAS)* was born October 08, 1833, and died October 04, 1912. He married (1) ELIZABETH JULIA WHITE March 16, 1856, daughter of MARTIN WHITE and ANNA BURDEN. She was born January 06, 1839, and died March 18, 1881. He married (2) SARAH ANN STEDMAN December 04, 1881 in Elbert Co, GA. She was born 1841, and died 1911.

Children of THOMAS MOORE and ELIZABETH WHITE are:
  i.   MARY FRANCES MOORE, b. December 31, 1861.
  ii. WILLIAM MARCUS BARTO MOORE, b. August 24, 1866; d. Abt. 1934.
  iii. MARY FRANCES NELSON "NETTIE" MOORE, b. December 31, 1861, Elbert Co, GA; d. July 02, 1964, Madison Co, GA.
  iv. SARAH LOUVENIA "LOU V" MOORE, b. February 21, 1864, GA; d. August 14, 1928; m. WILLIAM B. HEWELL.
  v.   JOSEPH THOMAS "JOE" MOORE, b. September 20, 1870; d. December 31, 1945, Elbert Co,
  vi. JAMES LEONIDAS "LON" MOORE, b. December 14, 1872; d. November 18, 1934.
  vii. ORA MOORE, b. February 14, 1875; d. May 04, 1950.
  viii. JASPER DAVID "JACK" MOORE, b. November 01, 1878; d. December 28, 1968, Elbert Co,
  ix. FRANK MARTIN MOORE, b. February 21, 1881; d. October 13, 1911.
  x.   MARTHA ANNE H. MOORE, b. September 28, 1859; d. June 16, 1929; m. WILLIAM THOMAS MOORE, November 21, 1875; b. October 03, 1848; d. January 04, 1928.

7. JOHN N. MOORE *(WILLIAM J, THOMAS)* was born December 22, 1836, and died October 27, 1859 in Madison Co Ga. He married HULDA ANN FAULKNER October 27, 1859 in Madison Co, GA. She was born Abt. 1837, and died September 26, 1906.

Children of JOHN MOORE and HULDA FAULKNER are:
  i.   GEORGE WASHINGTON MOORE, b. June 14, 1862, Elbert Co, GA; d. March 18, 1908, Homeland, Charlton Co, GA; m. SALLIE OLLIE DILLARD; b. April 1865, Oglethorpe Co Ga.
  ii. ANNA MOORE, b. Abt. 1865, Elbert Co, GA.
  iii. FUDGE B MOORE, b. Abt. 1869, Elbert Co, GA.
  iv. DORA E MOORE, b. September 02, 1870, Elbert Co, GA; d. December 22, 1954, Anderson, Anderson Co, SC.
  v.   MARY MOORE, b. Abt. 1874, Elbert Co, GA.
  vi. JOHN MOORE, b. Abt. 1876, Elbert Co, GA; d. NC.
  vii. FANNIE MOORE, b. Abt. 1877, Elbert Co, GA.
  viii. DOLLIE MOORE, b. Abt. 1880, Elbert Co, GA.

8. WILLIAM MOORE *(WILLIAM J, THOMAS)* was born Abt. 1838. He married CENIS HARRIS. She was born Abt. 1840. Military Service: Private Co. D 2nd Calvary.

Children of WILLIAM MOORE and CENIS HARRIS are:
- i.   GOSS MOORE, b. Aft. 1860.
- ii.   BILLIE MOORE, b. Aft. 1860.
- iii. WALKER MOORE, b. Aft. 1860.

9. MARY E MOORE *(WILLIAM J, THOMAS)* was born June 10, 1843 in Elbert Co, GA, and died July 03, 1897 in Madison Co, GA. She married WILLIAM ALEXANDER SORRELLS November 10, 1864. He was born December 02, 1828 in Madison Co, GA, and died January 08, 1883 in Madison Co, GA.

Children of MARY MOORE and WILLIAM SORRELLS are:
- i.   LUCRETIA C SORRELLS, b. February 13, 1866, Madison Co, GA.
- ii.   LEILA ALLELULIA ANN SORRELLS, b. December 22, 1867, Madison Co, GA.
- iii. OVIE FRANCES SORRELLS, b. July 06, 1869, Madison Co, GA.
- iv.   WILLIAM RICHARD SORRELLS, b. 1872, Madison Co, GA; d. 1948, Madison Co, GA.
- v.   GIBEON TABULUS REV SORRELLS, b. April 15, 1874, Madison Co, GA.
- vi.   EVELINA DESDEMONA SORRELLS, b. August 16, 1876, Madison Co, GA; d. 1956, Madison Co, GA.
- vii. SARAH E "SALLIE" SORRELLS, b. April 19, 1879, Madison Co, GA; d. November 17, 1902, Madison Co, GA.
- viii. VASSIE ANN SORRELLS, b. November 24, 1881, Madison Co, GA.

10. WOODSON V MOORE *(WILLIAM J, THOMAS)* was born 1845 in Elbert Co, GA. He married MARTHA M FAULKNER February 02, 1864 in Madison Co, GA. She was born 1843 in GA.

Children of WOODSON MOORE and MARTHA FAULKNER are:
- i.   ENOCH V MOORE, b. 1867, Madison Co, GA.
- ii.   JAMES O MOORE, b. 1868, Madison Co, GA.
- iii. ROSA B MOORE, b. 1870, Madison Co, GA.
- iv.   ALCHOLER MOORE, b. 1871, Madison Co, GA.
- v.   MARY LOU "MOLLIE" MOORE, b. December 08, 1873, Madison Co, GA; d. January 07, 1942, Madison Co, GA.

vi. WALTER GRIFFEY MOORE, b. November 18, 1874, Madison Co, GA; d. May 23, 1883, Madison Co, GA.

vii. MYRA J MOORE, b. 1876, Madison Co, GA.

11. NANCY CATHERINE MOORE *(WILLIAM J, THOMAS)* was born November 14, 1848, and died Abt. 1925. She married GEORGE WASHINGTON TURNER December 26, 1867. He was born April 25, 1845, and died March 26, 1927.

Children of NANCY MOORE and GEORGE TURNER are:

i. MARY LILLA TURNER, b. Abt. 1868.

ii. RENA EVADA TURNER, b. Abt. 1870.

iii. NORA LEE TURNER, b. Abt. 1871; d. May 02, 1954.

iv. WILLIE WASHINGTON TURNER, b. Abt. 1873.

v. JESSE LAFAYETTE TURNER, b. Abt. 1875; d. November 23, 1958.

vi. EDIE CARY TURNER, b. Abt. 1877.

vii. LONA DORA TURNER, b. Abt. 1879.

viii. PELLIE CORA TURNER, b. Abt. 1881; d. Abt. 1906.

ix. MAMIE DAISY TURNER, b. Abt. 1883.

x. JOHNIE GORDON TURNER, b. Abt. 1885.

xi. ESSIE ORA TURNER, b. Abt. 1887.

xii. GEORGE HENRY TURNER, b. Abt. 1889; d. Abt. 1914.

xiii. PEARLIE MAE TURNER, b. Abt. 1891.

12. WILLIAM M. MOORE *(JOHN NATHANIEL, THOMAS)* was born May 03, 1829 in Elbert Co Ga, and died May 09, 1907 in Franklin Co. Ga. He married KEZIAH H. DAVID May 01, 1850, daughter of BERRY DAVID and ELIZABETH VAUGHN. She was born 1827 in Madison Co Ga, and died Bet. 1894 - 1895 in Elbert Co Ga. **Military service: Private enlisted October 15, 1861 in Co H. 38th Ga. Appears last on roll for April 1863 Transferred to Co F 15th Georgia, Captured at Dandridge, Tenn. January 22,1864. Transferred from Rock Island, Ill. for exchange March 2,1865. No later record.**

Children of WILLIAM MOORE and KEZIAH DAVID are:

i. BERRY MATHEWS MOORE, b. Abt. 1853; d. October 29, 1920, Atlanta Ga; m. AURORA M THORNTON, Abt. 1873; b. Abt. October 1847; d. November 17, 1920, Atlanta Ga.

ii. FRANSANNA OPHELIA MOORE, b. 1858, Elbert Co. Ga; d. Abt. 1895, Dade Co Ga; m. WILLIAM THOMAS "BUD" GINN, November 23, 1876, Elbert Co Ga; b. Abt. 1852, Elbert Co, GA; d. 1923, Dade Co, GA.

iii.OWEN LAMAR MOORE, b. Abt. 1867; d. Abt. 1919, Birmingham, Ala;
  m. SAVANAH NEESE, December 10, 1891, Hart Co Ga.

13. THOMAS A MOORE *(JOHN NATHANIEL[2], THOMAS[1])* was born January 13, 1834. He married MARTHA E "BETSY" TUCKER, daughter of ROBERT TUCKER and MARTHA STAPLES. She was born Abt. 1830. **Military Service: Appointed 4th Corporal October 1862. Wounded at Fredericksburg, Virginia, December 13, 1862. Captured at Gettysburg, Pennsylvania, July 5, 1863. Paroled at DeCamp General Hospital, David's Island, New York, Harbor, September 1863. Received at City Point, Virginia, September 16,1863. Appointed 3rd Corporal in 1864. Surrendered at Appomattox, Virginia, April 9, 1865**
    Children of THOMAS MOORE and MARTHA TUCKER are:
    i.   MARTHA J MOORE, b. Abt. 1856; m. WILLIAM T. MOORE.
    ii. MALITA MOORE, b. Abt. 1859; m. GEORGE T. HALL.
    iii. ISAAC A MOORE, b. Abt. 1860.
    iv. PAULINA MOORE, b. Abt. 1864; m. CHARLES S. HALL, December 15, 1881.
    v.   JOHN W MOORE, b. Abt. 1866.
    vi. ELZINA P MOORE, b. Abt. 1869; m. MARK H TILLER, January 13, 1888.
    vii. A. LENA MOORE, b. Abt. 1871; m. LORENZO R. MOON.
    viii. EMMA L MOORE, b. Abt. 1875.

14. ELIZABETH MOORE *(JOHN NATHANIEL, THOMAS)* was born August 05, 1836. She married (1) BILLY JONES. She married (2) STEPHEN JOSHUA WHITE February 23, 1854, son of MARTIN WHITE and ANNA BURDEN. He was born October 05, 1825, and died May 23, 1862 in Savanah Ga during Civil War. **STEPHEN JOSHUA WHITE Military service: October 15, 1861, Co H 38th Georgia Inf**
    Children of ELIZABETH MOORE and STEPHEN WHITE are:
    i. JOHN MARTIN WHITE, b. March 10, 1855; d. February 05, 1938, Elbert Co Ga.
    ii. CHARLES H. WHITE, b. June 25, 1856; d. January 22, 1857, Elbert Co Ga.

15. JUDAH ANN MOORE *(JOHN NATHANIEL, THOMAS)* was born November 11, 1840 in Elbert Co Ga, and died February 27, 1858 in Elbert Co Ga. She married (1) THOMAS J STEPHENS January 29, 1850 in Elbert Co, GA. He was born Abt. 1835. She married (2) CHARLES H. GORDON October 07, 1855 in Elbert Co Ga. **Military Service: Jr. 2nd. Lieutenant, July 13, 1861. Appointed Adjutant of the 30th Batt. Ga. Cavalry. Transferred to the 11th**

Regt. Ga. Cavalry. Wounded Dec. 4, 1864. In Macon, Ga. hospital Feb. 1865. No later record. She married (3) EGBERT MARK HARWELL October 29, 1872 in Elbert Co, GA. He was born August 10, 1822 in Oglethorpe Co, GA, and died June 20, 1908 in Atlanta, Fulton Co, GA. **Military Service: 9th Regiment, Georgia Infantry (State Guards)**

Child of JUDAH MOORE and THOMAS STEPHENS is:

    i.   GEORGIA STEPHENS, b. 1861, Elbert Co, GA; d. Kannapolis, NC.

16. ISAAC "IKE" VAUGHN MOORE *(JOHN NATHANIEL, THOMAS)* was born November 17, 1830 in Elbert Co, GA, and died November 29, 1918 in Madison Co, GA. He married (1) ELIZABETH J SIMMONS October 18, 1852 in Madison Co, GA, daughter of FRANCIS SIMMONS and ELIZABETH POWER. She was born April 18, 1836 in Madison, Co Ga, and died February 17, 1897 in Madison, Co Ga. He married (2) SARAH FRANCES ALMOND Unknown, daughter of W.M. ALMOND and S. THORNTON. She was born Abt. 1836. **Military service: Sgt co E 37th Ga Inf**

Children of ISAAC MOORE and ELIZABETH SIMMONS are:

    i.   JOHN WILLIAM MOORE, b. July 12, 1853, Madison Co GA; d. May 07, 1917; m. MARY I STAMPS, February 01, 1876, Madison Co GA; b. December 10, 1858; d. April 15, 1936.

    ii.   FRANCIS S MOORE, b. April 17, 1855, Madison, Co Ga; m. FRANCES LOU MARTIN, December 09, 1880, Elbert Co Ga; b. Abt. 1855.

    iii.   MARTHA GREEN MOORE, b. Abt. 1857; d. March 14, 1930, Madison Co, GA; m. ALEXANDER BROWN; b. Abt. 1855.

    iv.   ISAAC DAVID MOORE, b. January 11, 1860, Madison Co GA; d. November 07, 1864, Madison Co GA.

    v.   MARY LOU MOORE, b. December 10, 1861; d. March 05, 1936; m. JOHN LOVIC MOON, February 01, 1877, Madison Co, GA; b. August 16, 1850, Elbert Co, GA; d. February 25, 1916, Madison Co, GA.

    vi.   ESTHER ANN MOORE, b. August 07, 1866, Madison Co GA; d. April 23, 1886; m. WILLIAM JOHNSON, December 27, 1881, Madison Co GA; b. Abt. 1860.

    vii.   ELIZABETH F MOORE, b. May 09, 1868; m. WILLIS NELMS, December 12, 1882, Madison Co GA; b. Abt. 1865.

    viii.   ELLEN MOORE, b. February 23, 1871; d. January 03, 1929; m. JAMES CARROUTH, October 22, 1885, Madison Co GA; b. Abt. 1870.

   ix. IDA VAUGHN MOORE, b. July 22, 1873; d. March 25, 1951; m. JOSEPH A. SAYER, June 06, 1894, Madison Co GA; b. Abt. 1870.

   x. HATTIE D. MOORE, b. Abt. 1877.

   xi. SUSIE MILDRED MOORE, b. July 22, 1878; d. April 05, 1953; m. TINSLEY JEFFERSON HULME, Aft. 1900; b. Abt. 1875.

   xii. MELVIN GOSS MOORE, b. July 10, 1882; d. September 28, 1919; m. CYNTHIA LELLIE SORROW.

17. PRISCILLA TULULLAH MOORE *(JOHN NATHANIEL, THOMAS)* was born December 27, 1865 in Elbert Co Ga, and died September 28, 1948 in Elbert Co Ga. She married ALLEN THOMAS GINN December 21, 1881, son of HENRY GINN and FRANCES DOBBS. He was born 1856 in Elbert Co Ga, and died August 23, 1940 in Elbert Co Ga.

    Child of PRISCILLA MOORE and ALLEN GINN is:

i.POPE BENTLEY GINN, b. September 06, 1892.

18. WILLIAM THOMAS MOORE *(JOEL WASHINGTON, THOMAS)* was born October 03, 1848, and died January 04, 1928. He married MARTHA ANNE H. MOORE November 21, 1875, daughter of THOMAS MOORE and ELIZABETH WHITE. She was born September 28, 1859, and died June 16, 1929.

Military service: Private Co H 1st Ga St Troops

Children of WILLIAM MOORE and MARTHA MOORE are:

   i. ELLA MOORE, b. August 18, 1876.

   ii. ALBERT GEORGE MOORE, b. December 01, 1878; d. April 16, 1949; m. UDAH LOU ADAMS, December 27, 1903; b. June 06, 1882; d. March 12, 1966.

   iii. LEONARD FRANKLIN MOORE, b. December 25, 1880; d. August 05, 1964; m. CARRIE SUSAN SHAW, July 14, 1912; b. May 07, 1894.

   iv. JOEL ALEXANDER MOORE, b. February 05, 1884; d. October 28, 1908.

   v. ESTES JULIAN MOORE, b. August 13, 1886; d. December 22, 1966; m. ANNIE PRATHER, July 12, 1908; b. May 10, 1886.

   vi. AGNES ZORA MOORE, b. September 03, 1889; m. WILLIAM ELMO ADAMS, August 10, 1904; b. June 20, 1885; d. June 26, 1966.

   vii. SARAH LOU MOORE, b. May 04, 1892; m. JOHN REESE ALEWINE, February 26, 1911; b. October 17, 1888; d. July 25, 1954.

viii. HERBERT THOMAS MOORE, b. November 19, 1894.
  ix. ATTICUS DEWITT MOORE, b. May 23, 1901; d. April 05, 1967; m. ADDIE SEYMOUR, August 01, 1938; b. February 04, 1902; d. March 07, 1967.
   x. BARTIE ELIZABETH MOORE, b. February 16, 1905.

19. MARY CATHERINE MOORE *(JOEL WASHINGTON, THOMAS)* was born October 10, 1850, and died December 24, 1922. She married MILTON POPE WEBB January 26, 1871 in Elbert Co Ga. He was born November 07, 1848, and died April 09, 1923.

Child of MARY MOORE and MILTON WEBB is:
   i. EDWARD C. WEBB, b. October 08, 1874; d. May 20, 1960; m. ROSA LEE AYRES, December 20, 1896; b. August 18, 1879; d. August 31, 1967.

DESCENDANTS OF ISAAC SIMMONS

Generation No. 1

1. ISAAC SIMMONS was born February 11, 1758 in NC, and died March 24, 1832 in Talbot Co, GA. He married MARY POWER Abt. 1795 in Prob Elbert Co, GA, daughter of FRANCIS POWER and ELIZABETH EVANS. She was born November 29, 1779, and died Abt. 1875 in Madison Co Ga.

Children of ISAAC SIMMONS and MARY POWER are:

2. i.   THOMAS SIMMONS, b. 1796, Madison Co, GA.
3. ii.   ELIZABETH SIMMONS, b. Abt. 1800, Madison Co Ga.
    iii. WILLIAM SIMMONS, b. Abt. 1800, Madison Co Ga; d. Abt. 1863, Madison Co Ga.
4. iv.   JOHN SIMMONS, b. Abt. 1803; d. December 1866.
    v.   ISAAC SIMMONS, JR, b. 1806; m. WILLIAM ANN WILLI-FORD.
5. vi.   FRANCIS SIMMONS, b. Abt. 1808; d. Abt. 1866.
6. vii. DAVID POWER SIMMONS, b. September 24, 1810, Madison Co Ga; d. March 20, 1887, Madison Co Ga.
    viii. PATSY SIMMONS, b. 1811; m. JACOB ALBRIGHT, December 11, 1825, Madison Co, GA; b. Abt. 1810.
7. ix.   MARY SIMMONS, b. Abt. 1815.
8. x.   SARAH SIMMONS, b. Abt. 1816.
9. xi.   BENNETT SIMMONS, b. Abt. 1820; d. Abt. 1876, Madison Co Ga.
10. xii. SUSAN PINKNEY SIMMONS, b. April 05, 1822, Madison Co, GA; d. July 19, 1908, Oglethorpe Co, GA.
11. xiii. TURNER SIMMONS, b. Abt. 1825, Madison, Co Ga; d. April 1862, died of disease in Goldsboro N.C. .

Generation No. 2

2. THOMAS SIMMONS *(ISAAC)* was born 1796 in Madison Co, GA. He married MARIAH W CHRISTIAN August 17, 1819 in Madison Co, GA. She was born March 26, 1806 in Madison Co, GA.

Children of THOMAS SIMMONS and MARIAH CHRISTIAN are:

i.   EDWARD CHARLES SIMMONS, b. 1824, Madison Co, GA; m. MARTHA A GREENWOOD; b. Abt. 1825.

  ii. MARTHA JANE SIMMONS, b. March 02, 1826, Madison Co, GA; m. JOSEPH MORRIS; b. Abt. 1825.

  iii. THOMAS WILLIAM SIMMONS, b. November 15, 1829, Madison Co, GA; m. MARY A CAUDLE; b. Abt. 1830. **Military service: Private Co B 9ᵗʰ Battalion Ga Infantry**

3. ELIZABETH SIMMONS *(ISAAC)* was born Abt. 1800 in Madison Co Ga. She married JOHN W MOON November 18, 1819. He was born 1796 in Elbert Co, GA, and died Aft. 1850 in Pickens Co, SC.

  Child of ELIZABETH SIMMONS and JOHN MOON is:

  i. BOLER MOON, b. 1822.

4. JOHN SIMMONS *(ISAAC)* was born Abt. 1803, and died December 1866. He married MILDRED "MILLIE" W DAVID January 18, 1827 in Madison Co, GA, daughter of HENRY DAVID and PERLINA DAVID. She was born May 1803 in GA, and died Aft. 1900.

  Children of JOHN SIMMONS and MILDRED DAVID are:

12. i. WYLEY C SIMMONS, b. October 1827, Madison Co, GA.

13. ii. MARY "POLLY" R SIMMONS, b. Jan 30, 1830, Madison Co,GA; d. Feb 08, 1901, Madison Co,

14. iii. SARAH E SIMMONS, b. July 05, 1835, Madison Co, GA; d. April 30, 1914, Madison Co, GA.

  iv. MILLEY JANE SIMMONS, b. November 16, 1847, Madison Co, GA; d. March 28, 1898, Madison Co, GA.

5. FRANCIS SIMMONS *(ISAAC)* was born Abt. 1808, and died Abt. 1866. He married ELIZABETH POWER, daughter of JESSE POWER and ESTHER TUGGLE. She was born Aft. 1810.

  Children of FRANCIS SIMMONS and ELIZABETH POWER are:

17. i. MARY G SIMMONS, b. 1827, Madison Co, GA; d. Madison Co, GA.

18. ii. ELIZABETH J SIMMONS, b. April 18, 1836, Madison, Co Ga; d. February 17, 1897, Madison, Co Ga.

6. DAVID POWER SIMMONS *(ISAAC)* was born September 24, 1810 in Madison Co Ga, and died March 20, 1887 in Madison Co Ga. He married HANNAH SIMS HALL January 27, 1831 in Madison Co GA, daughter of JEREMIAH HALL and NANCY UNKNOWN. She was born May 16, 1807, and died May 05, 1880 in Madison Co Ga.

  Children of DAVID SIMMONS and HANNAH HALL are:

19.   i.   SARAH ROSANNE SIMMONS, b. January 05, 1832, Madison Co, GA; d. July 30, 1917, Elbert Co, GA.

20.   ii. AMANDA C SIMMONS, b. May 04, 1833, Madison Co, GA; d. March 25, 1919, Elbert Co, GA.

21.   iii. WILLIAM C SIMMONS, b. April 14, 1835; d. October 23, 1909.

22.   iv. ISAAC B. SIMMONS, b. November 06, 1836; d. November 29, 1863, Knoxville,Tn.

23.   v.   DAVID T SIMMONS, b. January 25, 1838; d. July 11, 1927.

        vi. ELMIRA JANE SIMMONS, b. July 05, 1840, Madison Co, GA.

        vii. WYLEY JONES SIMMONS, b. January 25, 1842, Madison Co, GA; d. January 08, 1910, Confederate Soldier's Home in Atlanta, GA.
             Military service: Bet. March 04, 1861 - April 1865, Private Co E 37th Ga Inf wounded and captured at Franklin Tn 12/17/1864 Admitted to USA Post Hospital Savanna Ga 6/5/65 - Foot amputated - discharged 7/8/1865

24.   viii. MARTHA A SIMMONS, b. Abt. 1844; d. July 21, 1917, Hall Co, TX.

25.   ix. WALTON G SIMMONS, b. May 16, 1848, Madison Co, GA.

7. MARY SIMMONS *(ISAAC)* was born Abt. 1815. She married (1) WILLIAM GRAHAM March 18, 1845 in Madison Co, GA. He was born September 21, 1809 in Oglethorpe Co, GA. She married (2) HARVEY M. SIMMONS December 22, 1829 in Madison Co GA, son of ABRAHAM SIMMONS and SARAH UNKNOWN. He was born 1804 in Elbert Co, GA, and died 1836.
        Children of MARY SIMMONS and HARVEY SIMMONS are:
        i.   ELIZABETH C SIMMONS.

26.   ii. SARAH M SIMMONS, b. November 09, 1832, Madison Co, GA; d. March 15, 1918, Madison Co, GA.

8. SARAH SIMMONS *(ISAAC)* was born Abt. 1816. She married JOHN HALL December 06, 1832 in Madison Co GA, son of JEREMIAH HALL and NANCY UNKNOWN. He was born Abt. 1810, and died 1859.
        Children of SARAH SIMMONS and JOHN HALL are:
        i.   ISSAC L. HALL, b. Abt. 1834; m. ROSANNAH KING.
             Military service: Private Co H 34th Ga Inf
        ii. NANCY HALL, b. Abt. 1836.
        iii. MARY HALL, b. Abt. 1842.
        iv. SUSAN HALL, b. Abt. 1842; d. Abt. 1908; m. ROBERT LACY TAIT PORTERFIELD; b. September 17, 1837, Madison Co. Ga;

d. December 31, 1932. **Military service: Private Co E 37th Ga Infantry**

    v.   SARAH HALL, b. Abt. 1843.

    vi. JANE HALL, b. Abt. 1845.

27.   vii. JEREMIAH W HALL, b. Abt. 1847; d. November 12, 1914, Lindale, TX.

9. BENNETT SIMMONS *(ISAAC)* was born Abt. 1820, and died Abt. 1876 in Madison Co Ga. He married SUSAN BETHANY GHOLSTON December 06, 1849 in Madison Co GA. She was born December 15, 1830, and died December 25, 1910 in Madison Co, GA.

    Children of BENNETT SIMMONS and SUSAN GHOLSTON are:

    i.   SARAH E SIMMONS, b. November 25, 1850; d. April 15, 1885; m. RICHARD H SORRELLS, May 31, 1868, Madison Co, GA; b. 1849, Madison Co, GA.

28.   ii. FRANCES "FANNIE" E SIMMONS, b. November 19, 1854, Madison Co, GA; d. December 08, 1923, Madison Co, GA.

29.   iii. SUSAN "SUSIE" BETHANY SIMMONS, b. December 23, 1855, Madison Co, GA; d. December 19, 1899, Madison Co, GA.

    iv. FRANKLIN SIMMONS, b. 1857.

30.   v.   PARILEE LUCINDA SIMMONS, b. September 07, 1859, Madison Co, GA; d. May 01, 1926, Madison Co, GA.

    vi. BENNETT W SIMMONS, b. 1863; d. November 04, 1937, Madison Co, GA.

31.   vii. MARY LOU "MOLLIE" SIMMONS, b. 1866, Madison Co, GA; d. November 30, 1931, Madison Co, GA.

32.   viii. JOSEPH L SIMMONS, b. 1868; d. February 15, 1902, Madison Co, GA.

33.   ix. LUCINDA P "DOLLIE" SIMMONS, b. June 09, 1870, Madison Co, GA; d. February 18, 1938, Madison Co, GA.

    x.   LUTICA N "BABE" SIMMONS, b. November 1872, Madison Co, GA; d. 1944, Madison Co.

10. SUSAN PINKNEY SIMMONS *(ISAAC)* was born April 05, 1822 in Madison Co, GA, and died July 19, 1908 in Oglethorpe Co, GA. She married DAVID GRAHAM December 01, 1837 in Madison Co, GA. He was born January 09, 1815 in Oglethorpe Co, GA, and died October 23, 1893 in Oglethorpe Co, GA.**Military Service: Company B 1st Georgia Reserves (Fannin's)**

    Children of SUSAN SIMMONS and DAVID GRAHAM are:

    i.   MARY JANE GRAHAM, b. December 16, 1838, Oglethorpe Co, GA; d. November 02, 1908.

    ii.   JOHN WILLIAM GRAHAM, b. May 13, 1840, Madison Co, GA; m. (1) QUEEN NOELL; b. Abt. 1840, Oglethorpe Co, GA; m. (2) SARA TILLER; b. Abt. 1845. **Military Service: Capt. Tiller's Company, Georgia, (Echol's Light Artillery)**

    iii.   SARA FRANCES GRAHAM, b. March 04, 1842, Oglethorpe Co, GA; m. DAVID HOLOMAN; b. Abt. 1840. **Military Service: Private Co. I 61st Ga Infantry**

    iv.   SERENA ELIZABETH GRAHAM, b. November 09, 1843, Oglethorpe Co, GA; d. April 21, 1917, Lexington, Oglethorpe Co, GA; m. RICHARD BUTLER MATTHEWS, May 16, 1861, Oglethorpe Co, GA; b. February 02, 1841, Oglethorpe Co, GA; d. January 12, 1932, Oglethorpe Co, GA. **Military Service: Tiller's Company, Georgia, (Echol's Light Artillery)**

    v.   SUSAN PINKNEY GRAHAM, b. December 05, 1845, Oglethorpe Co, GA; m. J C G SEVENS; b. Abt. 1845.

    vi.   ANNIE T GRAHAM, b. December 05, 1845, Oglethorpe Co, GA; d. Bef. 1855, in Childhood.

    vii.   GEORGE THOMAS GRAHAM, b. March 20, 1847, Oglethorpe Co, GA; m. SARAH CUNNINGHAM; b. Abt. 1850.

    viii.   LUCY CLARENDA GRAHAM, , b. September 12, 1853, Oglethorpe Co, GA; d. August 27, 1928, Oglethorpe Co, GA. m. FRANK HILL; b. Abt. 1850.

    ix.   RHODA TALLULAH GRAHAM, b. November 25, 1856, Oglethorpe Co, GA; m. WILLIAM CUNNINGHAM; b. Abt. 1855.

    x.   FRANK DAVID GRAHAM, b. March 20, 1859, Oglethorpe Co, GA; d. Bef. 1962; m. (1) JESSIE THORNTON; b. Abt. 1860; m. (2) NANCY BRAY; b. 1880, Oglethorpe Co, GA; d. November 29, 1962, Clarke Co, GA.

    xi.   MARTHA BEAUREGARD GRAHAM, b. September 15, 1861, Oglethorpe Co, GA; m. JOSEPH H HARRIS; b. Abt. 1860.

11. TURNER SIMMONS *(ISAAC)* was born Abt. 1825 in Madison, Co Ga, and died April 1862 in died of disease in Goldsboro N.C. He married NICEY EMILY BARNETT August 31, 1845 in Oglethorpe Ga. She was born Abt. 1823, and died in Madison Co, GA.

    Military service: 7/11/1861 Private Co A 16th Ga Inf

    Notes for NICEY EMILY BARNETT: Amnesty Oath: 1865, Fair, dark hair, grey eyes, 5'4"

Children of TURNER SIMMONS and NICEY BARNETT are:
36.   i.   ISAAC D SIMMONS, b. 1846.
37.   ii.   JOHN B SIMMONS, b. 1853; d. 1930, Madison Co, GA.
38. iii.   WILLIAM T P SIMMONS, b. 1855.
39. iv.   FRANCIS HENRY SIMMONS, b. 1857; d. 1892, Madison Co, GA.
      v.   WILLIAM P SIMMONS, b. 1854, Madison Co, GA; m. MATTIE; b. 1858.

Generation No. 3

12. WYLEY C SIMMONS *(JOHN, ISAAC)* was born October 1827 in Madison Co, GA.
Note: Children were living with Wyley's parents in 1860 census no record of marriage in Madison Co.
    Child of WYLEY C SIMMONS is:
      i.   Sydney C. Simmons b. ca 1856
     ii.   THEODICEA A SIMMONS, b. July 07, 1859, Madison Co, GA; d. October 08, 1920, Madison Co, GA; m. JOHN H ASHWORTH; b. June 22, 1855; d. September 03, 1919.

13. MARY "POLLY" R SIMMONS *(JOHN, ISAAC)* was born January 30, 1830 in Madison Co, GA, and died February 08, 1901 in Madison Co, GA. She married WILLIAM ANDREW JACKSON BROWN May 25, 1848 in Madison Co, GA. He was born January 31, 1825 in Madison Co, GA, and died January 21, 1909 in Madison Co, GA.**Military Service:** *W A J Brown - Private Aug 6, 1863. Co E, 37th Regiment, Ga Volunteer Infantry, Surrendered at Greensboro, NC Apr 26,*
    1865. (Born in Oglethorpe County, Ga in 1825)
    Children of MARY SIMMONS and WILLIAM BROWN are:
      i.   JOHN FOGGY BROWN, b. December 11, 1851, Madison Co, GA; d. October 21, 1929, Madison Co, GA.
     ii.   WYLEY PINKNEY BROWN, b. June 13, 1856, Madison Co, GA; d. October 05, 1940, Madison Co, GA; m. SARAH CATHERINE POWER, December 22, 1881, Madison Co, GA; b. March 08, 1857, Madison Co, GA; d. March 14, 1945, Madison Co, GA.
    iii.   MYRTLE BROWN, b. February 16, 1861, Madison Co, GA; d. January 15, 1918, Madison Co, GA; m. WILLIAM DAVID, 1911; b. Abt. 1873; d. June 13, 1926, Madison Co, GA.

14. SARAH E SIMMONS *(JOHN, ISAAC)* was born July 05, 1835 in Madison Co, GA, and died April 30, 1914 in Madison Co, GA. She married JAMES LAWSON DUDLEY January 20, 1853 in Madison Co, GA. He was born March 07, 1831 in Madison Co, GA, and died September 07, 1893 in Madison Co, GA.

Military Service: Lawson Dudley - Private Mar 1862. Co B, 9th Battalion, Ga Volunteer Infantry Wounded. Transferred to Co E, 37th Regt Ga Inf. May 6, 1863. Surrendered at Greensboro, NC Apr 26, 1865

Children of SARAH SIMMONS and JAMES DUDLEY are:

   i.   JOEL G DUDLEY, b. November 22, 1853, Madison Co, GA; d. June 07, 1924, Madison Co, GA; m. MARY ELIZABETH "LIZZIE" BRUCE, December 09, 1917, Madison Co, GA; b. July 11, 1865, Madison Co, GA; d. April 19, 1947, Madison Co, GA.

   ii.   JOSEPH S DUDLEY, b. November 22, 1853, Madison Co, GA; d. Abt. 1853, Madison Co, GA.

        From family bible record; best guess is that he died as an infant.

   iii.   JOHN J DUDLEY, b. August 05, 1857, Madison Co, GA; d. January 24, 1923, Madison Co,

   iv.   JOSEPHINE T DUDLEY, b. January 24, 1860, Madison Co, GA; d. February 11, 1947, Madison Co, GA; m. WILLIAM A KING, October 17, 1878, Madison Co, GA; b. June 1857, Madison Co, GA; d. 1931, USA.

   v.   DELONIA OSCAR DUDLEY, b. February 18, 1866, Madison Co, GA; d. January 24, 1884, Madison Co, GA.

   vi.   DERNANDA ELISE DUDLEY, b. May 12, 1869, Madison Co, GA.

   vii.   MONTIE ALICE DUDLEY, b. 1871, Madison Co, GA; d. January 20, 1937, Madison Co, GA; m. JAMES C LIVELY, January 28, 1900, Madison Co, GA; b. 1881, Madison Co, GA; d. 1953, Madison Co, GA.

   viii.   WILEY JONAH DUDLEY, b. January 14, 1874, Madison Co, GA; d. October 10, 1954, Madison Co, GA; m. ALMA OMEGA SEYMOUR, January 03, 1897, Madison Co, GA; b. December 20, 1876, Elbert Co, GA; d. May 27, 1945, Madison Co, GA.

   ix.   MARY E DUDLEY, b. May 07, 1878, Madison Co, GA; d. October 30, 1965, Madison Co, GA; m. EDD R MITCHELL, October 04, 1914, Madison Co, GA; b. 1872, Rockdale Co, GA; d. January 04, 1935, Madison Co, GA.

17. MARY G SIMMONS *(FRANCIS, ISAAC)* was born 1827 in Madison Co, GA, and died in Madison Co, GA. She married JOHN F WITCHER September 26, 1844 in Madison Co, GA. He was born 1822 in Madison Co, GA, and died in Madison Co, GA. **Military Service: Private Co D. 16ᵗʰ Georgia Infantry**
> Children of MARY SIMMONS and JOHN WITCHER are:
>
> i. MARY E WITCHER, b. May 17, 1846, Madison Co, GA; d. 1912, Timpson, TX.
> ii. FRANCIS M WITCHER, b. Abt. 1850, GA.
> iii. BENJAMIN WITCHER, b. Abt. 1854, GA.
> iv. ISAAC WITCHER, b. Abt. 1857, GA.
> v. JANE WITCHER, b. Abt. 1859, GA.

18. ELIZABETH J SIMMONS *(FRANCIS ISAAC)* was born April 18, 1836 in Madison, Co Ga, and died February 17, 1897 in Madison, Co Ga. She married ISAAC "IKE" VAUGHN MOORE October 18, 1852 in Madison Co, GA, son of JOHN MOORE and MARTHA VAUGHN. He was born November 17, 1830 in Elbert Co, GA, and died November 29, 1918 in Madison Co, GA. **Military service: Sgt co E 37th Ga Inf**
> Children of ELIZABETH SIMMONS and ISAAC MOORE are:
>
> i. JOHN WILLIAM MOORE, b. July 12, 1853, Madison Co GA; d. May 07, 1917; m. (1) MARY I; b. October 28, 1858; d. April 15, 1936; m. (2) MARY I STAMPS, February 01, 1876, Madison Co GA; b. December 10, 1858; d. April 15, 1936.
> ii. FRANCIS S MOORE, b. April 17, 1855, Madison, Co Ga; m. FRANCES LOU MARTIN, December 09, 1880, Elbert Co Ga; b. Abt. 1855.
> iii. MARTHA GREEN MOORE, b. Abt. 1857; d. March 14, 1930, Madison Co, GA; m. ALEXANDER BROWN; b. Abt. 1855.
> iv. ISAAC DAVID MOORE, b. January 11, 1860, Madison Co GA; d. November 07, 1864, Madison Co GA.
> v. MARY LOU MOORE, b. December 10, 1861; d. March 05, 1936; m. (1) JOHN LOVIC MOON, February 01, 1877, Madison Co GA; b. Abt. 1860; m. (2) JOHN LONNIE MOON, February 01, 1877, Madison Co, GA; b. August 16, 1850, Elbert Co, GA; d. February 25, 1916, Madison Co, GA.
> vi. ESTHER ANN MOORE, b. August 07, 1866, Madison Co GA; d. April 23, 1886; m. WILLIAM JOHNSON, December 27, 1881, Madison Co GA; b. Abt. 1860.
> vii. ELIZABETH F MOORE, b. May 09, 1868; m. WILLIS NELMS, December 12, 1882, Madison Co GA; b. Abt. 1865.

viii. ELLEN MOORE, b. February 23, 1871; d. January 03, 1929; m. JAMES CARROUTH, October 22, 1885, Madison Co GA; b. Abt. 1870.

ix. IDA VAUGHN MOORE, b. July 22, 1873; d. March 25, 1951; m. JOSEPH A. SAYER, June 06, 1894, Madison Co GA; b. Abt. 1870.

x. HATTIE D. MOORE, b. Abt. 1877.

xi. SUSIE MILDRED MOORE, b. July 22, 1878; d. April 05, 1953; m. TINSLEY JEFFERSON HULME, Aft. 1900; b. Abt. 1875.

xii. MELVIN GOSS MOORE, b. July 10, 1882; d. September 28, 1919; m. CYNTHIA LELLIE SORROW.

19. SARAH ROSANNE SIMMONS *(DAVID POWER, ISAAC)* was born January 05, 1832 in Madison Co, GA, and died July 30, 1917 in Elbert Co, GA. She married WILLIAM PINKNEY GINN December 12, 1848 in Madison Co, GA, son of ISAAC GINN and MARTHA BURDEN. He was born January 12, 1827 in Elbert Co Ga, and died August 22, 1900 in Elbert Co Ga. **Military service: Co K 2nd Ga State Line Troops**

Children of SARAH SIMMONS and WILLIAM GINN are:

i. ISAAC D. GINN, b. December 14, 1849, Elbert Co Ga; d. November 04, 1892, Elbert Co Ga; m. MARY DENNY, October 06, 1872; d. Bef. 1880.

ii. WILLIAM THOMAS "BUD" GINN, b. Abt. 1852, Elbert Co, GA; d. 1923, Dade Co, GA; m. (1) FRANSANNA OPHELIA MOORE, November 23, 1876, Elbert Co Ga; b. 1858, Elbert Co. Ga; d. Abt. 1895, Dade Co Ga; m. (2) LIZZIE, Abt. 1898, Dade Co. Ga.

iii. AMANDA B. GINN, b. Abt. 1854; m. BENJAMIN T. ALGOOD, December 24, 1878; b. Abt. 1850.

iv. JONES WASHINGTON GINN, b. September 01, 1858, Elbert Co Ga; d. April 11, 1935, Elbert Co Ga; m. ETTA COLVARD; b. November 22, 1864; d. April 05, 1925.

v. CORA A. GINN, b. Abt. 1860; m. THOMAS ROBERT CRITTENDON?; b. Abt. 1860.

vi. JAMES M. GINN, b. Abt. 1864; d. August 05, 1892.

vii. LIBIA GINN, b. 1866, GA; d. 1952.

viii. PATRICK HENRY GINN, b. Abt. 1868, Elbert Co Ga; d. April 05, 1937; m. ELECTRA WHITE, February 13, 1889; b. Abt. 1875; d. Abt. 1958.

ix. ELURA "LULA" GINN, b. Abt. 1870; m. JOHN PULASKI BOND; b. Abt. 1870.

x. ROSE ELIZABETH "LIZZIE" GINN, b. March 03, 1873, GA; d. February 22, 1928, Franklin Co, GA; m. MOSES CHEEK, April 01, 1891; b. Abt. 1870.

20. AMANDA C SIMMONS *(DAVID POWER, ISAAC)* was born May 04, 1833 in Madison Co, GA, and died March 25, 1919 in Elbert Co, GA. She married SINGLETON SATTERWHITE GINN December 23, 1852 in Madison Co, GA. He was born December 04, 1831 in Elbert Co, GA, and died September 20, 1895 in Elbert Co, GA. **Military service: Bet. 1861 - 1865, Private - June 27, 1862. Wounded at Seven Days' Fight near Richmond, Virginia in 1862. Surrendered at Appomattox, Virginia, April 9, 1865**

Children of AMANDA SIMMONS and SINGLETON GINN are:
  i. TINSLEY ASBERY GINN, b. October 08, 1853, Elbert Co Ga; d. April 16, 1907; m. NANCY E. BERRYMAN, January 11, 1872, Madison Co GA; b. January 14, 1852, Madison, Co Ga; d. September 14, 1902.
  ii. NANCY ELIZABETH "BETTY" GINN, b. April 10, 1857; d. March 22, 1911.
  iii. WILLIAM C GINN, b. Abt. 1860, GA; d. Abt. 1885.
  iv. WHEELER GINN, b. Abt. 1862.
  v. LAURA JEANETTE GINN, b. December 25, 1866; d. May 28, 1940.
  vi. ELLEN MADORA GINN, b. October 11, 1869; d. April 04, 1945.
  vii. ISAAC S GINN, b. Abt. 1873, GA.
  viii. NANCY ELIZABETH GINN, b. April 10, 1857, Elbert Co Ga; d. March 22, 1911, Elbert Co Ga; m. WILLIAM H. BERRYMAN, February 22, 1897; b. January 23, 1850, Elbert Co Ga; d. September 24, 1910, Elbert Co Ga.
  ix. WILLIAM C. "BILLY" GINN, b. October 1859.
  x. ALEXANDER S. GINN, b. January 18, 1870.
  xi. ISAAC S. GINN, b. September 04, 1872.

21. WILLIAM C SIMMONS *(DAVID POWER, ISAAC)* was born April 14, 1835, and died October 23, 1909. He married ELIZABETH M POWER October 25, 1866 in Madison Co GA, daughter of WILLIAM POWER and MARTHA GRIMES. She was born June 05, 1832, and died November 16, 1893. **Military service: July 11, 1861, Private Co A 16th Georgia Inf Surrendered Appomattox, Va 4/9/1865**

Children of WILLIAM SIMMONS and ELIZABETH POWER are:
  i. MARTHA SIMMONS, b. Abt. 1870.

ii. INFANT SIMMONS, b. September 22, 1867; d. September 22, 1867.

22. ISAAC B. SIMMONS *(DAVID POWER, ISAAC)* was born November 06, 1836, and died November 29, 1863 in Knoxville,Tn. He married E. JANE. She was born Abt. 1841.
Burial: In unmarked grave in Confederate cemetary in Knoxville, Tn
Military service: Bet. July 11, 1861 - November 29, 1863, Private Co A 16th Georgia Inf
>   Child of ISAAC SIMMONS and E. JANE is:
>   i. LUCY SIMMONS, b. Abt. 1859.

23. DAVID T SIMMONS *(DAVID POWER, ISAAC)* was born January 25, 1838, and died July 11, 1927. He married DELILAH A. BURDEN Abt. 1865, daughter of NELSON BURDEN and NANCY GINN. She was born May 08, 1843, and died March 22, 1924. **Military service: Bet. March 04, 1861 - April 1865, Private Co E 37th Ga Inf Surrendered Greensboro N. C. 1865**
>   Children of DAVID SIMMONS and DELILAH BURDEN are:
>   i. ISAAC N SIMMONS, b. April 17, 1866, GA; d. April 09, 1917.
>   ii. VIOLA L SIMMONS, b. Abt. 1869.
>   iii. JAMES W SIMMONS, b. Abt. 1873.
>   iv. ISAAC N SIMMONS, b. April 17, 1866, GA; d. April 09, 1917.

24. MARTHA A SIMMONS *(DAVID POWER, ISAAC)* was born Abt. 1844, and died July 21, 1917 in Hall Co, TX. She married JEREMIAH W HALL August 22, 1865 in Madison Co, GA, son of JOHN HALL and SARAH SIMMONS. He was born Abt. 1847, and died November 12, 1914 in Lindale, TX.
1865 Amnesty Oath - dark, light hair, grey eyes, 5'7"Military service: Private Co A 16th Ga Inf In hospital Jan. 31, 1865.Released at Nashville, Tenn., May 22, 1865.
>   Children of MARTHA SIMMONS and JEREMIAH HALL are:
>   i. SUSAN J HALL, b. October 22, 1866, GA; d. Abt. 1876, Royston, Franklin Co, GA.
>   ii. WILLIAM T "WILLIE" HALL, b. November 12, 1867, Royston, Franklin Co, GA; d. August 26, 1938, Slidell, TX.
>   iii. OLLIE HANNAH LEE HALL, b. October 02, 1869, GA; d. March 06, 1950, Lindale, TX.
>   iv. LAURIE EMMA HALL, b. September 25, 1871; d. July 21, 1896, Royston, Franklin Co, GA of shot by Husband.
>   v. MATTIE M HALL, b. April 15, 1873.

vi. DAVID CARLTON (CROCKETT) HALL, b. May 04, 1875; d. June 1948, Hall Co, TX.

vii. MARY ELIZABETH HALL, b. June 07, 1877, Madison Co, GA; d. July 19, 1904, MA.

viii. JOHN SANFORD "SANTY" HALL, b. May 05, 1878, Banks Co, GA; d. April 19, 1930, Lindale, TX.

ix. ISAAC JONAH "JONEY" HALL, b. May 15, 1879, Royston, Franklin Co, GA; d. May 11, 1949, Lindale, TX.

x. ROBERT WALTON "ROBIN" HALL, b. December 08, 1881, Fairburn, GA; d. August 16, 1945, Lindale, TX.

xi. SAMUEL S HALL, b. September 05, 1883; d. Abt. 1890, GA accidently shot.

xii. LUBY L HALL, b. June 13, 1885; d. December 07, 1951, Tyler, TX.

xiii. PERRY G HALL, b. September 25, 1888; d. November 07, 1913, Lindale, TX.

25. WALTON G SIMMONS *(DAVID POWER, ISAAC)* was born May 16, 1848 in Madison Co, GA. He married SARAH CATHERINE BRIDGES August 19, 1869 in Madison Co, GA. She was born 1855.

Children of WALTON SIMMONS and SARAH O. are:

i. SARAH E SIMMONS, b. Abt. 1872.

ii. JAMES G SIMMONS, b. Abt. 1874.

iii. ILEY J SIMMONS, b. Abt. 1877.

iv. ELIZABETH SIMMONS, b. Abt. 1879.

26. SARAH M SIMMONS *(MARY, ISAAC)* was born November 09, 1832 in Madison Co, GA, and died March 15, 1918 in Madison Co, GA. She married THOMAS PETER BRUCE August 30, 1855 in Madison Co, GA, son of WALTER BRUCE and MARY DAVID. He was born October 18, 1828 in Madison Co, GA, and died September 11, 1896 in Madison Co, GA. **Military service: Private Co K 2nd Ga St. Line Trp**s

Children of SARAH SIMMONS and THOMAS BRUCE are:

i. HARVEY W BRUCE, b. July 26, 1856, Madison Co, GA; d. January 21, 1918, Madison Co, GA; m. ALLETHA FRANCES GUNNELLS, October 17, 1875, Madison Co, GA; b. May 31, 1858, Home, Madison Co, GA; d. May 18, 1927, Madison Co, GA.

ii. CLAYTON JONES BRUCE, b. September 06, 1858, Madison Co, GA; d. June 25, 1910, Madison Co, GA; m. AUGUSTA ANN

"AUNT SIS" //; b. January 03, 1856, Madison Co, GA; d. September 1928, Madison Co, GA.

iii.   LURENA F BRUCE, b. 1863, Madison Co, GA; m. J F CAREY, March 28, 1883, Madison Co, GA; b. Abt. 1860.

iv.   MARY ELIZABETH "LIZZIE" BRUCE, b. July 11, 1865, Madison Co, GA; d. April 19, 1947, Madison Co, GA; m. (1) MILES A SEXTON, September 01, 1896, Madison Co, GA; b. November 22, 1856; d. March 25, 1899, Madison Co, GA; m. (2) JOEL G DUDLEY, December 09, 1917, Madison Co, GA; b. November 22, 1853, Madison Co, GA; d. June 07, 1924, Madison Co, GA.

v.   BARBARA EMMA BRUCE, b. August 22, 1868, Madison Co, GA; d. May 17, 1903, Madison Co, GA; m. JOHN H LONG, September 26, 1888, Madison Co, GA; b. November 17, 1866; d. January 12, 1960, Madison Co, GA.

vi.   JOHN D BRUCE, b. October 16, 1869, Madison Co, GA; d. November 24, 1949, Madison Co, GA; m. HATTIE E GINN; b. May 26, 1876, Madison Co, GA; d. May 07, 1957, Madison Co,

vii.   HENRY L BRUCE, b. February 1875, Madison Co, GA; d. 1956, Madison Co, GA; m. TERRILA GINN; b. 1885, Banks Co, GA; d. December 11, 1932, Madison Co, GA.

27. JEREMIAH W HALL *(SARAH SIMMONS, ISAAC)* was born Abt. 1847, and died November 12, 1914 in Lindale, TX. He married MARTHA A SIMMONS August 22, 1865 in Madison Co, GA, daughter of DAVID SIMMONS and HANNAH HALL. She was born Abt. 1844, and died July 21, 1917 in Hall Co, TX.

1865 Amnesty Oath - dark, light hair, grey eyes, 5'7"

Military service: Private Co A 16th Ga Inf In hospital Jan. 31, 1865.Released at Nashville, Tenn., May 22, 1865.

Children are listed above under (24) Martha A Simmons.

28. FRANCES "FANNIE" E SIMMONS *(BENNETT, ISAAC)* was born November 19, 1854 in Madison Co, GA, and died December 08, 1923 in Madison Co, GA. She married JAMES THOMAS DAVID November 27, 1877 in Madison Co, GA, son of SAMUEL DAVID and EADY PORTERFIELD. He was born July 19, 1857 in Madison Co, GA, and died April 12, 1928 in Madison Co, GA.

Children of FRANCES SIMMONS and JAMES DAVID are:

i.   BENNETT LUTHER DAVID, b. Abt. 1878; m. MILDRED LARIE MCGOWAN; b. October 1892; d. 1931.

ii.   BANKS DAVID, b. Abt. 1880.

iii. ROBERT T "UNCLE BOB" DAVID, b. February 1881, Madison Co, GA; d. Atlanta, Fulton Co, GA; m. MAUDE ELISE CARRINGTON, June 30, 1907, Madison Co, GA; b. May 10, 1888, Madison Co, GA; d. January 04, 1984, Atlanta, Fulton Co, GA.

iv. CLAUD DAVID, b. Abt. 1885.

v. MAUD E DAVID, b. March 08, 1890; d. April 18, 1951.

vi. MAZELLE DAVID, b. November 22, 1893, Madison Co, GA; d. March 13, 1964, Madison Co

vii. DAVID, b. Abt. 1894; m. ELDO ADAMS; b. Abt. 1890.

viii. DAVID, b. Abt. 1896; m. H T HOPKINS; b. Abt. 1895.

ix. OLA DAVID, b. September 1888; d. Atlanta, GA.

x. FANNIE RUTH DAVID, b. September 11, 1898, Madison Co, GA; d. May 17, 1977, Atlanta, Fulton Co, GA.

xi. CLINTON DAVID, b. Abt. 1900, Madison Co, GA; d. Bef. 1951.

29. SUSAN "SUSIE" BETHANY SIMMONS *(BENNETT, ISAAC)* was born December 23, 1855 in Madison Co, GA, and died December 19, 1899 in Madison Co, GA. She married WILLIAM DAVID PORTERFIELD November 05, 1874 in Madison Co, GA, son of JAMES PORTERFIELD and MARY BRADBURY. He was born March 12, 1855 in Madison Co, GA, and died August 15, 1916 in Madison Co,

Children of SUSAN SIMMONS and WILLIAM PORTERFIELD are:

i. RICHARD B PORTERFIELD, b. December 11, 1875, Madison Co, GA; d. June 19, 1901, Madison Co, GA.

ii. MAGGIE PORTERFIELD, b. October 22, 1877, Madison Co, GA; d. June 11, 1903, Madison Co, GA; m. WEBB B MASON; b. Abt. 1877.

iii. JESSIE MAE PORTERFIELD, b. 1880, Madison Co, GA; d. 1972, Madison Co, GA; m. JOE L BOND; b. 1871, Madison Co, GA; d. 1929, Madison Co, GA.

iv. DELONEY PORTERFIELD, b. August 22, 1881, Madison Co, GA; d. May 21, 1901, Madison Co, GA.

v. REECE H PORTERFIELD, b. May 1884, Madison Co, GA; d. February 02, 1953, Madison Co, GA; m. JULIA A PORTERFIELD, March 24, 1907, Madison Co, GA; b. April 08, 1888, Madison Co, GA; d. June 24, 1967, Madison Co, GA.

vi. COLLIER PORTERFIELD, b. 1887, Madison Co, GA; d. 1947; m. MINNIE BRADLEY; b. 1876; d. 1955.

vii. GEORGIA A PORTERFIELD, b. February 1887, Madison Co, GA; d. 1971, Madison Co, GA; m. SEABORN "SEAB" WINFREY, July 20, 1921, Madison Co, GA; b. July 22, 1896, Madison Co, GA; d. April 1977, Madison Co, GA.

viii. GARNETT PORTERFIELD, b. Abt. 1892, Madison Co, GA.

ix. ROSCOE PORTERFIELD, b. September 15, 1894, Madison Co, GA; d. July 1966, Madison Co, GA; m. M HESSIE TYNER, August 29, 1915, Madison Co, GA; b. January 1895; d. 1966.

x. DAN PORTERFIELD, b. Abt. 1896; m. WILLIE COX; b. Abt. 1900.

xi. RUBEN PORTERFIELD, b. November 22, 1898, Madison Co, GA; d. September 19, 1905, Madison Co, GA.

30. PARILEE LUCINDA SIMMONS *(BENNETT, ISAAC)* was born September 07, 1859 in Madison Co, GA, and died May 01, 1926 in Madison Co, GA. She married JAMES THOMAS "TOM" PORTERFIELD December 20, 1877 in Madison Co, GA, son of JAMES PORTERFIELD and MARY BRADBURY. He was born December 18, 1857 in Madison Co, GA, and died November 22, 1925 in Madison Co, GA.

Children of PARILEE SIMMONS and JAMES PORTERFIELD are:

i. MINNIE MERTALLIE PORTERFIELD, b. November 15, 1878; d. January 26, 1905, Madison Co, GA; m. JAMES ELLIS GRIFFETH, December 20, 1900, Madison Co, GA; b. June 23, 1871, Madison Co, GA; d. June 18, 1932, Madison Co, GA.

ii. LOU ELLEN PORTERFIELD, b. February 06, 1881; d. January 25, 1948, Atlanta, DeKalb Co, GA; m. KING WILLIAM CARRINGTON, November 10, 1901, Comer, Madison Co, GA; b. January 09, 1880, Comer, Madison Co, GA; d. March 27, 1963, Atlanta, DeKalb Co, GA.

iii. THOMAS BENNETT KNOX PORTERFIELD, b. August 12, 1884, Madison Co, GA; d. December 26, 1953, Madison Co, GA.

iv. JEWELL ESTELLE PORTERFIELD, b. April 22, 1888; d. August 27, 1953, Clarke Co, GA; m. JAMES THOMAS CARITHERS, JR, January 20, 1907, Madison Co, GA; b. 1883, Madison Co, GA; d. February 04, 1950, Madison Co, GA.

v. RUBY LEE PORTERFIELD, b. December 13, 1892; d. September 04, 1949, Madison Co, GA; m. JAMES GRADY COOPER, April 25, 1914, Madison Co, GA; b. March 20, 1891, Madison Co, GA; d. September 21, 1965, Madison Co, GA.

vi. RALPH WALDO PORTERFIELD, SR, b. August 22, 1894; d. Albany, Dougherty Co, GA; m. JOSEPHINE REID BELCHER, January 03, 1924, Bainbridge, GA; b. Abt. 1895; d. GA.

vii. LOIS PORTERFIELD, b. July 03, 1898; m. JAMES FLOYD HEAD, April 14, 1923, GA; b. Abt. 1892, GA; d. 1963, Dahlonega, Lumpkin Co, GA.

viii. HERSCHEL PORTERFIELD, b. November 02, 1903; d. January 01, 1904.

ix. JAMES HERSCHEL PORTERFIELD, b. November 02, 1903.

31. MARY LOU "MOLLIE" SIMMONS *(BENNETT, ISAAC)* was born 1866 in Madison Co, GA, and died November 30, 1931 in Madison Co, GA. She married GEORGE WASHINGTON MERCIER December 09, 1883 in Madison Co, GA. He was born 1861 in Madison Co, GA, and died November 03, 1931 in Madison Co, GA.

    Child of MARY SIMMONS and GEORGE MERCIER is:

i. LORA DELL MERCIER, b. April 10, 1890, Madison Co, GA; d. August 1984, Madison Co, GA; m. FRANCIS "FRANK" GIPSON O'KELLEY, August 12, 1906, Madison Co, GA; b. December 31, 1888, Madison Co, GA; d. July 17, 1955, Madison Co, GA.

32. JOSEPH L SIMMONS *(BENNETT, ISAAC)* was born 1868, and died February 15, 1902 in Madison Co, GA. He married FLEETA H PORTERFIELD November 13, 1888 in Madison Co, GA. She was born June 10, 1871 in Madison Co, GA, and died January 18, 1926 in Royston, Franklin Co, GA.

    Children of JOSEPH SIMMONS and FLEETA PORTERFIELD are:

i. MARCUS SIMMONS, b. Aft. 1888.

ii. WILLIE SIMMONS, b. Aft. 1888.

iii. HOLLIS EUGENE SIMMONS, SR, b. July 1893, Madison Co, GA; d. August 24, 1961, Athens, GA; m. (1) LUCY ELLEN DEAN, November 14, 1915, Madison Co, GA; b. April 1896, Madison Co, GA; d. 1937, Madison Co, GA.

iv. CLAUDIE C SIMMONS, b. July 18, 1895, Madison Co, GA; d. Sept. 26, 1896, Madison Co,

v. ROBERT SIMMONS, b. November 08, 1901, Madison Co, GA; d. November 17, 1901, Madison Co, GA.

vi. WYLEY BENNETT SIMMONS, b. July 24, 1897, Madison Co, GA; d. December 08, 1901, Madison Co, GA.

vii. JOSEPH LEE SIMMONS, b. July 24, 1897, Madison Co, GA; d. March 24, 1950, Madison Co,

viii.   SUSAN M SIMMONS, b. August 1899, Madison Co, GA.

33. LUCINDA P "DOLLIE" SIMMONS *(BENNETT, ISAAC)* was born June 09, 1870 in Madison Co, GA, and died February 18, 1938 in Madison Co, GA. She married ROBERT FRANCIS O'KELLEY August 31, 1897 in Madison Co, GA. He was born December 06, 1864 in Madison Co, GA, and died February 19, 1941 in Madison Co, GA.
        Child of LUCINDA SIMMONS and ROBERT O'KELLEY is:
        i.   R SIDNEY O'KELLEY, b. April 26, 1906; d. January 1941.

36. ISAAC D SIMMONS *(TURNER, ISAAC)* was born 1846. He married ELIZABETH J WILSON October 13, 1864 in Madison Co GA. She was born 1838 in Madison Co, GA.
Military service: Co E 37th Ga Inf
        Children of ISAAC SIMMONS and ELIZABETH WILSON are:
        i.   WASHINGTON SIMMONS, b. 1869, Madison Co, GA.
        ii. HENRY SIMMONS, b. 1872, Madison Co, GA.
        iii. JOHN B SIMMONS, b. 1874, Madison Co, GA.

37. JOHN B SIMMONS *(TURNER, ISAAC)* was born 1853, and died 1930 in Madison Co, GA. He married MARY NANCY ?. She was born Abt. 1853, and died 1924 in Madison Co, GA.
        Children of JOHN SIMMONS and MARY ? are:
        i.   SARAH L SIMMONS, b. Abt. 1875.
        ii. MAMIE SIMMONS, b. Abt. 1876; d. 1952, Madison Co, GA; m. JOSEPH LOGAN "LOGE" COILE, January 03, 1895, Madison Co, GA; b. 1869, Madison Co, GA; d. 1952, Madison Co,
        iii. JOHN B DAN SIMMONS, b. November 1878, Madison Co, GA; m. CLARA LIVELY, May 15, 1900, Madison Co, GA; b. August 1883.
        iv. BEULAH SIMMONS, b. February 1884; m. GEORGE SMITH, September 12, 1915, Madison Co, GA; b. Abt. 1880.
        v.   DORA ELLA SIMMONS, b. September 1882, Madison Co, GA; d. 1945; m. THOMAS J GULLEY, June 24, 1908, Madison Co, GA; b. 1868; d. January 04, 1952, Hall Co. Hosp, Gainesville, GA.
        vi. MANLEY CLEVELAND SIMMONS, b. May 1887, Madison Co, GA; d. 1958, Madison Co, GA; m. MARY LEE MOORE; b. 1884; d. 1964, Madison Co, GA.

38. WILLIAM T P SIMMONS *(TURNER, ISAAC)* was born 1855. He married MATTIE R. . She was born Abt. 1858.

Children of WILLIAM SIMMONS and MATTIE R. are:
  i.   JAMES T SIMMONS, b. 1877.
  ii. FRED D SIMMONS, b. 1879.

39. FRANCIS HENRY SIMMONS *(TURNER, ISAAC)* was born 1857, and died 1892 in Madison Co, GA. He married MARY EMELINE PORTERFIELD December 12, 1878 in Madison Co, GA. She was born 1860 in Madison Co, GA, and died 1935 in Madison Co, GA.

Children of FRANCIS SIMMONS and MARY PORTERFIELD are:
  i.   CHARLIE E SIMMONS, b. September 1879, Madison Co, GA.
  ii.   LONNIE A SIMMONS, b. August 11, 1881, Madison Co, GA; d. November 24, 1916.
  iii. WILLIAM REESE SIMMONS, b. June 16, 1891, Madison Co, GA; d. Abt. 1893, Madison Co,
  iv.   EMMA SIMMONS, b. June 16, 1891, Madison Co, GA; d. June 03, 1989, Madison Co, GA; m. CLIFFORD CHARLIE SMITH, December 29, 1909, Madison Co, GA; b. January 10, 1889, Madison Co, GA; d. October 06, 1966, Madison Co, GA.
  v.   JAMES FATE SIMMONS, b. November 12, 1888, Madison Co, GA; d. October 25, 1914, Madison Co, GA.
  vi.   MARY LOU SIMMONS, b. September 06, 1883, Madison Co, GA; d. October 07, 1971, Clarke Co, GA; m. WILLIAM HOMER [^] COMPTON, December 15, 1900, Madison Co, GA; b. January 10, 1882, Madison Co, GA; d. November 18, 1937, Madison Co, GA.
  vii. MINNIE LEE SIMMONS, b. September 06, 1883, Madison Co, GA; d. 1944, Madison Co, GA; m. (1) WILLIAM DAVID BROWN, September 18, 1898, Madison Co, GA; b. December 28, 1879, Madison Co, GA; d. September 28, 1910, Madison Co, GA; m. (2) GEORGE THOMAS PATTEN, SR, March 22, 1924, Madison Co, GA; b. 1878, Madison Co, GA; d. 1956, Madison Co, GA.
  viii. ROBERT H SIMMONS, b. December 26, 1886, Madison Co, GA; d. March 20, 1938, Madison Co, GA; m. NEZZIE V PORTERFIELD, January 23, 1910, Madison Co, GA; b. February 1894, Madison Co, GA.
  ix.   WILLIAM FLETCHER SIMMONS, b. November 12, 1888, Madison Co, GA; d. July 02, 1936, Atlanta, GA.
  x.   TWIN BRO SIMMONS, b. June 16, 1891, Madison Co, GA; d. Bef. 1900, Madison Co, GA.

DESCENDANTS OF ALEXANDER VAUGHN

Generation No. 1

1. ALEXANDER VAUGHN was born Abt. 1784 in Amelia Co Virginia, and died May 28, 1880 in Georgia. He married ELIZABETH DAVID August 20, 1807 in Elbert Co Ga, daughter of ISSAC DAVID and MILDRED WHITE. She was born July 1788 in Wilkes Co, and died October 07, 1873 in Elbert Co. Ga.

Children of ALEXANDER VAUGHN and ELIZABETH DAVID are:

	i.	ISAIAH H VAUGHN.
2.	ii.	WILLIAM DAVID VAUGHN, b. May 12, 1808, Elbert Co Ga; d. Abt. 1855, Madison Co. Ga.
3.	iii.	ISSAC DAVID VAUGHN, b. Abt. 1810; d. June 1877, Elbert Co Ga.
4.	iv.	MARTHA ELIZABETH VAUGHN b. Mar 4, 1812, Elbert Co Ga; d. July 17, 1860, Elbert Co Ga.
5.	v.	MILDRED VAUGHN, b. Abt. 1814.
6.	vi.	JAMES W. VAUGHN, b. Abt. 1815, Elbert Co Ga.
	vii.	ELIZABETH PENDLETON VAUGHN, b. September 05, 1818; m. UNKNOWN BROWN.
7.	viii.	JACOB DAVID VAUGHN, b. March 24, 1823; d. May 31, 1862, Savanah Ga.

Military service: Private Co H 38th Ga Inf

ix. PERLINA VAUGHN, b. Abt. 1824; m. ISSAC D. GLORE, October 20, 1850; b. Abt. 1827.

Military service: Co F 15th Ga Inf private July 15,1861. Captured and paroled at Hartwell, Ga. May 19,1865.

8. x. ALEXANDER VAUGHN, b. Abt. 1826, Elbert Co Ga; d. July 06, 1863, Gettysburg, Pa.

Military service: Private Co H 38th Ga Inf

xi. JOHN HENRY VAUGHN, b. Abt. 1828, Elbert Co Ga; d. July 01, 1862, Charlottesville, Va; m. MALITTA P. TUCKER, July 11, 1850; b. Abt. 1828.

Military service: Private Co H 38th Ga Inf

xii. MARY CAROLINA VAUGHN, b. January 30, 1830; m. UNKNOWN HEWELL.

Generation No. 2

2. WILLIAM DAVID VAUGHN *(ALEXANDER)* was born May 12, 1808 in Elbert Co Ga, and died Abt. 1855 in Madison Co. Ga. He married PERLINA KEZIAH DAVID December 12, 1827, daughter of HENRY DAVID and MARY MATHEWS. She was born April 01, 1808.

Children of WILLIAM VAUGHN and PERLINA DAVID are:

     i. MARY CAROLINE VAUGHN, b. Abt. 1829; m. UNKNOWN HEWELL.

9.   ii. MILES B VAUGHN, b. Abt. 1830; d. December 13, 1862, Killed Fredericksburg Va.
       Military service: Co H 38th Georgia Infantry 3/1/1862

    iii. MATHEW A VAUGHN, b. Abt. 1832.

    iv. MARTHA A VAUGHN, b. Abt. 1835; d. Abt. 1910; m. WILLIAM W HEWELL, December 08, 1853.

     v. MARION VAUGHN, b. Abt. 1840.

    vi. MILLY VAUGHN, b. Abt. 1842.

    vii. SUSAN C VAUGHN, b. Abt. 1843; d. April 28, 1924, Provo, Utah; m. SANFORD M BRUCE, April 04, 1882; b. January 1861, Madison Co, GA.

    viii. WILLIAM H VAUGHN, b. Abt. 1844; d. June 27, 1862, Killed Cold Harbor, Va Peninsula Campaign. **Military service: Co H 38th Georgia Infantry 3/1/1862**

    ix. JAMES T VAUGHN, b. Abt. 1847; m. SAMANTHA A VAUGHN.

10.   x. PERLINA KEZIAH VAUGHN, b. June 14, 1849, Madison Co, GA; d. December 14, 1914, Madison Co, GA.

3. ISSAC DAVID VAUGHN *(ALEXANDER)* was born Abt. 1810, and died June 1877 in Elbert Co Ga. He married (1) HARRIET CAMPBELL after 1862. She was born About 1845. He married (2) RACHEL C DAVID February 15, 1832, daughter of PETER DAVID and ELIZABETH DAVID. She was born January 09, 1810, and died Abt. 1861 in Elbert Co Ga.

Child of ISSAC VAUGHN and HARRIET CAMPBELL is:

     i. ELLA S J VAUGHN, b. June 01, 1869; d. October 19, 1870.

Children of ISSAC VAUGHN and RACHEL DAVID are:

    ii. MARTHA J VAUGHN, b. January 01, 1834; d. January 06, 1834.

    iii. PETER DAVID VAUGHN, b. January 17, 1835; d. April 19, 1862.

Military service: private Co C 15th Ga, July 15, 1861. Died in 1st Ga. Hospital at Richmond, Va. April 19,1862

11.   iv.   ALEXANDER WILKS VAUGHN, b. November 08, 1837, Elbert Co. Ga; d. January 29, 1905.

v.   WILLIAM W. VAUGHN, b. May 07, 1840; d. Abt. August 1863. **Military service: Co H 38th Georgia Infantry 3/1/1862 Absent, sick, August 1863. Died in service.**

vi.   SARAH J. VAUGHN, b. December 15, 1842; d. February 09, 1850.

vii.   ELIZABETH C. VAUGHN, b. October 13, 1847; m. C. COLUMBUS HAYNES.

viii.   JOSEPH L. VAUGHN, b. January 12, 1846; d. February 06, 1846.

ix.   ISSAC J.M. VAUGHN, b. May 08, 1850; d. **April 20, 1863, Civil War**.

4. MARTHA ELIZABETH VAUGHN *(ALEXANDER)* was born March 04, 1812 in Elbert Co Ga, and died July 17, 1860 in Elbert Co Ga. She married JOHN NATHANIEL MOORE March 06, 1828, son of THOMAS MOORE and JUDITH BOOTH. He was born March 31, 1807 in Elbert Co Ga, and died January 27, 1887 in Elbert Co Ga.

Children of MARTHA VAUGHN and JOHN MOORE are shown under Descendants of Thomas Moore.

i.   WILLIAM M. MOORE, b. May 03, 1829, Elbert Co Ga; d. May 09, 1907, Franklin Co. Ga.

ii.   ISAAC V. MOORE, b. November 17, 1830, Elbert Co Ga; d. November 29, 1918, Madison Co

iii.   THOMAS A MOORE, b. January 13, 1834.

iv.   ELIZABETH MOORE, b. August 05, 1836.

v.   JUDAH ANN MOORE, b. November 11, 1840, Elbert Co Ga; d. February 27, 1858, Elbert Co Ga; m. CHARLES H. GORDON, October 07, 1855, Elbert Co Ga.

vi.   MARTHA J. MOORE, b. December 24, 1852; m. CHARLES JESSE VAUGHN, October 15, 1868.

5. MILDRED VAUGHN *(ALEXANDER)* was born Abt. 1814. She married WILLIAM W DAVID September 18, 1835 in Elbert Co Ga, son of PETER DAVID and ELIZABETH DAVID. He was born Abt. 1808, and died August 1864.

Children of MILDRED VAUGHN and WILLIAM DAVID are:

16.   i.   JAMES W DAVID, b. Abt. 1836.

      ii. PETER DAVID, b. 1842, Elbert Co, GA; d. Bef. August 1864, Elbert Co, GA. **Military Service private July 15, 1861. Wounded at Garnett's Farm, Va. June 27,1862. Died of wounds July 12,1862**

17.   iii. WILLIAM A DAVID, b. Abt. 1854; d. 1916, Elbert Co, GA.

6. JAMES W.VAUGHN *(ALEXANDER)* was born Abt. 1815 in Elbert Co Ga. He married ELIZABETH E. DAVID February 07, 1839 in Madison Co GA, daughter of PETER DAVID and ELIZABETH DAVID. She was born Abt. 1816, and died Abt. 1859.

      Children of JAMES VAUGHN and ELIZABETH DAVID are:

        i. RACHEL VAUGHN, b. Abt. 1847.

       ii. MARY JANICE VAUGHN, b. Abt. 1851.

     iii. LEWIS DAVID VAUGHN, b. Abt. 1854.

     iv. ISSAC DAVID VAUGHN, b. Abt. 1857; m. MARTHA UNKNOWN.

      v. MILLY DAVID VAUGHN, b. Abt. 1859.

7. JACOB DAVID VAUGHN *(ALEXANDER)* was born March 24, 1823, and died May 31, 1862 in Savanah Ga. He married MARTHA J HEWELL December 16, 1847 in Elbert Co Ga. **Military service: Co H. 38th Ga Inf Private - October 15, 1861. Died at Savannah, Georgia, May 31, 1862.**

      Children of JACOB VAUGHN and MARTHA HEWELL are:

        i. WILLIAM A VAUGHN, b. Abt. 1854.

       ii. JAMES W VAUGHN, b. Abt. 1858.

     iii. ISAAC W VAUGHN, b. Abt. 1856.

8. ALEXANDER VAUGHN *(ALEXANDER)* was born Abt. 1826 in Elbert Co Ga, and died July 06, 1863 in Gettysburg, Pa. He married NANCY WHITE. She was born Abt. 1831, and died January 04, 1922 in Franklin Co, Ga. **Military service: Private Co H 38th Ga Inf—Wounded severly in the lungs at Gettysburg, Pa 7/1/1863 died there on7/6/1863**

      Children of ALEXANDER VAUGHN and NANCY WHITE are:

        i. JAMES M VAUGHN, b. 1856.

       ii. LAURA VAUGHN, b. 1860; m. UNKNOWN MAYFIELD.

     iii. ALEXANDER J VAUGHN, b. 1861.

Generation No. 3

9. MILES B VAUGHN *(WILLIAM DAVID, ALEXANDER)* was born Abt. 1830, and died December 13, 1862 in Killed Fredericksburg Va. He married SUSAN ANN UNKNOWN. **Military service: Co H 38th Ga Inf Private - October 15, 1861. Killed at Fredericksburg, Virginia, December 13, 1862**

    Children of MILES VAUGHN and SUSAN UNKNOWN are:
- i. ISSAC D VAUGHN, b. Abt. 1852.
- ii. ANGELINA VAUGHN, b. Abt. 1854; m. J. D. FORD.
- iii. WILEY VAUGHN, b. Abt. 1856.
- iv. LACY B VAUGHN, b. Abt. 1860.
- v. CHRISTOPHER VAUGHN.

10. PERLINA KEZIAH VAUGHN *(WILLIAM DAVID, ALEXANDER)* was born June 14, 1849 in Madison Co, GA, and died December 14, 1914 in Madison Co, GA. She married JAMES HENRY BRUCE in Madison Co GA, son of JAMES BRUCE and MARY KING. He was born September 22, 1848, and died November 25, 1936 in Madison Co, GA.

    Children of PERLINA VAUGHN and JAMES BRUCE are:
- i. AGATHA W BRUCE, b. December 1871, Madison Co, GA; d. September 29, 1967, Atlanta, Fulton Co, GA.
  ial: Vineyards Creek Bapt Ch Cem, Madison Co, GA p308
- ii. WILLIAM N BRUCE, b. 1874, Madison Co, GA; d. August 04, 1955, Pavo, GA.
- iii. ADORA E BRUCE, b. 1876, Madison Co, GA; d. June 07, 1965, Savannah, GA.
- iv. MARY ELIZABETH "LIZZIE" BRUCE, b. March 1877, Madison Co, GA; d. Aft. 1967, Atlanta, GA.
- v. HASSIE BRUCE, b. January 1881.
- vi. JAMES LESTER BRUCE, b. March 04, 1887, Madison Co, GA; d. July 09, 1887, Madison Co, GA.

11. ALEXANDER WILKS VAUGHN *(ISSAC DAVID, ALEXANDER)* was born November 08, 1837 in Elbert Co. Ga, and died January 29, 1905. He married SARAH JANE CAMPBELL November 23, 1871. She was born Abt. 1850.
Military service: Co H 38th Ga Inf Private - September 10, 1862. Wounded at Fredericksburg, Virginia, December 13, 1862. Wounded and captured at Gettysburg, Pennsylvania, July 2,1863. Paroled at DeCamp General Hospital, David's Island, New York, Harbor in 1863.

    Child of ALEXANDER VAUGHN and SARAH CAMPBELL is:

i. EARLY CALLOWAY VAUGHN, b. August 22, 1872; d. 1942, Florida; m. LUCRETIA ELIZABETH SANDERS, December 31, 1893; b. July 29, 1872; d. June 14, 1968.

15. ELIZABETH MOORE *(MARTHA ELIZABETH VAUGHN)* was born August 05, 1836. She married (1) BILLY JONES. She married (2) STEPHEN JOSHUA WHITE February 23, 1854, son of MARTIN WHITE and ANNA BURDEN. He was born October 05, 1825, and died May 23, 1862 in Savanah Ga during Civil War. **Military service: October 15, 1861, Co H 38th Georgia Inf**
Children of ELIZABETH MOORE and STEPHEN WHITE are:
  i. JOHN MARTIN WHITE, b. March 10, 1855; d. February 05, 1938, Elbert Co Ga.
  ii. CHARLES H. WHITE, b. June 25, 1856; d. January 22, 1857, Elbert Co Ga.

16. JAMES W DAVID *(MILDRED VAUGHN, ALEXANDER)* was born Abt. 1836. He married MARY WHITE Abt. 1860. She was born May 31, 1837.
Military service: Private Co A Phillips Legion
Children of JAMES DAVID and MARY WHITE are:
  i. MILLY E DAVID, b. 1862, Ebert Co, GA.
  ii. SARAH T J DAVID, b. 1864, Ebert Co, GA.
  iii. ZEADA DAVID, b. 1867, Ebert Co, GA.
  iv. LOUISA L D DAVID, b. 1869, Ebert Co, GA.
  v. ISAIAH W DAVID, b. 1872, Ebert Co, GA.
  vi. MARTHA DAVID, b. 1874, Ebert Co, GA.
  vii. JOHN G DAVID, b. 1876, Ebert Co, GA.
  viii. ONNIE DAVID, b. 1879, Ebert Co, GA.

17. WILLIAM A DAVID *(MILDRED VAUGHN, ALEXANDER)* was born Abt. 1854, and died 1916 in Elbert Co, GA. He married EMMA A OGILVIE Abt. 1880. She was born February 1860 in Ebert Co, GA.
Children of WILLIAM DAVID and EMMA OGILVIE are:
  i. GROVER C DAVID, b. 1884.
  ii. JOHN G DAVID, b. 1886.
  iii. OGILVIE DAVID, b. 1899.

DESCENDANTS OF FRANCIS POWER

Generation No. 1

1. FRANCIS POWER was born February 21, 1756 in MD, and died Bef. August 03, 1818 in Madison Co Ga. He married ELIZABETH EVANS December 24, 1768 in Brunswick Co, VA. She was born Abt. 1753 in Probably in Maryland, and died Aft. 1818 in Prob Madison Co, GA.

Francis Power had a grant of land in Wilkes County, Ga, in the part that later became Madison County. He built a house on the land without nails. The split pine floors were still in good condition when his granddaughter, Anna Moon Patten, lived there in 1887.

He is buried on the land and there is a marker erected by Ralph "Doc" Power with the names of all the children of Francis and Elizabeth Power.

Children of FRANCIS POWER and ELIZABETH EVANS are:

	i.	WILLIAM POWER, b. Abt. 1770; m. SALLY GREEN MOON, Abt. 1785, Prob Wilkes Co, GA; b. Abt. 1770, Wilkes Co, GA.
	ii.	ELIZABETH POWER, b. January 25, 1776, VA; d. March 25, 1846, Monroe Co, GA.
	iii.	ROBERT POWER, SR, b. July 10, 1778; d. August 12, 1836, Butts Co, GA.
4.	iv.	MARY POWER, b. November 29, 1779; d. Abt. 1875, Madison Co Ga.
5.	v.	BENNETT POWER, b. Abt. 1780.
6.	vi.	JESSE POWER, b. April 30, 1788, Madison, Co Ga; d. October 18, 1881, Madison, Co Ga.
7.	vii.	DAVID B. POWER, b. Abt. 1790, Elbert Co. Ga; d. Aft. June 1840, Madison Co, GA.
8.	viii.	SUSAN POWER, b. Bet. 1790 - 1800, Elbert Co, GA; d. Bef. 1850, Prob Madison Co, GA.
9.	ix.	JAMES POWER, b. 1792, Elbert Co, GA; d. December 1838, Madison Co, GA.
10.	x.	ANNA POWER, b. December 07, 1793; d. December 07, 1879.

Generation No. 2

4. MARY POWER *(FRANCIS)* was born November 29, 1779, and died Abt. 1875 in Madison Co Ga. She married ISAAC SIMMONS Abt. 1795 in Prob

Elbert Co, GA. He was born February 11, 1758 in NC, and died March 24, 1832 in Talbot Co, GA.

   Children of MARY POWER and ISAAC SIMMONS are:
   i.   THOMAS SIMMONS, b. 1796, Madison Co, GA.
   ii.   ELIZABETH SIMMONS, b. Abt. 1800, Madison Co Ga.
   iii. WILLIAM SIMMONS, b. Abt. 1800, Madison Co Ga; d. Abt. 1863, Madison Co Ga.
   iv.   JOHN SIMMONS, b. Abt. 1803; d. December 1866.
   v.   ISAAC SIMMONS, JR, b. 1806; m. WILLIAM ANN WILLIFORD.
   vi.   FRANCIS SIMMONS, b. Abt. 1808; d. Abt. 1866.
   vii. DAVID POWER SIMMONS, b. September 24, 1810, Madison Co Ga; d. March 20, 1887, Madison Co Ga.
   viii. PATSY SIMMONS, b. 1811; m. JACOB ALBRIGHT, December 11, 1825, Madison Co, GA; b. Abt. 1810.
   ix.   MARY SIMMONS, b. Abt. 1815.
   x.   SARAH SIMMONS, b. Abt. 1816.
   xi.   BENNETT SIMMONS, b. Abt. 1820; d. Abt. 1876, Madison Co Ga.
   xii. SUSAN PINKNEY SIMMONS, b. April 05, 1822, Madison Co, GA; d. July 19, 1908, Oglethorpe Co, GA.
   xiii. TURNER SIMMONS, b. Abt. 1825, Madison, Co Ga; d. April 1862, died of disease in Goldsboro N.C. .

5. BENNETT POWER *(FRANCIS)* was born Abt. 1780.
   Child of BENNETT POWER is:
22.   i.   WILLIAM G POWER, b. 1803, Oglethrope Co, GA; d. Madison Co, GA.

6. JESSE POWER *(FRANCIS)* was born April 30, 1788 in Madison, Co Ga, and died October 18, 1881 in Madison, Co Ga. He married (1) ESTHER TUGGLE Abt. 1810. She was born Abt. 1790 in Madison, Co Ga, and died Bef. 1836 in Madison, Co Ga. He married (2) EMILY BROCHE July 31, 1836 in Madison Co GA. She was born July 07, 1809, and died February 1857. He married (3) SUSAN BRADBERRY December 27, 1859 in Madison Co GA, daughter of WILLIAM BRADBERRY. She was born Abt. 1808, and died Bef. 1880 in Madison, Co Ga.

   Jesse and Esther are both buried in the Fork Creek Cemetery in Madison Co. Ga.

   Notes for JESSE POWER: Amnesty Oath: 1865, Fair, grey hair, yellow eyes, 5'8," age 77, farmer

POWER, Jesse, 94 yrs, died 10/18/1881, Madison Co., Ga. - Christian Index, 11/3/1881, pg 6, line 3

The Obituary from the Christian Index: Power - Died at his residence in Madison county, Georgia on the 18th day of October, 1881. In his 94th year, Deacon Jesse Power. Brother Power united with the Baptist church at the Fork of Broad River when a young man. Settled as a farmer, procuring a good living by industry and economy. He raised a large family of sons and daughter. He was faithful and punctual in the discharge of all duties assigned him. He was ordained deacon fifty odd years ago, and filled the office well. Thus has passed away another one of the Lord's faithful servants, leaving a widow, sons and daughters, and many grand and great grandchildren, to mourn their loss. But not as those who have no hope, for we feel confident that he is in possession of that rest that remaineth to the people of God. W. R. Goss, Harmony Grove, GA October 24th, 1881

Children of JESSE POWER and ESTHER TUGGLE are:

    i.   CHARLES TUGGLE POWER, b. Abt. 1809, Elbert Co, GA; m. MARY ANN MORGAN, February 15, 1831, Madison Co, GA; b. Abt. 1812.

23.   ii.   ELIZABETH POWER, b. Aft. 1810.

    iii.   GREEN B POWER, b. Aft. 1810.

    iv.   JANE G POWER, b. Aft. 1810; m. DAVID MEADOWS.

    v.   MARY POWER, b. Aft. 1810; m. JOHN J CARITHERS; b. 1825, Madison Co, GA.
        Amnesty Oath: 1865, Ruddy, black hair, black eyes, 5'6"

    vi.   WELBORN POWER, b. Aft. 1810.

24.   vii.   FRANCIS EVANS POWER, SR, b. November 20, 1812, Madison Co, GA; d. September 01, 1877, Madison Co, GA.

    viii.   JESSE GREEN POWER, b. 1815, Madison Co, GA.

25.   ix.   WILLIAM THOMAS POWER, SR, b. Nov. 26, 1817, Madison Co, GA; d. 1861, Elbert Co, GA.

26.   x.   JAMES DUNCAN POWER, b. April 17, 1820; d. October 13, 1890.

    xi.   JANE GIBSON POWER, b. November 1822, Madison Co, GA; m. DAVID (MEADOW) MEADOWS, March 30, 1841, Madison Co, GA; b. 1817, Madison Co, GA.

27.   xii.   WYLEY BENNETT POWER, b. June 07, 1825, Madison Co, GA; d. April 25, 1899, Madison Co, GA. **Military Service: Private Co G. 3rd Regiment, Georgia Cavalry (State Guards)**

28.   xiii.   MARY M POWER, b. October 13, 1827, Madison Co, GA; d. Sept. 27, 1905, Madison Co, GA.

Children of JESSE POWER and EMILY BROCHE are:

xiv. JOSEPH B POWER, b. July 1837; d. November 23, 1862, Madison Co, GA; m. ANNA G POWER, December 04, 1856, Madison Co, GA; b. November 03, 1834, Madison Co, GA; d. January 04, 1893, Madison Co, GA .**Military Service: Private May 9, 1862. Died of chronic diarrhoea, at home in Madison County, Ga., Nov. 23, 1862**

xv. ASA POWER, b. Abt. 1838; m. JANE HAND, December 19, 1861, Talbot Co, GA; b. Abt. 1840. **Military Service: Private July 20, 1862. Transferred to Co. E, 37th Regt. Ga. Inf. May 6, 1863. Wounded at Chickamauga, Ga. Sept. 20, 1863. Sent to hospital. Received pay at Atlanta, Ga. Apr. 30, 1864. No later record.**

29. xvi. JOSIAH WELBORN POWER, b. January 26, 1840; d. November 21, 1921, Madison Co, GA.

30. xvii. THOMAS BOLTON POWER, b. Abt. 1842; d. Madison Co, GA.

xviii. OSBORN GOSS POWER, b. Abt. 1844; m. LUCY J MADDOX, Bef. 1869, Elbert Co, GA; b. 1848.

7. DAVID B. POWER *(FRANCIS)* was born Abt. 1790 in Elbert Co. Ga, and died Aft. June 1840 in Madison Co, GA. He married (1) SUSANNAH MOON October 15, 1807 in Elbert Co Ga, daughter of WILLIAM MOON and SARAH RICHARDSON. She was born Abt. 1790, and died Abt. 1827. He married (2) MARGARET PATTEN May 11, 1828 in Madison Co, GA. She was born 1798 in GA, and died Aft. 1860 in GA.

Children of DAVID POWER and SUSANNAH MOON are:

31. i. JESSE R POWER, b. 1808, Madison Co, GA; d. 1842, Madison Co, GA.

32. ii. WILLIAM POWER, b. Abt. 1810; d. 1834, Madison Co, GA.

33. iii. JAMES MANKIN [REV] POWER, b. 1812, Madison Co, GA; d. Aft. 1880.

34. iv. SARAH F POWER, b. 1815, Madison Co, GA; d. Aft. 1850, Madison Co, GA.

v. AMANDA ELIZABETH POWER, b. Abt. 1817, Madison Co, GA; m. WILLIAM A SIMS, 1846;

35. vi. FRANCIS E POWER, b. Abt. 1819.

vii. POLLY POWER, b. 1821, Madison Co, GA; m. ISHAM MURRAY, November 23, 1834, Madison Co, GA; b. Abt. 1820.

36. viii. MARTHA C POWER, b. 1823, Madison Co, GA; d. Bef. 1870, Madison Co, GA.

37.   ix.   SUSAN E POWER, b. May 04, 1824; d. September 30, 1908, Madison Co, GA.

       x.   DAVID M POWER, b. 1825, Madison Co, GA.

       Children of DAVID POWER and MARGARET PATTEN are:

       xi.   MATILDA CATHERINE[6] POWER, b. 1829, Madison Co, GA; m. JOHN G EVANS, January 03, 1846, Madison Co, GA; b. 1824, Madison Co, GA.

38.   xii.   SAMUEL PATTON POWER, SR, b. July 09, 1831, Madison Co, GA; d. October 27, 1911.

       xiii.   ROBERT T POWER, b. 1832, Madison Co, GA; d. July 29, 1917, Cartersville, Bartow Co, GA; m. ELIZABETH NICHOLS, February 07, 1858, Madison Co, GA; b. 1843, GA. **Military Service: Co B, 9th Battalion, Ga Volunteer Infantry, Army of Tenn. CSA**

       xiv.   MINERVA LOUISA POWER, b. 1836, Madison Co, GA; m. JESSE G POWER, November 29, 1859, Madison Co, GA; b. May 07, 1843, Madison Co, GA; d. May 29, 1862, Knoxville, TN.
       Co B, 9th Battalion, Ga Volunteer Infantry, Army of Tenn. CSA
       Jesse G Power - Private Mar 4, 1862. Died May 29, 1862. Knoxville, Tenn.

       xv.   MARGARET S POWER, b. November 15, 1838, Madison Co, GA; d. November 16, 1903; m. SYLVESTER GISSON WILEY, May 08, 1857, Madison Co, GA; b. July 04, 1824, GA; d. July 27, 1911, Jackson Co, GA. **Military Service: private July 15, 1861 Co F 15th Georgia Inf. Sick in hospital February 28,1865. No later record**

8. SUSAN POWER *(FRANCIS)* was born Bet. 1790 - 1800 in Elbert Co, GA, and died Bef. 1850 in Prob Madison Co, GA. She married ARCHELAUS P MOON SR Abt. 1804 in Elbert Co, GA. He was born 1776 in VA, and died Abt. 1842 in Madison Co, GA.

       Children of SUSAN POWER and ARCHELAUS MOON are:

       i.   ANNA MOON, b. 1809, Elbert Co, GA; d. Aft. 1887, Madison Co, GA; m. SAMUEL PATTEN, JR, December 26, 1826, Madison Co, GA; b. February 01, 1807, GA; d. January 10, 1882, Carlton, Madison Co, GA.

       ii.   ARCHELAUS P MOON, JR, b. 1816, Elbert Co, GA; d. October 1874, Madison Co, GA; m. (1) GABRILLA MOON, Abt. 1835, Elbert Co, GA; b. August 1817, Elbert Co, GA; d. Abt. 1867, Madison Co, GA; m. (2) NANCY L RIDGWAY, March 03, 1868, Madison Co, GA; b. Abt. 1820; d. Madison Co, GA.

iii. IRENTA MOON, b. 1810, Elbert Co, GA; m. JOHN T MITCH-ELL, November 14, 1826, Madison Co, GA; b. Abt. 1810.

iv. MARY MOON, b. 1805, Madison Co, GA; d. Abt. 1863, Stewart Co, GA; m. WILLIAM SIMS, December 24, 1822, Madison Co, GA; b. Abt. 1800.

v. ROBERT T MOON, b. 1814, Madison Co, GA.

39. vi. WILLIAM T MOON, b. April 13, 1824, Madison Co, GA; d. Jan. 26, 1883, Madison Co. Ga.

40. vii. MARTHA E MOON, b. 1823, Madison Co, GA.

9. JAMES POWER *(FRANCIS)* was born 1792 in Elbert Co, GA, and died December 1838 in Madison Co, GA. He married ELIZABETH WILLIAM-SON Abt. 1810 in Prob Jackson Co, GA. She was born in Jackson Co Ga, and died Aft. 1870 in Madison Co, GA.

Children of JAMES POWER and ELIZABETH WILLIAMSON are:

41. i. WILLIAM WILLIAMSON POWER, b. November 14, 1811; d. July 25, 1848.

42. ii. ANN MARIE POWER, b. 1815, Madison Co, GA.

iii. SUSAN POWER, b. Abt. 1820; m. JEPTHA H MOON, October 17, 1843; b. Abt. 1814; d. January 05, 1866.

43. iv. FRANCIS POWER, b. April 05, 1824; d. **1864, Killed at the battle of Chickamauga Ga.**

44. v. SUSANNA SUSAN POWER, b. 1830, Madison Co, GA; d. Madison Co, GA.

45. vi. LUCY JANE POWER, b. October 05, 1832, Madison Co, GA; d. January 14, 1903, Madison Co, GA.

10. ANNA POWER *(FRANCIS)* was born December 07, 1793, and died December 07, 1879. She married (1) THOMAS MINOR GRIMES June 15, 1809 in Elbert Co, GA. He was born Abt. 1785, and died October 1822 in Madison Co, GA. She married (2) MARTIN ROWE May 27, 1824 in Madison Co, GA. He was born March 12, 1795, and died May 31, 1885.

Children of ANNA POWER and THOMAS GRIMES are:

i. SUSAN GRIMES, b. Aft. 1809.

46. ii. ELIZABETH GRIMES, b. November 05, 1811, Madison Co, GA; d. May 30, 1854, Madison Co, GA.

47. iii. JOHN POWER GRIMES, b. January 22, 1814, Madison Co, GA; d. January 09, 1874, Tallapoosa Co, AL.

48. iv. MARTHA GRIMES, b. March 13, 1816; d. April 25, 1891.

Children of ANNA POWER and MARTIN ROWE are:

49.   v. STEPHEN ROWE, b. 1825, Madison Co, GA; d. September 04, 1864, Atlanta, GA in CSA.

50.   vi. JAMES POWER [REV] ROWE, b. 1827, Madison Co, GA; d. Bef. 1885.

Generation No. 3

22. WILLIAM G POWER *(BENNETT, FRANCIS)* was born 1803 in Oglethrope Co, GA, and died in Madison Co, GA. He married (1) NANCY BARNETT July 04, 1821 in Oglethorpe Co, GA. She was born 1805 in Oglethorpe Co, GA, and died Bef. 1831. He married (2) SARAH F POWER February 28, 1831 in Madison Co, GA, daughter of DAVID POWER and SUSANNAH MOON. She was born 1815 in Madison Co, GA, and died Aft. 1850 in Madison Co, GA.

Children of WILLIAM POWER and NANCY BARNETT are:

    i. WILLIAM DAVID POWER, b. Abt. 1822, Oglethorpe Co, GA; d. Aft. 1850; m. VIRGINIA CAROLINE TUCKER, November 17, 1844, Elbert Co, GA; b. Abt. 1825.**Military Service: Tiller's Company, GA Light Artillery (Echols Light Artillery**

    ii. JAMES BENNETT POWER, b. Abt. 1825, Oglethorpe Co, GA; m. (1) TABITHA HARRIETT HAYES, December 27, 1848, Oglethorpe Co, GA; b. Abt. 1825, Oglethorpe Co, GA;

    iii. SUSAN POWER, b. Abt. 1826, Oglethorpe Co, GA; d. Bef. 1861, Oglethorpe Co, GA.

Children of WILLIAM POWER and SARAH POWER are:

    iv. JESSE R POWER, b. 1836, Madison Co, GA; m. (1) SUSAN HALL, December 27, 1857, Madison Co, GA; b. Abt. 1840;

    v. JULIA A POWER, b. 1837, Madison Co, GA; m. WARREN W MEADOW, December 09, 1851, Madison Co, GA; b. 1834, Madison Co, GA.

    vi. DAVID P POWER, b. 1840, Madison Co, GA; d. Aft. 1880; m. EMILY, Bef. 1862; b. 1842; **Military Service: Co B. 1st Regiment, GA Cavalry**

    vii. MARY J POWER, b. 1842, Madison Co, GA.

    viii. FRANCES POWER, b. 1845, Madison Co, GA.

    ix. HENRY POWER, b. 1848, Madison Co, GA; m. (1) LAURA //; b. Abt. 1850; m. (2) MARY //; b. Abt. 1850; m. (3) MRS EMMA MARSHALL; b. Abt. 1850.

23. ELIZABETH POWER *(JESSE, FRANCIS)* was born Aft. 1810. She married FRANCIS SIMMONS, son of ISAAC SIMMONS and MARY POWER. He was born Abt. 1808, and died Abt. 1866.

Children are listed above under (15) Francis Simmons.

24. FRANCIS EVANS POWER SR *(JESSE, FRANCIS)* was born November 20, 1812 in Madison Co, GA, and died September 01, 1877 in Madison Co, GA. . He married ELIZABETH P WOODS February 17, 1837 in Madison Co, GA. She was born Abt. 1819, and died April 04, 1901 in Madison Co, GA.

Children of FRANCIS POWER and ELIZABETH WOODS are:

    i.   JESSE G POWER, b. May 07, 1843, Madison Co, GA; d. May 29, 1862, Knoxville, TN; m. MINERVA LOUISA POWER, November 29, 1859, Madison Co, GA; b. 1836, Madison Co, GA. **Notes for JESSE G. POWER: Co B, 9th Battalion, Ga Volunteer Infantry, Army of Tenn. CSA Jesse G Power - Private Mar 4, 1862. Died May 29, 1862. - Roster of Confederate Soldiers**

   ii.   MARY JANE POWER, b. September 16, 1845, Madison Co, GA; d. February 21, 1936, Madison Co, GA.

  iii.   MARTHA A POWER, b. May 29, 1847, Madison Co, GA; d. Bef. 1933; m. ISAAC D VAUGHN, Abt. 1863, Madison Co, GA; b. 1842. **Military Service: Private Co I 31st Regiment, Georgia Infantry**

   iv.   ELIZABETH FRANCES POWER, b. May 12, 1849, Madison Co, GA; d. December 08, 1933, Madison Co, GA; m. WILLIAM WYLEY CARITHERS, August 19, 1868, Madison Co, GA; b. November 30, 1846, Madison Co, GA; d. March 20, 1928, At Home in Madison Co, GA.

    v.   WILLIAM WILEY POWER, b. June 23, 1851, Madison Co, GA; d. November 29, 1937, Athens, Clarke Co, GA; m. SUSAN CLEMENTINE EVANS, December 01, 1871, Madison Co, GA; b. 1851, Madison Co, GA; d. May 28, 1938.

   vi.   SARAH CATHERINE POWER, b. March 08, 1857, Madison Co, GA; d. March 14, 1945, Madison Co, GA; m. WYLEY PINKNEY BROWN, December 22, 1881, Madison Co, GA; b. June 13, 1856, Madison Co, GA; d. October 05, 1940, Madison Co, GA.

  vii.   FRANCIS EVANS POWER, JR, b. December 31, 1860, Madison Co, GA; d. November 13, 1922, Madison Co, GA; m. (1) ELIZABETH LILA MOON, January 21, 1889, Madison Co, GA; b. November 1867, Elbert Co, GA; m. (2) MATTIE MCELROY, December 16, 1891, Madison Co, GA; b. Abt. 1860.

25. WILLIAM THOMAS POWER, SR *(JESSE, FRANCIS)* was born November 26, 1817 in Madison Co, GA, and died 1861 in Elbert Co, GA. He married SUSAN MILDRED OGLESBY November 25, 1852 in Elbert Co, GA, daughter of WILLIAM OGLESBY and PERLINA WILEY. She was born March 25, 1833, and died December 13, 1897.

Children of WILLIAM POWER and SUSAN OGLESBY are:

i. PURLINA J POWER, b. June 11, 1854; d. November 07, 1855.

ii. WILLIAM THOMAS POWER, JR, b. October 14, 1855, Elbert Co, GA; m. MAMIE BRADLEY; b. Abt. 1855.

iii. IDA A POWER, b. March 13, 1858, Elbert Co, GA; d. February 23, 1918, Columbus, Muscogee Co, GA; m. JOHN P SHANNON, December 06, 1876, Elbert Co, GA; b. August 04, 1850; d. September 16, 1900.

iv. JOHN OGLESBY POWER, b. November 11, 1859; d. June 10, 1864.

v. JOHN W POWER, b. 1861.

vi. MARY TURNER POWER, b. June 29, 1861, Elbert Co, GA; d. December 1950; m. BRITTAIN LEE PAYNE; b. 1861; d. 1888, Elbert Co, GA.

26. JAMES DUNCAN POWER *(JESSE, FRANCIS)* was born April 17, 1820, and died October 13, 1890. He married MARY ELIZABETH DAVID November 22, 1861 in Madison Co, GA, daughter of BERRY DAVID and ELIZABETH VAUGHN. She was born July 16, 1839, and died December 23, 1890.

More About JAMES DUNCAN POWER:Burial: Fork Cemetary, Madison Co

More About MARY ELIZABETH DAVID:Burial: Fork Cemetary, Madison Co

Children of JAMES POWER and MARY DAVID are:

i. MARY L POWER, b. Abt. 1866; d. September 07, 1894, Madison Co, GA; m. (1) LEONIDAS HARRISON EBERHARDT; b. Abt. 1865; m. (2) LEONIDAS HARRISON "HARRY" EBERHART, December 22, 1886, Madison Co, GA; b. July 1865, Elbert Co, GA; d. May 04, 1940, Madison Co, GA.

ii. LUELLEN POWER, b. Abt. 1868.

iii. ESTHER ELIZABETH "LIZZIE" POWER, b. March 12, 1869, Madison Co, GA; d. June 08, 1938, Madison Co, GA; m. ALEXANDER "LEK" LUCAS COMER, October 10, 1888, Madison Co, GA; b. January 31, 1871, Madison Co, GA; d. March 21, 1961, Madison Co, GA.

iv. JANE G POWER, b. Abt. 1871; d. July 01, 1947, Madison Co, GA; m. RICHARD HENLEY BULLOCK GHOLSTON, February 22, 1890, Madison Co, GA; b. February 08, 1867, Madison Co, GA; d. March 30, 1924, Madison Co, GA.

    v. HENRY C POWER, b. Abt. 1872.

    vi. NELL POWER, b. Abt. 1872; d. October 15, 1944; m. (1) STOVALL; b. Abt. 1870; m. (2) GEORGE M [MD] STOVALL; b. April 13, 1867; d. November 05, 1894.

    vii. CLARA POWER, b. Abt. 1874.

    viii. ALLEN POWER, b. Abt. 1876.

27. WYLEY BENNETT POWER *(JESSE, FRANCIS)* was born June 07, 1825 in Madison Co, GA, and died April 25, 1899 in Madison Co, GA. He married MARY JANE POWER October 18, 1852 in Madison Co, GA, daughter of JAMES POWER and ELIZABETH MOORE. She was born Abt. 1837, and died December 10, 1901. **Military Service: Private Co G. 3rd Regiment, Georgia Cavalry (State Guards)**

    Children of WYLEY POWER and MARY POWER are:

    i. ESTER ANN POWER, b. 1855, Madison Co, GA; d. 1896, Madison Co, GA; m. HEZEKIAH SMITH "SHUG" (WYNN) WINN; b. October 30, 1839, Madison Co, GA; d. September 17, 1925, Madison Co, GA.

    ii. WILLIAM WILEY POWER, b. October 12, 1862; d. June 01, 1927; m. LORENA POWER, October 04, 1881, Madison Co, GA; b. Abt. 1867; d. May 23, 1941.

    iii. ELIZABETH POWER, b. Abt. 1860.

    iv. WILLIE W POWER, b. Abt. 1863.

    v. L.E. POWER, b. Abt. 1866.

    vi. ADANA POWER, b. Abt. 1868.

    vii. JAMES G POWER, b. Abt. 1872; d. 1918; m. JESSIE E ARNOLD; b. 1871; d. 1950.

    viii. SUSAN E POWER, b. Abt. 1874.

    ix. MARY A POWER, b. Abt. 1877.

28. MARY M POWER *(JESSE, FRANCIS)* was born October 13, 1827 in Madison Co, GA, and died September 27, 1905 in Madison Co, GA. She married JOHN J CARITHERS January 29, 1846 in Madison Co, GA. He was born 1825 in Madison Co, GA.

Amnesty Oath: 1865, Ruddy, black hair, black eyes, 5'6"

    Children of MARY POWER and JOHN CARITHERS are:

    i. WILLIAM WYLEY CARITHERS, b. November 30, 1846, Madison Co, GA; d. March 20, 1928, At Home in Madison Co, GA; m. ELIZABETH FRANCES POWER, August 19, 1868, Madison Co, GA; b. May 12, 1849, Madison Co, GA; d. December 08, 1933, Madison Co, GA.

   ii. JANE "JANIE" P CARITHERS, b. January 22, 1849, Madison Co, GA; d. May 22, 1923, Madison Co, GA; m. JAMES THOMAS SIMS, February 04, 1869, Madison Co, GA; b. October 07, 1847, Madison Co, GA; d. March 10, 1889, Madison Co, GA.

29. JOSIAH WELBORN POWER *(JESSE, FRANCIS)* was born January 26, 1840, and died November 21, 1921 in Madison Co, GA. He married MARY W "POLLY" POWER September 06, 1861 in Madison Co, GA, daughter of WILLIAM POWER and MARTHA GRIMES. She was born May 20, 1839 in Madison Co, GA, and died June 07, 1911 in Madison Co, GA.
Notes for JOSIAH WELBORN POWER:Co B, 9th Battalion, Ga Volunteer Infantry, Army of Tenn. CSA Private Mar 4, 1862. Transferred to Co E, 37th Regt Ga Inf. May 6, 1863. Sent to hospital Aug 10, 1863. Received pay May 3, 1874. No later record. (Born in Ga in 1840)
   Children of JOSIAH POWER and MARY POWER are:
   i. EUGENIA POWER, b. 1864, Madison Co, GA; m. ROBERT COMER, March 01, 1888, Madison Co, GA; b. Abt. 1860.
   ii. ADA L POWER, b. January 29, 1866, Madison Co, GA; d. August 04, 1941, Madison Co, GA; m. JAMES T CHRISTIAN, October 04, 1883, Madison Co, GA; b. February 10, 1862, GA; d. November 08, 1926, Madison Co, GA.
   iii. JESSE W [MD] POWER, b. August 18, 1870, Madison Co, GA; d. August 04, 1925, Madison Co, GA; m. RUBY DELONEY COMER, October 05, 1892, Madison Co, GA; b. May 10, 1877, Madison Co, GA; d. June 27, 1937, Madison Co, GA.
   iv. MARTHA EMMA POWER, b. September 23, 1875, Madison Co, GA; d. January 15, 1943, Madison Co, GA; m. JOHN HENRY MITCHELL, SR, October 11, 1896, Madison Co, GA; b. December 04, 1875, Madison Co, GA; d. April 06, 1934, Madison Co, GA.
   v. JAMES G POWER, b. 1885.
   vi. OULA POWER, b. 1889.
   vii. JOSEPH L POWER, b. March 1868, Madison Co, GA; d. 1957, Madison Co, GA; m. (1) LILLIAN E. DAVID, November 01, 1892; b. Abt. 1872; m. (2) ELIZABETH LILLIAN DAVID, November 01, 1892, Madison Co, GA; b. September 1872, Madison Co, GA; d. November 30, 1940, Madison Co, GA.

30. THOMAS BOLTON POWER *(JESSE, FRANCIS)* was born Abt. 1842, and died in Madison Co, GA. He married GEORGIA ANN VIRGINIA DAVID

October 25, 1866 in Madison Co, GA, daughter of HENRY DAVID and ELIZABETH OGLESBY. She was born 1846 in AL, and died in Madison Co, GA. **Co B, 9th Battalion, Ga Volunteer Infantry, Army of Tenn. CSA Thomas B Power - Private July 1862. Transferred to Co E, 37th Regt Ga Inf. May 6, 1863. Surrendered at Greensboro NC Apr 26, 1865.**

Children of THOMAS POWER and GEORGIA DAVID are:

i. EMILY AUZIE POWER, b. August 11, 1867, Madison Co, GA; d. December 06, 1912, Madison Co, GA; m. WILLIAM THOMAS BRUCE, February 14, 1885, Madison Co, GA; b. September 21, 1858, Madison Co, GA; d. January 06, 1901, Madison Co, GA.

ii. THOMAS EDGAR POWER, SR, b. 1870, Madison Co, GA; d. 1900, Madison Co, GA; m. SARAH A DELIA COILE, March 15, 1894, Madison Co, GA; b. December 18, 1875, Madison Co, GA; d. December 24, 1935, Madison Co, GA.

iii. HENRY DAVID POWER, b. 1872, Madison Co, GA; d. October 02, 1908, Madison Co, GA of Typhoid Fever.

iv. OTHA LAMAR POWER, b. 1876, Madison Co, GA; d. 1950, Madison Co, GA; m. HULDAH M DAVID, January 08, 1901, Madison Co, GA; b. November 1877, Madison Co, GA; d. September 30, 1954, Madison Co, GA.

v. WILEY B POWER, b. 1881, Madison Co, GA; d. September 21, 1926, Grayson, Gwinnett Co, GA; m. ROSIE L MOORE, February 13, 1905, Madison Co, GA; b. 1878, Madison Co, GA.

vi. EARLIE L POWER, b. June 17, 1888, Madison Co, GA; d. February 27, 1920, Madison Co, GA; m. CYNTHIA KIDD, November 07, 1915, Madison Co, GA; b. July 17, 1887, Madison Co, GA; d. November 16, 1939, Madison Co, GA.

31. JESSE R POWER *(DAVID B., FRANCIS)* was born 1808 in Madison Co, GA, and died 1842 in Madison Co, GA. He married JULIA ANN HOPKINS December 14, 1834 in Madison Co, GA, daughter of DENNIS HOPKINS and MARGARET PATTEN. She was born 1819 in Madison Co, GA.

Children of JESSE POWER and JULIA HOPKINS are:

i. SUSAN M POWER, b. December 28, 1835, Madison Co, GA; d. April 22, 1899, Elbert Co, GA; m. WILLIAM SANFORD BUTLER, December 15, 1853, Madison Co, GA; b. March 17, 1831, Oglethrope Co, GA; d. March 29, 1901, Elbert Co, GA. **Military Service: Co I 15th Ga. Inf. private July 15,1861. Admitted to Chimborazo Hospital #1, at Richmond, Va. October 18, 1861. Transferred to 24th St. Hospital. Discharged at Richmond, Va. hosital January 3,1862**

    ii. MARGARET P POWER, b. February 1839, Madison Co, GA; d. Aft. 1920, Madison Co, GA; m. JAMES WESLEY RHODES, February 25, 1858, Madison Co, GA; b. 1835, Oglethrope Co, GA; d. Bef. 1900.
        James W Rhodes - Private May 10, 1862. Co B, 9th Battalion, Ga Volunteer Infantry Transferred to Co E, 37th Regt Ga Inf. May 6, 1863. Roll for Apr 1, 1864, last on file, shows he was detailed shoemaker by order of Gen Johnston Mar 10, 1864.

32. WILLIAM POWER *(DAVID B.· FRANCIS)* was born Abt. 1810, and died 1834 in Madison Co, GA. He married ELIZABETH GRIMES July 31, 1827 in Madison Co, GA, daughter of THOMAS GRIMES and ANNA POWER. She was born November 05, 1811 in Madison Co, GA, and died May 30, 1854 in Madison Co, GA.

    Children of WILLIAM POWER and ELIZABETH GRIMES are:
    i. SUSAN E M POWER, b. 1828, Madison Co, GA; d. 1907, Madison Co, GA; m. CHARLES O'KELLEY, SR, December 28, 1842, Madison Co, GA; b. December 28, 1815, Madison Co, GA; d. 1852, Madison Co, GA.
    ii. GEORGE W POWER, b. 1832, Madison Co, GA; m. (1) NANCY A CARITHERS, June 08, 1851, Madison Co, GA; b. 1834; m. (2) MARY A WILLIAMS, December 30, 1856, Madison Co, GA; b. March 24, 1836, Madison Co, GA; d. March 02, 1918, Madison Co, GA.
        Military Service: Private Co. A. 40th Regiment Volunteer Infantry

33. JAMES MANKIN [REV] POWER *(DAVID B., FRANCIS)* was born 1812 in Madison Co, GA, and died Aft. 1880. He married ELIZABETH R. MOORE August 06, 1829 in Madison Co GA. She was born 1813 in Madison Co, GA, and died Bef. 1880. He married (2) MARY ANN PATTEN Abt. 1880. She was born 1826.

    Children of JAMES POWER and ELIZABETH MOORE are:
    i. ELIZABETH A POWER, b. 1831, Madison Co, GA; d. Abt. 1872, Madison Co, GA; m. (1) LUKE H WHITE, November 06, 1856, Madison Co, GA; b. 1834, Madison Co, GA; **Military Service: private July 15, 1861. Appointed 5th Sergeant April 1863. Captured at Gettysburg, Pa. July 3, 1863. aroled at Point Lookout, Md. February 18, 1865. Received at Boulware & Cox's Wharves, James River, Va. for exchange, February 20 / 21,1865. No later record.** (2) JOHN HIRAM CHEEK, December 11, 1865, Madison Co, GA; b. January 02, 1848, Franklin Co, GA; d. May 13, 1923, Oconee

Co, GA.b. Abt. 1832. **Military Service: Private Co I. 41st Regiment, Georgia Infantry**

ii. JOHN MANKIN POWER, b. December 06, 1833, Madison Co, GA; d. June 11, 1888, Habersham Co Ga; m. MARTHA E. AMANDA CROOK, November 23, 1853, Elbert Co Ga; b. October 14, 1838; d. August 21, 1907, Walton Co. Ga; m.
   Military service: Private Co H 38th Ga Inf- October 15, 1861. Captured and paroled at Hartwell, Georgia, May 18, 1865

iii. MARY JANE POWER, b. Abt. 1837; d. December 10, 1901; m. WYLEY BENNETT POWER, October 18, 1852, Madison Co, GA; b. June 07, 1825, Madison Co, GA; d. April 25, 1899, Madison Co, GA.

iv. WINNIE A POWER, b. April 07, 1839, Madison Co, GA; d. Aft. 1920, Madison Co, GA; m. (1) GEORGE C BROWN, December 15, 1859, Madison Co, GA; b. August 06, 1836, Oglethrope Co, GA; d. December 06, 1882, Madison Co, GA; m.

v. MARTHA FRANCES POWER, b. May 01, 1843, Madison Co, GA; d. January 29, 1913, Madison Co, GA; m. JOHN SIMEON MOON, December 14, 1857, Madison Co, GA; b. October 13, 1836, Elbert Co, GA; d. February 19, 1911, Madison Co, GA **Military Service Co H. 38th GA.**

vi. ELIZA J POWER, b. Abt. 1845; d. May 10, 1909; m. (1) MARTIN T BUTLER, December 29,1865, Elbert Co, GA; b. 1843, Elbert Co, GA; d. 1878, Elbert Co, GA;

vii SARAH M POWER, b. 1845, Madison Co, GA; m. NATHANIEL H NELMS, January 16, 1868, Elbert Co, GA; b. Abt. 1840

viii. MARGARET J POWER, b. 1849, Madison Co, GA; d. Bef. 1871; m. (1) JOHN HENRY "JACK" OR "HUT" BOND, December 12, 1867, Elbert Co, GA; b. June 14, 1840, Madison Co, GA; d. April 11, 1918, On Farm in Madison Co, GA; m.

ix. WILLIAM L POWER, b. 1851, Madison Co, GA; m. DESDEMONIA BERRYMAN, November 14, 1867, Madison Co, GA; b. 1845, Madison Co, GA.

x. OPHELIA POWER, b. Abt. 1854.

xi. OLIVIA POWER, b. Abt. 1856.

34. SARAH F POWER *(DAVID B., FRANCIS)* was born 1815 in Madison Co, GA, and died Aft. 1850 in Madison Co, GA. She married WILLIAM G POWER February 28, 1831 in Madison Co, GA, son of BENNETT POWER. He was born 1803 in Oglethrope Co, GA, and died in Madison Co, GA.
   Children are listed above under (22) William G Power.

35. FRANCIS E POWER *(DAVID B., FRANCIS)* was born Abt. 1819. He married (1) ELIZABETH P WOODS. She was born Abt. 1819, and died April 04, 1901 in Madison Co, GA. He married (2) CATHERINE G SIMS December 19, 1843 in Madison Co, GA. She was born 1823.

Children of FRANCIS POWER and ELIZABETH WOODS are:

   i.   MARY J POWER, b. Abt. 1846.
   ii.   MARTHA POWER, b. Abt. 1847.
   iii.   WILLIAM W POWER, b. Abt. 1851.
   iv.   MENDER POWER, b. Abt. 1853.
   v.   JAMES B POWER, b. Abt. 1855; d. 1943, Madison Co, GA.
   vi.   FRANCIS E POWER, b. Abt. 1861.
   vii.   SARAH C POWER, b. Abt. 1857.

Child of FRANCIS POWER and CATHERINE SIMS is:

   viii.   NANCY[7] POWER, b. 1849.

36. MARTHA C POWER *(DAVID B., FRANCIS)* was born 1823 in Madison Co, GA, and died Bef. 1870 in Madison Co, GA. She married WILLIAM T MOON January 12, 1843 in Madison Co, GA, son of ARCHELAUS MOON and SUSAN POWER. He was born April 13, 1824 in Madison Co, GA, and died January 26, 1883 in Madison Co, GA.

Children of MARTHA POWER and WILLIAM MOON are:

   i.   SUSAN G MOON, b. 1847, Madison Co, GA.
   ii.   ELIZABETH ANN "ANNIE" MOON, b. October 27, 1850, Madison Co, GA; d. July 25, 1889, Madison Co, GA; m. JAMES OLIVER DANIEL, SR, December 21, 1871, Madison Co, GA; b. December 23, 1850, Madison Co, GA; d. June 21, 1928, At Home in Madison Co, GA.
   iii.   ARCHELAUS P MOON, b. 1858, Madison Co, GA.
   iv.   IRENA MOON, b. June 06, 1863, Madison Co, GA; d. March 06, 1895, Madison Co, GA; m. JEFF POWER; b. Abt. 1860.

37. SUSAN E POWER *(DAVID B., FRANCIS)* was born May 04, 1824, and died September 30, 1908 in Madison Co, GA. She married PLEASANT MOON, JR, June 13, 1842 in Madison Co, GA. He was born March 09, 1813 in Elbert Co, GA, and died February 21, 1891 in Madison Co, GA.

Burial: David Fam Cem, Madison Co, GA p72

Children of SUSAN POWER and PLEASANT MOON are:

   i.   SUSAN LOUISA MOON, b. November 09, 1843, Madison Co, GA; d. March 11, 1933, Madison Co, GA; m. ISAAC H MITCH-

ELL, July 05, 1863, Madison Co, GA; b. February 27, 1842; d. January 08, 1884, Madison Co, GA.

ii. JONATHAN D MOON, b. March 18, 1854, Madison Co, GA; d. May 13, 1921, Madison Co, GA; m. LAURA C POWER, November 21, 1878, Madison Co, GA; b. October 20, 1861, Madison Co, GA; d. March 13, 1924, Madison Co, GA.

38. SAMUEL PATTON POWER SR *(DAVID B., FRANCIS)* was born July 09, 1831 in Madison Co, GA, and died October 27, 1911. He married MARTHA ANN DAVID October 20, 1853 in Madison Co, GA, daughter of BERRY DAVID and ELIZABETH VAUGHN. She was born December 11, 1834 in Madison Co GA, and died December 03, 1922. **Military Service: Private May 10, 1862. Transferred to Co E, 37th Regt Ga Inf. May 6, 1863. Surrendered at Greensboro, NC Apr 26, 1865.**

SAM P. POWER, SR, Will, 1905, Madison County, GA

Will Records 1897–1922 page 132 Madison County, Georgia

Will of Sam P. Power, Sr. . . . . 7th day of March 1905

—- my wife M. A. Power should be the longest liver It is my will that my executors herein after named shall keep my estate together and manage and direct it according to their own judgment as may be best for the interest of the estate. My beloved wife is to have a life estate in all my property both real and personal and my said executors are hereby directed to pay over to her all of the rents and profits accruing to my estate during her lifetime

. . . I give and bequeath to the effect at the death of my wife as aforesaid my entire estate to the following children and Grand Children to wit. To Daisy Power and Clyde Power Children of my son B. D. Power jointly one share to Martha Power, Mary Power, Clifford Power, Gussie Power and Nellie Power children of my son W. H. Power jointly One share. To my son J. O. Power one share. To my daughter Lorena wife of W. W. Power one share. To my son Sam P. Power, Jr. One share, and to my son M. C. Power one Share.

. . . . It is my will and I so direct that if at the time of the distribution of my estate any one of my children named in the preceding item of this my will should be indebted to my estate that said indebtedness must be paid before distribution or deducted from their respective shares at the time of the distribution of my estate and I further will and direct that any indebtedness to my estate upon the part of my son B. D. Power or my son W. H. Power at the time of the distribution of my estate shall in like manner be accounted for and settled or deducted from the distributive shares of their respective children named in the third item of my will. And in the event that the mother of the said children of B. D. Power or the mother of said children of W. H. Power should be indebted to my estate a like account and settlement shall be made before or at the time my estate is distributed.

. . . . It is my will and I do give and bequeath in the event of either of Daisy or Clyde Powers death before the distribution of my estate the entire one share to the one then living and it is my will and I do give and bequeath in like manner and under like conditions the entire one share of my estate at the time of its distribution to the surviving children of my son W. H. Power.

. . . I do hereby nominate and appoint my sons Sam P. Power, Jr. and M. C. Power Executors of this my last will and testament. In Testimony whereof I have hereto set my hand this 7th Day of March 1905

S. P. Power Sr

Witnessed by J. C. Martin, A. P. Stevens, W. E. Whetted

(No date of probate given)

Children of SAMUEL POWER and MARTHA DAVID are:

i. BERRY DAVID POWER, b. Abt. 1855; m. MATTIE , Abt. 1880; b. July 1859.

ii. WILLIAM H POWER, b. Abt. 1857, Carlton, Ga; d. 1927, Carlton, Madison Co, GA; m. MARY ELLA POWER, Abt. 1877; b. Abt. 1861; d. 1925.

iii. JAMES OSCAR POWER, b. August 26, 1860; d. January 08, 1928; m. CARRIE BONNER CUNNINGHAM, December 24, 1889, Oglethorpe Co, GA; b. August 18, 1861; d. May 18, 1937.

iv. LORENA POWER, b. Abt. 1867; d. May 23, 1941; m. WILLIAM WILEY POWER, October 04, 1881, Madison Co, GA; b. October 12, 1862; d. June 01, 1927.

v. SAMUEL PATTON POWER, JR, b. March 03, 1873; d. March 21, 1938; m. (1) CORRIE A; b. September 26, 1877; d. December 30, 1960; m. (2) CORRIE A GULLEY, November 21, 1897, Madison Co, GA; b. September 26, 1877, GA; d. December 30, 1960, Madison Co, GA.

vi. MARCUS CLINTON POWER, b. January 1876, Madison Co, GA; m. AURLIE ORIE BELL, July 10, 1898, Elbert Co, GA; b. September 03, 1878, Elbert Co, GA; d. October 03, 1909, Elbert Co, GA.

39. WILLIAM T MOON *(SUSAN POWER, FRANCIS)* was born April 13, 1824 in Madison Co, GA, and died January 26, 1883 in Madison Co, GA. He married MARTHA C POWER January 12, 1843 in Madison Co, GA, daughter of DAVID POWER and SUSANNAH MOON. She was born 1823 in Madison Co, GA, and died Bef. 1870 in Madison Co, GA.

Children are listed above under (36) Martha C Power.

40. MARTHA E MOON *(SUSAN POWER, FRANCIS)* was born 1823 in Madison Co, GA. She married JAMES SIMS September 10, 1839 in Madison Co, GA. He was born Abt. 1820, and died Bef. 1860.

Children of MARTHA MOON and JAMES SIMS are:

i. WILLIAM A SIMS, b. 1840, Madison Co, GA; m. LUCY E; b. 1848.

ii. MARY S SIMS, b. 1842, Madison Co, GA.

iii. JAMES THOMAS SIMS, b. October 07, 1847, Madison Co, GA; d. March 10, 1889, Madison Co, GA; m. JANE "JANIE" P CARITHERS, February 04, 1869, Madison Co, GA; b. January 22, 1849, Madison Co, GA; d. May 22, 1923, Madison Co, GA.

41. WILLIAM WILLIAMSON POWER *(JAMES, FRANCIS)* was born November 14, 1811, and died July 25, 1848. He married MARTHA GRIMES, daughter of THOMAS GRIMES and ANNA POWER. She was born March 13, 1816, and died April 25, 1891.

Children of WILLIAM POWER and MARTHA GRIMES are:

i. ANNA G POWER, b. November 03, 1834, Madison Co, GA; d. January 04, 1893, Madison Co, GA; m. JOSEPH B POWER, December 04, 1856, Madison Co, GA; b. July 1837; d. November 23, 1862, Madison Co, GA.

ii. SUSAN P POWER, b. 1837, Madison Co, GA; d. July 26, 1853.

iii. MARY W "POLLY" POWER, b. May 20, 1839, Madison Co, GA; d. June 07, 1911, Madison Co, GA; m. JOSIAH WELBORN POWER, September 06, 1861, Madison Co, GA; b. January 26, 1840; d. November 21, 1921, Madison Co, GA.

iv. ELIZABETH M POWER, b. June 05, 1832; d. November 16, 1893; m. WILLIAM C SIMMONS, October 25, 1866, Madison Co GA; b. April 14, 1835; d. October 23, 1909.

42. ANN MARIE POWER *(JAMES, FRANCIS)* was born 1815 in Madison Co, GA. She married WILLIAM J SMITH December 14, 1835 in Madison Co, GA. He was born Abt. 1815 in Madison Co, GA, and died Bef. 1840 in Madison Co, GA.

Children of ANN POWER and WILLIAM SMITH are:

i. STEPHEN P SMITH, b. 1837, Madison Co, GA; m. MARY (WYNN) WINN, October 20, 1859, Madison Co, GA; b. December 13, 1842, Madison Co, GA. **Military Service: Private Mar. 4, 1862. Transferred to Co. E, 37th Regt. Ga. Inf. May 6, 1863. Surrendered at Greensboro, N.C. Apr. 26, 1865**

    ii. ELIZABETH W SMITH, b. 1838, Madison Co, GA; m. COLUM-
BUS W BENNETT, October 02, 1855, Madison Co, GA; b. 1837,
VA; d. October 11, 1863, Camp Douglas Prison, IL. **Military Service: Private May 10, 1862. Transferred to Co. E, 37th Regt. Ga.
Inf. May 6, 1863. Captured at Chickamauga, Ga. Sept. 19, 1863.
Died of diarrhoea at Camp Dougles, Ill. Oct. 11, 1863.**

43. FRANCIS POWER *(JAMES, FRANCIS)* was born April 05, 1824, and
died 1864 in Killed at the battle of Resaca Ga. . He married SARAH M GRA-
HAM December 08, 1843 in Madison Co, GA. She was born Abt. 1826, and
died Bet. 1870 - 1880 in Madison Co, GA.
**FRANCIS POWER: Co B, 9th Battalion, Ga Volunteer Infantry, Army of Tenn,
CSA**
**Francis Power - Jr 2d Lieutenant Mar 4, 1862. Elected 2d Lieutenant in 1862.
Transferred to Co E, 37th Regt. Ga Inf. as 1st Lieutenant May 6, 1863. Killed at
Chickamauga, Ga. Sept 19, 1863.** Burial: Fork Cemetery, Carlton, Madison Co,
GA p14
    Children of FRANCIS POWER and SARAH GRAHAM are:
    i. CHARLES POWER, b. Abt. 1849; d. December 30, 1896; m.
SARAH ELLA C LONG, November 30, 1880, Madison Co, GA;
b. 1851.
    ii. MARY F POWER, b. Abt. 1851; m. GROVER WILLIAMS,
December 25, 1873, Madison Co, GA; b. Abt. 1850.
    iii. GEORGIA A POWER, b. Abt. 1853; d. Bef. 1879; m. JACOB
A AMBROSE, Abt. 1870; b. July 25, 1854; d. November 21,
1926.
    iv. JOSEPHINA POWER, b. Abt. 1856.
    v. JAMES G POWER, b. 1845, Madison Co, GA; m. MARY
FRANCES LONG, December 24, 1867, Madison Co, GA; b.
1846, Madison Co, GA.
    vi. WILLIAM WILLIAMSON POWER, b. July 12, 1846, Madison
Co, GA; d. August 22, 1922, Buford, Gwinnett Co, GA.
    vii. HARRIETT JOSEPHINE POWER, b. October 18, 1855; m.
JACOB A AMBROSE, Abt. 1879; b. July 25, 1854; d. November
21, 1926.
    viii. ELIZABETH J POWER, b. 1858, Madison Co, GA; m. AFT
STREET; b. Abt. 1855.

44. SUSANNA SUSAN POWER *(JAMES, FRANCIS,)* was born 1830 in Madison Co, GA, and died in Madison Co, GA. She married JAMES N EVANS

December 31, 1845 in Madison Co, GA. He was born 1819 in Madison Co, GA, and died 1855 in Madison Co, GA.

Children of SUSANNA POWER and JAMES EVANS are:

    i. ELIZABETH POWER EVANS, b. February 08, 1847, Madison Co, GA; d. June 02, 1932, Madison Co, GA; m. JAMES ALEXANDER HART, December 05, 1872, Prob Athens, Clarke Co, GA; b. March 26, 1849, Madison Co, GA; d. July 01, 1918, Madison Co, GA.

    ii. MARY F EVANS, b. 1848, Madison Co, GA; m. FRANCIS MARION WILEY, 1866; b. 1838, Jackson Co, GA.

    iii. SUSAN CLEMENTINE EVANS, b. 1851, Madison Co, GA; d. May 28, 1938; m. WILLIAM WILEY POWER, December 01, 1871, Madison Co, GA; b. June 23, 1851, Madison Co, GA; d. November 29, 1937, Athens, Clarke Co, GA.

    iv. LUCY A EVANS, b. 1854, Madison Co, GA.

45. LUCY JANE POWER *(JAMES, FRANCIS)* was born October 05, 1832 in Madison Co, GA, and died January 14, 1903 in Madison Co, GA. She married CHARLES C GRAHAM May 24, 1849 in Madison Co, GA. He was born 1828 in Madison Co, GA, and died May 25, 1863 in Home in Madison Co, GA. **Military Service: Co B. 9th Georgia Batallion Private May 10, 1862. Sent to hospital as nurse Jan. 4, 1863. Died of chronic diarrhoea, at home in Madison County, Ga. May 25, 1863.**

Children of LUCY POWER and CHARLES GRAHAM are:

    i. JAMES P GRAHAM, b. February 27, 1853, Madison Co, GA; d. April 15, 1887, Madison Co, GA; m. SUSAN "SUSIE" ANN DANIEL, January 24, 1878, Madison Co, GA; b. August 13, 1860, Madison Co, GA; d. August 23, 1915, Madison Co, GA.

    ii. FRANCIS "FRANK" WILLIAMSON GRAHAM, b. October 20, 1856, Madison Co, GA; d. December 06, 1949; m. FRANCES AMELIA DANIEL, Abt. 1881, Madison Co, GA; b. March 16, 1863; d. March 02, 1935.

    iii. ALICE F GRAHAM, b. May 1860, Madison Co, GA; m. ROBERT T DANIEL, December 25, 1878, Madison Co, GA; b. July 1856, Madison Co, GA.

    iv. LOU CHARLIE GRAHAM, b. April 09, 1862, Madison Co, GA; d. November 19, 1934, Madison Co, GA; m. WILLIAM PALMER ROWE, December 01, 1878, Madison Co, GA; b. May 21, 1859, Madison Co, GA; d. April 19, 1928, Home in Madison Co, GA.

46. ELIZABETH GRIMES *(ANNA POWER, FRANCIS)* was born November 05, 1811 in Madison Co, GA, and died May 30, 1854 in Madison Co, GA. She married (1) WILLIAM POWER July 31, 1827 in Madison Co, GA, son of DAVID POWER and SUSANNAH MOON. He was born Abt. 1810, and died 1834 in Madison Co, GA. She married (2) HENRY P SMITH February 1839 in Madison Co, GA. He was born 1809 in Madison Co, GA, and died Aft. 1870.

Notes for HENRY P SMITH: Amnesty Oath: 1865, Dark, grey hair, grey eyes, 6,' age 57, farmer.

Children of ELIZABETH GRIMES and HENRY SMITH are:

    i.   ROBERT MILTON SMITH, b. 1839, Madison Co, GA; m. MARY JANE WOODS, February 16, 1871, Madison Co, GA; b. April 11, 1842, Madison Co, GA; d. January 11, 1928, Madison Co, GA. Amnesty Oath: 1865, Fair, light hair, blue eyes, 5'5," age 24

    ii.   SIDNEY ANN "LOU" SMITH, b. August 21, 1841, Madison Co, GA; d. December 03, 1886, Madison Co, GA; m. JOHN RUSSELL, February 07, 1867, Madison Co, GA; b. October 17, 1839, Madison Co, GA; d. March 21, 1897, Madison Co, GA.
Co B, 9th Battalion, Ga Volunteer Infantry, Army of Tenn. CSA John Russell - Private Mar 4, 1862. Transferred to Co E, 37th Regt Ga Inf. May 6, 1863. Surrendered at Greensboro, NC Apr 26, 1865.

    iii.   WILLIAM H "BILLY" SMITH, b. December 02, 1843, Madison Co, GA; d. Aft. 1920, Madison Co, GA; m. ELIZA ARTEMISSIE WOODS, January 05, 1871, Madison Co, GA; b. November 21, 1850, Madison Co, GA; d. December 05, 1919, Madison Co, GA.
Co B, 9th Battalion, Ga Volunteer Infantry, Army of Tenn. CSA **William H Smith - Private Mar 4, 1862. Transferred to Co E, 37th Regt Ga Inf. May 6, 1863. In hospital, wounded, close of war. (Born in Ga Dec 2, 1843)**
William H Smith, 1865 Amnesty Oath - fair, auburn hair, grey eyes, 5'10," age 21, farmer

    iv.   JASPER JONES SMITH, b. August 03, 1845, Madison Co, GA; d. November 25, 1915, Confederate Soldiers' Home in Atlanta, GA; m. ZEMULA FRANCES WOODS, Jan. 05, 1871, Madison Co, GA; b. July 12, 1843, Madison Co, GA; d. Aug. 01, 1910, Madison Co, GA.
Co E, 37th Regiment, Ga Volunteer Infantry, Army of Tenn. CSA

Jasper J Smith - Private Aug 10, 1863. Surrendered at Greensboro, NC Apr 26, 1865. (Born in Madison County, Ga Aug 3, 1845. Died at Confederate Soldiers' Home in Atlanta, Ga Nov 15, 1915.)

   v.   PERMELIA JANE SMITH, b. March 25, 1847, Madison Co, GA; d. July 21, 1933, Madison Co, GA; m. JAMES THOMAS CARITHERS, SR, August 06, 1874, Madison Co, GA; b. December 31, 1852, Madison Co, GA; d. April 15, 1928, Madison Co, GA.

   vi.   STEPHEN T SMITH, b. 1849, Madison Co, GA; d. Bef. 1910; m. LUCINDA MARGARET PORTERFIELD, Abt. 1876; b. 1851, Madison Co, GA; d. 1928, Madison Co, GA.

47. JOHN POWER GRIMES *(ANNA POWER, FRANCIS)* was born January 22, 1814 in Madison Co, GA, and died January 09, 1874 in Tallapoosa Co, AL. He married (2) LINDA ROWE August 03, 1834 in Madison Co, GA, daughter of MARTIN ROWE. She was born July 03, 1815 in Madison Co, GA, and died February 29, 1884 in Tallapoosa Co, AL.

   Children of JOHN GRIMES and LINDA ROWE are:

   i.   FANNIE NORTH GRIMES, b. November 02, 1835, Madison Co, GA; d. December 27, 1883, Tallapoosa Co, AL; m. RICHARD HENRY HUNT, October 23, 1870, Tallapoosa Co, AL; b. November 06, 1818, GA; d. August 08, 1884, New Site, AL.

   ii.   ANNIE MINOR GRIMES, b. July 12, 1837, Madison Co, GA.

   iii.   THOMAS MARTIN GRIMES, b. May 13, 1839, Madison Co, GA; d. March 13, 1913, Weogufka, AL.

   iv.   MARTHA JUDSON GRIMES, b. March 20, 1841, Madison Co, GA; d. August 14, 1922; m. JEREMIAH JONES, April 30, 1878; b. July 26, 1851; d. August 14, 1922.

   v.   STEPHEN ROWE GRIMES, b. February 25, 1843, Madison Co, GA; d. August 03, 1898; m. MARTHA A RIDDLE, September 28, 1866, Tallapoosa Co, AL; b. February 1846.

   vi.   JAMES EBER GRIMES, b. November 18, 1845, Madison Co, GA; d. 1930; m. MARTHA L GOSS, January 03, 1867, Tallapoosa Co, AL; b. July 1849, AL; d. 1925.

   vii.   WILLIAM TAYLOR GRIMES, b. July 18, 1848, Madison Co, GA; d. August 17, 1923; m. MARTHA MATILDA FOSHEE, December 24, 1867, AL; b. July 11, 1845; d. February 13, 1927, AL.

   viii.   CHARLES BRITTAN GRIMES, b. February 17, 1851, New Site, AL; d. January 23, 1926, New Site, AL; m. ALMETIA MAR-

ZEE GILLIAM, November 23, 1873, Tallapoosa Co, AL; b. Abt. 1855.

ix.   JOHN PALMER GRIMES, b. September 14, 1853, New Site, AL.

x.   GEORGE W GRIMES, b. June 23, 1856, New Site, AL.

xi.   DOCK GRIMES, b. August 27, 1858, New Site, AL.

48. MARTHA GRIMES *(ANNA POWER, FRANCIS)* was born March 13, 1816, and died April 25, 1891. She married WILLIAM WILLIAMSON POWER, son of JAMES POWER and ELIZABETH WILLIAMSON. He was born November 14, 1811, and died July 25, 1848.

Children are listed above under (41) William Williamson Power.

49. STEPHEN ROWE *(ANNA POWER, FRANCIS)* was born 1825 in Madison Co, GA, and died September 04, 1864 in Atlanta, GA in CSA. He married FRANCES P LANDERS September 07, 1850 in Madison Co, GA. She was born 1832 in Madison Co, GA. **Military Service: Private Cp G. 3rd Regiment, Georgia Cavalry (State Guards)**

Children of STEPHEN ROWE and FRANCES LANDERS are:

i.   JAMES T "JIM" ROWE, b. March 13, 1852, Madison Co, GA; d. April 04, 1924, Madison Co, GA; m. MARTHA ANN THOMPSON, January 06, 1878, Madison Co, GA; b. September 30, 1858, Madison Co, GA; d. September 02, 1926, Madison Co, GA.

ii.   JOHN M ROWE, b. 1854.

iii. WILLIAM J ROWE, b. September 02, 1856; d. August 12, 1916; m. MARIA MAUDE POWER; b. August 05, 1869, Madison Co, GA; d. June 15, 1914.

50. JAMES POWER [REV] ROWE *(ANNA POWER, FRANCIS)* was born 1827 in Madison Co, GA, and died Bef. 1885. He married MARY ANN M GRAHAM November 23, 1848 in Madison Co, GA. She was born June 06, 1830 in Madison Co, GA.

Children of JAMES ROWE and MARY GRAHAM are:

i.   HARRIETT GRAHAM ROWE, b. October 08, 1849, Madison Co, GA; d. May 17, 1909; m. GABRIEL WILHITE GRIMES, October 24, 1867, Madison Co, GA; b. March 03, 1836, Madison Co, GA; d. August 10, 1895, Jackson Co, GA.

Gabriel Wilhite Grimes served the Confederacy during the Civil War. He volunteered on July 10, 1861, and was a sergeant in the 16th Georgia Volunteer Infantry Regiment. He was a prisoner of war held at Elmira, New York, captured June 1, 1864. He was

released May 19, 1865, and signed an Oath of Allegiance while in New York. On this oath, he is described as being from Athens, GA, having a blonde (?) complexion, light hair, grey eyes, and being 6 feet tall. On one of the copies of the "Roll of Prisoners of War," there is the remark that he "was over persuaded to do so by misrepresentations, etc. (?) Desires to go to (illegible) where he has some friends residing.

  ii. ANN ROWE, b. December 05, 1851, Madison Co, GA; m. W GRADY JOHNSON; b. Abt. 1850.

 iii. MARTIN A "BUD" ROWE, b. February 07, 1853, Madison Co, GA.

 iv. MARTHA J ROWE, b. January 17, 1855, Madison Co, GA.

  v. SARAH FRANCES ROWE, b. February 10, 1858, Madison Co, GA.

 vi. WILLIAM PALMER ROWE, b. May 21, 1859, Madison Co, GA; d. April 19, 1928, Home in Madison Co, GA; m. LOU CHARLIE GRAHAM, December 01, 1878, Madison Co, GA; b. April 09, 1862, Madison Co, GA; d. November 19, 1934, Madison Co, GA

DESCENDANTS OF ISAAC DAVID

Generation No. 1

1. ISSAC DAVID was born May 30, 1756 in Virginia, and died March 1840 in Madison Co GA. He was the son of Peter David and Elizabeth Morrisette. He married (1) MILDRED "MILLY" WHITE Abt. 1774, daughter of HENRY WHITE and CELIA PAGE. She was born January 23, 1755 in Virginia, and died February 26, 1798 in Oglethorpe Co. Ga. He married (2) SUSANNAH WILKINS VAUGHN October 14, 1798, daughter of JAMES WILKINS and ARABELLA SMITH. She was born Abt. 1754 in Virginia, and died Abt. 1855 in Madison, Co Ga.

Military service: Revolutionary War Veteran

Children of ISSAC DAVID and MILDRED WHITE are:

2.   i.   PERLINA WHITE DAVID, b. June 28, 1776, VA; d. November 06, 1857, Jackson Co, GA.
3.   ii.   ISAIAH DAVID, b. Abt. 1778; d. Abt. 1839.
       iii. CELIA DAVID, b. Abt. 1780; m. UNKNOWN BALDWIN; b. Abt. 1775.
4.   iv.   HENRY DAVID, b. Abt. 1782; d. Abt. 1808.
       v.   CHARITY DAVID, b. Abt. 1784; m. BAILEY BROOKS; b. Abt. 1788.
5.   vi.   ELIZABETH DAVID, b. July 1788, Wilkes Co; d. October 07, 1873, Elbert Co. Ga.
6.   vii. MILDRED DAVID, b. Abt. 1790; d. Bef. 1839.
7.   viii. LOCKY DAVID, b. Abt. 1791.
8.   ix.   CAROLINE DAVID, b. Abt. 1792, Virginia.
9.   x.   JACOB WHITE DAVID, b. Abt. 1794, Elbert Co. Ga; d. August 30, 1871, Elbert Co. Ga.

Generation No. 2

2. PERLINA WHITE DAVID *(ISSAC)* was born June 28, 1776 in VA, and died November 06, 1857 in Jackson Co, GA. She married HENRY [REV] DAVID January 10, 1800 in VA, son of PETER DAVID and MARY WHITE. He was born January 11, 1781 in VA, and died June 15, 1845 in Franklin Co, GA.

Children of PERLINA DAVID and HENRY DAVID are:

10.   i.   JAMES HORATIO DAVID, b. August 27, 1799, Franklin Co Ga; d. January 21, 1878.

      ii. WILLIAM A DAVID, b. September 30, 1801, Franklin Co, GA; m. SARAH NEAL; b. Abt. 1810.

11.   iii. MILDRED "MILLIE" W DAVID, b. May 1803, GA; d. Aft. 1900.

12.   iv. HENRY FRANKLIN DAVID, b. September 09, 1805; d. November 17, 1887, Franklin Co, GA.

      v. JONATHAN DAVID, b. March 18, 1807, Franklin Co Ga; d. August 27, 1808.

13.   vi. ISSAC MORRISETT DAVID, b. August 26, 1809, Franklin Co Ga; d. March 20, 1865, Banks Co

    vii. Polly J DAVID, b. February 05, 1811, Franklin Co, GA; m. RICHARD NEAL, JR, November 13, 1842, Jackson Co, GA; b. Abt. 1810.

14.   viii. NANCY W DAVID, b. February 06, 1813, Franklin Co Ga.

    ix. SIMEON DAVID, b. September 14, 1814, Franklin Co Ga; d. September 28, 1814, Franklin Co Ga.

    x. PALLINA WHITE DAVID, b. May 06, 1818, Franklin Co, GA; m. MARION SEWELL, December 03, 1836, Franklin Co, GA; b. Nov. 23, 1816, Banks Co, GA; d. Oct. 25, 1883, Polk Co, GA.

    xi. MARY H DAVID, b. May 28, 1819, Franklin Co Ga.

3. ISAIAH DAVID *(ISSAC)* was born Abt. 1778, and died Abt. 1839. He married SUSANNAH DAVID. She was born Abt. 1780.

    Children of ISAIAH DAVID and SUSANNAH DAVID are:

    i. MARY DAVID, b. Abt. 1800.

    ii. SUSANNAH DAVID, b. Abt. 1801.

    iii. MILLY DAVID, b. Abt. 1803.

    iv. SINTHA DAVID, b. Abt. 1805; m. SAMUEL BARGO; b. Abt. 1800.

    v. CHARITY DAVID, b. Abt. 1809; m. CHRISTOPHER COBLE.

    vi. ELIZABETH DAVID, b. Abt. 1809; m. ALLEN WILSON.

    vii. ISAIAH DAVID, b. Abt. 1813.

    viii. MARY JANE DAVID, b. Abt. 1821; m. SIMON CRADDOCK; b. Abt. 1815.

4. HENRY DAVID *(ISSAC)* was born Abt. 1782, and died Abt. 1808. He married MARY MATHEWS, daughter of WILLIAM MATHEWS and MARY MILLER. She was born Abt. 1787 in of Wilkes Co., Georgia, and died Abt. 1835.

    Children of HENRY DAVID and MARY MATHEWS are:

15.   i. BERRY MATHEWS DAVID, b. Abt. 1807, Oglethorpe Co Ga; d. Abt. 1853, Madison Co Ga.

16.   ii.   ELIZABETH DAVID, b. Abt. 1805, Madison Co GA.
17.   iii. PERLINA KEZIAH DAVID, b. April 01, 1808.

5. ELIZABETH DAVID *(ISSAC)* was born July 1788 in Wilkes Co, and died October 07, 1873 in Elbert Co. Ga. She married ALEXANDER VAUGHN August 20, 1807 in Elbert Co Ga, son of JAMES VAUGHN and SUSANNAH VAUGHN. He was born Abt. 1784 in Amelia Co Virginia, and died May 28, 1880 in Ga.

 Children of ELIZABETH DAVID and ALEXANDER VAUGHN are:
(See Descendants of Alexander Vaughn)
  i.   ISAIAH H VAUGHN.
18.   ii.   WILLIAM DAVID VAUGHN, b. May 12, 1808, Elbert Co Ga; d. Abt. 1855, Madison Co. Ga.
19.   iii. MARTHA ELIZABETH VAUGHN, b. March 04, 1812, Elbert Co Ga; d. July 17, 1860, Elbert Co Ga.
20.   iv.   MILDRED VAUGHN, b. Abt. 1814.
21.   v.   JAMES W. VAUGHN, b. Abt. 1815, Elbert Co Ga.
  vi. ELIZABETH PENDLETON VAUGHN, b. September 05, 1818; m. UNKNOWN BROWN.
22.   vii. JACOB DAVID VAUGHN, b. March 24, 1823; d. May 31, 1862, Savanah Ga.
  viii. PERLINA VAUGHN, b. Abt. 1824; m. ISSAC D. GLORE, October 20, 1850; b. Abt. 1827. More About ISSAC D. GLORE: **Military service: Co F 15th Ga Inf private July 15,1861. Captured and paroled at Hartwell, Ga. May 19,1865.**
23.   ix.   ALEXANDER VAUGHN, b. Abt. 1826, Elbert Co Ga; d. **July 06, 1863, Gettysburg, Pa.**
  x.   JOHN HENRY VAUGHN, b. Abt. 1828, Elbert Co Ga; d. July 01, 1862, Charlottesville, Va; m. MALITTA P. TUCKER, July 11, 1850; b. Abt. 1828. **Military service: Private Co H 38th Ga Inf.**
  xi. MARY CAROLINA VAUGHN, b. January 30, 1830; m. UNKNOWN HEWELL.
24.   xii. ISAAC D VAUGHN, b. Bet. 1810 - 1815, Elbert Co, GA; d. June 1877, Elbert Co Ga.

6. MILDRED DAVID *(ISSAC)* was born Abt. 1790, and died Bef. 1839. She married GEORGE WILEY February 04, 1808 in Elbert Co Ga. He was born Bet. 1770 - 1780 in Georgia.

 Children of MILDRED DAVID and GEORGE WILEY are:
  i.   FLEMING WILEY, b. Aft. 1808.

    ii.   GEORGE W WILEY, b. Aft. 1808.

    iii. ISSAC DAVID WILEY, b. Aft. 1808.

    iv. JANE WILEY, b. Aft. 1808; d. Aft. 1842; m. STEPHEN BEN-NETT.

    v.   JOHN J WILEY, b. Aft. 1808.

    vi. JOSEPHUS WILEY, b. Aft. 1808.

    vii. JULY ANN WILEY, b. Aft. 1808; m. SAMUEL B HAY.

    viii. LUCINDA WILEY, b. Aft. 1808; m. RILEY A WILLINGHAM.

    ix. NANCY WILEY, b. Aft. 1808; m. THOMAS NICHOLS.

    x.   SILVANUS G WILEY, b. Aft. 1808. **Military service: private Co F 15th Ga July 15, 1861. Sick in hospital February 28,1865. No later record**

    xi. UNKNOWN WILEY, b. Aft. 1808.

    xii. WILLIAM SCOTT WILEY, b. Abt. 1809.

25.   xiii. PERLINA JOHNSON WILEY, b. Abt. 1810.

7. LOCKY DAVID *(ISSAC)* was born Abt. 1791. She married BIRD MOON May 01, 1814 in Madison Co GA. He was born Abt. 1790. Military service: War of 1812—- Served Capt M. Boon's Co Georgia Militia

    Children of LOCKY DAVID and BIRD MOON are:

    i.   JEPTHA H MOON, b. Abt. 1814; d. January 05, 1866; m. SUSAN POWER, October 17, 1843; b. Abt. 1820.

    ii. ELIZABETH MOON, b. Abt. April 16, 1814; d. 1898; m. WIL-LIAM PARHAM.

    iii. MARY A MOON, b. Abt. 1815; m. JAMES PHELPS, July 19, 1835.

    iv. SUSAN A MOON, b. Abt. 1821; m. JOHN WOFFORD PHELPS.

    v.   WILLIAM H MOON, b. Abt. 1822; d. June 17, 1862. **Military service: private Co C 15th Ga Inf June 17,1862. Died in camp June 17,1862.**

    vi. JACOB D MOON, b. Abt. 1824; d. June 28, 1864, Kennesaw Mt Ga; m. SARAH WHITE, December 03, 1846, Elbert Co Ga; b. Abt. 1825. **Military service: Co E 2nd Ga State Troops Killed Kennesaw Mt. 6/28/1864**

    vii. PERLINA W MOON, b. November 07, 1824; m. JAMES W KING, August 09, 1848; b. 1824; d. March 16, 1865, Richmond, Va. **Military service: Private Co A 16th Ga Captured at Deep Bottom, Va. Aug. 16, 1864. Paroled at Elmira, N.Y., for exchange Mar. 2, 1865. Died of chronic diarrhoea and pneumonia in Jackson Hospital, Richmond, Va., Mar. 16, 1865.**

    viii. THIRSTY MOON, b. Abt. 1825; m. JAMES D MEAD; b. April 06, 1848.

    ix. ISSAC M MOON, b. Abt. 1827; d. Bef. 1860; m. ELIZABETH BUTLER.

    x. JESSE M MOON, b. Abt. 1828; m. MARTHA WHITE, December 07, 1847, Elbert Co Ga; b. Abt. 1828. **Military service: Co C 15th Georgia**

    xi. BIRD A MOON, b. Abt. 1832; d. December 24, 1864, Murfreesboro, Tn; m. EMALINE BOOTH, October 17, 1851; b. Abt. 1830. **Military service: Private Co E 37th Ga Infantry Transferred to Co G May 6 1863 Killed Dec. 1864 at the 2nd Battle of Murfreesboro**

8. CAROLINE DAVID *(ISSAC)* was born Abt. 1792 in Virginia. She married ABNER GLORE. He was born Abt. 1792 in Virginia.

    Children of CAROLINE DAVID and ABNER GLORE are:

    i. MELISSA GLORE, b. Abt. 1822; m. GEORGE NATHANIEL EVANS, November 02, 1845, Madison Co GA.

    ii. JACOB W D GLORE, b. Abt. 1824; m. NANCY M. .

    iii. SUSAN GLORE, b. Abt. 1825; m. WILSON PENN BERRYMAN, February 02, 1854, Madison Co GA; b. Abt. 1820.

    iv. PALINA GLORE, b. Abt. 1826.

    v. JOSEPH GLORE, b. Abt. 1833. **Military service: Private Co E 37th Ga Inf**

    vi. JOHN S. GLORE, b. Abt. 1833. **Military service: private Co F 15th Ga Inf July 15,1861. Captured at Morristown, Tenn., January 18,1864. Enlisted in U. S. Army October 6,1864**

    vii. ISSAC D. GLORE, b. Abt. 1827; m. PERLINA VAUGHN, October 20, 1850; b. Abt. 1824. **Military service: Co F 15th Ga Inf private July 15,1861. Captured and paroled at Hartwell, Ga. May 19,1865.**

9. JACOB WHITE DAVID *(ISSAC)* was born Abt. 1794 in Elbert Co. Ga, and died August 30, 1871 in Elbert Co. Ga. He married MARGARET ALMOND January 02, 1817 in Elbert Co Ga. She was born Abt. 1793, and died January 31, 1857 in Harris Co Ga. **Military service: Private Co K 12th Ga Cavalry State Guards**

    Children of JACOB DAVID and MARGARET ALMOND are:

    i. SUSAN DAVID, b. September 30, 1820, Elbert Co. Ga; d. October 15, 1906.

    ii. JOHN ISSAC DAVID, b. Oct. 12, 1824, Elbert Co Ga; d. Sept. 08, 1888, Muscogee Co, Ga.

26.   iii.   JACOB WHITE DAVID, JR., b. May 05, 1825, Elbert Co. Ga; d. Jan 05, 1873, Huntsville, Ala.
       iv.   LIVONIA DAVID, b. Abt. 1827.
        v.   JAMES A DAVID, b. Abt. 1828, Elbert Co. Ga; m. MARY E FULLER, October 13, 1848.
       vi.   JANE EMILIA DAVID, b. February 22, 1828; d. September 20, 1905.
      vii.   ELIZABETH DAVID, b. Abt. 1830, Elbert Co. Ga; m. GREEN MCCREARY.
     viii.   SARAH H DAVID, b. Abt. 1830, Ga.
       ix.   WILLIAM JEROME DAVID, b. February 12, 1830; d. September 12, 1889. **Military service: Private Co K 12th Ga Cavalry St Troops**
        x.   CLEMENTINE DAVID, b. Abt. 1831.
       xi.   MARGARET LOUISE DAVID, b. January 28, 1835; d. September 08, 1908; m. JAMES CLINTON BLACKMON, February 12, 1867.
      xii.   FRANCIS COLUMBUS DAVID, b. March 10, 1837, Elbert Co. Ga; d. July 23, 1911, Huntsville, Ala. **Military service: Ensign, 10th Div. 1st Brigade , Ga Militia**
     xiii.   HENRY CLAY DAVID, b. Abt. 1844; d. March 20, 1888. **Military service: Private Co H 38th Ga Inf October 23, 1863. Roll dated November 6, 1864, last on file,shows him present. No later record.**
      xiv.   JOSEPHINE AUGUSTA DAVID, b. July 11, 1845; d. March 08, 1894; m. HENRY CLAY BLACKMON; b. Abt. 1840.

Generation No. 3

10. JAMES HORATIO DAVID *(PERLINA WHITE, ISSAC)* was born August 27, 1799 in Franklin Co Ga, and died January 21, 1878. He married (1) NANCY HENRY December 09, 1819. She was born Bef. 1803 in Elbert Co, GA. He married (2) THIRZA BOWEN July 31, 1823. She was born Abt. 1803.
       Children of JAMES DAVID and THIRZA BOWEN are:
        i.   ELEANOR E DAVID, b. May 10, 1825.
       ii.   MARY JULIETTE DAVID, b. December 07, 1826; m. // NEAL; b. Abt. 1820.
      iii.   PALINA CHARITY DAVID, b. Abt. 1828; m. // BELL; b. Abt. 1825.
       iv.   SIMEON BOWEN DAVID, b. January 29, 1829.
        v.   THIRZA A. DAVID, b. Abt. 1833.

vi.   OWEN THOMAS DAVID, b. September 06, 1835, Jackson Co
      Ga; d. October 05, 1864.

vii. PILLONA WHITE DAVID, b. November 19, 1839; m. // ALEX-
      ANDER; b. Abt. 1830.

viii. HORATIO JAMES DAVID, b. April 1842. **Military Service:
      private July 17,1861. Appointed 4th Cor- poral September 1861.
      Elected Jr. 2d Lieutenant March1, 1863. Wounded at Chancellors-
      ville, Va. May 3, 1863. Wounded in eye, resulting in loss of sight, at
      Deep Bottom, Va. August 16,1864. Retired on account of wounds
      February 1865. Roll for February 1865, shows he was elected 1st
      Lieutenant of Co. C, March 1,1863, but name does not appear on
      rolls of this company. Captured and paroled, Athens, Ga. May
      8,1865. (Born in Georgia December 4, 1842.)**

11. MILDRED "MILLIE" W DAVID *(PERLINA WHITE, ISSAC)* was born
May 1803 in GA, and died Aft. 1900. She married JOHN SIMMONS January
18, 1827 in Madison Co, GA, son of ISAAC SIMMONS and MARY POWER.
He was born Abt. 1803, and died December 1866.

Children of MILDRED DAVID and JOHN SIMMONS are:

i.   WYLEY C SIMMONS, b. October 1827, Madison Co, GA.

ii. MARY "POLLY" R SIMMONS, b. January 30, 1830, Madison
     Co, GA; d. February 08, 1901, Madison Co, GA; m. WILLIAM
     ANDREW JACKSON BROWN, May 25, 1848, Madison Co,
     GA; b. January 31, 1825, Madison Co, GA; d. January 21, 1909,
     Madison Co, GA.
     **Military Service: Co E, 37th Regiment, Ga Volunteer Infantry,
     Army of Tenn. CSA
     W A J Brown - Private Aug 6, 1863. Surrendered at Greensboro,
     NC Apr 26, 1865. (Born in Oglethorpe County, Ga in 1825)**

iii. SARAH E SIMMONS, b. July 05, 1835, Madison Co, GA; d.
     April 30, 1914, Madison Co, GA; m. JAMES LAWSON DUD-
     LEY, January 20, 1853, Madison Co, GA; b. March 07, 1831,
     Madison Co, GA; d. September 07, 1893, Madison Co, GA.
     **Milirary Service: Co B, 9th Battalion, Ga Volunteer Infantry, Army
     of Tenn. CSA
     Lawson Dudley - Private Mar 1862. Wounded. Transferred to Co
     E, 37th Regt
     Ga Inf. May 6, 1863. Surrendered at Greensboro, NC Apr 26,
     1865.**

iv. MILLEY JANE SIMMONS, b. November 16, 1847, Madison
     Co, GA; d. March 28, 1898, Madison Co, GA; m. JOHN T WIL-
     SON; b. February 26, 1854; d. June 26, 1935, Madison Co,

v.   SYDNEY C SIMMONS, b. October 1827.

vi. MILLY JANE "JANIE" SIMMONS, b. November 16, 1847, Madison Co, GA; d. March 28, 1898, Madison Co, GA; m. JOHN THOMAS WILSON; b. February 24, 1854; d. June 26, 1935, Madison Co, GA.

12. HENRY FRANKLIN DAVID *(PERLINA WHITE, ISSAC)* was born September 09, 1805, and died November 17, 1887 in Franklin Co, GA. He married MARY SMITH CRISLER September 07, 1826. She was born February 02, 1809 in Franklin Co, GA, and died September 11, 1892 in Franklin Co, GA. **Military service: Col Mitchell's Regiment Ga Militia**

Children of HENRY DAVID and MARY CRISLER are:

i.   NANCY JOHNSON DAVID, b. August 09, 1828, Franklin Co, GA; d. 1902, Madison Co, GA; m. JAMES P FITZPATRICK, November 20, 1845, Oglethorpe Co, GA; b. 1824, Oglethorpe Co, GA; d. August 1864.

Madison Co, Ga Will Book "B," pg 190–191 11/3/1862: 8/20/1864

JAMES P. FITZPATRICK: Going into Confederate Service. Names wife, Nancy J; children: Georgia Fitzpatrick, Addison B Fitzpatrick, Henry T Fitzpatrick, Nancy J, James A, Mary F P, Elizabeth S Fitzpatrick, William B M, Rhoda C V B Fitzpatrick. **Military service: Private Co A 16th Georgia Inf.**

ii. MARY ANN PALINA DAVID, b. January 06, 1831, Franklin Co, GA; d. December 05, 1904; m. WILLIAM G WADE, October 13, 1850, Franklin Co, GA; b. Abt. 1830, Franklin Co, GA. **Military Service: private September 17,1862 . Co H 15th Georgia Infantry Died in Edray, W. Va. hospital May 5,1864 .**

iii. THEODOSIA ALLEN DAVID, b. January 26, 1834, Franklin Co, GA; d. March 18, 1911; m. JAMES V WALKER, December 19, 1852, Franklin Co, GA; b. Abt. 1830.

iv. VIRGINIA JACKSON DAVID, b. March 1835, Franklin Co, GA; d. August 1864; m. JAMES WILSON, January 13, 1857, Franklin Co, GA; b. Abt. 1835.

v.   HENRY DAVID, b. April 22, 1837, Franklin Co, GA; d. February 22, 1842, Franklin Co, GA.

vi. LUCY ARTIMESIA DAVID, b. September 28, 1838, Franklin Co, GA; d. June 10, 1904; m. (1) WILLIAM DAVID DALRYMPLE; b. Abt. 1835; m. (2) JOHN COLUMBUS CARSON, November 19, 1855, Franklin Co, GA; b. 1833, Franklin Co, GA; d. 1863, Civil War in E TN. **Military Service: Co E 13 Georgia Cavalry**

vii.   ROSANA CRISTLER DAVID, b. June 1840, Franklin Co, GA; d. July 1840, Franklin Co, GA.

viii. LOIS MENTARIA DAVID, b. July 1841, Franklin Co, GA; d. November 1889; m. HENRY DAVID CARSON, August 21, 1860; b. April 25, 1837, Franklin Co, GA; d. April 23, 1916, Benton, AR. **Military Service: Co E 13 Georgia Cavalry**

ix.   ABSALOM N DAVID, b. 1843.

x.   ELIZABETH CARSON DAVID, b. August 27, 1844, Franklin Co, GA; m. ? WILSON; b. Abt. 1830.

xi.   HENRY FRANKLIN DAVID, JR, b. July 27, 1847, Franklin Co, GA; d. December 27, 1914, Madison Co, GA; m. JULIA T ? ; b. March 1847, GA; d. Madison Co, GA. **Military service: Private Co A 11th Cavalry**

xii.   EMILY WORTH DAVID, b. January 20, 1849, Franklin Co, GA; d. February 08, 1936; m. CULBERTSON; b. Abt. 1845.

xiii. ZABIAH CAROLINE DAVID, b. January 05, 1852, Franklin Co, GA; d. November 20, 1878; m. ? MILLER; b. Abt. 1850.

xiv.   HIRAM AUGUSTUS DAVID, b. December 25, 1853, Franklin Co, GA; d. October 18, 1922; m. (1) ? CARTWRIGHT; b. Abt. 1855; m. (2) ALICE C FIELDS, December 04, 1887; b. December 13, 1859; d. September 27, 1934.

xv.   IRA MAE DAVID, b. 1854.

xvi.   WILLIAM G DAVID, b. 1855.

13. ISSAC MORRISETT DAVID *(PERLINA WHITE, ISSAC)* was born August 26, 1809 in Franklin Co Ga, and died March 20, 1865 in Banks Co Ga. He married ARTEMACY HARDY August 10, 1831 in Jackson Co Ga. She was born Aug 20, 1813 in Jackson Co Ga, and died July 31, 1878 in Banks Co Ga.

Children of ISSAC DAVID and ARTEMACY HARDY are:

i.   JOSEPH A DAVID, b. August 07, 1832, Franklin Co Ga; d. August 11, 1832. **Military service: Private in Co D Inf. battn.,Smith's Legion,Ga. vols. Aug. 26,1862. Transferred to Co H, 1/1/1863: to Co F. 65th Regt.Ga Inf. Mar. 1863. Appointed 5th Sergeant May or June 1863; 2nd Sergeant Nov. 1863: Sgt. Major and transferred to Field Staff and Band 12/1**

ii.   PILLINA WHITE DAVID, b. August 08, 1833, Franklin Co Ga; d. July 22, 1862.

iii.   SARAH H DAVID, b. May 03, 1835, Franklin Co Ga; d. August 10, 1853.

iv. MINERVA CLEMENTINE DAVID, b. February 16, 1837, Franklin Co Ga; d. September 25, 1891, Gwinnett Co Ga; m. WALTER SUDDETH SIMS, January 01, 1852, Franklin Co, GA; b. July 18, 1825, Franklin Co, GA; d. June 11, 1901, Jackson Co, GA.

v. WILLIAM DAVID, b. November 24, 1838, Franklin Co Ga; d. October 27, 1861.

vi. ISSAC C DAVID, b. February 17, 1841, Franklin Co Ga; d. December 19, 1846.

vii. ELIZABETH A DAVID, b. December 04, 1842, Franklin Co Ga; d. October 11, 1856.

viii. CHARLES F DAVID, b. Abt. 1845, Franklin Co Ga.

ix. ERASTUS C DAVID, b. Abt. 1848, Franklin Co Ga; m. MARY EMMA UNKNOWN.
Military service: Private Co A 11th Cavalry

x. JAMES H DAVID, b. Abt. 1851, Franklin Co Ga.

xi. PALLINA WHITE DAVID, b. August 08, 1833, Franklin Co, GA; d. July 22, 1862, Franklin Co, GA; m. REUBEN D NUNN, July 11, 1850, Franklin Co, GA; b. Abt. 1830; d. 1864.

Reuben D Nunn, Banks Co, Ga Will Book A, pg 52, 3/12/1863: 2/1863

"If I should die or be killed in battle." Wife: Jemica, my five children: William E, Sarah J, Prena A, Olivia A, Eliza. Exr: J M David **Military Service: Co D. 16th Infantry Regiment.**

xii. ISAAC C DAVID, b. February 17, 1841, Franklin Co, GA; d. December 19, 1846, Franklin Co,

xiii. ELIZA A DAVID, b. December 04, 1842, Franklin Co, GA; d. October 11, 1856, Franklin Co,

xiv. CHARLES P DAVID, b. 1845, Franklin Co, GA.

14. NANCY W DAVID *(PERLINA WHITE, ISSAC)* was born February 06, 1813 in Franklin Co Ga. She married DAVID J NEAL December 15, 1836 in Franklin Co, GA. He was born 1814 in Franklin Co, GA.

Children of NANCY DAVID and DAVID NEAL are:

i. HENRY D NEAL, b. 1838.

ii. PERLINA F NEAL, b. 1839, Franklin Co, GA; m. WILLIAM WALKER, November 18, 1856, Franklin Co, GA; b. Abt. 1835.

iii. RICHARD NEAL, b. 1840.

iv. LOUIZA A W NEAL, b. 1847.

15. BERRY MATHEWS DAVID *(HENRY, ISSAC)* was born Abt. 1807 in Oglethorpe Co Ga, and died Abt. 1853 in Madison Co Ga. He married ELIZA-BETH VAUGHN October 10, 1825 in Madison Co GA, daughter of JAMES VAUGHN and SUSANNAH VAUGHN. She was born Abt. 1791 in Laurens District S. C.

Children of BERRY DAVID and ELIZABETH VAUGHN are:

  i.   KEZIAH H. DAVID, b. 1827, Madison Co Ga; d. Bet. 1894 - 1895, Elbert Co Ga; m. WILLIAM M. MOORE, May 01, 1850; b. May 03, 1829, Elbert Co Ga; d. May 09, 1907, Franklin Co. Ga

  ii. HENRY DAVID, b. Abt. 1828, Madison Co GA. Died before 1860

  iii. JAMES W. V. DAVID, b. Abt. 1831; d. July 31, 1862, Scottsville, Va; m. MARY M. RAY, September 28, 1854, Hart Co Ga. **Military service: Enlisted 5/7/1862 Co B. 24th Ga Inf. Died Scottsville Va. 7/31/1862 Chronic Diarrhea**

  iv. SUSANNAH DAVID, b. Abt. 1833; m. JAMES S. OGLESBY.

  v.   MARTHA ANN DAVID, b. December 11, 1834, Madison Co GA; d. December 03, 1922; m. SAMUEL PATTON POWER, SR, October 20, 1853, Madison Co, GA; b. July 09, 1831, **Military service: Private Co E. 37th Ga Inf**

  vi. MARY ELIZABETH DAVID, b. July 16, 1839; d. December 23, 1890; m. (1) JAMES DUNCAN POWER, November 22, 1861, Madison Co, GA; b. April 17, 1820; d. October 13, 1890;

16. ELIZABETH DAVID *(HENRY, ISSAC)* was born Abt. 1805 in Madison Co GA. She married JOHN BELL. He was born Abt. 1800.

Children of ELIZABETH DAVID and JOHN BELL are:

  i.   BERRY BELL, b. Abt. 1829.

  ii. MARY BELL, b. Abt. 1833.

  iii. MATHEW BELL, b. Abt. 1835.

  iv. MILLY A BELL, b. Abt. 1841.

  v.   MARTHA BELL, b. Abt. 1846.

17. PERLINA KEZIAH DAVID *(HENRY, ISSAC)* was born April 01, 1808. She married (1) WILLIAM DAVID VAUGHN December 12, 1827, son of ALEXANDER VAUGHN and ELIZABETH DAVID. He was born May 12, 1808 in Elbert Co Ga, and died Abt. 1855 in Madison Co. Ga.

Children of PERLINA DAVID and WILLIAM VAUGHN are:

  i.   MARY CAROLINE VAUGHN, b. Abt. 1829; m. UNKNOWN HEWELL.

ii. MILES B VAUGHN, b. Abt. 1830; d. December 13, 1862, Killed Fredericksburg Va; m. SUSAN ANN UNKNOWN. **Military service: Co H 38th Ga InfPrivate - October 15, 1861. Killed at Fredericksburg, Virginia, December 13, 1862**

iii. MATHEW A VAUGHN, b. Abt. 1832.

iv. MARTHA A VAUGHN, b. Abt. 1835; d. Abt. 1910; m. WILLIAM W HEWELL, Dec 08, 1853.

v. MARION VAUGHN, b. Abt. 1840.

vi. MILLY VAUGHN, b. Abt. 1842.

vii. SUSAN C VAUGHN, b. Abt. 1843; d. April 28, 1924, Provo, Utah; m. SANFORD M BRUCE, April 04, 1882; b. January 1861, Madison Co, GA.

viii. WILLIAM H VAUGHN, b. Abt. 1844; d. June 27, 1862, Killed Cold Harbor, Va—Peninsula Campaign. **Military service: Co H 38th Georgia Infantry 3/1/1862**

ix. JAMES T VAUGHN, b. Abt. 1847; m. SAMANTHA A VAUGHN.

x. PERLINA KEZIAH VAUGHN, b. June 14, 1849, Madison Co, GA; d. December 14, 1914, Madison Co, GA; m. JAMES HENRY BRUCE, Madison Co GA; b. September 22, 1848; d. November 25, 1936, Madison Co, GA.

25. PERLINA JOHNSON WILEY *(MILDRED DAVID, ISSAC)* was born Abt. 1810. She married WILLIAM OGLESBY May 21, 1830 in Elbert Co Ga. He was born Abt. 1774 in Bedford Co., Va.

Children of PERLINA WILEY and WILLIAM OGLESBY are:

i. JOHN OGLESBY, b. August 10, 1831. **Military Service: 2nd Lieutenant Co H. 38th Georgia Inf - October 15, 1861. 1st lieutenant September 22, 1862. Killed at Gettysburg, Pennsylvania, July 2,1863**

ii. LUCINDA OGLESBY, b. Abt. 1832.

iii. SUSAN MILDRED OGLESBY, b. March 25, 1833; d. December 13, 1897; m. WILLIAM THOMAS POWER, SR, November 25, 1852, Elbert Co, GA; b. November 26, 1817, Madison Co, GA; d. 1861, Elbert Co, GA.

iv. THOMAS OGLESBY, b. September 16, 1834. **Military Service Co D 9ᵗʰ Battalion Ga Inf private March 4, 1862. Died of disease June 15, 1862.**

v. ABDA OGLESBY, b. June 09, 1836. **Military Service: 38th Georgia Inf 4th Sergeant - October 15, 1861. Captured at Spotsylvania, Virginia, May 12, 1864. Paroled at Fort Delaware, Delaware and sent to Aiken's Landing, Virginia for exchange September 18,**

1864. Received at Varina, Virginia, September 22, 1864. Admitted to Jackson Hospital at Richmond, Virginia, with abscess on arm, September 22, 1864 and furloughed for 30 days September 26, 1864. Enlisted as a private in Company H, 2nd Battalion Georgia Militia Cavalry October 1, 1864. Appointed 1st Lieutenant and Acting Adjutant. Surrendered at Macon, Georgia, April 22, 1865

vi.   DRURY PATRICK OGLESBY, b. May 30, 1838. **Military Service Co D 9th Battalion Ga Inf 3rd Corporal May 10, 1862. Elected Jr. 2d Lieutenant December 1, 1862. Wounded at Murfreesboro, Tenn. December 31, 1862. Transferred to Co. G, 37th Regiment Ga. Inf. May 6, 1863. Elected 1st Lieutenant June 27, 1863. Wounded at Franklin, Tenn. December 17, 1864. Pension records show he was at home on wounded furlough close of war. (Resident of Ga. since 1839.)**

vii.   NANCY ANN OGLESBY, b. September 03, 1840.

26. JACOB WHITE DAVID, JR. *(JACOB WHITE, ISSAC)* was born May 05, 1825 in Elbert Co. Ga, and died January 05, 1873 in Huntsville, Ala. He married PARTUNIA BRANTLEY. She was born Abt. 1825. **Military service: Private Co A Phillips Legion**

Child of JACOB DAVID and PARTUNIA BRANTLEY is:

i.   OTIS DAVID, b. Abt. 1850.

DESCENDANTS OF PETER DAVID

Generation No. 1

1. PETER DAVID was born July 01, 1748 in King Williams Parrish Goochland Va, and died Abt. 1812 in Madison Co GA. He was the son of Peter David and Elizabeth Morrisette. He married (1) MARY ELIZABETH WHITE Abt. 1771 in Virginia, daughter of HENRY WHITE and CELIA PAGE. She was born August 21, 1751 in Bedford, Va, and died Abt. 1790 in Virginia. He married (2) ELIZABETH HALE November 08, 1793 in Bedford Co. Va, daughter of RICHARD HALE and ELIZABETH. She was born Abt. 1775 in Virginia, and died Abt. 1845 in Madison Co GA.

      Children of PETER DAVID and MARY WHITE are:

2.	i.	WILLIAM DAVID, b. 1775, Buckingham Co, VA; d. November 05, 1822, Madison Co GA.
3.	ii.	LUCY DAVID, b. Abt. 1774; d. Bef. 1824, Putnam Co, GA.
4.	iii.	HENRY DAVID, REV., b. January 11, 1780, Virginia; d. June 16, 1845, Franklin Co. Ga.
5.	iv.	JUDITH DAVID, b. Abt. 1784; d. October 15, 1828, Putnam Co, GA.
6.	v.	NANCY DAVID, b. August 09, 1785, Petersburg, Va; d. February 06, 1875, Conyers/Newton, Ga.
7.	vi.	PETER DAVID, b. September 23, 1787, Virginia; d. June 22, 1872, Madison Co GA.

      Children of PETER DAVID and ELIZABETH HALE are:

8.	vii.	MORASSETT[5] DAVID, b. January 09, 1795, Elbert Co, GA; d. January 08, 1864, Madison Co
	viii.	SARAH S DAVID, b. Abt. 1797.
	ix.	ISSAC DAVID, b. Abt. 1799, Virginia; d. Abt. 1880, Madison Co GA; m. PATSY SARTAIN; b. Abt. 1798.
9.	x.	MARY DAVID, b. September 10, 1801; d. Aft. 1860.
10.	xi.	SAMUEL DAVID, b. Abt. 1805, Virginia; d. Abt. 1888, Madison, Co Ga.

Generation No. 2

2. WILLIAM DAVID *(PETER)* was born 1775 in Buckingham Co, VA, and died November 05, 1822 in Madison Co GA. He married LUCY WHITE Abt. 1802, daughter of JESSE WHITE and ELIZABETH BROWN. She was born Abt. 1786, and died Abt. 1857.

      Children of WILLIAM DAVID and LUCY WHITE are:

	i.	JOHN WHITE DAVID, b. Abt. 1803, Madison, Co Ga; d. Bef. 1840; m. ELIZABETH T. POWER, 1828; b. Madison, Co Ga.
11.	ii.	ELIZABETH DAVID, b. May 29, 1804; d. August 15, 1878.
12.	iii.	MARY DAVID, b. 1806, Madison Co, GA; d. Madison Co, MS.
	iv.	SARAH A DAVID, b. Abt. 1807, Madison, Co Ga; m. COLEMAN PITTS, 1824; b. Abt. 1800.
	v.	JOSEPH DAVID, b. Aft. 1807, Madison Co, GA.
13.	vi.	WILLIAM DAVID II, b. November 13, 1811; d. Aft. 1870.
	vii.	BENJAMIN DAVID, b. Abt. 1812, Madison Co, GA.
14.	viii.	HAYDEN JUBAL DAVID, SR, b. November 07, 1813; d. June 04, 1899, Nicholson, Jackson Co, GA.
	ix.	JESSE DAVID, b. Abt. 1814, Madison Co, GA.
15.	x.	FRANCIS MARION DAVID, b. May 06, 1816; d. January 29, 1891.
	xi.	HENRY PAGE DAVID, b. March 04, 1818; d. June 09, 1860; m. (1) M. ZUGLAR; b. Abt. 1820; m. (2) NANCY J. SMITH.
16.	xii.	JONATHAN SAUNDERS DAVID, b. December 06, 1819; d. July 26, 1871.

3. LUCY DAVID *(PETER)* was born Abt. 1774, and died Bef. 1824 in Putnam Co, GA. She married JOHN ALLEN February 04, 1794 in Franklin Co, GA. He was born Abt. 1760 in VA, and died 1827 in Putnam Co, GA.

      Children of LUCY DAVID and JOHN ALLEN are:

	i.	CELIA ALLEN, b. Abt. 1795.
	ii.	FRANCES ALLEN, b. Abt. 1795.
17.	iii.	LELAND ALLEN, b. February 11, 1799, Lynchburg, VA; d. January 22, 1891, Lee Co, AL.

4. HENRY DAVID, REV. *(PETER)* was born January 11, 1780 in Virginia, and died June 16, 1845 in Franklin Co. Ga. He married PERLINA WHITE DAVID January 10, 1800, daughter of ISSAC DAVID and MILDRED WHITE. She was born June 28, 1776 in VA, and died Nov. 06, 1857 in Jackson Co, GA.

      Children of HENRY DAVID and PERLINA DAVID are:

18.   i. JAMES HORATIO DAVID, b. August 27, 1799, Franklin Co Ga; d. January 21, 1878.

       ii. WILLIAM B. DAVID, b. September 30, 1801.

      iii. MILDRED "MILLIE" W. DAVID, b. May 1803, GA; d. Aft. 1900.

19.   iv. HENRY FRANKLIN DAVID, b. September 09, 1805; d. November 17, 1887, Franklin Co, GA.

       v. JONATHAN DAVID, b. March 18, 1807, Franklin Co Ga; d. August 27, 1808.

20.   vi. ISSAC MORRISETT DAVID, b. Aug 26, 1809, Franklin Co Ga; d. March 20, 1865, Banks Co

      vii. POLLY J. DAVID, b. June 05, 1811, Franklin Co Ga.

21.   viii. NANCY W DAVID, b. February 06, 1813, Franklin Co Ga.

      ix. SIMEON DAVID, b. Sept 14, 1814, Franklin Co Ga; d. September 28, 1814, Franklin Co Ga.

       x. PILLINA W DAVID, b. May 06, 1818, Franklin Co Ga; m. MARION SEWELL, 1836; b. November 23, 1816, Banks Co, GA; d. October 25, 1883, Polk Co, GA.

      xi. MARY H DAVID, b. May 28, 1819, Franklin Co Ga.

5. JUDITH DAVID *(PETER)* was born Abt. 1784, and died October 15, 1828 in Putnam Co, GA. She married (1) MICAJAH WHITE 1806 in VA, son of JESSE WHITE and ELIZABETH BROWN. He was born Abt. 1788, and died July 16, 1825 in Putnam Co, GA. She married (2) ELIJAH ANDERSON November 07, 1826 in Putnam Co, GA. He was born Abt. 1792.

    Children of JUDITH DAVID and MICAJAH WHITE are:

       i. JEPE M WHITE, b. Aft. 1806.

      ii. JESSE MARION WHITE, b. March 01, 1807.

22.   iii. ELIZABETH BROWN WHITE, b. May 26, 1808, Elbert Co, GA; d. November 11, 1851, Roanoke, AL.

      iv. JOHN B WHITE, b. November 11, 1811.

       v. MARY WHITE, b. November 13, 1813.

      vi. JAMES WHITE, b. September 17, 1816.

6. NANCY DAVID *(PETER)* was born August 09, 1785 in Petersburg, Va, and died February 06, 1875 in Conyers/Newton, Ga. She married (1) BUTLER. She married (2) THOMAS SIMEON ALMOND Abt. 1801, son of THOMAS ALMOND and ANN USSERY. He was born August 16, 1779 in Rockingham,N.C., and died June 29, 1846 in Newton, Ga.

    Children of NANCY DAVID and THOMAS ALMOND are:

    i. JOHN BUTLER ALMOND, b. April 09, 1802; d. August 14, 1838, Newton Co, GA; m. MARY V DILLARD; b. October 06, 1795; d. October 18, 1863, Newton Co, GA.

    ii. MARY ALMOND, b. August 12, 1803; m. JOHN DENNARD, July 21, 1819, Elbert Co, GA; b. Abt. 1800.

    iii. MARTHA ALMOND, b. April 03, 1805; d. October 20, 1883, Chambers Co, AL; m. THOMAS M HARRIS; b. 1802, GA; d. Chambers Co, AL.

    iv. WELCOME USSERY ALMOND, b. December 30, 1806; d. February 04, 1878, Newton Co, GA; m. (1) NANCY GRAY, July 17, 1828, Newton Co, GA; b. Abt. 1811; d. Bef. 1849, Newton Co, GA; m. (2) SUSAN HARRIS, July 12, 1849; b. September 19, 1810.

    v. ANN ALMOND, b. October 13, 1808; m. WILLIAM HARRIS, February 20, 1824, Newton Co, GA; b. October 08, 1802.

    vi. SARA ANN ALMOND, b. September 27, 1810; m. ELISHA SPARKS, February 12, 1829, Newton Co, GA; b. Abt. 1810.

23.   vii. PETER BENNETT ALMOND, b. August 14, 1812; d. September 18, 1887.

    viii. JAMES F ALMOND, b. October 18, 1814.

    ix. JOSEPH HAMILTON ALMOND, b. November 15, 1818; d. October 24, 1897.

    x. HENRY PRYOR ALMOND, b. January 07, 1821; d. January 13, 1903.

    xi. JAMES T ALMOND, b. May 12, 1823.

    xii. SIMEON DOCK ALMOND, b. July 07, 1825; d. October 09, 1899.

    xiii. GRAVES BENNETT ALMOND, b. June 18, 1827; d. 1864, Lynchburg, Campbell Co, VA.

    xiv. SOPHRONIA E ALMOND, b. June 18, 1827.

    xv. DAVID BUTLER ALMOND, b. Sept 17, 1816, Elbert Co, GA; d. September 12, 1873, NV, AR.

7. PETER DAVID *(PETER)* was born September 23, 1787 in Virginia, and died June 22, 1872 in Madison Co GA. He married ELIZABETH ?. She was born Abt. 1785, and died Aft. 1850.

    Children of PETER DAVID and ELIZABETH ? are:

24.   i. WILLIAM W DAVID, b. Abt. 1808; d. August 1864.

25.   ii. RACHEL C DAVID, b. January 09, 1810; d. Abt. 1861, Elbert Co Ga.

26.   iii. HENRY H DAVID, b. Abt. 1811; d. Bef. 1860.

27. iv. MARY WHITE DAVID, b. Abt. 1814; d. Abt. 1850, Madison Co, GA.

28. v. ELIZABETH E. DAVID, b. Abt. 1816; d. Abt. 1859.

29. vi. JOHN MORRISETT "MURRAY" DAVID, SR, b. November 18, 1816, Madison Co, GA; d. October 03, 1896, Madison Co, GA.

30. vii. SARAH ANN DAVID, b. Abt. 1817; d. Prob Oglethorpe Co, GA.

viii. ELIZABETH E DAVID, b. 1820, Madison Co, GA; d. Bef. 1867, Madison Co, GA; m. JAMES W VAUGHN, February 07, 1839, Madison Co, GA; b. Abt. 1820.

31. ix. JAMES M. DAVID, b. Abt. 1825; d. September 1862, Sharpsburg,Md.

x. LEWIS M DAVID, b. March 12, 1829; d. September 29, 1874, Madison Co, GA.

8. MORASSETT DAVID *(PETER)* was born January 09, 1795 in Elbert Co, GA, and died January 08, 1864 in Madison Co GA. He married ELIZABETH DAVID May 02, 1819 in Elbert Co, GA, daughter of WILLIAM DAVID and LUCY WHITE. She was born May 29, 1804, and died August 15, 1878. Amnesty Oath: 1865, Light, grey hair, 5'7," age 61, housekeeper

Children of MORASSETT DAVID and ELIZABETH DAVID are:

i. JOSEPH J DAVID, b. February 22, 1829; d. September 30, 1860; m. NANCY E MEADOW, September 09, 1852, Madison Co, GA; b. 1836, Madison Co, GA.

ii. MORASSETT DAVID, JR, b. 1835, Madison Co, GA; d. November 25, 1863, Missonary Ridge, Tennessee. **Military ServiceCo B, 9th Battalion, Ga Volunteer Infantry, Private Mar 4, 1862. Transferred to Co E, 37th Regt Ga Inf. May 6, 1863. Died at Missionary Ridge, Tenn November 25th 1863**

iii. JONATHAN S DAVID, b. 1838, Madison Co, GA. Amnesty Oath: 1865, Dark, black hair, grey eyes, 5'1" age 28, farmer **Military service: Private Co G 3rd Cavalry Ga State Trps**

32. iv. WILLIAM G DAVID, b. August 24, 1839; d. January 28, 1929. **Military ServiceCo B, 9th Battalion, Ga Volunteer Infantry, Private Mar 4, 1862. Transferred to Co E, 37th Regt Ga Inf**

v. SARAH DAVID, b. Abt. 1842.

33. vi. LUCINDA A DAVID, b. May 22, 1820, Madison Co, GA; d. May 07, 1867, Madison Co, GA.

viii. SARAH ELIZABETH DAVID, b. 1842, Madison Co, GA; d. Died Young.

34.   ix.   LUCY ELIZABETH DAVID, b. December 26, 1845, Madison
                 Co, GA; d. February 10, 1898, Madison Co, GA.

9. MARY DAVID *(PETER,)* was born September 10, 1801, and died Aft. 1860.
She married WALTER H BRUCE September 24, 1822 in Elbert Co, GA, son
of THOMAS H. BRUCE. He was born August 30, 1798 in Virginia, and died
Bet. 1835 - 1840 in Georgia.
        Children of MARY DAVID and WALTER BRUCE are:
        i.   WILLIAM J BRUCE, b. Abt. 1823, Madison Co. Ga; d. Aft.
              1860, Madison Co. Ga; m. FRANCES E GRAHAM, September
              10, 1856; b. 1837, Madison Co, GA.
35.   ii.   JOHN M BRUCE, b. Abt. 1824, Madison Co. Ga; d. Aft. 1880,
              Madison Co. Ga.
36.   iii. CELIA BRUCE, b. Abt. 1825, Madison Co. Ga; d. October 17,
              1900, Jackson Co, GA.
37.   iv.   JAMES HENRY BRUCE, b. July 19, 1826, Madison Co. Ga; d.
              November 28, 1864.
        v.   MARY BRUCE, b. Abt. 1831; d. 1860, Madison Co. Ga.
38.   vi.   SARAH BRUCE, b. Abt. 1831, Madison Co. Ga; d. 1886, Elbert
              Co, GA.
39.   vii. FRANCES BRUCE, b. Abt. 1834, Madison Co. Ga; d. Bef. 1900,
              Madison Co, GA.
        viii. LUCINDA BRUCE, b. Abt. 1835.
40.   ix.   THOMAS PETER BRUCE, b. October 18, 1828, Madison Co,
              GA; d. September 11, 1896, Madison Co, GA.
        x.   SINGLETON BRUCE, b. Abt. 1831.

10. SAMUEL DAVID *(PETER)* was born Abt. 1805 in Virginia, and died Abt.
1888 in Madison, Co Ga. He married HARRIETT THRELKELD May 25,
1826 in Elbert Co, GA. She was born 1807 in SC, and died Bef. 1887.
        Amnesty Oath: 1865, Dark, black hair, yellow eyes, 5'6," age 60
        Children of SAMUEL DAVID and HARRIET THRELKELD are:
41.   i.   MARSHALL DAVID, b. October 02, 1828; d. September 20,
              1897.
        ii   MARION DAVID, b. 1832
42.   iii. PETER DAVID, b. Abt. 1834, Madison, Co Ga; d. Abt. May
              1862, Knoxville, Tenn.
44.   iv.   SAMUEL C DAVID, JR, b. 1837, Madison Co, GA; d. Bet. 1862
              - 1865, CSA.
        v.   DELILAH DAVID, b. Abt. 1843.

45.   vi. ISSAC DAVID, b. Abt. 1843; d. May 11, 1910, Madison Co.
Military service: private Co D 16th Ga Inf. September 12,1862.
Roll dated December 15,1864, shows him absent without leave
since October 1,1864. Captured and paroled, Greenville, S. C. May
23,1865
vii. MARY DAVID, b. 1842.

Generation No. 3

11. ELIZABETH DAVID *(WILLIAM, PETER)* was born May 29, 1804, and
died August 15, 1878. She married MORASSETT DAVID May 02, 1819 in
Elbert Co, GA, son of PETER DAVID and ELIZABETH HALE. He was born
January 09, 1795 in Elbert Co, GA, and died January 08, 1864 in Madison Co
GA.

12. MARY DAVID *(WILLIAM, PETER)* was born 1806 in Madison Co, GA,
and died in Madison Co, MS. She married (1) ELIJAH PATTEN September
27, 1821 in Madison Co, GA. He was born 1800 in Madison Co, GA, and died
in Madison Co, MS.
    Children of MARY DAVID and ELIJAH PATTEN are:
     i. SAMUEL H PATTEN, b. 1825, Madison Co, GA; d. MS; m.
        ANN //; b. 1832, MS.
    ii. EDWARD L W PATTEN, b. 1828, Madison Co, GA; d. Madison
        Co, MS; m. MARGARET //; b. 1829, AL.
   iii. JONATHAN PATTEN, b. 1830, Madison Co, GA.
   iv. JAMES PATTEN, b. 1833, Madison Co, GA; d. MS.
    v. MARY M PATTEN, b. 1836, Madison Co, GA; d. MS.

13. WILLIAM DAVID II *(WILLIAM, PETER)* was born November 13, 1811,
and died Aft. 1870. He married (1) MARY POWER. She was born Abt. 1812,
and died Bef. 1860. He married (2) SARAH E. CHAMBERS Abt. 1863. She
was born Abt. 1835.
    Children of WILLIAM DAVID and MARY POWER are:
     i. JAMES CLARK DAVID, b. Abt. 1833; d. September 01, 1916;
        m. LUCY ADDIE GARLAND; b. Abt. 1839; d. Aft. 1916.
    ii. WILLIAM H DAVID, b. Abt. 1835; d. October 27, 1861, Frank-
        lin Co, GA; m. ELIZABETH JANE GARLAND. **Military ser-**
        vice: Private Co A 24th Ga Inf
   iii. JOHN W DAVID, b. Abt. 1839.
   iv. MARY E DAVID, b. Abt. 1841.
    v. SARAH A DAVID, b. Abt. 1845.

   vi.   JOSEPHINE DAVID, b. Abt. 1848.

   vii. JONATHAN S DAVID, b. Abt. 1851.

  viii. SUSIE JANE DAVID, b. April 04, 1853.

Children of WILLIAM DAVID and SARAH CHAMBERS are:

   ix. EMMA DAVID, b. Abt. 1863.

    x. JOHN W DAVID, b. Abt. 1866.

14. HAYDEN JUBAL DAVID SR *(WILLIAM, PETER)* was born November 07, 1813, and died June 04, 1899 in Nicholson, Jackson Co, GA. He married (1) SARAH ADELINE STRICKLAND Abt. 1835, daughter of KNICHEN STRICKLAND. She was born Abt. 1816, and died Bef. 1860. He married (2) SARAH "SALLIE" STRICKLAND January 12, 1836 in Madison Co, GA. She was born Abt. 1815 in SC. He married (3) PRISCILLA LUCINDA PITTMAN April 03, 1860 in Jackson Co, GA. She was born November 03, 1826, and died December 02, 1896 in Nicholson, Jackson Co, GA.

        Children of HAYDEN DAVID and SARAH STRICKLAND are:

    i. JAMES M DAVID, b. Abt. 1836. Died 6/29/1862 **Military service: Cpl Co G 43rd Ga Vol Infantry Volunteered at Jefferson, Jackson Co. Ga 3/4/1862 for 3 years or the War. Died 6/29/1862 in Atlanta, Ga**

    ii. JOHN W DAVID, b. Abt. 1838; d. February 15, 1865. **Enlisted 8/1/1861 at Athens Ga for the duration of the War. Taken prisoner May 29,1864 at Hanover Courthouse Va. On roll of prisoners at Point Lookout, Md June 11,1864. Transferred to Elmira, NY 7/12/1864. Died of Typhoid Fever 2/15/1865**

   iii. MARY E DAVID, b. Abt. 1843.

   iv. KINTCHEN DAVID, b. Abt. 1845.

    v. JOSEPHINE DAVID, b. Abt. 1847.

   vi. LUCY ANN DAVID, b. Abt. 1849.

Children of HAYDEN DAVID and PRISCILLA PITTMAN are:

   vii. HAYDEN J. DAVID, b. April 05, 1867; d. August 04, 1937, TX; m. ANNA ROPER, September 14, 1890; b. Abt. 1867.

  viii. LETITIA PRISCILLA DAVID, b. January 08, 1862; d. April 06, 1947, Jackson Co, GA; m. JOEL WALTER FREEMAN, February 14, 1884, Jackson Co, GA; b. September 16, 1859, Madison or Jackson Co, GA; d. May 17, 1952, Jackson Co, GA.

   ix. LEUTITIA DAVID, b. January 08, 1862.

15. FRANCIS MARION DAVID *(WILLIAM, PETER)* was born May 06, 1816, and died January 29, 1891. He married CATHERINE BORUM October 19, 1836. She was born Abt. 1822. **Enlisted at Jefferson, Jackson Co for 6 months 7/25/1863 Present 1/25/1864**

Children of FRANCIS DAVID and CATHERINE BORUM are:

   i.   SARAH DAVID, b. Abt. 1839.
  ii.   LUCY DAVID, b. Abt. 1843.
 iii.   MARTHA E DAVID, b. Abt. 1845.
 iv.   ELIZABETH D DAVID, b. Abt. 1847.

16. JONATHAN SAUNDERS DAVID *(WILLIAM, PETER)* was born December 06, 1819, and died July 26, 1871. He married (1) AMANDA FRANCES BRAWNER. He married (2) MARTHA RICHARDSON. She was born Abt. 1820. He married (3) MARTHA JANE RICHARDSON Abt. 1854.

Child of JONATHAN DAVID and MARTHA RICHARDSON is:

   i.   HOSEA BALLEW DAVID, b. January 21, 1859; d. December 09, 1884.

17. LELAND ALLEN *(LUCY DAVID, PETER)* was born February 11, 1799 in Lynchburg, VA, and died January 22, 1891 in Lee Co, AL. He married ELIZABETH BROWN WHITE February 01, 1823 in Putnam Co, GA, daughter of MICAJAH WHITE and JUDITH DAVID. She was born May 26, 1808 in Elbert Co, GA, and died November 11, 1851 in Roanoke, AL.

Child of LELAND ALLEN and ELIZABETH WHITE is:

   i.   JUDAH ALLEN, b. July 30, 1826, Newton Co, GA; d. January 20, 1920, Cooke Co, TX; m. WILLIAM HODGES DANIEL; b. March 08, 1822, Clarke Co, GA; d. December 12, 1901, Cooke Co, TX.

18. JAMES HORATIO DAVID *(HENRY, PETER)* was born August 27, 1799 in Franklin Co Ga, and died January 21, 1878. He married (1) NANCY HENRY December 09, 1819. She was born Bef. 1803 in Elbert Co, GA. He married (2) THIRZA BOWEN July 31, 1823. She was born Abt. 1803.

Children of JAMES DAVID and THIRZA BOWEN are:

   i.   ELEANOR E DAVID, b. May 10, 1825.
  ii.   MARY JULIETTE DAVID, b. December 07, 1826; m. // NEAL; b. Abt. 1820.
 iii.   SIMEON BOWEN DAVID, b. January 29, 1829.
 iv.   PILLINA CHARITY DAVID, b. April 22, 1831.
  v.   THIRZA A. DAVID, b. Abt. 1833.
 vi.   OWEN THOMAS DAVID, b. September 06, 1835, Jackson Co Ga; d. October 05, 1864.
 vii.   PILLONA WHITE DAVID, b. November 19, 1839.

    viii. HORATIO JAMES DAVID, b. April 1842. **Military service: Co B 16th Georgia Inf private July 17,1861. Appointed 4th Cor- poral September 1861. Elected Jr. 2d Lieutenant March1, 1863. Wounded at Chancellorsville, Va. May 3, 1863. Wounded in eye, resulting in loss of sight, at Deep Bottom, Va. August 16,1864. Retired on account of wounds February 1865. Roll for February 1865, shows he was elected 1st Lieutenant of Co. C, March 1, 1863, but name does not appear on rolls of this company. Captured and paroled, Athens, Ga. May 8, 1865. (Born in Georgia December 4, 1842.)**

19. HENRY FRANKLIN DAVID *(HENRY, PETER)* was born September 09, 1805, and died November 17, 1887 in Franklin Co, GA. He married MARY SMITH CRISLER September 07, 1826. She was born February 02, 1809 in Franklin Co, GA, and died September 11, 1892 in Franklin Co, GA. **Military service: Col Mitchell's Regiment Ga Militia**

    Children of HENRY DAVID and MARY CRISLER are:

    i. NANCY JOHNSON DAVID, b. August 09, 1828, Franklin Co, GA; d. 1902, Madison Co, GA; m. JAMES P FITZPATRICK, November 20, 1845, Oglethorpe Co, GA; b. 1824, Oglethorpe Co, GA; d. August 1864. **Military service: Private Co A 16th Georgia Inf.**

    ii. MARY ANN PALINA DAVID, b. January 06, 1831, Franklin Co, GA; d. December 05, 1904; m. WILLIAM G WADE, October 13, 1850, Franklin Co, GA; b. Abt. 1830, Franklin Co, GA. **Military Service: private September 17,1862 . Co H 15th Georgia Infantry Died in Edray, W. Va. hospital May 5,1864 .**

    iii. THEODOSIA ALLEN DAVID, b. January 26, 1834, Franklin Co, GA; d. March 18, 1911; m. JAMES V WALKER, December 19, 1852, Franklin Co, GA; b. Abt. 1830.

    iv. ELIZABETH CARSON DAVID, b. August 27, 1834, Franklin Co, GA; m. ? WILSON; b. Abt. 1830.

    v. HENRY DAVID, b. April 22, 1837, Franklin Co, GA; d. February 22, 1842, Franklin Co, GA.

    vi. LUCY ARTIMESIA DAVID, b. September 28, 1838, Franklin Co, GA; d. June 10, 1904; m. (1) WILLIAM DAVID DALRYMPLE b. Abt. 1835; m. (2) JOHN COLUMBUS CARSON, November 19, 1855, Franklin Co, GA; b. 1833, Franklin Co, GA; d. 1863, Civil War in E TN. **Military Service: Co E 13 Georgia Cavalry**

    vii. ROSANA CRISTLER DAVID, b. June 1840, Franklin Co, GA; d. July 1840, Franklin Co, GA.

    viii. LOIS MENTARIA DAVID, b. July 1841, Franklin Co, GA; d. November 1889; m. HENRY DAVID CARSON, August 21,

1860; b. April 25, 1837, Franklin Co, GA; d. April 23, 1916, Benton, AR. **Military Service: Co E 13 Georgia Cavalry**

   ix. ABSALOM N DAVID, b. 1843.

   x. VIRGINIA JACKSON DAVID, b. March 1845, Franklin Co, GA; d. August 1864; m. JAMES WILSON, January 13, 1857, Franklin Co, GA; b. Abt. 1840.

   xi. HENRY FRANKLIN DAVID, JR, b. July 27, 1847, Franklin Co, GA; d. December 27, 1914, Madison Co, GA; m. JULIA T //; b. March 1847, GA; d. Madison Co, GA. **Military service: Private Co A 11th Cavalry**

   xii. WELD EMILY WORTH DAVID, b. January 20, 1849, Franklin Co, GA; d. February 08, 1936; m. ? CULBERTSON; b. Abt. 1845.

   xiii. ZABIAH CAROLINE DAVID, b. January 05, 1852, Franklin Co, GA; d. November 20, 1878; m. ? MILLER; b. Abt. 1850.

   xiv. HIRAM AUGUSTUS DAVID, b. December 25, 1853, Franklin Co, GA; d. October 18, 1922; m. (1) ? CARTWRIGHT; b. Abt. 1855; m. (2) ALICE C FIELDS, December 04, 1887; b. December 13, 1859; d. September 27, 1934.

   xv. IRA MAE DAVID, b. 1854.

   xvi. WILLIAM G DAVID, b. 1855.

20. ISSAC MORRISETT DAVID *(HENRY, PETER)* was born August 26, 1809 in Franklin Co Ga, and died March 20, 1865 in Banks Co Ga. He married ARTEMACY HARDY August 10, 1831 in Jackson Co Ga. She was born August 20, 1813 in Jackson Co Ga, and died July 31, 1878 in Banks Co Ga.

    Children of ISSAC DAVID and ARTEMACY HARDY are:

   i. JOSEPH A DAVID, b. August 07, 1832, Franklin Co Ga; d. August 11, 1832. **Military service: Private in Co D Inf. battn.,Smith's Legion,Ga. vols. Aug. 26,1862. Transferred to Co H, 1/1/1863: to Co F. 65th Regt.Ga Inf. Mar. 1863. Appointed 5th Sergeant May or June 1863; 2nd Sergeant Nov. 1863: Sgt. Major and transferred to Field Staff and Band 12/1**

   ii. PILLINA WHITE DAVID, b. August 08, 1833, Franklin Co Ga; d. July 22, 1862.

   iii. SARAH H DAVID, b. May 03, 1835, Franklin Co Ga; d. August 10, 1853.

   iv. MINERVA CLEMENTINE DAVID, b. February 16, 1837, Franklin Co Ga; d. September 25, 1891, Gwinnett Co Ga; m. WALTER SUDDETH SIMS, January 01, 1852, Franklin Co, GA; b. July 18, 1825, Franklin Co, GA; d. June 11, 1901, Jackson Co, GA.

    v. WILLIAM DAVID, b. November 24, 1838, Franklin Co Ga; d. October 27, 1861. **Military Service: Private Co A 24th Georgia Infantry**

    vi. ISSAC C DAVID, b. February 17, 1841, Franklin Co Ga; d. December 19, 1846.

    vii. ELIZABETH A DAVID, b. December 04, 1842, Franklin Co Ga; d. October 11, 1856.

    viii. CHARLES F DAVID, b. Abt. 1845, Franklin Co Ga.

    ix. ERASTUS C DAVID, b. Abt. 1848, Franklin Co Ga; m. MARY EMMA UNKNOWN. Military service: Private Co A 11th Cavalry

    x. JAMES H DAVID, b. Abt. 1851, Franklin Co Ga.

21. NANCY W DAVID *(HENRY, PETER)* was born February 06, 1813 in Franklin Co Ga. She married (1) DAVID NEAL December 15, 1836. She married (2) DAVID J NEAL December 15, 1836 in Franklin Co, GA. He was born 1814 in Franklin Co, GA.

    Children of NANCY DAVID and DAVID NEAL are:

    i. HENRY D NEAL, b. 1838.

    ii. PERLINA F NEAL, b. 1839, Franklin Co, GA; m. WILLIAM WALKER, November 18, 1856, Franklin Co, GA; b. Abt. 1835.

    iii. RICHARD NEAL, b. 1840.

    iv. LOUIZA A W NEAL, b. 1847.

22. ELIZABETH BROWN WHITE *(JUDITH DAVID, PETER)* was born May 26, 1808 in Elbert Co, GA, and died November 11, 1851 in Roanoke, AL. She married LELAND ALLEN February 01, 1823 in Putnam Co, GA, son of JOHN ALLEN and LUCY DAVID. He was born February 11, 1799 in Lynchburg, VA, and died January 22, 1891 in Lee Co, AL.

    Child is listed above under (17) Leland Allen.

23. PETER BENNETT ALMOND *(NANCY DAVID, PETER)* was born August 14, 1812, and died September 18, 1887. He married PERMELIA B DORSEY March 15, 1835. She was born February 11, 1816.

    Child of PETER ALMOND and PERMELIA DORSEY is:

    i. PETER JACKSON ALMOND, b. October 28, 1852; m. JOHANNA VASTI DANIEL, August 16, 1872; b. February 22, 1856; d. June 1917.

24. WILLIAM W DAVID *(PETER, PETER)* was born Abt. 1808, and died August 1864. He married MILDRED VAUGHN September 18, 1835 in Elbert Co Ga, daughter of ALEXANDER VAUGHN and ELIZABETH DAVID. She was born Abt. 1814.

Children of WILLIAM DAVID and MILDRED VAUGHN are:

i. JAMES W DAVID, b. Abt. 1836; m. MARY WHITE, Abt. 1860; b. May 31, 1837. **Military service: Private Co A Phillips Legion**

ii. PETER DAVID, b. 1842, Elbert Co, GA; d. Bef. August 1864, Elbert Co, GA.

iii. WILLIAM A DAVID, b. Abt. 1854; d. 1916, Elbert Co, GA; m. EMMA A OGILVIE, Abt. 1880; b. February 1860, Ebert Co, GA.

25. RACHEL C DAVID *(PETER, PETER)* was born January 09, 1810, and died Abt. 1861 in Elbert Co Ga. She married ISSAC DAVID VAUGHN February 15, 1832, son of ALEXANDER VAUGHN and ELIZABETH DAVID. He was born Abt. 1810, and died June 1877 in Elbert Co Ga. She married

Children of RACHEL DAVID and ISSAC VAUGHN are:

i. MARTHA J VAUGHN, b. January 01, 1834; d. January 06, 1834.

ii. PETER DAVID VAUGHN, b. January 17, 1835; d. April 19, 1862. **Military service: private Co C 15th Ga, July 15, 1861. Died in 1st Ga.Hositsl at Richmond, Va. April 19,1862**

iii. ALEXANDER WILKS VAUGHN, b. November 08, 1837, Elbert Co. Ga; d. January 29, 1905; m. SARAH JANE CAMPBELL, November 23, 1871; b. Abt. 1850.

More About ALEXANDER WILKS VAUGHN:

Military service: Co H 38th Ga Inf Private - September 10, 1862. Wounded at Fredericksburg, Virginia, December 13, 1862. Wounded and captured at Gettysburg, Pennsylvania, July 2,1863. Paroled at DeCamp General Hospital, David's Island, New York, Harbor in 1863. Received at City Point, Virginia, September 16, 1863. Captured and paroled at Hartwell, Georgia, May 19, 1865.

iv. WILLIAM W. VAUGHN, b. May 07, 1840; d. Abt. August 1863.

Military service: Co H 38ᵗʰ Georgia Infantry March 01, 1862, Absent, sick, August 1863. Died in service.

v. SARAH J. VAUGHN, b. December 15, 1842; d. February 09, 1850.

vi. ELIZABETH C. VAUGHN, b. October 13, 1847; m. C. COLUMBUS HAYNES.

   vii. JOSEPH L. VAUGHN, b. January 12, 1846; d. February 06, 1846.

  viii. ISSAC J.M. VAUGHN, b. May 08, 1850; d. April 20, 1863, Civil War.

26. HENRY H DAVID *(PETER, PETER)* was born Abt. 1811, and died Bef. 1860. He married ELIZABETH OGLESBY December 27, 1838 in Elbert Co Ga. She was born Abt. 1820 in Elbert Co, GA.

     Children of HENRY DAVID and ELIZABETH OGLESBY are:

    i. MARY E DAVID, b. Abt. 1839; m. THOMAS HERNDON, October 30, 1859; b. Abt. 1835.

   ii. FRANCIS M DAVID, b. Abt. 1842; d. January 09, 1863; m. (1) CELIA R. BLACK, Madison Co GA; m. (2) CELIA C BLACK, October 21, 1856, Madison Co, GA; b. 1836, Madison Co, GA. Military Service: Co B, 9th Battalion, Ga Volunteer Infantry, Private May 10, 1862. Sent to Atlanta, Ga hospital Nov 12, 1862. Died Jan 9, 1863.

  iii. HENRY C DAVID, b. Abt. 1844; d. Abt. 1890; m. (1) JOSEPHINE M ?; b. Abt. 1850; m. (2) EURINA EMALINE MOON, December 20, 1866, Madison Co, GA; b. 1845, Madison Co, GA; d. Bef. 1891, Madison Co, GA. **Military service: Waddell's Bttry Al Arty**

  iv. JOHN W DAVID, b. Abt. 1849.

   v. MARY DAVID, b. Abt. 1840; m. // HERNDON, AL??; b. Abt. 1840.

  vi. JOHN M DAVID, b. 1849, AL.

27. MARY WHITE DAVID *(PETER, PETER)* was born Abt. 1814, and died Abt. 1850 in Madison Co, GA. She married NOAH W MEADOW March 13, 1834 in Madison Co, GA. He was born 1812 in Madison Co, GA, and died in Madison Co, GA.

     Children of MARY DAVID and NOAH MEADOW are:

    i. ELIZABETH MEADOW, b. 1835, Madison Co, GA.

   ii. SARAH S MEADOW, b. 1837.

  iii. MARTHA E MEADOW, b. 1839, Madison Co, GA; m. JAMES L BOLTON, December 11, 1859, Madison Co, GA; b. 1838, Madison Co, GA.

  iv. MARY JANE MEADOW, b. April 05, 1842, Madison Co, GA; d. May 18, 1913, Madison Co, GA; m. DAVID RICHARD MOSLEY, September 01, 1859, Madison Co, GA; b. January 10, 1832, GA; d. September 26, 1907, Madison Co, GA.

Military Service: Co B, 9th Battalion, Ga Volunteer Infantry May 10, 1862. Pension records show he was wounded,right arm permanenty disabled, at Utoy Creek, Ga Aug 6, 1864.

   v. SUSANNAH MEADOW, b. 1844, Madison Co, GA.

  vi. WILEY ISAAC MEADOW, b. January 05, 1847, Madison Co, GA; d. July 08, 1927, Madison Co, GA; m. SARAH ELIZABETH LOUVINIA WHITE, July 29, 1871, Madison Co, GA; b. August 20, 1853, Madison Co, GA; d. January 09, 1924, Madison Co, GA.

 vii. CHARLES MEADOW, b. 1848, Madison Co, GA.

28. ELIZABETH E. DAVID *(PETER, PETER)* was born Abt. 1816, and died Abt. 1859. She married JAMES W. VAUGHN February 07, 1839 in Madison Co GA, son of ALEXANDER VAUGHN and ELIZABETH DAVID. He was born Abt. 1815 in Elbert Co Ga.

      Children of ELIZABETH DAVID and JAMES VAUGHN are:

   i. RACHEL VAUGHN, b. Abt. 1847.

  ii. MARY JANICE VAUGHN, b. Abt. 1851.

 iii. LEWIS DAVID VAUGHN, b. Abt. 1854.

  iv. ISSAC DAVID VAUGHN, b. Abt. 1857; m. MARTHA UNKNOWN.

   v. MILLY DAVID VAUGHN, b. Abt. 1859.

29. JOHN MORRISETT "MURRAY" DAVID, SR *(PETER, PETER)* was born November 18, 1816 in Madison Co, GA, and died October 03, 1896 in Madison Co, GA. He married OLIVIA M B MOON March 15, 1866 in Madison Co, GA. She was born November 26, 1842 in Madison Co, GA, and died August 26, 1924 in Madison Co, GA. **Military Service: Co C. 4th Ga Reserves**

      Children of JOHN DAVID and OLIVIA MOON are:

   i. SUSAN E DAVID, b. September 14, 1870, Madison Co, GA; d. June 21, 1949, Madison Co, GA; m. JAMES L MERCIER, December 19, 1900, Madison Co, GA; b. October 24, 1868, Madison Co, GA; d. October 03, 1942, Madison Co, GA.

  ii. GEORGE P DAVID, b. June 30, 1880, Madison Co, GA; d. May 12, 1916, Home in Paoli, Madison Co, GA; m. ETHEL EVELYN //; b. January 19, 1880; d. August 18, 1969, Madison Co, GA.

 iii. MARY DAVID, b. Abt. 1875; m. (1) I. L. GOSS; m. (2) ISHAM LEONARD GOSS; b. May 24, 1882, Bowman, Hart Co, GA; d. April 16, 1920, Atlanta, GA.

iv.   OTHA DAVID, b. Abt. 1867; d. September 21, 1922, Madison Co, GA; m. LEILA ALICE CORNELIA "NELA" CARRINGTON; b. July 1876.

v.   LILLIAN E. DAVID, b. Abt. 1872; m. JOSEPH L POWER, November 01, 1892; b. March 1868, Madison Co, GA; d. 1957, Madison Co, GA.

vi.   WILLIAM DAVID, b. Abt. 1873; d. June 13, 1926, Madison Co, GA; m. (1) LOLA BELL RIDGWAY, August 11, 1903, Madison Co, GA; b. December 23, 1878, Madison Co, GA; d. November 13, 1911, Madison Co, GA; m. (2) MYRTLE BROWN, 1911; b. February 16, 1861, Madison Co, GA; d. January 15, 1918, Madison Co, GA; m. (3) LEE BELL, Aft. 1918; b. August 02, 1870; d. September 07, 1963, Madison Co, GA.

vii.   JOHN M DAVID, b. Abt. 1879; d. June 27, 1887, Madison Co, GA.

viii.   GEORGE P.DAVID, b. June 30, 1880, Madison Co GA; m. ETHEL E UNKNOWN.

30. SARAH ANN DAVID *(PETER, PETER)* was born Abt. 1817, and died in Prob Oglethorpe Co, GA. She married RAINEY EADES February 17, 1848 in Madison Co, GA, son of JOHN EADES. He was born 1814 in Oglethorpe Co, GA, and died in Prob Oglethorpe Co, GA.

Children of SARAH DAVID and RAINEY EADES are:

i.   SARAH ANN EADES, b. Abt. 1849; d. Abt. 1901.

ii.   ELIZABETH EADES, b. 1849.

iii.   REUBEN EADES, b. 1851.

iv.   AMERICA EADES, b. 1852.

v.   JOHN H EADES, b. 1855.

vi.   MARY F EADES, b. 1856.

vii.   MARTHA EADES, b. 1858.

viii.   SARAH EADES, b. 1860.

31. JAMES M. DAVID *(PETER, PETER,)* was born Abt. 1825, and died September 1862 in Sharpsburg,Md. He married ELIZABETH GHOLSTON October 25, 1849 in Madison Co GA. She was born June 16, 1827 in Madison Co, GA, and died May 22, 1900 in Madison Co, GA.
Military Record: Co. A 16ᵗʰ Georgia Infantry 2nd Sergeant July 11, 1861. Killed at Crampton's Gap, Md. September 14, 1862.

Children of JAMES DAVID and ELIZABETH GHOLSTON are:

i.   BETHANY DAVID, b. Abt. 1850; m. WALTER JONES FREEMAN; b. 1847, Madison Co, GA.

ii. ELIZABETH P. DAVID, b. Abt. 1851; d. July 31, 1927, At home in Poca, Madison Co, GA; m. JOSEPH WILEY FREEMAN; b. February 04, 1852, Madison Co, GA; d. August 25, 1901, Madison Co, GA.

iii. SARAH M. DAVID, b. Abt. 1852; m. (1) BRDY SEAGRAVES; m. (2) JOHN EDWARD COLLIER, November 02, 1879; b. Nov 07, 1852, Oglethrope Co, GA; d. April 27, 1920, Madison Co,

iv. JAMES THOMAS DAVID, b. July 19, 1859; m. (1) FRANCES SIMMONS; m. (2) HOPE WILKINS; b. Abt. 1865.

v. LUTITIA DAVID, b. Abt. 1862.

vi. JAMES P DAVID, b. 1861, Madison Co, GA; m. HOPE WILKINS, January 25, 1890, Madison Co, GA; b. Abt. 1865.

32. WILLIAM G DAVID *(MORASSETT, PETER)* was born August 24, 1839, and died January 28, 1929. He married MARY M GHOLSTON. She was born June 15, 1838 in Madison Co, GA, and died September 20, 1884 in Madison Co, GA.

Military Service: Co B, 9th Battalion, Ga Volunteer Infantry, Private Mar 4, 1862. Appointed 4th Corporal in 1862. Transferred to Co E, 37th Regt Ga Inf. as 4th Corporal May 6, 1863.

Surrendered at Greensboro, NC Apr 26, 1865. (Born in Madison Co Ga Aug24, 1839)

Amnesty Oath: 1865, Dark, black hair,6'1" , age 26, farmer

Children of WILLIAM DAVID and MARY GHOLSTON are:

i. WILLIAM J DAVID, b. April 16, 1863, Madison Co, GA; d. March 08, 1885, Madison Co, GA; m. SARAH ALICE BOND, January 28, 1883, Madison Co, GA; b. June 16, 1868, Madison Co, GA; d. September 20, 1950, Madison Co, GA.

ii. SARAH ELIZABETH DAVID, b. July 1866, Madison Co, GA; d. 1943, Madison Co, GA; m. THOMAS F LANDERS, December 26, 1886, Madison Co, GA; b. 1864, Madison Co, GA; d. March 02, 1920, Madison Co, GA.

iii. MARY ALMA DAVID, b. January 1868, Madison Co, GA; d. July 04, 1957, Athens, GA; m. JACKSON M LANDERS, January 29, 1888, Madison Co, GA; b. September 1860, Madison Co, GA; d. 1935, Madison Co, GA.

iv. JOHN M DAVID, b. December 18, 1869, Madison Co, GA; d. August 02, 1962, Madison Co, GA; m. LILLIE LANDERS; b. December 24, 1878; d. January 15, 1943.

    v. LEUDORA E DAVID, b. December 1874, Madison Co, GA; m. J M BREEDLOVE, January 29, 1901, Madison Co, GA; b. Abt. 1870.

    vi. HULDAH M DAVID, b. November 1877, Madison Co, GA; d. September 30, 1954, Madison Co, GA; m. OTHA LAMAR POWER, January 08, 1901, Madison Co, GA; b. 1876, Madison Co, GA; d. 1950, Madison Co, GA.

    vii. CHARLES E DAVID, b. March 04, 1880, Madison Co, GA; d. October 10, 1902, Madison Co,

33. LUCINDA A DAVID *(MORASSETT, PETER)* was born May 22, 1820 in Madison Co, GA, and died May 07, 1867 in Madison Co, GA. She married WILBURN JUDSON O'KELLEY January 27, 1842 in Oglethorpe Co, GA. He was born March 30, 1818 in Beaverdam Dist, Oglethorpe Co, GA, and died 1899 in Lincoln, Talladega Co, AL.
Amnesty Oath: 1865, Dark, black hair, hazel eyes, 5'3–1/2," age 45
Amnesty Oath: 1865, Dark, black hair, dark eyes, 6'2–1/2"
    Children of LUCINDA DAVID and WILBURN O'KELLEY are:

    i. LUCY ELIZABETH O'KELLEY, b. November 24, 1842, Madison Co, GA; d. OK; m. CHRISTOPHER W BENNETT, August 30, 1868, Madison Co, GA; b. 1848, Madison Co, GA; d. March 1900.
      Amnesty Oath: 1865, Fair, black hair, grey eyes, 5'7," age 22

    ii. JAMES DAVID O'KELLEY, b. 1851, Madison Co, GA; d. Abt. 1934, Jacksonville, AL; m. NANCY J BURROUGHS, August 10, 1871, Madison Co, GA; b. 1853, Madison Co, GA; d. Abt. 1932, Jacksonville, AL.

    iii. REV MORASETT JOSEPH [REV] O'KELLEY, b. October 26, 1861, Madison Co, GA; d. November 09, 1921, Madison Co, GA; m. ALICE LENORA FORTSON, March 23, 1883, Madison Co, GA; b. January 25, 1861, Hart Co, GA; d. October 02, 1930, Madison Co, GA.

34. LUCY ELIZABETH DAVID *(MORASSETT, PETER)* was born December 26, 1845 in Madison Co, GA, and died February 10, 1898 in Madison Co, GA. She married JAMES P HALL, SR November 15, 1866 in Madison Co, GA. He was born January 01, 1846 in Madison Co, GA, and died April 27, 1883 in Madison Co, GA. **Military Service: Co B, 9th Battalion, Ga Volunteer Infantry, Private Mar 4, 1862. Transferred to Co G, 37th Regt Ga Inf May 6, 1863. Captured at Nashville, Tenn. Dec 16, 1863. Released at Camp Chase, O June 12, 1865.**

Children of LUCY DAVID and JAMES HALL are:

i. LAURA E HALL, b. 1867.
ii. WILLIAM HENRY HALL, b. 1872, Madison Co, GA; d. 1925, Madison Co, GA.
iii. JAMES P HALL, JR, b. 1874.
iv. CORA MAE HALL, b. April 28, 1876, Madison Co, GA; d. June 03, 1880, Madison Co, GA.
v. ORPHIE ANN HALL, b. July 04, 1877, Madison Co, GA; d. July 05, 1877, Madison Co, GA.
vi. MARY L HALL, b. May 1880.

35. JOHN M BRUCE *(MARY DAVID, PETER)* was born Abt. 1824 in Madison Co. Ga, and died Aft. 1880 in Madison Co. Ga. He married BARBARA R ANTHONY January 02, 1853 in Madison Co, GA. She was born December 31, 1833 in Oglethorpe Co, GA, and died Aft. 1906.
Military Service: Co B, 9th Battalion, Ga Volunteer Infantry Private Mar 4, 1862. Roll dated Jan 14, 1863, last on file, shows him present. No later record.

Child of JOHN BRUCE and BARBARA ANTHONY is:

i. WILLIAM H L BRUCE, b. 1865, Madison Co, GA; m. EMMA L SCARBOROUGH, March 22, 1888, Madison Co, GA; b. 1869, Madison Co, GA.

36. CELIA BRUCE *(MARY DAVID, PETER)* was born Abt. 1825 in Madison Co. Ga, and died October 17, 1900 in Jackson Co, GA. She married MATTHEW S FREEMAN September 20, 1857 in Madison Co, GA. He was born April 05, 1812 in Madison Co, GA, and died June 17, 1886 in Madison Co, GA.

Amnesty Oath: 1865, Fair, light hair, blue eyes 5'2," age 36
Amnesty Oath: 1865, dark, black hair, blue eyes, 5'11," age 53, farmer

Child of CELIA BRUCE and MATTHEW FREEMAN is:

i. JOEL WALTER FREEMAN, b. September 16, 1859, Madison or Jackson Co, GA; d. May 17, 1952, Jackson Co, GA; m. LETITIA PRISCILLA DAVID, February 14, 1884, Jackson Co, GA; b. January 08, 1862; d. April 06, 1947, Jackson Co, GA.

37. JAMES HENRY BRUCE *(MARY DAVID, PETER)* was born July 19, 1826 in Madison Co. Ga, and died November 28, 1864. He married MARY KING December 23, 1848 in Madison Co GA, daughter of JOHN KING and MARY HALL. She was born August 26, 1828, and died February 14, 1907.

Children of JAMES BRUCE and MARY KING are:

i. JOHN B BRUCE, b. 1849, Madison Co, GA.

    ii. NANCY C BRUCE, b. 1852, Madison Co, GA; m. JOHN H MITCHELL; b. 1851, Madison Co,

   iii. MARY F BRUCE, b. 1856, Madison Co, GA; m. JOSEPH F CRIDER; b. 1810.

   iv. WILLIAM THOMAS BRUCE, b. September 21, 1858, Madison Co, GA; d. January 06, 1901, Madison Co, GA; m. (1) AUZIE POWER, February 14, 1885, Madison Co, GA; b. August 11, 1867; d. December 06, 1912, Madison Co, GA; m. (2) EMILY AUZIE POWER, February 14, 1885, Madison Co, GA; b. August 11, 1867, Madison Co, GA; d. December 06, 1912, Madison Co, GA.

    v. MATTHEW W BRUCE, b. 1859, Madison Co, GA.

   vi. CARSON BRUCE, b. 1863, Madison Co, GA.

  vii. ISAAC E BRUCE, b. August 1865, Madison Co, GA; d. Madison Co, GA; m. FRANCES KING; b. July 1874.

 viii. SANFORD M BRUCE, b. January 1861, Madison Co, GA; m. SUSAN C VAUGHN, April 04, 1882; b. Abt. 1843; d. April 28, 1924, Provo, Utah.

   ix. JAMES HENRY BRUCE,JR. b. September 22, 1848; d. November 25, 1936, Madison Co, GA; m. PERLINA KEZIAH VAUGHN, Madison Co GA; b. June 14, 1849, Madison Co, GA; d. December 14, 1914, Madison Co, GA.

38. SARAH BRUCE *(MARY DAVID, PETER)* was born Abt. 1831 in Madison Co. Ga, and died 1886 in Elbert Co, GA. She married WILLIAM GREEN TUCKER February 25, 1864 in Madison Co, GA. He was born Sept 28, 1807 in Abbeville, SC, and died 1882 in Elbert Co, GA.

    Child of SARAH BRUCE and WILLIAM TUCKER is:

    i. HENRY THOMAS TUCKER, b. March 12, 1872, Elbert Co, GA; d. June 08, 1934, Elbert Co, GA; m. LUNA FRANCES MOSS; b. August 1873, Elbert Co, GA; d. Elbert Co, GA.

39. FRANCES BRUCE *(MARY DAVID, PETER)* was born Abt. 1834 in Madison Co. Ga, and died Bef. 1900 in Madison Co, GA. She married SOLOMON WISE BROWN August 19, 1855 in Madison Co, GA. He was born 1830 in Madison Co, GA, and died in Madison Co, GA.

    Children of FRANCES BRUCE and SOLOMON BROWN are:

    i. WILLIAM A [SR] BROWN, b. 1856, Madison Co, GA; d. Bef. 1900.

   ii. HENRY W BROWN, b. 1858, Madison Co, GA.

iii. SAMUEL M BROWN, b. 1859, Madison Co, GA; m. JOSE-PHINE FORD, December 26, 1880, Madison Co, GA; b. 1861.

iv. MARY L BROWN, b. November 1861, Madison Co, GA.

v. SOLOMON S J BROWN, b. 1866, Madison Co, GA.

vi. JAMES W BROWN, b. March 1867, Madison Co, GA; m. CYN-THIA R //; b. September 1881.

vii. JOHN WILLIAM BROWN, b. December 25, 1868, Madison Co, GA; d. September 11, 1945, Madison Co, GA; m. TEMPLE "TEMPIE" ANN FORD, Abt. 1883, Madison Co, GA; b. August 17, 1864; d. July 13, 1954, Madison Co, GA.

viii. MAJOR OSCAR BROWN, b. 1872, Madison Co, GA; m. SARAH E DRAKE, July 22, 1888, Madison Co, GA; b. 1868, Madison Co, GA.

ix. ISAAC LEE BROWN, b. April 28, 1874, Madison Co, GA; d. 1939, Madison Co, GA; m. ANNA L SANDERS, October 08, 1893, Madison Co, GA; b. 1876; d. 1946, Madison Co, GA.

x. JOEL B BROWN, b. April 28, 1874, Madison Co, GA; d. February 06, 1934, Madison Co, GA; m. (1) ALLIE BOOTH, April 20, 1892, Madison Co, GA; b. Abt. 1875; d. Bef. 1894, Madison Co, GA; m. (2) HULDA ANN DRAKE, April 08, 1894, Madison Co, GA; b. June 24, 1877, Madison Co, GA; d. January 07, 1942, Madison Co, GA.

xi. FRANCIS E BROWN, b. October 1877.

xii. LAVONIA BROWN, b. 1878, Madison Co, GA.

40. THOMAS PETER BRUCE *(MARY DAVID, PETER)* was born October 18, 1828 in Madison Co, GA, and died September 11, 1896 in Madison Co, GA. He married SARAH M SIMMONS August 30, 1855 in Madison Co, GA, daughter of HARVEY SIMMONS and MARY SIMMONS. She was born November 09, 1832 in Madison Co, GA, and died March 15, 1918 in Madison Co, GA. **Military service: Private Co K 2nd Ga St. Line Trps**

Children of THOMAS BRUCE and SARAH SIMMONS are:

i. HARVEY W BRUCE, b. July 26, 1856, Madison Co, GA; d. January 21, 1918, Madison Co, GA; m. ALLETHA FRANCES GUNNELLS, October 17, 1875, Madison Co, GA; b. May 31, 1858, Home, Madison Co, GA; d. May 18, 1927, Madison Co, GA.

ii. CLAYTON JONES BRUCE, b. September 06, 1858, Madison Co, GA; d. June 25, 1910, Madison Co, GA; m. AUGUSTA ANN "AUNT SIS" ; b. January 03, 1856, Madison Co, GA; d. September 1928, Madison Co, GA.

   iii. LURENA F BRUCE, b. 1863, Madison Co, GA; m. J F CAREY, March 28, 1883, Madison Co, GA; b. Abt. 1860.

   iv. MARY ELIZABETH "LIZZIE" BRUCE, b. July 11, 1865, Madison Co, GA; d. April 19, 1947, Madison Co, GA; m. (1) MILES A SEXTON, September 01, 1896, Madison Co, GA; b. November 22, 1856; d. March 25, 1899, Madison Co, GA; m. (2) JOEL G DUDLEY, December 09, 1917, Madison Co, GA; b. November 22, 1853, Madison Co, GA; d. June 07, 1924, Madison Co, GA.

   v. BARBARA EMMA BRUCE, b. August 22, 1868, Madison Co, GA; d. May 17, 1903, Madison Co, GA; m. JOHN H LONG, September 26, 1888, Madison Co, GA; b. November 17, 1866; d. January 12, 1960, Madison Co, GA.

   vi. JOHN D BRUCE, b. October 16, 1869, Madison Co, GA; d. November 24, 1949, Madison Co, GA; m. HATTIE E GINN; b. May 26, 1876, Madison Co, GA; d. May 07, 1957, Madison Co,

   vii. HENRY L BRUCE, b. February 1875, Madison Co, GA; d. 1956, Madison Co, GA; m. TERRILA GINN; b. 1885, Banks Co, GA; d. December 11, 1932, Madison Co, GA.

41. MARSHALL DAVID *(SAMUEL, PETER)* was born October 02, 1828, and died September 20, 1897. He married (1) NANCY CAROLINE GUEST November 11, 1851 in Madison Co, GA. She was born 1832 in SC, and died Bet. 1860 - 1865. He married (1) FRANCES A DUDLEY December 01, 1868 in Madison Co, GA. She was born Abt. 1830. He married (2) SARAH A PAYNE November 19, 1865 in Madison Co, GA. She was born 1840 in GA, and died Abt. 1867.

Amnesty Oath: 1865, Fair, dark hair, yellow eyes, 6,' age 37, farmer
Military service: private June 17, 1862. Captured at Cedar Creek, Va. October 19,1864. Exchanged at Point Lookout, Md. March 28,1865. Captured, Greenville, S. C. May 23,1865

   Child of MARSHALL DAVID and NANCY GUEST is:

   i. BERRY G DAVID, b. Abt. 1859.

   Children of MARSHALL DAVID and FRANCES DUDLEY are:

   ii. JOEL T DAVID, b. 1873, Madison Co, GA.

   iii. JULIUS A DAVID, b. 1876, Madison Co, GA.

   iv. SARAH W DAVID, b. November 1879, Madison Co, GA.

42. PETER DAVID *(SAMUEL, PETER, PETER)* was born Abt. 1834 in Madison, Co Ga, and died Abt. May 1862 in Knoxville, Tenn. He married MARY M COOPER November 29, 1853 in Madison Co, GA. She was born Abt. 1835 in Madison Co, GA. **Military Service: Co B, 9th Battalion, Ga Volunteer Infan-**

try, - **Private Mar 4, 1862. Received $50 bounty Apr 17, 1862. Died of measles in Knoxville Tenn May 1862**

    Child of PETER DAVID and MARY COOPER is:
      i. HARRIETT DAVID, b. 1857.

44. SAMUEL C DAVID JR. *(SAMUEL, PETER)* was born 1837 in Madison Co, GA, and died Bet. 1862 - 1865 in CSA. He married EADA CAROLINE PORTERFIELD October 09, 1856 in Madison Co, GA. She was born February 29, 1836 in Madison Co, GA, and died October 01, 1924 in Madison Co, GA. **Military service: Private Co A 10th Ga Inf**

    Child of SAMUEL DAVID and EADA PORTERFIELD is:
      i. JAMES THOMAS DAVID, b. July 19, 1857, Madison Co, GA; d. April 12, 1928, Madison Co, GA; m. FRANCES "FANNIE" E SIMMONS, November 27, 1877, Madison Co, GA; b. November 19, 1854, Madison Co, GA; d. December 08, 1923, Madison Co, GA.
      ii. JOHN F DAVID, b. Abt. 1858.
      iii. GEORGE M DAVID, b. Abt. 1860; d. January 10, 1929, Madison Co, GA; m. ELIZA C; b. April 07,1859, Madison Co, GA; d. July 14, 1900, Madison Co, GA.

45. ISAAC DAVID *(SAMUEL, PETER)* was born Abt. 1844 in GA, and died May 11, 1910 in Madison Co, GA. He married ELIZABETH J . She was born Abt. 1850.
Amnesty Oath: 1865, Fair, dark hair, yellow eyes, 5'8," age 22, farmer

    Child of ISAAC DAVID and ELIZABETH is:
      i. Hattie David, b. October 28, 1881, Madison Co, GA; d. September 14, 1904, Madison Co, GA.

Contact Ron Jones
or order more copies of this book at

TATE PUBLISHING, LLC

127 East Trade Center Terrace
Mustang, Oklahoma 73064

(888) 361 - 9473

Tate Publishing, LLC

www.tatepublishing.com